Praise for the Novels
of Tracy Wolff

TEASE ME

"A tightrope of edgy suspense and taut sensuality. One fiery-hot read with nail-biting tension—I couldn't put it down!"

—Jaci Burton, national bestselling author of *Riding on Instinct*

"Holy cow! Tracy Wolff's *Tease Me* is one scorching-hot read! Don't miss this one, and don't forget to bring the ice."

—Lauren Dane, national bestselling author of *Coming Undone*

TIE ME DOWN

"Snares you in the first chapter with its detail of the desperation and need of the characters, and then keeps you enthralled as the plot unravels. Wolff grabs your attention and doesn't let you go. A great read!" —Fresh Fiction

"All I can say is that it is hot, hot, hot! Murder, mystery, and sex that sizzles—what more can a gal ask for? Warning—read this story with a fan ready at hand."

—Sunny, author of *Lucinda, Dangerously*

"An intoxicating blend of suspense and eroticism that will leave readers breathless!" —Maya Banks, author of *Sweet Persuasion*

"The sex is wild, exotic, and inventive in Wolff's serial-killer thriller."

—*Romantic Times Book Reviews*

"Hot, intense, and downright good, *Tie Me Down* is a page-turner that gives a huge adrenaline rush. . . . Tracy Wolff has created a superb story that hooked this reader from the first page, and didn't let go until the dramatic conclusion."

—The Romance Studio

continued . . .

"Tracy Wolff provides an engaging erotic police procedural romance filled with suspense and sex."   —Genre Go Round Reviews

"*Tie Me Down* is a very well-written novel that has sizzling suspense with several unexpected twists . . . an enthralling but somewhat disturbing read."

—Night Owl Romance

FULL EXPOSURE

"Wolff ratchets up the tension in her debut novel, a first-rate tale set in the hot and steamy Louisiana bayou. She combines the adrenaline of a psychological thriller with the intensity of an exquisitely sensual romance while skillfully exploring the deepest emotions of her characters. The erotic encounters lead to a passionate love affair that will have readers sighing with satisfaction. Intriguing twists keep the pages turning and pave the way for an unforgettable conclusion."

—*Romantic Times* (4½ stars, top pick)

"Edgy and erotic . . . A sultry, red-hot read."

—*New York Times* bestselling author Shannon McKenna

"This book kept me on the edge of my seat. . . . I recommend *Full Exposure* wholeheartedly."   —Fresh Fiction

"I adored *Full Exposure*. I found it extremely suspenseful and, in fact, I did not guess the villain until the very end. I LOVE when that happens because as a reader, it means that the author thought through the plot and came up with a viable and highly enticing ending. Add in two characters that fit together so completely they could have been stuck together with glue, and you have the perfect read."   —Romance Junkies

"The suspense in *Full Exposure* is as important to this story as the romance, and Ms. Wolff does a splendid job weaving the intrigue throughout the plot, peppering the book with slight hints to the villain's identity. The climactic ending is a heart-stopper, with moments that will make you gasp in fear before leaving you breathing a sigh of relief at the happy ending."   —Wild on Books

"Sexy, scorching, tender, poignant, and absolutely unputdownable . . . blends the steamy sensuality of Shannon McKenna and Lori Foster with the nail-biting romantic suspense of Nora Roberts and Linda Howard. Fast-paced, wickedly sensual, and captivating from start to finish . . . not to be missed!"

—Sensual Erotic Romance and Erotica 24/7

"The Bayou never looked so good . . . dynamic characters and a story line with a bite."   —Romance Novel TV

"*Full Exposure* is an on-your-toes erotic thriller that is as hot as the setting. . . . Tracy Wolff can write some hot sex scenes, and don't be surprised if you want to break out a fan while you read them."   —Fallen Angel Reviews

"*Full Exposure* is a breathtaking story. . . . I had a hard time putting this book down to do anything else. Tracy Wolff has done an amazing job of bringing her characters to life and making you pray for the best. Prepare for a wild ride with *Full Exposure*."   —Manic Readers

"With extremely hot and steamy sex scenes and a stalker all mixed together, *Full Exposure* sucks you in . . . a thrill ride that keeps you on the edge of your seat until the very end."   —Coffee Time Romance

"*Full Exposure* is a riveting read that will keep you in the dark until the last frame is fully developed. . . . Tracy Wolff has garnered my attention with her dazzling debut, and I will most assuredly be on the lookout for what she plans to offer next."   —Novel Talk

TEASE ME

TRACY WOLFF

HEAT

HEAT

Published by New American Library, a division of
Penguin Group (USA) Inc., 375 Hudson Street,
New York, New York 10014, USA
Penguin Group (Canada), 90 Eglinton Avenue East, Suite 700, Toronto,
Ontario M4P 2Y3, Canada (a division of Pearson Penguin Canada Inc.)
Penguin Books Ltd., 80 Strand, London WC2R 0RL, England
Penguin Ireland, 25 St. Stephen's Green, Dublin 2,
Ireland (a division of Penguin Books Ltd.)
Penguin Group (Australia), 250 Camberwell Road, Camberwell, Victoria 3124,
Australia (a division of Pearson Australia Group Pty. Ltd.)
Penguin Books India Pvt. Ltd., 11 Community Centre, Panchsheel Park,
New Delhi - 110 017, India
Penguin Group (NZ), 67 Apollo Drive, Rosedale, North Shore 0632,
New Zealand (a division of Pearson New Zealand Ltd.)
Penguin Books (South Africa) (Pty.) Ltd., 24 Sturdee Avenue,
Rosebank, Johannesburg 2196, South Africa

Penguin Books Ltd., Registered Offices:
80 Strand, London WC2R 0RL, England

First published by Heat, an imprint of New American Library,
a division of Penguin Group (USA) Inc.

First Printing, April 2010
10 9 8 7 6 5 4 3 2 1

HEAT is a trademark of Penguin Group (USA) Inc.

LIBRARY OF CONGRESS CATALOGING-IN-PUBLICATION DATA:

Wolff, Tracy.
Tease me/Tracy Wolff.
p.   cm.
ISBN 978-0-451-22925-0
1. Women authors—Fiction.   2. Carpenters—Fiction.   3. New Orleans (La.)—Fiction.
I. Title.
PS3623.O57T43 2010
813'.6—dc22   2009040781

Set in Sabon
Designed by Alissa Amell

Printed in the United States of America

PUBLISHER'S NOTE
This is a work of fiction. Names, characters, places, and incidents either are the product of the author's imagination or are used fictitiously, and any resemblance to actual persons, living or dead, business establishments, events, or locales is entirely coincidental.
The publisher does not have any control over and does not assume any responsibility for author or third-party Web sites or their content.

For Adam

Acknowledgments

Thanks to everyone at NAL who makes my books possible, especially my intrepid and wonderful editor, Becky Vinter, who always knows what's best for my books—even when I don't. You're the greatest!

And to my family, who put up with missed breakfasts and football games, late dinners and dirty clothes when I'm in full book-writing mode. Thanks for hanging in there with me.

TEASE ME

Chapter One

I feel you watching me, feel your eyes through the cold glass of my window and the sheer curtain that does such a poor job of covering it. You don't know that I sense you, that I revel in your burning eyes as they run over me.

To torment you—and myself—I open the pearl buttons of my blouse. I toy with them, sliding each through the buttonhole more slowly than the one before it. I can feel your impatience. Your rage. Your need, racing through the humid night until it slams into me as you long to do.

I slide my blouse from my shoulders, then slip out of my skirt, until I stand before you covered only by my white bra and panties, which are no cover at all.

I cup my breasts, rub my nipples through the stiff lace that has been a torment—and a delight—through the endless day.

You growl, low in your throat, and I swear I can hear you despite the courtyard separating us. I slide my fingers down my stomach, over the lace and silk that barely covers the secret, aching heart of me.

And imagine it is you.

Imagine that it is your hands caressing me. Imagine that it is your mouth upon me.

I rejoice in your strength—in the hardness of your muscles and the sweet se-duction of your mouth. I run my fingers down your naked back, cup your ass in my hands and pull you to the very center of me so that you can feel my hard nipples and the wild, staccato pounding of my heart.

So that you can feel my damp, heated core and know that you are respon-sible. That you have done this to me. That it is you, and only you, that I want.

That I need.

That I crave.

"Fuck!" Byron Hawthorne slammed his laptop shut as need ran through him like a goddamn freight train. But closing the computer couldn't make him forget what he'd read—or cool the desire shooting through his veins. But then, nothing ever did. Or ever would, he was afraid—save a random case of complete and total amnesia.

Striving to put some distance between himself and the words spinning in his head, he shoved himself away from his desk with a curse, only to find that his legs were almost too shaky to hold him. Goddamn it. His cock was on fire, his entire body so hard and turned on that it was impossible to breathe with-out pain.

Why did he continue to torture himself? Why, when he knew he'd spend the rest of the night so hard and horny that he would barely be able to function, did he continue to read her damn blog?

Because he was obsessed, that's why. Obsessed, delusional and completely fucking masochistic. There was no other answer for it. No other excuse as to why he—like the thousands of other morons who were ruled by their dicks instead of their brains—couldn't go a day without visiting her damn Web site.

What had begun as a lark had become the very best—and worst—part of his day. A friend of his, who was big into the New Orleans Internet scene, had intro-duced him to the blog months ago, while they were hanging out during halftime of one football game or another. Mike had told him the site was becoming another piece of New Orleans' ever-changing, sexually based culture, and that as a newly single transplant to the Big Easy, he should have his finger on the pulse of what the city considered sexy.

At first Byron had made fun of Mike for going to the blog, had laughed at him for being so pathetically wrapped up in the words of a woman he'd never get the chance to meet. Had even wondered aloud what she got out of such a blatant fuck-you to the men of the world.

But he'd logged on. He'd told himself it was just because he wanted to harass Mike, but as the days passed and he continued to read the fantasies, he'd had to admit that he was hooked on the blog. Hooked on and obsessed with What a Girl Wants—as the mystery blogger had named her site.

It was a place where she could anonymously post her deepest, darkest fantasies. Where she could tell the world—or at least her small corner of it—what she'd never have the guts to tell anyone else. Or so she said . . .

But it was so much more than that. At least to him. It was like she had a window into his soul, like she knew exactly what *he* wanted. What *he* needed. The idea that she needed it too—well, that's what kept him up at night, his body aching for release no matter how many times he jacked off.

It drove him insane—the knowledge that she was out there, that she lived in the same damn city as him, and he would never be able to meet her. Never have a chance with her. Hell, he couldn't even try to find her, unless he wanted to look like some fucked-up, crazy stalker.

Which he wasn't, he assured himself as he strode to the fridge and pulled out a beer. At least not yet. But if this insane sexual frustration kept up, who knew what the hell he'd end up being in a month or two. He could give up his gig as a carpenter and become a full-time psycho instead. He shook his head with disgust at the thought.

As it was, he'd been through five girlfriends in the last four months as he tried, desperately, to focus on a real, live woman instead of his fantasies. But he couldn't connect to any of the women he'd dated lately, and while a year ago he would have at least tried to forge a relationship with one of them, these days he couldn't be bothered. There was nothing wrong with any of the women he'd seen—they were nice, attractive, smart. But they weren't *her*.

His laugh, when it came, was strangled—more angry than amused. Of course they weren't. Because, really, who could be? Even this woman—who seemed to be the living, breathing epitome of every fantasy he'd ever had—couldn't be real. Her writings were just words, her online personality just a persona that she'd adopted.

Or at least that's what he tried to believe. *What he* had *to believe*, he corrected himself as he downed the beer in two long swallows. Otherwise he'd go insane thinking that his perfect woman was out there and he'd never have more of her than her fantasies. Never have any more of her than thousands of other men had too.

Just the thought of other men reading her words made him feel vaguely homicidal—a surefire sign that he was closer to insanity than he liked to admit. Because he wanted to go back to the laptop and read today's blog entry again, he forced himself to stay on the other side of the room from it. It wasn't nearly as explicit as some of the ones she'd written in the past, yet her list of wants—of needs—was so close to his own that he couldn't help responding to it.

Pissed off, out of sorts, and still more than a little turned on, he grabbed another beer and headed out to his balcony. It was late August in New Orleans, which meant it was already hot as hell and twice as humid, but at least a storm was coming in and the fry-your-brain temperatures of earlier in the day had receded a little bit.

Once he got outside, he felt some of the tension ease. There was something about being out here, as day slowly faded to twilight, that relaxed him. In fact, it was this balcony, and the peaceful, narrow courtyard it overlooked, that had sold him on this building when he'd moved to the city last year.

To this day, he didn't know if it was the magnolia-scented air or the soft trickle of water in the fountain down below that calmed him. Nor did he care. All that mattered was that for a little while, he had surcease from the painful, clawing need that enveloped him every time he thought about his fantasy woman. The fact that he was pretty much the only one who ever came out here made the whole thing just a little better.

Yet even as the thought formed, he heard the soft snick of a door opening and then closing. Annoyed at the disturbance, he bent forward until his forearms were resting on the wrought iron of the balcony railing, his beer dangling from loose fingertips.

Scanning the area where the sound had come from, he finally found the unexpected intruder. It was the sexy redhead from across the courtyard, the one who had moved in to the building last month and had caught his attention from his very first glimpse of her.

For a while, he'd thought about asking her out, about using her to help him get *her* and her dick-twisting fantasies out of his head. But the redhead had never even acknowledged Byron's existence, even when they passed in the parking lot or took out their trash at the same time, and he hadn't been interested enough to try to get her attention.

But looking at her now—a little mussed, a little sweaty, and much more than a little sexy—he was more than interested. He was downright intrigued. With her red hair tumbling down her back and her sheer blouse plastered to her breasts, she looked like a fantasy. Add the pissed-off scowl on her face, and she just might *be* his fantasy. At least for tonight.

Lacey Adams was hot, tired and more than a little irritated. She'd spent all day tracking down leads on her current book, only to be given the runaround time and time again. It was ridiculous, really, how all her original sources had closed ranks, especially since so many of them had been willing to talk about their roles in the Crescent City Escort Service/prostitution ring—and subsequent arrests— when she'd interviewed them over the phone a few weeks before.

Ridiculous and weird and very, very suspicious. She didn't have a clue what had changed, but something obviously had—especially considering the fact that everyone else she'd managed to dig up was being just as closemouthed. She knew most of them were hoping she'd give up and go away, but their reticence only made her want to dig deeper—until she found whatever it was they were hiding.

The research for the book should have been a slam dunk—she basically wanted to write about the formation of the escort service, the names in its Rolodex and how and why it managed to operate for so long without drawing the attention of law enforcement. She'd expected a little trouble when it came to getting some of the important people in the files to open up, but the names had already been leaked, so it wasn't like they had so much to protect. Yet trying to get more than the most basic information was turning into a nightmare.

With a groan of absolute frustration, Lacey flicked her hair over her shoulder as she flopped down on the upscale lounge chair she'd bought herself last year for her twenty-seventh birthday. It had been way too expensive, but so comfortable that she'd managed to talk herself into the splurge. She hadn't regretted it once—had, in fact, spent many nights out here writing, or simply whiling away the hours when her insomnia was in full swing.

Her long peasant skirt had ridden up to the middle of her thighs when she'd sat down, but she didn't bother to fix the soft cotton. In the evening's oppressive heat, the slight breeze felt nice on her legs. Besides, there was almost never anyone out here. She and the guy across the courtyard were the only two who used their balconies for anything besides storage. But then, they were also two of the only single people in the entire building.

Because the apartments in the building were large, most of them were taken up by families with small children. And, judging from the amount of noise that came from her neighbors' places, they had plenty to do in the evenings besides hanging out on their balconies—especially in this heat.

And God, it was hot, so hot that she could actually feel the sweat beginning to bloom on the small of her back. It was stupid to sit out here, baking, when her air-conditioned apartment was only a few steps away. But the frustrations of the day were still looming large, and the idea of sitting in her living room as the walls slowly closed in held no appeal.

Leaning her head against the back of the lounger, she let her eyelids flutter closed and her mind drift. But the heat wouldn't let her relax; the humidity so stifling that it was hard to breathe. She could only hope the rainstorm that was due later that night would hurry up and arrive sooner.

Without conscious thought, she brought her fingers to the buttons of her blouse and quickly undid them before stripping it off, so that the only thing between her and the sticky air was the ivory silk camisole she'd shrugged into that morning.

With a sigh—of pleasure this time—she picked up a glass of water and took a long swallow, then rolled it slowly down her cheek and across her breastbone.

As the cold glass bolstered her flagging energy, life suddenly seemed a whole lot more bearable, even if her latest book *was* currently dead in the water. But how could she have known that in a city like New Orleans—which wore its many sins and bad behaviors like badges of honor—people would clam up so completely over a prostitution ring? Sure, it was a very large, very high-reaching prostitution ring, but it was *still* just a prostitution ring. Or so the papers and the police said.

Still, something about this whole thing just wasn't sitting right with her. Everyone was being too closemouthed about the situation, even now, eighteen months after the prostitution ring had been busted up. A year after the Mardi Gras Madam and some of her girls had been arrested and spent only a couple months in jail, thanks to a suspicious-as-hell plea bargain.

But this was New Orleans, she reminded herself, a city whose crime rate bordered on the obscene. Stranger things had happened here before—and would again.

In the years she'd been writing true-crime books, Lacey had found that the payoff of notoriety was often more than enough to convince people to give up their secrets. That same formula had proven true as she'd begun to investigate this story, begun to dig into the prostitution ring that hinted at reaching all the way to the top levels of various industries, not to mention the government.

Right up until last week, when every source she had had dried up. Nearly everyone she'd previously spoken to had suddenly developed amnesia—and those who hadn't simply refused to say anything on the record. Or off.

It was enough to drive her investigative radar crazy, enough to convince her that something darker was at work here. And everything she'd found—everything she'd experienced lately—only made her more determined to get that story. When this many people refused to talk, it was usually for a good reason. She wanted—needed—to find out what that reason was.

Too bad she was back at square one.

Taking another sip of water, Lacey sighed in disgust at the entire predicament. Then forced it from her mind for the moment, as dwelling on it was doing nothing but getting her more and more upset.

She let her eyes wander over the building and balconies across from her. Mrs. Rochet needed to water her flowers—they were dying in the heat, despite the frequent rainstorms. And Mr. Andalukis really should—

Her thought process came to a screaming halt as she suddenly realized that she wasn't alone. That she was, in fact, being watched—by the same sinful eyes that had haunted her dreams, and her blog, for the last few weeks. Dark, dangerous and more than a little wild, they never failed to send shivers down her spine, and today was no exception.

For long moments, she could do nothing but return his stare, her gaze locked on his like a guided, heat-seeking missile.

There was power in those eyes. Power and sex and an edgy desire that set her blood humming in a way she hadn't felt in far too long. For one endless moment, she wondered what it would be like if she took him up on the blatant offer in his too-hot stare. If she let him do all the wicked, wonderful, *wanton* things those eyes promised.

It would be good. She knew that much from the way she'd seen him move these last few weeks, when he didn't know she was watching. She'd noticed her neighbor right after she moved in—with his broad shoulders, big hands and terrific ass, it would have been impossible not to. Add in the shaggy blond hair, too-pretty face and devil-may-care grin, and he'd been damn near irre-sistible.

But she *had* resisted him. For five long weeks, she'd ignored the interested glances he'd shot her way, had denied her own interest in him, even as he figured prominently in her most recent fantasies.

But this flirtation wasn't make-believe, and she wasn't the same woman who trusted every pretty face that came along anymore. Who gave everything to a man—and let him take far too much—just because she loved him. And she never would be again.

Lacey started to look way—to pretend a disinterest she was far from feeling—but he wouldn't let her, his eyes so steady and sexy that she could practically feel them moving over her skin.

She couldn't do this, her sluggish brain tried to tell her body. Not now. Not with *him*. No matter how out of sorts she was or how hot he made her, she couldn't start this. Couldn't let him start it. Because tomorrow was only a few hours away, and he had the word *complicated* written all over him. From his too-fierce eyes and grim mouth to his hardworking truck and straitlaced friends, he was *everything* she wasn't looking for. No wham, bam, thank you, ma'am for this guy. He'd want to take all night and then start again in the morning, and she just didn't have the time for that. Or the inclination.

Too messy.

Too involved.

Too much potential for emotional complications—something Curtis had cured her of wanting once and for all.

Besides, this guy was way too good-looking for her. He was out of her league, out of her division. Out of her whole fucking stratosphere. She'd watched him enough to know that—and to know that there was no way he'd put up with being a one-shot deal. She'd seen him around, seen a couple of the women he'd dated. The way he was when he was with them—serious, intense, interested—was the opposite of the kind of relationship she was looking for.

Curtis had carried around that same kind of intensity, and look where that had gotten her. All fucked up with nowhere to go.

No, she was much better off playing it fast and loose—something she had a feeling her too-sexy neighbor with the possessive eyes knew nothing about.

Which meant that they were at an impasse, whether he recognized it or not.

She took another sip of her water, but didn't look away. The sexual magnetism he exuded was amazing, so intense that she could almost feel his fingers stroking down the slender column of her throat despite the courtyard that separated them.

He didn't look away either. Didn't move, didn't blink, didn't shift from that indolent pose against his railing. Just kept her in his sights, his gaze an odd mix of predator and partner.

It was strange and flattering—and oh, so arousing—to be the object of that heated stare.

But those are the wrong reactions, she told herself. She should be indignant or wary or at least concerned that he'd been staring at her as she took off her shirt, as she fanned herself with her skirt. She should be annoyed that he'd let her half strip and had done nothing to alert her to his presence.

It wasn't like she was naked, her sense of fair play reminded her, or even showing as much as she would on the shores of Lake Pontchartrain. And it wasn't like he'd been skulking in the shadows. No, his stare was a blatant, in-your-face come-on. One she'd been stupid to miss.

One she had a sinking feeling she wouldn't be able to resist.

Besides, the way he looked at her—like he was the big, bad wolf and she was the most succulent sheep in the herd—intrigued her. More, it turned her on. It had been a long time since she'd paid attention to that look on a man's face—and even longer since she'd given a damn.

One more time Lacey tried to convince herself to leave him hanging. To simply pick up her glass and head inside, where she would make sure to close her blinds behind her.

It was what she should do. What she *normally* would do, as she had absolutely no interest in encouraging any man—even one as hot as this one.

And yet she didn't want to go. Not now, when her toes were curling and her nipples tingling. Not now, when he was smiling a slow, wicked smile that had her fists clenching and her stomach turning somersaults.

Returning his stare with the hottest one she could muster, Lacey sat up and straddled the narrow lounger, placing her feet flat on the ground, but making no move to pull her skirt over her knees. She knew he couldn't see much, if anything at all, but she felt wanton sitting there with her pink lace panties exposed.

His eyes flared, grew darker, and she felt a little thrill all the way to her toes. Her nipples peaked and wetness pooled between her thighs. She knew she shouldn't be here, shouldn't be doing this. But it was like something out of one of her fantasies, and just once she wanted to be that woman she so often imagined.

Just once she wanted to live in the moment and say, "To hell with the consequences." Eyes still locked with his, she took a long, slow swallow from her glass, and then tipped it so that a stream of cold water poured onto the hollow of her throat. Ran over her collarbone and trickled down between her breasts, until her nipples hardened even more and her camisole clung wetly to her chest.

Then she closed her eyes and let her head loll back on her neck while she arched her back, knowing that she was spotlighting her rock-hard nipples, that even with the courtyard between them, he was close enough to see the dark shadow of her nipples beneath the thin silk.

Wondering if he liked what he saw.

Byron's brain shut down as he stared at the siren across from him. She was stunning, more beautiful than he had ever imagined, with her diamond-hard nipples and pink lace panties. More tempting than he had ever thought possible.

He felt his dick twitch, felt himself grow harder still, and it was all he could do to keep himself from leaping the two stories to the courtyard below, just so he could climb up to her. So he could bury his hands in those lush, red curls and run his lips over those full, tempting breasts.

He was more than aware that his thoughts echoed those on his fantasy blog, that the situation was eerily reminiscent of the one he'd just finished reading about, but for once, he wasn't imagining doing these things to *her*. No, for the first time in six, long months he was completely in the present. Completely wrapped up in the gorgeous, desirable woman who was, at this very moment, watching him, watching her.

The only question was, What was he going to do about it?

Chapter Two

Lacey shivered despite the heat, her body trembling under her neighbor's intense scrutiny. Part of her wanted to look away, wanted to pick up her water glass and head indoors. But she couldn't move, couldn't think. Could barely breathe, as her entire body lit up from the inside.

What was it about this man, with his black eyes and roguish grin, that turned her on so much? That held her transfixed on her balcony when she should be doing anything but this? She knew better—had known better since Curtis had used and abused her—and yet here she was, unable to look away. Worse, she was enjoying every second of watching him watch her. Was reveling in the arousal arcing through her body.

In the distance, lightning flashed. Once, twice, followed quickly by the sharp crack of thunder. The air around her grew heavier, wetter—as did her body at the sudden advent of the storm. The wind picked up, whipped through her loose hair and down her bare arms. Lifted her skirt and flirted with the soft, damp skin of her upper thighs.

And she let it.

Then watched, fascinated, as across the courtyard her neighbor's eyes

narrowed dangerously. She nearly grinned as he focused on her open thighs—
and, she hoped, the small scrap of pink lace that was the only thing separating
her from his view.

Desire escalated to need, and she felt her breath catch. Sweat bloomed on
her skin, ran in rivulets between her breasts and down her back, and still she
didn't go inside. Didn't cover herself. Didn't so much as move.

She couldn't.

Watching him watch her was the most erotic experience she'd ever had.

The breeze felt good as it caressed her thighs, as it slid between her breasts
and crept softly down her neck. She imagined it was his hands touching her—that
it was his long fingers trailing so languorously over her most private parts—and
nearly whimpered.

Biting her lip to keep the sound from escaping, she watched as his jaw
clenched at the telltale movement. Watched as his entire body tensed.

He knew exactly how she was feeling, knew exactly how turned on she was.
His knowledge was dangerous, disconcerting, and would have been completely
unbearable—after all, knowledge was power when it came to love and war—
except for the fact that he was as turned on as she was.

Maybe more—although Lacey wasn't sure that was possible.

The wind picked up, its caresses growing stronger. If she closed her eyes, she
could pretend that it was him teasing and tormenting her. That it was him bringing her one step closer to crazy.

But she couldn't look away, couldn't let her eyelids fall. His hands, clenched
on the iron railing, made the muscles of his forearms stand out in stark relief—a
silent testament to the fact that he was burning, as she was.

The need was building in her—teasing her, tantalizing her, taking her over
with the promise of sensual satisfaction. Suddenly, her nipples were so tight that
even the light fabric of her camisole chafed them, and her lower body ached with
the need to be filled. To be taken after so many long months of celibacy.

This time she couldn't stop the whimper that escaped, any more than she
could stop herself from stroking the back of her hand down her neck and over

her chest. With a sigh, she moved her hand even lower until she was cupping her left breast—massaging slowly and firmly as her thumb glanced across her nipple. Once, twice. Then again and again as her body spiraled up and nearly out of her control.

And still she watched him. Still she maintained eye contact as his body stiffened and his hands clutched the wrought-iron railing with the desperation of an addict looking for a much-delayed fix.

Setting her water glass down on the table beside her, she brought her right hand to her stomach. Lifted the soft cotton of her camisole so that she could trail her fingers up and down the sensitive skin of her stomach. She shivered at the first touch of cold fingers on hot skin, but the chill didn't last long. It couldn't— not when her neighbor stared at her with fiery eyes. Not when her own need was growing more desperate with every second that passed.

As she moved her hand lower, skimming it over the bare skin of her upper thighs, a little voice in the back of her head started clamoring. *What was she doing?* it asked. *Was she insane? She didn't know this man, didn't know anything about him. And she was out in the open, where any of her neighbors could see.*

Out in the open, where *anyone* could see.

She tuned the voice out, didn't listen. *Couldn't* listen, as her body continued to operate on a frequency her conscious mind no longer reached. She was too far gone, desire and need and the months of self-denial all tied together as her body searched for release. She'd deal with the consequences later, put up with his knowing looks and sly smiles if she had to. Right now she needed to come, and for reasons completely unknown to her, it had to be here.

Had to be in front of his passion-glazed eyes.

Had to be with *this* man, whose desire was making hers burn hotter and brighter than it ever had before.

With a sigh, she let her head fall back against the longue, then let the chaise take the weight of her upper body as she skimmed her fingers closer and closer to her inner thighs. Part of her wanted to just do it, to rush for the prize—the sweet release—that was only a few finger strokes away.

But there was something addictive about the power she felt in these moments, about the incredible raptness she was inspiring in her audience of one.
His gaze was intense, his jaw rigid. His muscles so tight that she could see them
bunch and ripple even across the courtyard. The knowledge that he was as cap-
tivated by her as she was by him moved through her; right now a bomb could go
off and he wouldn't flinch, wouldn't move. Hell, he probably wouldn't even hear
it. That's how intent he was on her.

After months—years—of being the good little girl, it felt good to be wanted.
After a lifetime of playing the innocent for men like Curtis—and taking whatever
they gave her—it was fabulous to wield total control over her own pleasure.

And over his.

The tension inside of her built at the thought, had her teetering on the edge
of a truly unbelievable orgasm before she'd so much as run a finger over her clit.
Deciding she'd waited long enough, and feeling more powerful—and more
aroused—than she could remember, Lacey slipped her index finger beneath her
pink lace thong and scooted the material out of the way so that she was totally
open, totally bare. So that there was nothing between her most secret flesh and
his most enthralled gaze.

And then, when she was sure she had his undivided attention, she began to
stroke.

With the first caress of her finger, the tip of his cock damn near blew right off.

Shit. Fuck. Goddamn, holy hell. Was this really happening?

Was his prim little neighbor about to get herself off in front of him?

Was she really going to let him watch?

Dear God, he certainly hoped so, because otherwise he was going to fucking
die from disappointment.

As his little redhead—somewhere in the middle of this he'd definitely begun
to think of her as *his*—slipped a finger between her slick folds, Byron groaned.
And nearly came.

Palming his dick through the heavy material of his jeans, he squeezed it tightly and did his best not to blow his whole fucking wad. But it was damn hard—no pun intended—as everything he'd ever wanted was spread before him like a fucking fantasy.

Only this wasn't a film. It was real, and all the more arousing because of it. As she touched herself, one delicate finger circling her clit again and again, he nearly lost it. Would have, except he wasn't ready for this to end, any more than he was ready to come in his jeans like an adolescent in the throes of his first real hard-on.

But he couldn't help imagining what she could feel like, couldn't help imagining that it was his finger caressing her to orgasm.

She'd feel like silk—wet, soft and so fucking rich that he wouldn't be able to resist her. He wouldn't be able to stop himself from burying his face between her thighs and his tongue in her gorgeous, glistening pussy.

The fantasy was so real—the need so alive—that he could almost taste her. Sweet, rich honey flowing over his tongue and down his throat. Thick and warm and delicious.

His cock tightened even more, until it was a miracle he could even stand. Until pain pierced him with every shallow breath he took. And when she slipped a finger inside herself, and then another—her hips rocking gently against her hand—he knew he was done for.

With another groan, he lowered his zipper slowly, then shuddered in relief as his dick sprang free from the restraining fabric. Fisting it, he stroked himself then stopped as that simple touch brought him right to the edge of orgasm. Any more and he'd go over, something he flat-out refused to do—at least until she did. They might not be lovers in the traditional sense, but "ladies first" had been his motto from his very first time with Jennifer Mason in the backseat of his daddy's BMW, and he saw no reason to change it now.

Besides, she couldn't last much longer. Her hips were rocking faster now, harder, and her skin had turned that pretty rose color that told him her orgasm was coming up fast. And it couldn't get here quickly enough for him—he was dying to see her shatter, desperate to watch her take her pleasure.

Pulling his eyes away from the sweet, sexy flesh between her thighs, he concentrated on her face. On her eyes. And was at once gratified to find her as focused on his cock as he'd been on her pussy.

Her green eyes were dark as emeralds, sexy as all hell. He felt himself start to come, his orgasm beginning at the base of his spine and then blowing down his cock with the force of a fucking cannon, and he gritted his teeth in an effort to stop it. Squeezed hard to make himself last just another minute.

Her lips parted in a moan, and he longed to hear it. Was pathetically grateful when the wind whipped the sound close enough for him to catch a breathy sigh.

She came with a strangled scream, her body stiffening as her curves arched off the longue. Her skin flushed pink—the prettiest pink he'd ever seen—while her wet dream of a mouth formed a perfect O.

Her gaze jerked up to his, clung, as the orgasm rolled through her, and that was all it took to blast his control to hell and back. With a yell of his own, he let the climax rip through him, and reveled in wave after wave of sensation that swamped him. Hard, rough, nearly brutal in its intensity, the orgasm took him with more force than anything ever had.

His knees actually trembled, and for one long moment he was afraid they wouldn't support him. Was afraid that he'd collapse on the wood boards of his balcony even as his cock continued to spume.

Locking his knees in place, he grabbed the railing with his free hand and let the sensations take him. Let them wash over him, again and again, in the most intense orgasm of his life. And still he didn't look away from her. Still he kept his eyes locked on the wild jade of hers as the pleasure went on and on and on.

Thunder boomed above them, shaking the building with its force, but he barely noticed. Just as he hardly noticed the rain suddenly lashing against his skin, against hers. But as the weather worsened, as the rain came down with more and more force, it became harder to keep up the eye contact. Harder to see her clearly.

The pleasure finally ebbed and he glanced around for something to clean himself up with. He grabbed a towel he'd left to dry on the balcony after his morning swim and did just that. Then turned back to her, wanting to regain their connection—needing to do so, with a desperation that bordered on insanity.

But she wasn't there, had instead taken his momentary distraction as a chance to slip away.

Cursing viciously, he studied her balcony with narrowed eyes. And told himself that he hadn't dreamed it. Hadn't dreamed her. She *had* been there—and would be again, if he had anything to say about it.

Chapter Three

Geez, Lace, what's got your panties in such a wad?"

"My panties are *not* in a wad!" Lacey looked across the narrow café table at Sandra, the first friend she'd made when she moved to New Orleans. A librarian at Tulane University, she'd helped Lacey with a lot of the initial information gathering she'd done weeks before.

Sandra knowingly eyed the second order of beignets Lacey was in the middle of devouring. Café du Monde was famous for the square, French doughnuts, and usually Lacey contented herself with one order, but today her nerves had her scarfing down anything she could get her hands on.

"If you say so." Sandra flipped her hair and started scoping out the prospects at the surrounding tables. The pickings were slim—mostly tourists and teenagers—but Lacey watched in amusement as her friend managed to garner the interest of the only hot guy in the place.

Of course, Sandra was good at getting male attention. And unlike Lacey, she knew exactly what to do with it when she had it. Petite, blond, and cute as a button, she was everything Lacey wasn't—including interested in a long-term relationship.

"I do say so," Lacey reiterated firmly, after she'd shoved the last beignet in her mouth. "This has nothing to do with a guy—the book's just been giving me trouble lately."

As soon as the words passed her mouth, Lacey felt guilty for the lie. While the book was turning into a nightmare of epic proportions, that wasn't what had her so out of sorts. No, her sexy neighbor was what had Lacey so stressed-out. He was also the reason she'd suggested this trip to Café du Monde for breakfast instead of eating on her balcony as she and Sandra had a tendency to do when they made an early morning breakfast date.

For the last two days she'd done everything but dive for cover in an effort to avoid him; she'd even kept the blinds on her balcony firmly closed. She didn't usually spook so easily, but she was too embarrassed to face him. She still couldn't believe she'd actually let that whole scene happen the other night—it was so unlike her. Shocking, impulsive, insane—the encounter was everything she wasn't. And then some.

"Well, if it's the book, stop by the library and we'll do some digging together. Summer's always quiet, and I'm sick of staring at the walls and inventing things to do."

"I might do that." Lacey jumped on the lifeline, thrilled to have her friend's attention turned away from the subject of men. "I'm having a terrible time getting anyone to talk to me. Maybe you can help me come up with some more names to contact."

"Sure." Sandra pushed back from the table gracefully and swung her stylish hobo bag over her shoulder. "I've got a meeting until eleven, but after that I should be free for the rest of the day."

"I'll stop by sometime after lunch."

"Excellent." Sandra headed toward the opening in the wrought-iron gates that surrounded the sidewalk café. Half a dozen male heads turned to watch her go, and she worked the attention for all it was worth.

Lacey sipped her café au lait and concentrated on following her friend's progress, in a desperate attempt to focus on something, anything, besides the steamy encounter she'd had on her balcony the night before last.

She almost laughed, would have if she wasn't so damned annoyed with herself. What kind of woman was brave enough to share that kind of intimate sexual experience with a total stranger, yet too cowardly to stick around to see what might happen next?

A *smart one*, she told herself as she polished off the last of the beignets. One who knew that real life rarely lived up to fantasy.

A *lonely one*, the little voice in the back of her head chastised her. One who no longer trusted her own judgment when it came to men but who still had all the needs of a woman who was much less afraid than she.

Completely disgusted—with herself, the situation, the whole damn world—Lacey reached into the ratty brown messenger bag that went almost everywhere with her and ripped a few sheets of paper from her binder. If she couldn't get her devastatingly sexy neighbor out of her mind, then maybe she could channel all her pent-up desire for him into her latest blog entry. God knew, the way she was feeling, she could probably light up an entire block of Bourbon Street with the sexual energy pumping through her.

I lay in bed at night, naked, and dream you. Dream your mouth sliding over my breasts, your hands smoothing down my stomach, your fingers playing with my clit. As she wrote, Lacey struggled to immerse herself in the words. To remember the fantasy she'd had last night as she'd stretched out in her own bed, staring at the ceiling and searching desperately for sleep.

But, for once, she wasn't able to get lost in the fantasy—or the sexy heat spiraling through her. She tried to blame it on the sidewalk café, tried to tell herself she was struggling with her blog entry because she was in public, surrounded by strangers.

But her breasts were achy and her pussy damp despite the public venue, and she couldn't shake the awkward, frightened feeling that had been with her ever since she'd realized late last night that she was no longer fantasizing about an imaginary lover.

No, today—like last night—she was thinking about *him*. Imagining *him*, with his chest bare and his cock in his fist as he stared at her across that damn courtyard. Wanting *him* to slowly lick his way down her body.

That was what was really bothering her, she finally admitted. Not the fact that she was in a public place, but rather that her imaginary lover had a face for the first time in longer than she wanted to admit.

To see *him* when she closed her eyes, to think of *him* when she touched herself, was more than strange. More than disconcerting. It was downright alarming, especially since her body wanted nothing more than to be watched by him again.

From the moment she'd seen him come—the moment she'd let him see her do the same—she hadn't been able to get him out of her mind. And now, as she tried to put her latest fantasy into words, he was still right there.

Ugh. Lacey folded the papers in half and stuffed them back in her notebook. Why couldn't that one encounter be enough? She wasn't looking for more—didn't want more—so she should have just been able to enjoy it and move on. But instead here she was, having spent the last hour shoving French doughnuts in her face as she tried to pretend she wasn't so turned on that it hurt to breathe.

She was still cursing herself when her sixth sense had her looking up just in time to spy her very hot neighbor stroll into the open-air café and up to the long front counter to place his order.

Heat flashed through her body at her first glimpse of him, though she didn't know if it was residual lust or simply out-and-out embarrassment. Probably a little bit of both, she decided, while her heart started to beat double time in a panicked tattoo. Either way, she had to get out of there—and quickly—before he finished ordering and ran right into her.

Maybe it *was* stupid, but she couldn't face him, not now. Not when she hadn't figured out what to say to him or how to act. She didn't know if she'd ever find the right words, but until she came up with something, it seemed like a good idea, all around, to stay as far away from sexy courtyard guy as humanly possible.

Gathering up her things as fast as she could, and leaving a brand-new, steaming cup of café au lait on the table in the process, Lacey darted for the opening in the low, black iron fence that surrounded the café.

Sure that she was going to make it, positive that he'd be held up by the line at the front for the couple of minutes it would take her to mount her getaway, Lacey relaxed her guard as she got closer to the exit. There was no need for a confrontation here, no need to assume that he was as aware of her as she was of him. She'd just walk out and be on her way without him ever knowing she'd been in his vicinity.

Besides, for all she knew, he wouldn't care even if he did see her. It wasn't like he'd come knocking on her door to introduce himself any time in the last few days. He was probably as interested in avoiding her as she was him.

Calmer now that rationalization had set in, and that freedom was within her grasp, Lacey breathed a huge sigh of relief. Then froze when a strong hand grabbed her elbow and pulled her to a stop. Startled, she could do nothing but watch as everything in her hands—including her trusty bag, her book of the moment, and the papers she'd been writing her blog on—slid right out of her hands and onto the ground between them.

"Sorry. I didn't mean to startle you," said her hotter-than-hell neighbor as he crouched down and began gathering up her stuff.

That she let him, and didn't even try to help, showed just how far gone she really was. Normally she'd freak out if anyone handled the rough drafts of her blog entries; while she loved writing the blog, she was almost obsessed with keeping her identity secret. Not just because of the safety issue, but because the blog was her sexual outlet. Her deepest, darkest fantasies on display. Her psyche laid wide open, and she'd rather have a root canal without anesthetic than let someone inside her head again. God knew, Curtis had done enough damage to last a lifetime.

"But I didn't want you to leave before I had a chance to talk to you. I've been trying to run into you for a couple of days now."

His dark brown eyes were nearly black as they studied her, and she felt her stomach tremble in response—as if an entire flock of rabid vultures had taken up residence there. Or, at the very least, one rabid vulture with an attitude problem.

As his words sunk in, she could feel her cheeks flaming. Of course he'd been looking for her—how often did a guy come across a woman more than willing to give him a balcony peep show? And one he didn't have to pay for, at that. He probably wanted to arrange an encore.

Wanting nothing more than to escape, yet deathly afraid that it was far too late for that, Lacey all but ripped her things from his outstretched hands. "Thanks," she mumbled, then turned to go before she died of abject humiliation. Or jumped him out of the rampant horniness that only seemed to surface around him.

"Hey, wait." Once again those strong fingers curled around her elbow. Once again, her stomach flip-flopped crazily. "I don't even know your name."

Taking a deep breath in an effort to ignore the embarrassment—and, God help her, arousal—that jangled along her nerve endings, Lacey gave him her most intimidating stare, the one she'd mastered after ten years as a true-crime investigator and writer. "Is there some reason you want to know it?"

Those bittersweet chocolate eyes turned assessing, then narrowed dangerously, as if he didn't like her attitude. "I don't normally sleep with a woman until I know her name."

Arching an eyebrow, she tried to tug her elbow away, but his fingers tightened. Not enough to hurt; just enough to let her know that he wasn't planning on letting her go anytime soon.

Heat gathered in her lower body, and she nearly shook her head in despair. What did it say about her that the thought of being trapped by him was at least as arousing as it was upsetting? Maybe more so.

Think of Curtis, she told herself grimly, as she tried to ignore the arousal winding through her. *Think of how sexy he'd been at the beginning—strong, masterful, hotter than hell. And he'd turned out to be the fucking Marquis de Sade—both physically and emotionally.*

She couldn't go through that again.

She *wouldn't* go through it.

Which meant she had absolutely no business being this turned on. This intrigued. Not by any man and certainly not by *this* one, no matter what had happened between them on those stupid balconies. He was trouble with a capital *T*, and she wanted nothing more to do with him.

Liar, the little voice in the back of her mind said, but she tuned it out. Sometimes denial was a girl's best friend.

"I wasn't aware we'd slept together." Using every ounce of willpower she had, Lacey kept her voice cool, her eyes level. Her self-control was rewarded when his charming smile turned into a not-so-nice scowl.

"You know what I mean."

"Do I?" She cocked her head to one side as if puzzled, and waited for his fury to ignite. Unlike with Curtis, it seemed to take more than a smart mouth to set him off.

He leaned forward until his face was only an inch or two from hers, until his perfect mouth was well within kissing distance. She jerked her head back at the thought, but he followed her, closing any distance she tried to put between them.

"You know exactly what I'm talking about." The words were low, husky, and instantly evoked images from the Great Balcony Escapade in her head. Images that had her breath hitching in her throat and her nipples tingling inside her flimsy excuse for a bra.

For long seconds she had no comeback, her brain so scrambled by sexual awareness that she couldn't do much but stare at him and drool. And damn it, he knew it, knew how he affected her, the edgy frustration in his eyes giving way to a sexual satisfaction that was nearly palpable.

His fingers relinquished their hold on her elbow and slid slowly, languorously down her arm to her wrist. They lingered there, stroking softly, until the spark of need inside her had become a five-alarm fire.

Once again, Lacey tried to pull away, self-preservation paramount in her head.

Once again, he held her trapped—as much with the dark power of his gaze as with the sensual hold of his fingers around her too-sensitive wrist.

"I'm Byron Hawthorne."

"Lacey Adams." She choked out the words before she could think better of them, and even as she told herself she was being an idiot, she couldn't bring herself to regret them. Standing here with Byron felt better than anything had—Tuesday night excluded—in a very long time.

"It's nice to meet you, Lacey Adams." His fingers uncurled from her wrist, and she felt an alien sense of disappointment at their loss. Until his other arm wrapped around her, so that his right hand rested on the small of her back.

"You too." *Is that my voice?* she wondered frantically of that soft, breathy intonation that was barely more than a whisper.

"Come sit down. Have a cup of coffee with me." As he spoke, his hand exerted a subtle pressure on her lower back and he began to steer her toward a nearby table.

And she let him, despite the warning bells clamoring in her head.

Let him guide her, though every instinct she had told her he was dangerous.

Let him direct her like a lamb to slaughter, though the rational side of her brain was telling her to get out and get out fast. This was a man she could lose herself in, and she'd worked too damn hard to find herself after Curtis to ever let that happen again.

"I ordered you a café au lait and some beignets. The waiter should be by with them any minute now." He stopped in front of a small garden table and pulled a chair out for her.

She almost sat, almost gave up her vow to swear off men, just that easily.

Almost forgot Curtis and everything she'd suffered at his hands in an effort to appease the blazing sexual need that just wouldn't go away.

But as Byron's words—as well as the command behind them—sunk in, she froze in place. Then jerked out from beneath his restraining hand before he could stop her.

As she did, a bunch of thoughts whirled in her head, each one fighting for supremacy.

He'd ordered without consulting her.

He'd ignored her when she came in, even though he'd obviously seen her.

He was sure of her—so sure that he'd bought her doughnuts she didn't want and a coffee that she did.

He expected her to do exactly as he told her.

The thoughts circled faster and faster, until a new one came to the forefront, coalescing out of months and years of annoyance and fear and more pain than any woman should have to endure.

He was just like Curtis. Just like the man she'd fought so hard, and for so long, to escape.

He had the same sexual magnetism.

The same lack of concern for her wishes.

The same need for control—ordering for her, ignoring what she said, guiding her to do what he wanted her to do and to hell with what she wanted. And she'd almost gone along with it—just like she had with Curtis. Almost followed him like a good little girl without a brain—or a will—of her own.

Had she learned nothing?

After all this time—and all the pain—was she just as stupid and self-destructive as she'd always been? It had taken her months to get away from Curtis, well over a year to get her self-confidence back. Was she really going to give all that up just because she was attracted to a man? Just because he wanted her to?

Self-disgust had her spine stiffening and her jaw locking. Oh no, she *wasn't* going back there. Not now, not ever again. She'd come too far to just throw her newfound confidence away on the first easy grin to come her way. Even if it did belong to the sexiest man she'd ever seen.

Or maybe *because* it did.

"I don't have time for coffee." Her voice wasn't as forceful as she would have liked, but it got the job done. Made his eyebrows draw down in confusion and annoyance. Made him frown unhappily, as if he wasn't used to his orders being thwarted.

And he probably wasn't. Curtis sure as hell hadn't been. But that was just too damn bad.

"One more cup—"

"No." She pulled away from him, this time refusing to let Byron's scowl—or his tantalizing fingers—stop her. "Thanks for the thought, but I have work to do."

"Don't go, Lacey. Have some breakfast." He held out a hand, palm up, in entreaty, and she almost fell for it. Almost stayed because he looked disconcerted and lost, like a little boy who had just misplaced his brand-new toy.

But she wasn't a toy, and she never would be again. "I already had breakfast—which you would have known had you bothered to ask." She shoved her book and papers into her bag with trembling hands, more concerned with getting away than she was about making sure she had all her belongings. Then she gave Byron a smile she was far from feeling, and turned and headed for the sidewalks of Decatur like her favorite pair of Manolos depended on it.

The more she wanted to turn around, the faster she walked.

Well, that sure as hell hadn't gone the way he'd planned it. Byron watched Lacey walk away, appreciating the sexy sway of her curvy ass despite his overwhelming sense of frustration. And failure.

What had he done wrong? He didn't know, but he must have done something—Lacey had left so fast it was amazing she hadn't sprained an ankle in the ridiculously sexy four-inch heels she was wearing.

He continued to stare in her direction long after she'd disappeared into the midmorning crowds. Why did her interest—or lack thereof—matter so much to him anyway? If the lady wasn't interested, then he was man enough to move on.

Bullshit! He slammed a hand through his hair in irritation. Did she really expect him to believe that she was as unconcerned as she tried to appear? He snorted. All women should be so unconcerned. Did she think he hadn't seen her nipples harden when he touched her? That he hadn't felt the hitch in her breath or the sudden warmth of her skin when he'd held her wrist in his hand?

And, God knew, his body hadn't lit up like this—at least not for a flesh-and-blood woman—in longer than he could remember. His dick was so hard it was impossible to breathe without pain, and every single thing he wanted to do with Lacey was running double time through his head.

Sinking into the small, almost doll-like chair next to the table he'd selected, he went over the scene from the balcony for what had to be the fiftieth time in two days.

Replayed it like a favorite song.

Savored it like a fine wine.

The fact that he'd been reliving it probably made him a loser. But he was okay with that—more than okay. That half hour with Lacey had been, bar none, the hottest sexual experience of his life, and he could only imagine what it would be like when he finally got inside her.

And I will get inside her, he vowed grimly as the waiter delivered his order for two. There was no way he'd let sexual chemistry like this go to waste, not when it was this rare. And this powerful.

Not when she wanted him as badly as he wanted her.

Picking up the small, white cup of café au lait, he took a long swig as he contemplated what he'd done wrong in approaching her. And how the hell he was going to fix it.

Because one thing was for sure: He *needed* to fix it.

She was the first woman he'd been interested in since he'd discovered that damn blog—the first one who could take his mind off his fantasy woman and her deepest desires—and he wasn't about to let her slip through his fingers.

"Excuse me?" At the tentative voice, he loosened his death grip on the coffee cup and turned to see a young girl of maybe fifteen staring at him. She had dark hair and blue eyes and looked more than a little wary. Not that he blamed her—he probably looked like a cross between a thundercloud and a pissed-off serial killer.

"Yes?" He tried for his most reassuring voice, but it must not have been very convincing. The girl looked like she wanted to be anywhere but where she was.

"This fell out of your friend's bag when she was leaving." The words came out in a rush as she held out a couple sheets of notebook paper. "It looks like she spent some time on it, so I figured maybe you could return it to her."

He stared at the slightly crumpled papers for a minute, nonplussed, then forced a smile as he took them. "Thanks. I'll see that she gets them."

"Okay." The girl turned to leave with a palpable air of relief, and again he wondered what he had done to make her so nervous. He felt bad—after all, she'd given him the perfect reason to seek out Lacey again, and he was going to take it.

He didn't even want to think about how desperate this would make him look. Hell, he *was* desperate. Why should he bother to hide it? Something about Lacey lit him up like the floor of the New York Stock Exchange on a big trading day, and he wasn't going to fight it. Not this time.

Failure simply wasn't an option.

Pushing the uncomfortable memories of his old life to the back of his mind, he glanced down at the top piece of paper. Read a few words out of curiosity. Then read them again as his entire body stiffened into one giant hard-on.

I lay in bed at night, naked, and dream you. Dream your mouth sliding over my breasts, your hands smoothing down my stomach, your fingers playing with my clit.

I follow the path I want you to take, let the tips of my fingers brush my nipples as my palms cup my breasts.

I tug on the tight crests, feel lightning shoot through me, and imagine you sliding into me. I'm wet and aching and the promise of you only makes me crazier. I feel your cock brush against my inner thigh, feel—

Byron drew his own shaky breath as the words abruptly came to an end. Smoothing one far-from-steady hand through his hair, he let the harmless-looking piece of notebook paper settle onto the table. No wonder the girl who had given it to him had been wary; he was shocked she'd managed to work up the nerve to come over here at all after reading what Lacey had written. If—

He cut his thoughts off abruptly, refusing to spend one more second dodging the holy-shit realization that had grabbed him by the balls as he'd begun to read what Lacey had written. That same realization was currently shaking the shit out of him like a great white shark, and no matter how many times he told himself that what he was thinking couldn't be true, he knew that it was.

The woman he'd been fantasizing about for months lived right across the courtyard from him.

The woman who wrote the blog entries that had him tossing and turning all night lived in the same damn apartment building as him.

The woman who had given him the hottest sexual experience of his life was also the woman who had become his most devastating fantasy.

After all his agonizing, all his frustration, it was one more kick in the ass to realize she'd been within his reach all along.

What were the chances of that?

Unable to look away from the paper, he read the beginning of Lacey's newest fantasy one more time, each word whipping through his mind like wildfire. Emblazoning itself on his brain until he couldn't forget it if he tried.

Draining the second cup of coffee in one gulp, he folded the papers and shoved them into his back pocket before heading on to Decatur. Sliding past a group of kids dressed entirely in black—all of whom were white enough against the dark clothes to pass for the vampires they obviously aspired to be—he ambled toward the studio where he built his furniture and wondered what he was going to do with his newfound knowledge. Because one thing was for certain: Doing nothing was completely out of the question.

Chapter Four

Lacey ground her teeth in frustration as she stared at the Mardi Gras Madam herself, Veronique Rosen. The woman who was credited with single-handedly running the largest prostitution ring in American history looked somewhat different in person—a little older, a little grittier, a little more used—but she was definitely the same woman whose picture had been plastered all over every supermarket tabloid in the country eighteen months before.

She had the same bleached-blond hair, the same cornflower blue eyes. Same big—obviously fake—boobs. And yet it was like the woman had complete and total amnesia, as if the conversation they'd had over the phone weeks before had been nothing more than a figment of Lacey's overactive imagination.

"Veronique, come on." Lacey slammed her glass of iced tea on the table harder than she'd intended as she struggled to keep the anger from her voice. "You can't seriously expect me to believe this 'I don't recall' routine that you've suddenly got going on."

Veronique took a long drag off her cigarette and stared at her with eyes so glazed and flat that Lacey had to remind herself she wasn't talking to a dead woman. Veronique might be stoned—and more than a little drunk—but she was still alive and kicking. At least for now. "I don't really care what you believe. You're the one who's been hassling *me*."

Lacey bit her tongue against the blatant falsehood. When she'd gotten hold of Veronique weeks before, the other woman had been very accommodating—not to mention extremely interested in telling her part of the story to Lacey in exchange for some free publicity, in order to wrangle herself a book deal from a major New York publisher. Now all that seemed to have disappeared. Veronique's unwillingness to discuss even the most basic details of the case bordered on the obsessive. Or the terrified. It was just one more suspicious instance in a long line of them that was raising Lacey's hackles.

Veronique took another long drag off her cigarette, and when she spoke again, her voice was lower, younger than it had ever sounded before. "There's a lot more going on here than you think. A lot more than the press reported on."

Lacey's stomach clenched as excitement, pure and undiluted, ripped through her. "Like what?" she asked in the softest, most soothing voice she could summon.

"Like all those girls I had working for me. They were well-trained, expensive. Where do you think they came from?"

"You told the police most of them were college students."

"Yeah. College girls. Right." Veronique's laugh was anything but humorous.

"They were enrolled at UNO. Loyola. Tulane. The story checks out—I've done the research."

"Exactly. That's what I'm trying to tell you. You're dealing with men who can turn lies into truth. Men who can make stories check out, even when they're full of gigantic holes. What makes you think you can change that?"

"The cops—" Veronique stopped abruptly. Looked away.

Lacey leaned forward, lowered her voice. "What about the cops?"

"They've come around, warned me and some of the other girls off."

"Warned you off about what?"

"What do you think?" For the first time, Veronique looked angry. "Ever since you got your hands on that police file, they've been damn nervous."

"They asked you not to talk to me?" Lacey's stomach clenched as she thought of all the doors she'd had slammed in her face in the past two weeks.

Veronique's laugh was sarcastic. "Yeah, they *asked* us."

"What would happen if you did tell me something?"

For long seconds, Veronique was silent. Then, just when Lacey was sure she wouldn't answer, she murmured, "We'd end up like the other girls—missing or dead. And no offense, Lacey, no book is worth that."

"They threatened to kill you?"

"They threatened worse than that."

"What's worse than dead?" Lacey asked intently.

"If you have to ask, you don't know half as much about this case as the cops are afraid of." Veronique took another long drag off her cigarette and leaned back in her chair.

As Veronique's words sank in, merging slowly with the ugly suspicions Lacey had been dancing around for months, Lacey's mind raced to assimilate the new facts. Originally, she'd told herself she didn't have enough proof to leap to conclusions, but the more she learned, the harder it was to ignore her instincts screaming at her.

Which was why she had spent the last month scouring every news report, tabloid article, and blog posting on the subject. Had gotten her hands on the trial transcripts and police files and pored over every word in them. Had talked to everyone she could find who was involved in the case. Nothing—nothing—had so much as hinted at what her gut told her was going on.

"This isn't your garden-variety prostitution ring, is it, Veronique?" she asked when she was able to speak around the sudden lump in her throat.

Lacey kept her voice steady through sheer strength of will, when everything inside of her was a maelstrom of confusion. She didn't know what had gone on here—didn't know what was still going on—but she was smart enough to smell a cover-up when she saw one. And in this case, there was more than one. "This is more. It has to be. Girls are disappearing. You're scared to death. It's—"

"Don't say it!" Veronique cut her off sharply, then glanced over Lacey's shoulder to the street beyond the window. When their eyes met, Veronique's were once again glazed. Once again afraid. "Don't even think it." She picked up her purse and stepped unsteadily away.

"What happened to your girls, Veronique? The records said you had hundreds of girls working for you, yet only a handful went to prison. Most of the others disappeared into thin air. Nobody could track them down."

"You're making it sound really bad." She ground out her cigarette, then quickly lit up another one, all without taking her eyes from Lacey's. "And it's not like that at all. I treated my girls well. They were happy."

"If you continue with this, if you keep pushing, all you're going to do is get yourself killed—and maybe a whole bunch of other people as well. Find something else to write a book about, before you end up in over your head. This is too dangerous."

"Like you?" Lacey spoke softly, as if her tone would somehow negate the destructive power of her words.

Veronique smiled, and it was the saddest sight Lacey had ever seen. "Over my head? Honey, I'm in so deep I'll probably never see the surface again. Listen to what I'm telling you before it's too late. Trust me, you don't want to end up like me."

She turned away.

"I can help you." The words shot out of Lacey's mouth before she knew she was going to say them, but once they were out, she knew she wouldn't take them back even if she could. The offer was impulsive and impractical and wouldn't do a damn thing to help her write her book. But Veronique needed help, and it really didn't matter if she'd gotten herself into the mess she was currently in. It was obvious she wanted out, but didn't know how to go about getting there.

"You can't help me." Veronique stumbled back, and there was anger in her face now. Anger and a fear so deep it could only be called terror. Lacey winced away from it before she could stop herself. "In a few more days, you won't even be able to help yourself."

"Veronique." She reached for her, but the former madam shrugged her off like she was a particularly persistent gnat, and kept walking.

Out of the dining room.

Out of the restaurant.

Straight out of luck.

Lacey kept watching her—too skinny, too drugged, too *scared* to do herself any good—until she was completely out of sight.

Then picked up her own bag and started walking home, anger and confusion and her own fear churning in her stomach as Veronique's words—and her own questions—ran through her head again and again.

Dangerous.

Where did the girls come from?

More than prostitution.

Police involved.

Where did the girls come from?

Dangerous.

Can't help me.

In over your head.

Where did the girls come from?

The longer Lacey walked, the more furious she became. Continuing down Decatur to Conti, she turned left at the narrow street and headed toward her apartment. Tourists thronged around her, brightly colored beads at their necks and yard-long drinks in their hands in an effort to combat the late-afternoon heat. They were an interesting sight, and she was new enough to New Orleans that on a normal day she would have enjoyed the spectacle. But today, when all she wanted to do was get to her apartment and her computer and her research, the crowds just annoyed her.

She swung an absent right onto Bourbon, passing by a couple of the Big Easy's more notorious strip clubs. Pictures of half-naked girls in compromising positions adorned the windows, and for a minute it was all she could do to keep from getting sick. All she could do not to cry as she finally allowed her suspicions free rein.

With Veronique's words echoing in her head, Lacey ran over what she knew, along with what she could only guess at. If this wasn't just a prostitution ring—as Veronique had admitted to her—then what was it?

A drug ring? Were the girls somehow involved in drug smuggling? What else could have scared Veronique so badly? What else could have made every witness, every source she'd managed to uncover clam up so completely? The world of drugs was a dirty, disgusting one—more than one of the books she'd written in the past eight years had touched on the subject—and most of the kingpins stopped at nothing to keep their secrets. To many of them, murder was nothing more than a means to an end. And torture—torture was considered an amusing pastime.

Approaching a beautifully restored building that looked more like an antebellum mansion than a strip club, she studied the lewd pictures on the outside wall and windows, as her mind went over the evidence she'd managed to accumulate so far.

With everyone clamming up on her, there wasn't as much as she'd like. But there was enough for her to start building the foundations of her book. Though logic told her this was about drugs, her instincts told her it wasn't—or, at least, that it wasn't solely about drugs. But maybe her instincts were wrong. Maybe it *was* drug running that had Veronique so freaked out. God knew, she wasn't the first woman involved in the case who had been higher than a kite while Lacey had interviewed her. And she wouldn't be the last.

But it didn't feel like that, didn't have the same characteristics she'd seen when she'd written her books on the San Diego/Tijuana and Miami drug trades. Besides, simple, low-level drug trafficking didn't bring the kind of fear she'd seen in Veronique's eyes, any more than it bought the kind of police and district attorney cover-up that she was becoming convinced had gone on here.

If this case reached as high as she thought it did—past the New Orleans and Louisiana politicians already exposed, and into the most elite of Washington's upper echelon—then she couldn't imagine that it was really about the drugs. Most politicians were too savvy—and too scared—to get involved with high-level drug trafficking.

She continued looking at the pictures of girls in various states of undress, doing any number of sexually suggestive things. Her gaze was drawn again and again to the picture of a young woman dressed as a schoolgirl. She was wearing a very short plaid skirt, white knee-highs and saddle shoes. Her hair was in pig-tails and she was licking a long, phallic-shaped lollipop. She was also topless.

In any other city, the club owner would have been arrested for breaking public decency laws. In New Orleans, he was celebrated.

Her stomach churned as her gaze landed on the old-fashioned light pole not more than three feet away from her. And, more specifically, on the flyer attached to it.

The flyer was like any number she'd seen in her life—bright pink, with a HAVE YOU SEEN THIS GIRL? message at the top. But it wasn't the message, or even the information beneath the picture or even the information beneath the picture, that kept her transfixed. Anne Marie Winston. Last seen on March 19, 2007, on the University of Calgary campus. Last heard from on May 23, 2007. Call came from a Bourbon Street pay phone.

No, it was the photo of the young, beautiful blonde that took up most of the eleven-by-seventeen-inch sheet of paper that had her staring, her mind racing. Reaching out with great care, she pulled the flyer free from the lamppost. She'd seen this girl before—she just knew it. She was one of the girls who'd been busted in the prostitution ring, but had disappeared before she had a chance to stand trial.

The hair was wrong. If this was the girl she thought it was, her mug shot had shown her with much shorter, dark hair. Lacey had spent hours studying those photos, and she knew this girl was one of them.

She was a missing person? Lacey looked at the flyer again. Last seen going to school in Canada. How did a Canadian college student end up hooking in New Orleans? And why?

She turned around, stared blindly at the wall of photos and tried to find an explanation that didn't involve kidnapping and sexual slavery. She couldn't.

As her mind worked, she became aware of what she was staring at, and the investigative instincts that had helped her so many times before kicked in with a vengeance. Walking closer to the wall, she began to search through the vast collage of snapshots that covered the windows of the club. The photos were small and run-together, the faces almost indistinguishable as the various photographers had been more concerned with other parts of the girls' anatomies.

She studied picture after picture, wondering if she was losing her mind. None of the photos matched the face of the girl on the missing-persons flyer. She was about to give up, convinced her imagination was running away with her, when she found what she was looking for in the top row of pictures.

She studied the photo for a second, her face all but pressed up against the glass, and tried to tell herself she was wrong. That the girl dressed in a pair of skimpy black panties, spread-eagled and handcuffed to the bed, wasn't Anne Marie Winston, the same girl on the missing-persons flyer. But when she held up the flyer, the resemblance between the two photos was clear: The eyes were the same, the cheekbones, the fine gold necklace and butterfly around her neck.

She ignored the disgusting pose Anne Marie was in, ignored the lack of clothes and too heavy makeup, and tried again to figure out the ins and outs of how this girl had ended up on this wall. How she'd ended up in this city when she'd gone missing from a school that was on the other side of the continent.

Legs buckling, she sank to the ground with a sigh, wrapping her arms around her stomach as all the information she had so far come across worked through her mind. She didn't know how long she sat on the dirty curb at the corner of Bourbon and Toulouse, locked in her own little world, while unfazed tourists passed her by. Sweat trickled down her neck, down her back, but she ignored it. Just like she ignored the smell of urine and puke that saturated the humid street.

She let all the information she had so far come across stream through her mind. As she sorted it out, refocusing her attention from prostitution to slavery, she grew more and more convinced that she was finally on the right track.

She was knee-deep into plans to change the focus of her investigation—and the book—before it hit her that what she was considering wasn't the book she'd been contracted to write. It wasn't the story the publisher was expecting, and it wasn't the story she'd originally wanted to tell.

It was a million times uglier.

A million times more dangerous.

And yet, she knew she couldn't walk away. Not if what she suspected was true, that young girls were being kidnapped and forced into sex slavery. Not if everyone who had the power to stop it—the NOPD, the DA's office, the FBI—was willing to look the other way.

And why are they willing to look the other way? she asked herself viciously. *Money? Fear? Involvement? All three?*

Whipping out her notebook, she made a few quick notes, putting her thoughts down in a stream-of-consciousness style that she hoped would help her piece the puzzle together. But she couldn't concentrate. The street was spinning and she was having a horrible time keeping her balance. Reaching out, she braced a hand on the building and took a few slow, easy breaths until the Tilt-A-Whirl in her head started to slow down.

She had to do something, had to call someone. But who? The NOPD, whose spectacular lack of cooperation had already left her in a bind writing-wise? The FBI? But the girl wasn't a U.S. citizen, wasn't officially their problem.

So who? She glanced down at the flyer one last time and realized she didn't have a choice. She would have to start by calling Mark and Carrie Winston, the contacts listed on the flyer.

Maybe they'd be able to tell her that Anne Marie was home safe, that the suspicions of sex slavery running through her head were just that.

As she turned to head home, movement from the balcony two stories above the strip club caught her eye.

Glancing up, she froze as she realized she was being watched by a man who, despite his suave and sophisticated appearance, had an air of brutality about him. Dressed in a tailored black suit and dress shirt, an expensive watch gleaming at his wrist, he looked like he could be anything from a stockbroker to a doctor. But the ice in his blue eyes, the cruel twist of his lips, told her he was something a lot more sinister. Something she'd do better to avoid.

Yet she didn't look away, didn't start moving down the street toward home as had been her original intention. Though his scrutiny caused ice to skitter down her spine like the sharpest of razor blades, she couldn't help returning the perusal.

Instead of aggravating him, her attention seemed to amuse him and his lips twisted into a smile that was both interested and sadistic. Unwilling to give an inch, she wiggled her fingers in a brief but purely feminine wave. A quirk of one blond eyebrow was his only response, but it was enough to tell her that she had surprised him.

Tossing him a small smile that didn't meet her eyes, she turned and headed down the street. As she walked, she wondered who he was. And why he had found her so interesting.

Gregory watched with a smile of pure enjoyment as the redhead walked away. She had spirit, that one, and a fire that could keep a man warm in a Siberian prison. Or, he acknowledged with a wary tilt of his head, burn the hell out of him if he let his guard down.

But what had she been doing out there? He'd noticed her when she was still half a block up—strolling down Bourbon Street with purpose in her stride and heat in her eyes. She'd looked like she'd known exactly where she was going, and he'd pitied the poor tourists who'd crossed her path. For a minute, he'd thought she was going to beat the old guy in the Hawaiian shirt who'd stopped directly in her path.

He'd continued watching as she'd skirted the old geezer, because he was fascinated by the way she moved. By the passion that vibrated inside of her. By— and he was being completely honest here—the sheer power of her beauty.

She was a looker, no doubt about that. Long red hair, big green eyes, a delicate body that cried out for domination; she was every fantasy he'd ever had and never known he was missing.

When she'd stopped in front of his club, he'd been astounded. Had wondered if she felt his interest the way he felt the siren call she issued with every slap of her hot-pink stilettos against the pavement. But she hadn't glanced up, hadn't revealed an awareness of him as she'd stared, transfixed, at the pictures on the outside of his club. .

But then she'd reached for one of the flyers that had been on the pole outside his club for months. He'd never paid any attention to it—after all, since Katrina, flyers papered every pole in the Quarter, advertising services, looking for people who had gone missing in the floods, promising to rebuild the city to its former glory.

Yet the way she'd looked at the flyer and his walls—not to mention whatever she'd written in that little notebook—had ice skittering up his spine. What had been on that flyer that was so interesting to her? And what did it have to do with his club?

Despite his concerns, when she'd sunk to the curb in front of the club, he'd almost bounded down the two flights of stairs that separated them to see if he could be of assistance. Which was quite a role reversal from him, as he was much more used to playing the big, bad wolf than he was the prince who rescued damsels in distress.

He knew the prudent thing to do would be to find out what was in that notebook. If it was damning, he could have Jim dispose of the body in the lake. But even as he told himself to give the order, he didn't do it. There was something about her that got to him. Something that made all the beautiful women downstairs pale in comparison.

If he killed her, he would never discover what it was that made her so attractive, and he knew himself well enough to know he wouldn't be able to rest until he figured out what that quality was.

Until he possessed it. Possessed her.

"Jim." He spoke quietly, but his bodyguard/assistant heard him and came through the balcony doors in a hurry.

"Yes, Mr. Alexandrov?"

"Have her followed." He gestured to the woman who had so intrigued him.

Jim didn't question him, didn't argue, didn't point out the fact that she was almost out of sight. He just picked up the phone and barked orders into it. Less than a minute later, two men moved deliberately onto Bourbon, their eyes scanning the clumps and streams of bustling humanity for her bright red hair.

As his men went to work, Gregory amused himself by continuing to watch the redhead sweep down Bourbon Street. She was smaller and more slender than he usually liked his women, but there was a passion about her he found enticing. And the sway of her gently rounded ass wasn't bad either.

Still, she was up to something, and somehow he doubted it was anything as innocuous as wanting a job at his club—even if Seductions was the finest one of its kind in the city. No, a woman with her kind of fire would probably punch the first guy who tried to get close enough to slip a twenty into her G-string. Besides, the look on her face as she'd studied those pictures hadn't been curious or interested or revolted or scandalized—like so many of the people who passed by here. No, except for a brief moment right at the beginning, it had been clinical. Removed. Studious.

That in and of itself was so odd—most people had some sort of reaction to his club—that he found himself wanting to know more about this woman with the fiery hair and cool green eyes. This woman who was so full of contradictions he couldn't help but be intrigued, even as he wondered if he was going to have to kill her—after he'd had his fill of her, naturally.

He didn't like people who took an unusual interest in any aspect of his business; it led to problems. And this one, this one definitely had an agenda. He just needed to figure out what it was.

He continued watching that flame-red hair bob through the crowd, felt himself grow hard as he observed her. She walked quickly, without any excess motion, and yet the simple movements were more sensuous than anything he'd seen on the stage downstairs. As if she heard music no one else could and her body couldn't help but respond to it.

"Tell them to find out her name and where she lives. What she does for a living. And tell them to find out if she's involved with anyone."

He felt more than saw Jim's head jerk toward him, knew his bodyguard's eyes were boring holes through the back of his Armani suit. But he didn't turn around, didn't take his eyes from the slight figure with the miles of bright red hair until she finally turned a corner and was gone from his view.

Then he turned to Jim and barked, "Do it!" before reaching into his pocket and pulling out a Cuban. He lit it with the gold lighter one of his girlfriends had gotten him—he could remember the shape of her tits but not her name—and waited for the information to pour in.

He found himself hoping that the little redhead was unattached, then nearly laughed at the absurdity of the whole thing. After all, it wasn't like it mattered.

Chapter Five

Fuck it. He didn't need this shit, and he sure as hell didn't want it. Life was supposed to have gotten easier after he'd quit his job on Wall Street, not more difficult. It was supposed to have become slower, more relaxed. The last couple of days had been anything but, and today had actually given new meaning to the term *FUBAR*.

Fucked Up Beyond All Recognition. Yep, that seemed to sum up his life quite nicely of late, and Byron blamed it all on Lacey. Ever since he'd met her, Fuckup seemed to be his middle name—one he sincerely did not appreciate.

Ignoring his screaming muscles, Byron did another set of push-ups in an effort to work off the frustration—sexual and otherwise—that had been eating him alive for the past three days.

First, he'd managed to screw up the conference table he'd spent days working on—the table that the governor had ordered to replace the one that had been in the governor's mansion in Baton Rouge for nearly one hundred years.

It was all part of her new campaign to get Louisianans back to work. In order to promote her brainstorm, she'd picked several local artisans and commissioned each one to make a separate piece of furniture or art that would become a permanent fixture in the mansion for many years to come.

He'd been excited as hell when he'd gotten the commission, as it was a perfect spotlight for his work—especially since it came with a full photo spread in *Southern Living* magazine. Already, numerous other projects had come his way because of the commission, and he was damn grateful to have been one of the seven people chosen.

Not to mention the fact that he'd worked damn hard on that table—damn hard on his little piece of history—and today he had screwed it up. Royally. So royally that he doubted there was going to be any way to get the huge scratch that ran down the middle of the tabletop out. He was going to have to start over. And with time running short—he'd promised the governor the piece in pretty short order—he was almost completely screwed.

It was all *her* fault, he thought resentfully, as he punished himself with another brutal set. If he hadn't been thinking of her, wondering what she was doing, wondering where she was, he never would have screwed up so irreparably. Never would have—

Damn it, where *was* Lacey? It had been three days since he'd caught so much as a glimpse of her. Three days since she'd walked out on him at Café du Monde without another word. Three days since she'd posted a fantasy on her blog—and he should know; he'd been checking it every couple hours like some kind of fucking addict.

Glancing across the courtyard at her dark apartment, he wondered—again—if she was all right. Wondered where she was. What she was doing. And who she was doing it with . . .

The questions beat in his brain, keeping time with the music pumping through the speakers behind him. *One ninety-seven, one ninety-eight, one ninety-nine, two hundred.* Byron finished off the last of the killer, one-armed push-ups just as Aerosmith's "Helter Skelter" filled the room around him.

He sprang to his feet with a groan and headed over to the weight bench he kept beside the door to the balcony. Didn't it just figure that he was nearly killing himself in an effort to take his mind off Lacey, and then a song like this had to show up and bring her right back, front and center?

What the hell kind of bad karma did he have going on anyway? Had he been a serial puppy kicker in a former life, or what?

Setting the bench press at 240, he lay flat underneath it and gritted his teeth as the song lyrics started to get to him. "Do you, don't you want me to love you."

Not that he was obsessed or anything. He was just concerned. And horny. And . . . obsessed. He groaned as he admitted the truth to himself, then pressed the bar up fast and hard as Steven Tyler seemed to be directing his taunts directly at him. "I'm coming down fast but I'm miles above you."

And his father's phone call earlier hadn't helped his mood in the slightest. But then, the old man never did, no matter how hard Byron tried not to get into something with him.

"So, when are you going to give up this pipe dream of yours and head back to New York? I didn't spend all that money putting you through Princeton so you could be some common laborer, boy."

"I'm a carpenter, Dad. I make furniture."

"I am well aware of what you're doing now. It's embarrassing. If you had kept your old job you wouldn't have to do that shit. You could hire people to do that kind of work for you."

If he'd kept his old job, he'd probably be dead by now—or at least halfway there. He'd worked twenty-hour days under incredibly stressful conditions. He'd had high blood pressure and insomnia, and had been working on a nice little ulcer. The doctor had told him he needed to change his lifestyle, or he might very well not make it to thirty-five, let alone forty.

So he had done what the doctor had ordered, done what he'd wanted to do all along. And he was happy for the first time in his adult life. That more than anything else made him want to tell his father to go to hell, to tell him it didn't matter what he thought. But it would only have caused a fight, so he'd bitten his tongue until it bled in an effort to keep from telling his father off. One, because it never did him any good, and two, because he knew how upset his mother got when they fought. But it had been hard not to hang up on the guy; harder still not to tell him to mind his own damn business.

But he *was* his father, for better or worse, and Byron had struggled to remember that even when the man had—for all intents and purposes—called him a pussy.

"Dad, my old job was killing me. I couldn't face the stress anymore, couldn't face the twenty-hour days and the high-pressure stakes."

"High pressure doesn't seem to bother your brother."

"He's a doctor. It's different from being on the floor of the New York Stock Exchange."

"Yeah, he's actually saving lives, while you're cutting up wood. Damn right it's different."

Byron had suppressed a snort at his father's words. His brother was a plastic surgeon in Beverly Hills. And while he did do some work on burn victims, 90 percent of his practice was made up of boob, butt and nose jobs—not exactly life-saving procedures.

When he'd had enough of the same old song and dance—his father criticizing the hell out of him, and him trying to argue before finally giving up—he'd ended the conversation.

"Look, Dad, I know you're not happy about my choices. You've made that abundantly clear in the last nine months. But I'm not living my life for you. I'm doing it for me."

"Well, that's obvious. You—"

"I'm not doing this anymore. I'm not. I'm happy with my life, happy with my job in a way I never was in New York. And who cares if I'm not making a ton of money right now? I made more than enough in New York to last me for a damn long time."

"That's not the point."

"Then what is the point? I'm doing what I love—I won't apologize for that."

"Of course you won't. If you did that you'd have to admit you were a failure, just like you always have been. You're too soft to make it in the real world, boy."

They'd hung up a few minutes after his father's pronouncement, and though Byron tried like hell not to let it get to him—he was more than happy with his career and the new life he was building for himself here—it was hard. Just once it would be nice if his father laid off the criticism, if he saw him as something more than his fuckup of a second son.

Before he could stop himself, he turned his head—yet again—so he could see Lacey's apartment. Once again, he cursed as he realized it was still dark.

Where *was* she? It wasn't like her to stay out this late, and it made him nervous as hell. New Orleans, while beautiful, wasn't the safest city around. Not by a long shot, and it bothered him to think of Lacey out in it alone and unprotected.

Lifting and lowering the bar in time to the music, he tried to ignore the lyrics that hit far too close to home. Bad enough that it felt like half his time these days was spent trying to find Lacey, chase her, track her down so that he could talk to her like a normal person. Maybe ask her out on a real date or just hang with her awhile. The last thing he needed was for his favorite band to remind him of what a piss-poor job he'd done in accomplishing his goals so far.

How was it that she didn't seem to share his interest, despite their interlude on the balcony? How could she just walk away without giving them a chance to play this thing out? Especially when they were so in tune sexually?

When her deepest fantasies matched his so beautifully?

When what she wanted was exactly what he needed to give?

"Tell me, tell me, tell me the answer." The bar clattered down with a bang, and Byron picked up a nearby can of tennis balls and fired one at the OFF button of his stereo. Joe Perry stopped in mid–guitar riff and blessed quiet filled the room for the first time since he'd started working out—thank God.

It was one thing to wallow in his own self-pity; it was quite another to have one of his favorite bands mock him while he did it.

Lying back down, he did another rep of ten presses and was just about to start a fourth when a light finally came on in Lacey's apartment. Sitting up so fast he nearly hit his head on the weight bar, Byron reached for his water and swigged half the bottle down in one gulp. Then tried his damnedest not to stare at her through her open blinds like some kind of Peeping Tom.

He failed.

With his tongue all but hanging out of his mouth like the dog he was, he watched Lacey kick off her killer shoes before heading out of sight. Narrowing his eyes, he squinted in an effort to see where she had gone, and nearly crushed his damn fingers as he absently rolled the bar over in the stand.

"Fuck!" He stood up with a growl, then shook out his right hand as he waited for the pain to go away. While he waited, he contemplated how desperate it would make him look if he went over and knocked on Lacey's door. Probably less desperate than if he hung around and tried to orchestrate another "chance" meeting. Then again, that wasn't saying a whole hell of a lot.

With another muttered curse, he grabbed his free weights and started doing biceps curls. This whole thing was ridiculous—absolutely absurd. He'd never suffered from a lack of confidence with women before, so the fact that it was starting now was a real pain in the ass. Especially since his dream girl was less than fifty yards away.

Maybe it was the new career, new city, new life that was throwing him off his game. Back in New York he'd been in familiar territory—doing a job he was good at, making tons of money, living in a city he knew like the back of his hand. Women had been the least of his problems.

But since he'd dropped out of the rat race and moved to New Orleans, things had been different. Easier in some ways, but more difficult than he had imagined in others. He couldn't get used to the slow pace of the South, couldn't find a comfortable rhythm to settle into. In New York, life came at you at two hundred miles an hour, but at least he understood that. Could accommodate for it and find his groove.

Here he was lusting after a woman who ran hot and cold and back again so fast he could barely keep up. It irked him, almost as much as his own inability to move on did. In New York, he would have been gone already. But here it just wasn't that easy.

Maybe it was because he'd never met a woman in New York who mattered to him. There he'd dated when he'd had time, but there had been no woman as

important to him as his job. No woman who kept him awake nights as he struggled with his feelings for her.

His arms were burning, felt like they were on the verge of falling off, but he
pushed through it, hoping if he exhausted himself, then maybe he'd be able to
find some peace. Some surcease from the raging demands of his body.

His laugh, when it came, was bitter. Yeah, right. He hadn't had any peace
since that balcony scene a couple of days before; had had even less since he'd
found that damn blog this morning.

Even as he told himself not to look, he couldn't stop himself from glancing
into Lacey's apartment to see if she'd emerged from wherever she'd gone. And
nearly dropped a weight on his foot when he saw her standing in front of her
open balcony door, dressed in a pair of skimpy black shorts and a white tank top.
She was carrying a large glass of wine, and the look on her face said he wasn't the
only one who'd had one hell of a day.

Fighting down the instinctive urge to go to her—to comfort her—he continued his curls and did everything but stand on his head in an effort to ignore her.
She'd obviously had a rough time of it, and the last thing she needed was him
messing with her. He could handle a few more nights of sexual frustration. After
all, it hadn't killed him yet.

Byron did four more sets in quick succession, pumping fast in an effort to
alleviate the hard-on that seemed to be a permanent condition whenever Lacey
was around. By the time he set down the weights, his arms were screaming and
sweat was pouring off him like he'd been caught in a goddamned rainstorm.

He reached for the towel he'd put next to the weight bench when he'd
started this whole misadventure, but stopped dead when he realized that Lacey
was out on her balcony.

And that this time, *she* was watching *him*.

Lacey's eyes nearly glazed over as she watched Byron pumping iron. His chest
was bare and his muscles bulged under the rapid assault of the weights. Sweat ran

in rivulets down the tanned skin of his abdomen, pooled under the unbuttoned waist of his jeans. Had her aching for a taste of him when she should be running in the other direction.

Hadn't she decided she wasn't going to get involved with him? With any guy, until she was sure she wasn't going to make the same mistakes she'd made with Curtis?

She had, but as her eyes roamed over every one of Byron's deliciously exposed muscles, she couldn't bring herself to care. Besides, he'd make a hell of a diversion as she waited for Anne Marie Winston's parents to call her back.

She'd called them as soon as she'd gotten home, hoping for what, she wasn't exactly certain. All she knew was that she needed to talk to them, needed to know what had happened to Anne Marie and if she was in any way connected to Crescent City Escort Service. The fact that she was on the strip club wall proved that she'd been involved in something sexual in nature. Now Lacey needed to see if she could find anything connecting the girl to the escort service and the service to the club.

God, she really didn't want her suspicions to be true, really didn't want to be this close to a story on human trafficking. Her writer's instincts told her if things had played out here the way she thought they had—and she could survive proving it—she was looking at a bestselling book for sure. But just the thought made her feel guilty, the idea that she might somehow be capitalizing on innocent girls' terrible misfortune was more than enough to keep her up at night.

She thought back to the Web site she'd just stumbled on earlier when she'd been researching variations of Crescent City Escort Service. She'd clicked on what she'd assumed was a defunct link to the service's Web site and had found instead a series of pornographic pictures, each one linked to a request for payment and a guarantee of more to come. There'd even been a discount offered for frequent users.

It wasn't the link between porn and prostitution that was bothering her, though. It was the fact that at least three of the most violent pictures on the site had been of girls who had been arrested for working at Crescent City Escort

Service, but who had disappeared after they'd been released on bail. Yet if the dates on the pictures were to be believed, two of them had been taken in the last few weeks.

Lacey wasn't sure yet what the pictures meant, except that someone knew where the girls were—despite the fact that their family and friends, not to mention the police, were clueless of their whereabouts. It was just one more piece of a rapidly darkening puzzle.

Taking a long swallow of wine, she told herself that she would be doing the girls a favor if she managed to figure this thing out. Told herself that she would save countless other young girls from a fate worse than death. But the guilt still ate at her like a cancer.

Across the courtyard, Byron reached for a towel to wipe the sweat away, and she nearly protested. Would have, if he'd been close enough to hear her. She liked him the way he was—hot and sweaty and deliciously inviting. If she had her way, he'd walk around like that all the time. Of course, she'd have a hard time keeping her tongue in her mouth if he did, but sometimes sacrifices had to be made.

Long seconds passed as she imagined running her tongue down his glistening neck to his well-padded shoulders before moving on to his glorious chest and the dark blond happy trail that disappeared beneath his jeans. Just thinking of what was waiting for her there had her breasts swelling, her nipples tingling. Her thighs aching.

She knew she was using him as a distraction, knew she was thinking about Byron in an effort to keep her mind off that poor girl on the flyer and her parents. But she didn't care. If something didn't give between the two of them, she just might die of pure out-and-out sexual frustration.

Squeezing her legs together in an effort to stop the burn, Lacey struggled to look away. After the way she'd shut him down at Café du Monde, she had no business looking at him. No business wanting him—or any other man, for that matter.

But for the first time since she had gotten away from Curtis, she felt like a fraud telling herself that. She *did* want a man. Worse, she wanted Byron. The comments she'd gotten on her last blog entry had proven that to her.

As she'd been going through the normal response posts to her latest fantasy blog, all she'd been able to think about was Byron. She wanted Byron to do the things to her the other men promised, wanted Byron to tease her into a frenzy and make her scream and cry with pleasure.

With a moan, Lacey squeezed her legs together and tried to concentrate on something besides sex. But it was hard, damn hard, when Byron was directly across from her—half-naked and raring to go.

What was even more difficult was knowing that when she'd read the mystery responder's comments, when she'd imagined him doing all the wicked, wonderful things he'd promised her, it had been Byron's face that came to mind. Byron whom she'd imagined hovering over her. Byron whom she'd imagined touching and kissing and licking her all over.

Ugh. She ran a hand over her eyes in an effort to block Byron's hot, ripped body from her view. But the image was burned into her retinas, and it was all she could do to stop herself from getting his attention. From beckoning him over to her.

What was wrong with her that she was suddenly having such a rough time distinguishing fantasy from reality? One of the things she loved about her blog was her ability to live out her fantasies, even if it was only on a computer screen. She'd spent so much of her life picking boring men, men like Curtis who didn't want her suggestions in the bedroom, that she loved having access to men who weren't disgusted by what she wanted.

On her blog, she could act out everything she'd ever imagined. She could get comments from men who did like her suggestions, did like her ideas. And she could imagine what it was like to be touched by men like that, could imagine that she was actually trusting enough—healed enough—to open herself up to another man after everything that had happened with Curtis.

But that was fantasy, her blogging personality an alter ego she'd made up to satisfy her sexual nature without any risk to her heart. Never before had she had a specific man in mind to fulfill those fantasies. Never had she pictured the face of the man she fantasized about.

Now she did. Now when she closed her eyes, all she could see was Byron. When she imagined calloused hands running over her body, she wanted them to be his. When she imagined taking someone inside her, she *needed* it to be him.

It was embarrassing—humiliating, really—how much she wanted this guy. Wanted his attention. Wanted his body. Wanted him, when what she should want was anything but.

But allowing those fantasies to encompass her neighbor, to bleed into her real life, was dangerous territory.

After all, she'd done this before, Lacey reminded herself before she could get totally off track. She'd been drawn in by a smoldering look, a sexy voice. A great body. Had tried to live out all of her sensual fantasies as she had given herself totally to a man. All she'd gotten in return was more grief than any woman should have to handle.

As memories of her time with Curtis started to invade the sensual haze surrounding her, Lacey felt herself grow cold despite the heat. The crappiness of her day came back to her, had her gulping her wine as all the mug shots she'd pored over of the girls who had been arrested swam sickeningly in front of her eyes.

Most of them had been released on bail and disappeared before they had to stand trial, but the ones who had gone through court—the ones who had served time—surveyed the world with haunted looks that kept her up at night, especially after her talk with Veronique. Like the Mardi Gras Madam herself, these girls were terrified of something—and she needed to find out what it was.

For the story, for her own peace of mind, but mostly for the girls who hadn't been able to help themselves. She knew what it was to be helpless, knew what it was to be powerless when—

She cut off her thoughts with another big sip of wine. It slid down her throat smoothly, warmly, and it randomly occurred to her that she was abusing a very costly bottle of wine. Fine wine was meant to be savored, not swigged. Meant to be enjoyed slowly, not used to anesthetize all thoughts and feelings.

But right now she wanted to be anesthetized, needed it with a passion that couldn't be denied. And if she couldn't do it with sex—with the incredible release of tension that came from surrendering her body to a lover, with driving a lover wild—then she might as well do it with a fine bottle of red.

Lacey took another sip, but the ache inside of her only grew stronger. She was sad, lonely, horrified. Desperate for the comfort that only came with the touch of another.

It had been so long since she'd been held by a lover—by anyone. Too long since she'd trusted a man enough to give herself over to him. Certainly those last months with Curtis had been more about sheer survival than pleasure.

She ached to feel strong arms around her once again. To feel soft lips brush over her skin. To feel steady hands clamp on her thighs and open her fully to her lover's gaze.

She glanced at her computer, thought about blogging her frustrations out. After all, it certainly wouldn't be the first time in the last year she'd done just that. But the cold computer screen held no interest for her.

Byron set down one of the weights and guzzled a bottle of water, and desire ripped through her like a finely wrought blade as she watched his throat work. She told herself to turn away, told herself it was disgusting to watch a man who didn't know she was there. But she didn't move. She *couldn't*.

The sight of Byron, half-naked and ready to go, held her transfixed.

And when he lifted the navy blue towel to his face, then ran it over the back of his neck, she did whimper. The movement highlighted his washboard abs and thickly muscled chest, and it was all she could do to keep from panting.

She forced herself to move, to head back inside, but she couldn't resist one last glance in his direction. One last stare at everything she was giving up so that she could stay the course she'd put herself on eighteen months before. And that's when he caught her gaping like a schoolgirl looking at her very first crush.

Their eyes connected and for a second she swore she could feel the pop and sizzle of the electricity flowing between them. Her cheeks burned in embarrassment at being caught, and she wanted nothing more than to duck inside and never show her face again.

Except he didn't seem to mind the fact that she'd been watching him, didn't seem to care that she had invaded his privacy. He smiled at her—a warm, welcoming kind of grin that seemed totally at odds with the control freak she'd met at Café du Monde—and she couldn't help responding to it.

Her lips curved of their own volition, and while her smile was a little more sheepish than his, it was still genuine. Still pleased. Still capable of getting her into trouble.

They stayed that way for long seconds, neither one of them moving as they watched each other in perfect accord. And then he was finishing what he'd started, was running the towel over his face and chest before rubbing it quickly over his stomach and reaching for a black T-shirt. He pulled it over his head with a determination that couldn't be denied.

Lacey found herself wanting to protest, to tell him to stay exactly as he was. Her fantasy: strong and sweaty and half-naked. But he was more than a fantasy—much more—and she'd do well to remember it.

Her smile faded and she took a step back, followed by a second and a third. A little harmless flirtation was okay. Fantasizing late at night, when she was hurting no one, was even better. But thinking of Byron as her real-life fantasy? Letting herself get caught up in the dream? That was just asking for trouble. And if there was one thing she didn't need more of, it was trouble.

She moved back one last step, until she once again hovered in the doorway of her apartment. Pausing, she watched as the smile drained from his face. As his laughing eyes grew darker, more intense. As he stiffened in that I-can't-believe-she's-doing-this-again way that so many men did.

And then he was raising his hand, pointing one lone, tanned finger at her in a *You stay right there* kind of gesture. The order stiffened her spine in a way little else could, had her wanting nothing more than to tell him to go to hell.

But she didn't. She didn't argue, didn't tell him off, didn't do anything but stare at the empty space where he had last been standing. And when there was a knock on her front door a few minutes later, she knew she never would.

But what *would* she do?

Would she let him in or tell him off?

As she shuffled slowly to the front door, even she didn't know the answer to those questions. All she knew was that she'd better figure things out—and fast. Or her life would, once again, be spinning completely out of her control.

Chapter Six

You come to me when I least expect it. When my heart is pumping and my blood boiling and I expect anything but you. I open the door and see that wonderful, crooked smile of yours and everything that has come before this moment is gone.

You don't say hello, don't make small talk, don't do anything but ask permission with a quirk of your eyebrow, a tilt of your perfectly formed chin.

Yes, yes, yes. You know the answer before you ask, and as you pull me against you I know that things will never again be the same.

I want to touch you. To run my hands over your chest and back and ass until I understand the hardness that is you.

I want to taste you. To lick my way down your stomach, to take your cock in my mouth, to tease and torment your balls with flicks of my tongue until you are as familiar to me as my own breath.

I want to give you pleasure. To make you come in my mouth and my body again and again and again until I'm drowning in you and you are lost in me.

I want the same for you. From you.

Your hands in my hair.

Your mouth on my breast.

Your body backing mine against the wall as you thrust so deeply inside me that I will never get you out.

I want you.

I need . . .

You.

Byron's heart was pounding fast and hard as he stood outside Lacey's door. As he waited for her to let him in, the words of one of his favorite fantasies from What a Girl Wants ran through his head—one that he'd read over and over again until he'd had it memorized.

The first time he had read it, it had reached inside him, sunk its claws in good and hard. So that every time he thought of making love, every time he thought of her, it was there in his mind. Begging to be fulfilled. Begging to be made reality with the right lover—one who wanted the same things from him that he wanted from her.

Lacey would be that lover. He knew it—felt it—and couldn't let himself believe for one second that a woman as passionate as needy as she was would turn him away. Not when he was willing to fulfill every single fantasy she'd ever had.

Willing? He laughed grimly at the mediocre word. He was *eager* to fulfill her fantasies. *Dying* to fulfill them, and he didn't know what he'd do if she turned him away again. The idea of her doing those things with someone else had his stomach tightening, his jaw clenching. She was his fantasy, and he would do whatever it took to see that she got what she wanted. What they both needed.

The apartment door cracked open and he watched hungrily as Lacey was revealed to him, one tantalizing sliver at a time. First one delicate foot, with toes tipped in scarlet. Then the smooth expanse of a leg ending in the smallest pair of short-shorts he'd ever had the privilege to encounter.

As the door continued to open—one slow inch at a time— he was treated to a quick view of her bare stomach followed by an expanse of white tank top that hugged her small breasts, much as he would like to. And finally, when the door was fully ajar, he got to see the best part. Her glorious pixie face, surrounded by miles and miles of hair so red it was nearly crimson.

Her verdant eyes locked with his, sparkling with enough desire and mischief to have his cock throbbing in rhythm with his too-fast breathing. She wasn't smiling, but then, neither was he. The desire was too intense for anything as tepid as a grin; too overwhelming for anything but the intensity flowing between them.

At his first full glimpse of her, he wanted nothing more than to grab her, to shove her shorts down and take her in every way a man could take a woman. But there was more than desire in her eyes, more than the lust that was threatening to overwhelm him. There was a touch of fear that calmed him faster than anything else could, an uncertainty that warned him he had to take things much more slowly than he'd originally intended.

Suppressing his groan—as well as the sexual yearning that made every muscle in his body ache—he leaned against the doorframe and tried for a smile. "Hi, there."

"Hi." The word was breathy, a little high-pitched, and he couldn't help the spurt of satisfaction that shot through him at the knowledge that she was as aroused—as out of control—as he was.

Casting around for something to say that didn't begin with *Wanna fuck?* he cleared his throat, then said, "I was going to head down to the pool for a swim. Do you want to come with me?"

Those emerald eyes widened—first with surprise and then with a disappointment that made him happier than anything had in a very long time. "I, umm—" She paused; stared at him in confusion. "Really? A swim?"

"Sure. It's hot as hell outside, in case you haven't noticed."

Her look said that it was also hot as hell inside, the flames between them raging like a five-alarm fire. But all she said was, "You don't exactly look ready for a swim." She looked him over from the top of his black T-shirt to the tips of his jeans.

He laughed; he couldn't help it. He was just so delighted with Lacey and the fact that she hadn't shut the door in his face. Thrilled that she was going to invite him into her apartment, and that very soon, he might actually have a shot at getting inside of her as well. That, more than anything else, put an indelible grin on his face.

"I can change."

She nodded slowly. "Yes, but—" Her voice broke.

"But what?" He kept his voice deliberately low, so as not to spook her—or jar her out of the accommodating mood she seemed to be in.

"But—" She took a deep breath, then another and another until he feared for a second that she might actually hyperventilate. She didn't, and the odd breathing pattern actually seemed to give her courage; for when their eyes met again, the wariness was absent from hers. In its place was a determination—and a desire—that couldn't be denied.

"I don't want to swim right now."

"No?" He cocked an eyebrow and prayed that he wouldn't humiliate himself by losing it before he ever got his hands on her.

She shook her head. "No." And then turned and headed deeper into her apartment, leaving the door wide open behind her.

His heart slammed in his chest and his cock tightened to the point of insanity as he followed her inside like a pet on a leash. For a moment, he wondered what had changed her mind—she'd seemed so dead set against this when they'd spoken the other day. But then she stopped next to the couch, held out a hand to him. And every thought—every worry—flew right out of his head until nothing existed but the need to touch her. To hold her. To make her cry out in ecstasy again and again.

Reaching out, he grabbed her hand and gave one sharp tug that had her stumbling forward. First one step, then another, until she was pressed against him. But she was so small that they didn't quite match up. Cupping his hands under her glorious ass, he lifted her so that they were touching from breast to thigh.

It felt better than he could have imagined to have her against him like this, her soft breasts flush against his chest, her flat stomach resting against his, her plump, sexy mouth almost on the level with his.

"Hi," he whispered, leaning forward so that only centimeters separated his lips from hers.

"Hello, yourself," she whispered back with a grin.

"Is this okay?" He was dying to get inside her, but he didn't want to push. Didn't want to take things too quickly. As he looked into her wary eyes, he began to understand for the first time why Lacey put her fantasies on the Internet. She was too shy or too scared—he wasn't sure which one yet—to live them in real life.

"Yeah," she said as her arms went around his neck while her legs circled his waist in an attempt to steady herself. "I think so."

The first touch of her pussy—so hot and inviting—over his denim-clad cock had desire rushing through him. Clenching his teeth, fighting down the need to slam her against the nearest wall and bury himself in her, Byron lowered his head and touched his lips to hers. In that moment, with that first almost innocent connection, he realized that nothing in his life had ever felt so right. It scared the hell out of him, even as it made him burn hotter still.

Lacey trembled at the first touch of Byron's mouth on her own. For one brief second, panic flared, and she started to tell him to stop. To explain that she shouldn't be doing this, *couldn't* be doing this. She wasn't ready yet—not for a relationship and certainly not for the overwhelming need that clawed through her at the touch of Byron's hard, sculpted body against her own.

But he felt so good pressed against her—hot and firm and so solid she wanted to stay right where she was for as long as he would have her. The thought had warning bells sounding in her head, and she put her hands on his shoulders and began to push him away.

She *had* to end this.

Had to apologize for leading him on.

Had to—

He chose that moment to deepen the kiss, and she ended up pulling him closer instead of shoving him away. Her fingers curled into the soft cotton of his shirt, relishing the play of muscles beneath her questing hands. Anchoring him to her when she should be disconnecting. Getting closer when she should be backing away.

But his mouth was warm and tender and he tasted *so* good—like licorice and coffee and sweet summer rainstorms. Like desire and need and everything else she'd gone too long without.

She wanted more of it, more of him.

It had been so long since she'd let a man touch her, so long since she'd done anything but fantasize, and her body was on fire, her nerve endings screaming for the pleasure they knew Byron could provide.

The decision made—like there had ever been a choice—she let her fingers tighten on his shirt, dig into his skin, and what had started out gentle turned ravenous from one breath to the next.

Hard, hungry, filled with a desire she hadn't experienced in far too long, his mouth devoured hers, and she let it. Lips, tongue, teeth—he used them all to bring her to a frenzied state where nothing mattered but the feel of him against her, above her, inside her. Until he was all she wanted, all she needed. Everything she had to have.

"Lacey." He growled her name—low, deep, and so harsh it whipped right through her. She whimpered in response and opened to him, gave him everything he wanted. Took what she needed in return.

His tongue slipped between her parted lips, licked at the roof of her mouth before tangling with her own. Somehow her hands were in his hair, her fingers twisting in the too-long locks in an effort to pull him even closer.

He groaned, and his mouth grew hotter and harder against hers, demanding entrance. Demanding everything she had to give and more.

He bit at her lips, sharp little nips that made fire gather low in her belly. Then sucked her tongue deep into his mouth and stroked it. Stroked her. Again and again until all she could feel, want, need, was him. Until all her fears and all her objections were nothing but a memory.

He slid his tongue between her upper lip and her gums, fluttered it, and she lit up like a bonfire, light and heat pouring through her. Enveloping her. Stoking the flames inside her until she feared spontaneous combustion.

"Byron." She ripped her mouth from his and sucked huge gasps of air into her starving lungs as she tried to gain some kind of control over her out-of-control libido. But she was too far gone. Her body cried out for everything—anything—he could give it. And more. Always more.

Her hands tightened in his hair, and she tugged once, twice. Again and again, harder and harder as she struggled to get closer to him. To take what she wanted from him and give the same in return. Frustrated, desperate, Lacey bit down hard on Byron's lower lip.

She was against the wall in a heartbeat, his body straining against her, holding her in place. Touching her everywhere. His erection—hot, hard, huge—pushed against the apex of her thighs as he lifted and lowered her.

"Tighten your legs around me," he snarled as his hand tangled in her hair, forcing her head back.

She did, and the feel of him was arousing, tantalizing, even through the denim of his jeans and the soft cotton of her shorts.

"Fuck, Lacey!" One hand squeezed her ass, pulled them so tightly together that he was almost inside her. She could feel him pushing against her and she rode him through the fabric, her hips lifting and lowering in time to the blood roaring through her ears.

His other hand was still in her hair, forcing her head back so that she was completely open to him. His mouth skimmed over her cheeks, down her jaw to the tender skin of her throat before moving lower.

Before she could prepare herself, Byron's mouth closed over her nipple and she could feel even through her tank top the warmth of it, the incredibly seductive heat of him. He sucked at her, bit at her, ran his tongue in little circles around her nipple until she was frantic with the need to be skin to skin with him. Until nothing mattered but feeling him, naked, against her.

"Stop," she gasped, pushing him away as the tension continued to build in her. "I need—"

"What do you need, baby?" he murmured against her breast, refusing to relinquish his prize so easily.

"God, Byron, stop!" She shoved more forcefully this time, and his head snapped back, his eyes meeting hers. There was a question in them, and genuine concern. When he took a few deep, shuddering breaths, she realized suddenly that he was trying to get himself under control. That he thought she wanted him to stop for good.

Trusting him to hold on to her, she eased her upper body away from his even as she kept her legs locked around his waist. In one fluid movement, she stripped her tank top over her head. Then reached for his T-shirt and did the same.

His chest was smooth, sculpted, and so hard it made her mouth water with the need to taste him. To run her tongue over the heavy muscles of his pecs before taking his nipples in her mouth.

Leaning forward, she did just that, allowing her teeth to sink into his well-defined chest. He stiffened, cursed, so she swirled her tongue over the little hurt once, then again and again. His reaction was explosive, immediate, desperate. Thrusting his hands into her hair, he yanked none too gently until her face was on the same level as his.

Her first glimpse of his eyes had Lacey gasping, growing wetter. His gaze had turned to sleek obsidian—dark as midnight, dangerous as sin. She could see his need for her flickering in its depths, as well as the razor-thin edge of his control. She knew he was hanging on by his fingertips, knew she should let him keep a leash on himself just a little longer.

But it was a fantasy come true to know that she could push him to the brink, push him over. Not to mention how good it felt to realize that she wasn't alone in this desperate maelstrom of need.

She licked her lips, watched as his gaze followed her every movement like he was a starving man and she the only sustenance around. Did it again, and reveled in the groan he didn't even try to hold back. Did it once more, this time allowing her tongue to linger on her lower lip as she used her eyes to devour him.

Lightning crackled in the air between them and Lacey felt the heat of it rip through her body, through her mind and heart, through her veins and muscles. Through every part of her until Byron was all she could think of, all she could ever desire.

His harsh tugs on her hair only made her crazier, and she pressed her lips to his with a desperation she hadn't thought herself capable of. She'd never felt like this before, had never felt this wanton. This desperate. This needy. Not even with Curtis, who wielded his sexual power like a weapon, had she been this aroused.

But that was the difference between the two men, the difference she had failed to see the other day when Byron had all but ordered her to sit with him. Curtis was a club, bludgeoning her with his desires and requirements, whereas Byron was so much more sophisticated. He was a razor-sharp sword, a finely designed instrument of cunning and desire. And while she knew he was as dangerous—and probably more so—to her peace of mind as Curtis ever was, she couldn't bring herself to care. Not when he was careening out of control as fast, or faster, than she was herself.

"I have to feel you," she murmured, pressing her breasts to his bare chest and reveling in the heat pouring off him. Her fingers slipped to the waistband of his jeans, tore at the button there in a desperate attempt to get at his rock-hard erection. At the same time, she took his mouth with hers, devouring him. Taking everything he could give her and more—kissing, biting, sucking, using her lips and teeth and tongue on him.

Byron shuddered as lust ripped through him like a goddamn Molotov cocktail, burning, smoldering, getting ready to take him in one giant explosion. This was going too fast. He wasn't going to be able to hold on if he didn't slow it down; was going to explode like a teenager with his first girl if he couldn't gain a little distance.

But distance was impossible with Lacey wrapped around him, her delicate fingers ripping at his jeans like they contained the secret to the promised land. All he could do was feel and want and take whatever he could get.

Pulling away from her questing hands and mouth, he stared at her breasts with hungry eyes, his mouth actually watering with the need to taste her. She was small but perfectly round, and so firm his palms itched with the desire to feel her. Bending his head, unable to wait for one more second, he licked at her nipple until she was trembling and arching against him.

Lacey cried out as her hands slid up his chest to tangle in the hair at the nape of his neck. "Please," she gasped, rocking her lower body against his. "Please, Byron. I need—"

"What do you need, baby?" he asked as he toyed with first one nipple and then the other. "What do you want?"

"You." Her voice was high-pitched, breathy, and it shot another ball of adrenaline through his system. It skated up and down his nerves until there was no part of him unaffected by the passion she brought forth in him.

"You have me," he answered, flicking his tongue over her diamond-hard nipples again and again.

"I need— I need—"

"What?" he growled, desperate to take her inside his mouth. The need to taste her sweetness created a terrible urgency in him, one he knew he wouldn't be able to resist much longer. But he wanted to hear her say it, needed to know that she was on this crazy ride right along with him.

"More," she shrieked as she arched her back, using her body to plead with him as well.

It was what he'd been waiting—no, dying—to hear, and he almost swallowed her whole, his mouth closing around her nipple with a fierceness he wouldn't have tempered even if he could have.

He sucked hard and her hips bucked harshly against him, the muscles of her stomach contracting as her fingers twisted painfully in his hair. The small pain only made him more ravenous, and he held her there for long minutes, suckling one nipple and then the other until she was nearly incoherent with need. She tasted amazing—like warm caramel and spicy cinnamon. It was a combination he doubted he'd ever get enough of, one that was slowly and completely driving him out of his mind.

Part of him wanted to take her right then, to shove his jeans down, rip her flimsy excuse for shorts off and plunge inside of her. In only a second or two, they could both be coming.

But he wasn't ready for it to end so soon, wasn't ready to let her come so easily. Not when he'd spent the past seven months in an agony of aching, unfulfilled desire, courtesy of her.

With each swipe of his tongue, each pull of his mouth, he felt her vicious need to come. She moaned, begged, cried out again and again as her body rode his through her shorts, through his jeans. He could feel her heat even with the heavy denim between them, and for a minute he didn't think he'd be able to stop himself from ripping them away.

"Take them off, take them off," she chanted as she bucked and twisted against him.

"Soon, baby," he murmured between strong pulls on her nipple. "I'll—"

"Now!" she screamed, her fingers ripping at her shorts in near hysteria. "I need you now!"

Fuck! His hips surged at her obvious desperation, his control flying out the window as his body took over. He stripped her roughly, his hands rending her shorts in two in an effort to get at her. The sound of the fabric tearing only aroused him more, until his blood was boiling and he was in a near frenzy to be inside her.

"Byron, please!" She was almost incoherent, her head thrashing back and forth against the wall as she ground her hips against him.

"Okay, baby, okay." He didn't bother to pull his jeans all the way off—he would have had to set her down to do it, and that was never going to happen. So he just shoved them down enough to free his cock, quickly sheathed himself with the condom he'd stuck in his back pocket on the way out of his apartment and then pushed home in one hard thrust.

Lacey whimpered at the invasion, her body erupting at the first stroke of Byron inside of her. For long moments, everything around her went black as she was locked in the most amazing orgasm of her life, pleasure rippling through every part of her. It robbed her of the ability to think, to move, even to breathe. All she could do was take it—take him—as he thrust into her again and again—ratcheting up her pleasure with each movement of his hips.

Before her first climax had come to an end, she could feel a second one building, this one sharper than the first. As he plunged inside her, she dug her nails into his shoulder, hanging on for dear life as he took her with all his power and passion.

He came as she called his name, his body jerking and straining as he emptied himself inside her. His pleasure sent hers careening upward, until she teetered on the edge of an even more powerful release.

"Don't stop," she sobbed as she rocked against him. "Please, don't—"

He didn't. Reaching between their bodies, he rolled her clit between his thumb and forefinger and she whimpered, pressing herself against him as he continued to thrust.

He was still hard, as if his release had done nothing to dull his desire for her, and he surged against her again and again, each thrust a little more powerful than the one that came before it. She felt her back scraping against the wall, felt herself rising and falling as he tilted her hips forward to get a deeper position, and still she begged him not to stop.

Locking her ankles around his waist, she let her head fall back against the wall as she sobbed Byron's name again and again. She was spinning out of control—her mind, her body, everything that she was. It was all his for the taking.

It should have frightened her—would have terrified her at any other time, with any other man. But here, now, all she could do was open herself up to him, let him take all that he wanted.

She wanted it to end, to feel him empty himself totally and completely within her. She wanted it to go on forever, wanted his strong, hard body plunging into hers until she'd had her fill. Until her body no longer clamored for his. Until she didn't know where he started and she left off.

His fingers dug deeply into her hips and she shuddered with pleasure, admitting to herself that she wasn't sure a time would ever come when she didn't want Byron. He was so thick, so hard, so unbelievably strong that she couldn't think beyond the moment. Each powerful thrust of his body had her climbing higher, had her teetering on the edge of yet another orgasm.

"Lacey, look at me." His voice was deep, distorted, but so insistent she knew she didn't have a choice. Opening her eyes through sheer strength of will, she stared into Byron's dark ones, and shuddered at the pleasure and the pain of the connection.

She wanted to look away, needed to look away. This connection between them was too powerful, too overwhelming. But he wouldn't let her, his eyes capturing hers, taking her prisoner, as his body did the same. She couldn't break away, was completely, utterly in his thrall. The only thing keeping her sane was the knowledge that he was as vulnerable as she was, that he had no more control over his body at the moment than she did over hers.

He pressed more firmly on her clit, and she cried out as an answering wave of sensation whipped through her, sending her over the edge for a second time. She came, screaming his name, and still he refused to relinquish her gaze. Still he kept her pinned with those black-magic eyes that seemed capable of seeing all the way to her soul.

And when he followed her seconds later—his own release crashing through him with the all the power and finesse of a hydroplaning eighteen-wheeler—his gaze demanded more than she wanted to give. More than she *could* give.

As he continued to pulse within her, Lacey pushed the unwanted thoughts away. She had Byron now, and she was going to enjoy him. The future could take care of itself.

Chapter Seven

Minutes or maybe hours later—his sense of time was shot, along with every other sense he had—Byron became aware of Lacey pushing against his shoulders.

Holy shit was all he could think as he slowly pulled away from Lacey. *Holy shit*, he'd just had the best sex of his life. *Holy shit*, she'd ruined him for any other woman. Holy shit, what on earth was he supposed to do now? *Holy shit, holy shit, holy shit.*

"Come on, Byron, this wall is starting to hurt."

Her voice was low, breathy, and he struggled to focus on her words, but they weren't making much sense. His brain must have stopped functioning when everything else had—about thirty seconds after he'd had the most explosive orgasm of his life. Which was surprisingly okay with him. He was more than willing to stay right here forever; being inside Lacey while her small body cushioned his was the most comfortable, exciting experience he could remember.

Too bad the same couldn't be said for her. "Byron, I swear, I'm running out of oxygen here."

"Sssh, I think I'm having an out-of-body experience." He nuzzled her graceful neck, catching with his tongue the single drop of sweat that was rolling down. "Mmm, salty."

"Well, you're about to have an in-body experience—and a painful one at that—if you don't move. I would prefer it if you didn't have to explain to the police or my family how you smothered me against the wall after an incredible bout of sex."

"It was pretty great, wasn't it?" He worked his way up to the delicate shell of her ear. "A little fast, but that can be remedied next time."

"Not if every rib I have is broken from this time, it can't." Her hands tangled in his hair and tugged. Hard.

"Ow!" He pulled back, letting Lacey's feet settle on the wood floor as he gave her a disgruntled look. "That wasn't nearly as sexy as when you do it while screaming my name." He rubbed the sore spot.

"It wasn't supposed to be sexy," she answered, shoving at his shoulder so that she could pass. "Just necessary—at least if you're hoping for an encore."

Amazing enough, after his recent orgasm to end all orgasms, his body sprang to life at the mere possibility of getting inside Lacey again, his cock hardening like it had been hours instead of minutes since he'd come inside her.

What was it about Lacey that touched every part of him? That made him feel good—about his life and the whole freaking world?

Maybe it was because her fantasies had let him into her head in a way that didn't happen very often, and he could see how very similar they were. Maybe it was because making love to her seemed like more than just sex. Or maybe it was because she was fucking fantastic—smart and feisty and sexy as hell—and he wanted to see just how far they could take this thing.

As his thoughts echoed in his head, Byron tried to put the brakes on, tried to tell himself it was way too early for him to be thinking like that—especially since he hadn't yet told her that he knew about her blog. He wanted to, had even thought about doing so before he'd knocked on her door, but what was he supposed to say? *Hey, baby, let's work on fantasy number twenty-seven tonight?* She'd probably kill him. And he wouldn't blame her.

Stepping aside so Lacey could pass, Byron trailed her across the living room and down the hall to her bedroom, admiring the sexy sway of her ass with every step she took. "God, you're beautiful." The words were out before he'd even known he was going to say them.

"You don't have to say that—you already got me into bed." The look she shot him over her shoulder was amused.

"*Technically*"—he grabbed her arm and pulled her toward him—"I haven't gotten you into bed yet. But with a little encouragement, I'd be more than willing to fix that."

"I just bet you would."

"Now, see, there you've done it." He advanced on her threateningly.

"Done what?" she asked, her voice taking on the same breathless note she'd had when he'd been inside her. It sent shivers down his spine even as it turned him rock hard.

"That sounded suspiciously like a dare." Picking her up with a grin, he stepped a little closer to her bed and then let her fly. She landed with a startled scream in the middle of her bed, and he immediately lowered himself on top of her, being careful this time to brace most of his weight on his elbows. "I never could resist a dare."

"That wasn't a dare, you idiot! It was a statement of fact." He took the fact that she hadn't shoved him off her as encouragement, and bent his head to nibble on her smooth, sexy jaw.

"Sorry, my mistake," he whispered in between love bites.

"Yes, it was." But even as she said it, she was sliding her legs open so that he could rest between them, and looping her arms around his neck with a crooked smile. "Weren't we just here?"

"Not precisely." He returned her smile with one of his own, happier than he could remember being in a damn long time. Maybe forever. He dropped a kiss on her swollen lips, then traced the smattering of freckles on her nose with his tongue.

"Eew, gross!" She slapped at him, but was giggling too hard to actually connect.

He pretended to consider. "Actually, you taste pretty good—not gross at all. And you *are* beautiful. Completely, totally stunning." He let his gaze turn serious so she could see that he meant every word. "I thought so the first time I saw you, and time—and lack of distance—has only cemented the opinion."

Lacey's heart stuttered in her chest, and she actually had to turn her head so he wouldn't see the tears that had cropped up at his words. It had been so long since a man had even told her she was attractive. For Byron to say she was beautiful, and to mean it, meant more than she could ever tell him. Curtis had spent so much of their time together denigrating her, tearing her down one small sliver at a time, that she'd forgotten what is was like to be with someone who actually cared about making her feel good. Who actually cared about *her*.

As soon as the thought slipped into her consciousness, she could have kicked herself. One night did not equal caring—even if it was with a totally amazing guy. One who made her feel better, body and soul, than she had in a very long time.

But thinking that great sex meant he cared about her—or worse, thinking it meant she cared for him—was dangerous territory. And completely not in her game plan. Bad enough that she had broken her celibate-until-emotionally-self-sufficient rule, but to fall for the first guy she'd slept with in nearly two year was more than just plain dumb. It was emotional suicide, and she so wasn't going to go there. Not ever again.

"Hey, I didn't mean to freak you out. It's not like I was stalking you or anything." When she still didn't answer, he continued, "Lacey, are you okay?"

She came back from her little trip to Nightmare Island to find Byron peering at her anxiously. "Yeah, I'm fine."

"Are you sure? You don't look so good."

"It's just—" She took a deep breath. "I don't want you to read more into this than there is."

He pulled back a little, his eyes simmering despite the smile on his face. "What makes you think I've got a different script than you do?"

"I don't." She could feel her cheeks start to burn. "I just want to make sure there's no misunderstanding."

"By all means, then, enlighten me." His grin grew wider, his eyes warmer, as she fumbled for an explanation.

"I don't do things like this often. I'm not—"

"I never thought you were." He smoothed a hand down her face. "Is that what you're worried about? That I don't want anything but this?"

"No!" She shoved frantically at his shoulders. "I don't want more. I don't want anything from you but this, tonight."

His brows drew together, and she felt her stomach clench. "You're saying you don't want anything more than a one-night stand? You just want to fuck and move on?"

"It sounds awful when you say it like that!"

"Trust me. It sounds a hell of a lot worse when you say it." Byron rolled off her onto his back, making sure that no part of him touched any part of her. Though the distance was what she wanted, emptiness yawned inside her. Still, she didn't make any move toward him. He needed to understand, needed to know her boundaries.

Silence stretched between them for long seconds, and when he finally spoke, his voice was low, controlled. "So, do you want me to leave?"

"No! That's not what I meant." She rolled to her side to face him. "I just want to make sure you understand. I don't want to get serious."

"Who said I was serious?"

"Nobody!" Her cheeks burned even hotter. "But in case you wanted, you know—"

"No, I don't know. I think you're going to have to spell it out for me."

Was he seriously going to make her say it? Lacey sighed in exasperation and tried to stare him down, but the tense set of his jaw told her he was prepared to be more stubborn than she was.

"I'm not in the market for a relationship right now."

Byron pulled back abruptly, glanced around the purely feminine room. "What exactly does that mean, not in the market?" He seemed to choke a little. "You aren't married or something, are you?"

"No! Of course not. I meant that I'm only interested in . . . you know."

"Well, thank God for that. You were starting to freak me out." He reached over, trailed a soft finger down the bridge of her nose. "So, tell me more about this 'you know.'"

"Byron!"

"Lacey!" He mimicked, the wicked gleam in his eye telling her better than words that she'd been had.

"So, you're okay with this, then?"

"Okay with what?"

It was her turn to choke, and his eyes grew darker, more serious. "You seem to be very clear on what you don't want. But you're having a hell of a time asking for whatever it is you do want."

"That's not true."

"Sure it is." He rolled over so that she was once again beneath him. Settled his hands on either side of her face and his lean hips between her thighs. It was an unmistakable assertion of dominance, one that should have pissed her off, but instead had her melting.

He leaned down so that his lips were next to her ear, and her breath caught. He didn't move for a second. Two. Time seemed to stretch, to become elastic, and with each moment that passed her heart threatened to pound out of her chest. When he finally—finally—licked a path around the sensitive shell of her ear, she arched against him and moaned.

"Tell me what you want from me, Lacey," he whispered against her ear. "Tell me what you want me to do and I'll do it."

Fear swept through her at the question, mixed with the desire he was rekindling within her. Had a man ever asked her what she wanted before—in bed or out?

Did she even know what she wanted?

As unsure of what to say as she was about her own needs, Lacey finally whispered the only thing she knew for certain: "I want you inside me again. I want to feel you inside me, around me."

"Just for tonight?" His fingers tangled in her hair, dragged along her scalp, and electric shocks swept through her.

"Yes." She pressed her head more firmly against his magic fingers, nearly purred as he increased the pressure. "No."

"Which is it? Yes?" He nipped sharply at her jaw, sent heat careening through her. "Or no?"

"I don't know!"

He tugged at her hair, dragged her lips up to meet his. "Well, you'd better figure it out," he said through clenched teeth, his mouth taking hers in a brief but ravenous kiss. "Or I'll end up taking as much as I can."

"I want it to be all about the sex." The words burst from her on a tide of self-preservation.

"Excuse me?" He pulled back, arched one blond brow.

"I don't want to have to worry about hurting your feelings. I don't want you to have to worry about hurting mine." Once she got started, the words kept tumbling out. "I want us to be together—like this—whenever it's convenient, whenever we both want it, but that's it. No pressure, no relationship. Nothing serious. Just sex."

"If we're both in the mood, great. If we're not, that's fine too. No guilt, no expectations. Just . . ."

"Fun?"

"Exactly! Just fun!"

She looked up at him, expecting approval—after all, wasn't this what all guys wanted?—but his eyes were dark, shuttered. She found herself holding her breath, waiting for him to say something. Anything. But he simply stared at her until she had to fight the urge to squirm.

Long seconds passed, and when he still didn't move, she was certain that she'd blown it. Certain that in trying to lay down rules for them, she'd chased him away.

It's better that way, she told herself fiercely as she tried to ignore the chill moving through her. Better to know now if he couldn't handle her speaking up about their relationship—or lack thereof.

But when he finally spoke, his voice was soft, teasing. "So, are you sure you're completely recovered from nearly being smothered against the wall? Because I could check you out, you know, just to make sure you're really all right. We wouldn't want any injuries to go unrecognized."

"Is that all you have to say?" she demanded incredulously.

"I thought that's all you wanted me to say." He reached down, tickled a rib. "Just fun and games, right?"

Relief swamped her. "Right."

"So, about that collision with the wall. Do I need to play doctor?"

"Oh, well. Maybe you should." She tightened her arms around his neck, thrilled at his easy acquiescence. When his lips slid tenderly over her cheek to linger at her jaw, then at the hollow of her throat, she even managed to joke, "But, and believe me when I say I'm not trying to criticize your bedside manner, that's not the part of my anatomy that was in jeopardy."

"Just lie back and relax," he murmured as he swept gentle hands over her body, his touch somehow both soothing and arousing. "I'm very thorough in my examinations."

"I bet." She closed her eyes and let him do his thing, luxuriating in every soft kiss and caress he gave her. And minutes—or was it hours?—later, when he gentled her into a softer, smoother, but no less intense climax, it took all her willpower not to sob at the care he took with her.

Chapter Eight

Byron awoke in a conflagration of need. Desire raced through him— hot, greedy, all-consuming, and burning him alive with each touch of its white-hot flame.

Moving restlessly, he searched for some relief, but any movement he made only made the fire worse. His heart raced. His body throbbed. His lungs begged for air, and his skin felt so tight he thought he would explode. His cock was hard and aching, fully erect, his body spiraling up and out of his control even as he struggled toward full consciousness.

Awareness came slowly, on the heels of overwhelming obsession and unspeakable pleasure. He was in bed with Lacey and she was stoking the fire inside him, her hands and mouth and body driving him to the point of madness and beyond.

"Lacey, baby." His hands fumbled for her as he tried desperately to gain control of the situation, of himself. "Give me a second. Let me—"

He broke off as she licked a sizzling trail over his painfully full cock. He still ached from the conversation she'd insisted on earlier; her words were sharp little darts that had left bruises that were no less real for their invisibility. But seriously, what were the odds that when he finally found a woman he was interested in, she wouldn't want anything from him but his ability to make her come?

Part of him wanted to shove Lacey away at the thought, but as she swirled her tongue around him like he was an ice-cream cone, any prayer he had of slowing her down went up in a searing, scorching blaze.

"Do it again," he growled, in a demand he never would have issued if he'd been in his right mind. If he'd had even one iota of control left.

But she didn't seem to mind the order, as she did exactly what he said—again and again.

Quick little licks of her soft, sweet tongue over his dick.

Longer, deeper swipes that were meant to inflame instead of satisfy, torment instead of soothe. He took it for as long as he could, until he was as close to begging as he had ever been in his adult life, and then he tangled his hands in her hair. Fisted them in the flaming waves and tugged hard enough to get her attention.

She merely laughed, then circled her tongue around him so slowly he feared he would spontaneously combust. "Lacey!" His voice was harsh, desperate, but she ignored him as she continued to tease. Continued to stoke his desire with light, deliberate touches that had him trembling with the need to bury himself inside her.

He fought the burn, struggled to hold on to some small semblance of sanity. Tried desperately to stay in control so that he could give Lacey what she wanted, what she needed.

But when she pulled him into her mouth, one slow inch at a time, his breath slammed out of him in a strangled groan. This wasn't how it was supposed to go, wasn't how he'd planned it. He'd wanted to give Lacey *her* fantasies, to make each and every one of them come true. Instead, she was ripping him apart, giving to him instead of taking. Fulfilling his needs instead of her own.

He wanted to stop her, planned to stop her. But it felt so good, so incredibly fucking amazing, as she wrapped herself around him that he couldn't protest. Couldn't pull away. Couldn't do anything but lie there and let her pleasure him.

Which she did—hotter and sweeter than anyone else ever had. Sweat poured off of him as she taunted him, her talented tongue stroking over his balls, his dick, the sensitive spot behind his sac again and again, before she finally took his testicles into her mouth and began to suck.

At the first sweet suction of her mouth, he nearly came off the fucking bed—and would have if it hadn't meant that she would stop doing whatever wicked thing she was doing. "Jesus, Lacey." His voice was hoarse, more animal than human. Lust was a driving force within him as the pleasure threatened to overwhelm him.

His hands tightened in her hair as every muscle in his body contracted. He fought for control, fought for restraint, but there was nothing for him to hold on to. Only Lacey and the incredible warmth of her mouth as she brought him right up to the edge again and again.

Once again, his fingers tangled in her glorious hair and he tried to pull her away before he lost it completely, but she was having none of it. She slid her hands beneath him and cupped his ass as she continued to torture him with each stroke of her tongue on the tender skin of his balls. Once, twice, she caressed him, then again and again until the urge to fight her was gone. Until everything was gone except the burning-hot pleasure of her mouth.

When she finally pulled back, giving his balls one last, lingering kiss, he was a sweating, trembling mess. His cock was on fire, his body completely under her thrall, and he didn't know whether to thank her for stopping or plead with her to continue.

Before he could make up his mind, the decision was taken out of his hands as her sweet, sexy mouth swallowed him whole.

"I dreamed of you doing this," he whispered as she began to suck. "Dreamed of your hair in my hands, your mouth on my dick, your tongue licking me into a frenzy of desire. Of need."

He whispered his fantasy to her, feeling it was only fair that he give her something back for all the dreams she'd shared, unwittingly, with him. "Ever since the night on the balcony, I dreamed of having you like this. Naked, in bed, taking me as I'm dying to take you."

She moaned at his words, the little sound sending shock waves of sensation through his cock, and he lost the ability to talk, to think, to fucking breathe. And when she ran her tongue over and around the head of his dick, he wasn't sure how much longer he could go without imploding. The pleasure—the goddamned, unbelievable pleasure—was like nothing he'd ever felt before. Incredible, amazing, unending, and before he knew what he was doing, he was shoving himself into her mouth again and again, begging her to take more of him. To take all of him.

And she was doing it, her glorious mouth pulling him deeper into the flames of desire. Taking him so completely that he couldn't imagine anything ever measuring up to her—to this—again.

Lifting his head so he could see her, he watched as Lacey sucked him off. It was the most erotic thing he'd ever seen, her pale pink lips closing around him as he thrust between them. Her eyes open and glazed with a need that shot straight through him, a need that had his cum boiling up inside him. What was it about this woman with the wary eyes and delicate build that took him places he'd never dreamed of going?

He didn't know, and in that moment didn't care. All that he was was held in thrall by Lacey and her hotter-than-hell sex appeal.

His teeth clenched and his jaw locked as the moist, sexy heat of her mouth drew him in deep. Her tongue ran in circles around his throbbing cock—up and down and around until all he could think about was coming in her mouth while she milked him with lips and tongue and throat.

Pleasure swept through him at the thought, moving from his balls to the base of his cock, taking him over as she pulled him all the way in, her tongue stroking the sensitive spot at the underside of his cock in a rhythm that had his fists clenching and his eyes crossing.

"Lacey, you need to stop." The words were so low and guttural he barely understood them, but she seemed to know what he was saying and she refused to yield. He cupped her cheeks in his hands, tried to pull her up, but she tightened her hold on his ass even as she drew him deeper into her mouth.

"Lacey, I'm going to come. I'm going to—"

He broke off as she made a low, approving sound at the back of her throat, and that moan was all it took to slam him over the edge of ecstasy. And then he was coming, spurting inside her, his cum jetting furiously into her mouth. She took all of it, all of him, with a grace that had him climaxing hard and deep.

And still it wasn't enough.

He wanted more. Needed more with an obsession he didn't understand. All he knew was that he had to taste Lacey, had to take her, had to make her his in every way there was.

He wanted her to come on his fingers, on his lips, against his tongue, around his cock. He wanted to savor her sweetness on his tongue, to suck her incredible honey down his throat and swallow it. Swallow her, so that her taste—her pleasure—would always be with him.

Pulling her up until they were face-to-face, he traced his finger over her bottom lip, reveling in the heat that poured from her like a furnace. Then he took her mouth the way he wanted to take her body.

It wasn't a gentle kiss, wasn't sweet or careful or any of the other things he'd told himself he would be. It was hungry, ravenous, filled with need and lust and enough fire to burn the whole damn Quarter down.

He wanted to pull back, to take it slower, to show her how he felt about her, but she was having none of it. Her hands fisted in his hair, her fingers dug into his scalp and a sharp, furious cry tore from her throat.

That cry sent him soaring past the boundaries of the control he'd just managed to regain. With a groan, he ran his tongue over her lips and then went deep—taking her mouth the way he was dying to take her body. Licking, sucking, savoring the sweet taste of her. Nipping at her, delving deep, exploring all of her and loving every second of it.

When he couldn't take any more, when the need to thrust his tongue inside her and hear her scream was nearly overwhelming, he pulled away. And she fought him with her hands and lips and body, struggling to keep him where he was.

"Lacey, baby, I want more of you." He ran his lips down her neck, paused for long seconds at her breasts, where he ran his tongue over her gorgeous little nipples. Teased them, nipped at them, sucked them, licked them, until she was screaming his name.

Lacey's heart was beating so fast and hard that she was afraid it would jump right out of her chest. "Byron, please," she whimpered as she ran her hands over the smooth muscles of his back. He was pushing her right to the brink of madness again and again. His mouth on her breast felt so good, so hot, so right that it took all her concentration not to scream, not to beg.

"Please what, baby?" He skimmed his mouth over her breast, down her stomach to the curve of her hip. "Tell me what you want."

"I want—" Her voice broke as embarrassment welled within her. Writing her desires down in her fantasies was one thing, even if she posted them on the Internet. That was okay. *That* was anonymous. But looking at her lover as he prepared to go down on her, and telling him how she liked it? That was too much, especially as she had no idea how to answer him. The question had never come up before; none of her other lovers had ever bothered to ask.

Byron's tongue stroked over her stomach, circled her belly button before he worked his way lower. But just when she thought he would take her in his mouth, he paused and looked at her with his fallen-angel eyes and whispered, "Tell me, Lacey. Tell me how you like it. Soft and sweet?" His tongue made one long, lingering caress over her bare mons, and had her moaning.

"Hard and hot?" He spiked his tongue, played with her clit.

"Slow and deep?" He moved lower and licked along the lips of her pussy before stabbing his tongue deep inside her.

She screamed at the first touch of his tongue inside her, moving restlessly against him as her hips came off the bed.

"Is that it, baby?" he asked, his breath hot against her. "You want my tongue inside you?"

"Yes!" The word escaped before she knew she was going to say it, and Lacey would have been embarrassed if what Byron was doing to her didn't feel so damn good. His tongue was inside her, stroking the walls of her vagina with strong, powerful motions that had stars dancing in front of her eyes. Again and again he stroked, and she rose higher and higher.

But when she was on the brink of coming—when orgasm beckoned to her with rosy promise—he stopped dead. Left her hanging on the edge without a safety net, her nerve endings screaming for a relief he refused to provide.

"Byron, please!" The words were nearly incoherent with need, but he must have understood, because once again his tongue began to move. But this time, he took it slower, softer. Moved his tongue in gently fluttering motions that sent a whole new range of sensations spinning through her.

Once again, he took her right to the brink. Once again, he stopped right before she went crashing over. Grabbing his hair in her hands, she tugged sharply, then reveled in his sharp gasp. "Do it," she demanded, her hips moving wildly against his mouth.

She felt, more than saw, his grin. "Do what?" he whispered as he pulled out and ran his tongue over her in leisurely strokes.

"You know what." It was a plea, when she'd sworn to herself that she would never again beg a man for anything. But here now, in Byron's arms, she didn't mind begging, didn't mind humbling herself in front of him.

How could she, when he took such pleasure from driving her insane?

When he gave her such pleasure in return?

"I don't think I do," he answered with a teasing flick of his tongue that had her breath hitching in her throat. "Why don't you tell me?"

"Byron, come on."

"Lacey, come on." He mimicked her in between soft, sweet swipes of his tongue.

The pleasure was building, taking her higher, but still he didn't let her come. Finally, when she could take no more, when the pleasure was so intense it was almost pain, she cried, "Make me come. Please, Byron, let me come!"

He laughed and with one swirl of his tongue on her clit sent her careening into orgasm. A few more flicks and the quick slide of his fingers inside her had her spiraling up and over again.

And still he wasn't done.

Rolling onto his back, he lifted her in his strong arms and held her open and vulnerable above him.

"Byron, what are you—"

"Sssh, baby. Let me take care of you." He lowered her until her knees were on either side of his head and her pussy poised directly above his amazing mouth.

She laughed, but it came out as a half sob. "I thought you just did."

She felt more than saw him smile. "Oh, baby, I'm just getting started." Then he whispered something low and guttural and vaguely obscene, his breath steamy hot against the heart of her right before he pulled her clit into his mouth and began to suck.

She came like a freight train, her body spiraling up and over so quickly that she hadn't seen it coming. Hadn't felt it coming until it was too late, until the hard shell she kept around her thoughts and emotions simply shattered into myriad pieces. She couldn't breathe, couldn't think. Couldn't do anything but wait for whatever he was going to do next, as she spun outside herself to a place where only pleasure existed.

Wave after wave of the stuff crashed through her, taking her over. Frightening her with its intensity. Making her wonder how she'd ever lived without the sensations currently flooding her. The pleasure was so real, so raw, so all-encompassing that she couldn't help being scared, certain it was going to take over every part of her.

For long moments, she struggled to regain control. To hold on to something that had been lost with the first soft touch of Byron's mouth. She'd worked so hard to find herself that losing control now—at his hands—seemed faintly sacrilegious. At the same time, the never-ending pleasure was addictive, and there was a part of her that wanted nothing more than to wrap it around herself and just enjoy.

Byron sucked harder, swirling his tongue around the hard bud of her clitoris, and she bucked against his mouth in an effort to get closer, to get away. But he was having none of it. His hands fastened on her upper thighs, spread her wider, held her in place with the strength evident in his long, lean, muscular frame.

Need built in her again, sharp and all-consuming, and she didn't know what to do. She was going to lose her mind, lose her heart, lose control right here and now, and there was nothing she could do to stop it. He was taking her, and in doing so had knocked down every wall she'd built between herself and the world.

"Byron, stop. I can't—"

"You can." His voice was lower, harsher than she'd ever heard it. And when she glanced into his eyes, she was trapped by the flames flickering there, building to a towering inferno that threatened to consume every part of her.

His tongue—his wanton, wicked tongue—went from quick swirls to long, luxurious licks that had her hurtling, inconceivably, toward yet another climax. Ecstasy trembled along nerve endings that hadn't yet recovered from his first assault as he used his teeth, his tongue, his lips on her.

"Look at me," he demanded, and her eyes flew open. Met his turbulent black ones, and what she saw there took her higher even as it scared her to death. This wasn't ordinary lovemaking; with every kiss, he was claiming her, branding her, demanding something from her she hadn't wanted to give him. Hadn't wanted to give any man.

A high, keening sound came from within her, filling the room and making Byron's eyes and hands harden with desire. Moving one hand, he thrust first one finger and then another inside her. Found her sweet spot and stroked—once, twice—before pulling out to spread the liquid heat of her desire over and around her anus. He circled the tight bud again and again and she whimpered, nearly out of her mind with the need for more. The need for everything.

Just when she was certain he wasn't going to do it, when she was certain she would lose her mind, he thrust one long, calloused finger inside her and started to rub. Another orgasm whipped through her—quick and powerful and so all-consuming that there was no way she could hold back the screams that welled in her throat. She felt Byron smile against her as her cries bounced off the walls.

Fast and hard and never-ending. This time she screamed in total abandon.

Still, he continued to push her, trying—she assumed—to bring her to the irrevocable edge of total and complete madness.

"Stop," she gasped, as she grabbed on to the headboard and tried desperately to lift herself away from him. But he held on tight, his hands bearing down on the smooth silkiness of her hips and thighs, and she gave up on the fight she was very quickly beginning to understand was unwinnable.

Before the night was over, Byron was going to have her every way a man could have a woman, and she was going to let him. Was going to beg him, if things continued in this vein. The only thing that kept her grounded was seeing the need and desire in his own eyes.

He was as desperate for her as she was for him, and the fact made the unbelievable whirlwind of her emotions so much more palatable. He continued to torment her as his hands held her open to him—sucking, licking, spearing his tongue deep inside her—until one orgasm blended into another. And another. The more sensitive she grew, the more deliberate he became until she couldn't do anything but take it. Take him.

She couldn't talk, couldn't think, couldn't function, and still he persisted. No matter how she twisted and begged, pulled and whimpered, he wouldn't let her escape from his questing, ravenous mouth.

"Byron, no," she finally gasped. He had to stop. He *had* to. She couldn't survive another—

He laughed, a dark rich sound that raced through her bloodstream, right before his tongue speared deep inside her and hurtled her—that easily—into another climax.

She wondered vaguely how many times she'd come, as she'd lost count at four, and knew she'd left that number behind at least three orgasms ago. But it was nearly impossible to focus on anything but the ecstasy ravaging her body with each seductive movement of Byron's mouth. He was *devouring* her, pushing her beyond any and all limits, until she couldn't recognize the tormented, pleading woman she was fast becoming.

"Not yet," he growled while his tongue flicked deliberately from her clit to her anus and back again. "I'll never get enough of tasting you, never get enough of watching you unravel in my arms. I could go down on you all night."

Once again, he slid his tongue between her slick folds, and once again, she came, stars exploding in front of her blind eyes as she whimpered and sobbed and pleaded with him to take her.

Finally—finally—when she was on the brink of losing herself and everything she'd worked so hard for, when control was a nebulous concept she could no longer understand, he released her.

She slid bonelessly to the bed, into his embrace and half into sleep, but he wasn't done with her. Suddenly, they were rolling and she was beneath him, her body shaking with the need to feel him inside her.

Grabbing on to his shoulder with shaky hands, she pleaded with him to finish it. "I can't take any more, Byron. I'll die. You have to do it."

"Do what?" he asked, cupping her chin in one large hand so that she had no way of looking at anything but him.

The dam inside her burst, sweeping her up in the overwhelming tumble of sensations rushing through her. "Fuck me!" she all but screamed. You have to take me. You have to—"

Lacey's breathy pleas ran through him like a hit of electricity, and Byron nearly trembled in relief. She tasted so sweet and spicy as he'd taken her with his mouth that he was on the brink of losing total control. Running his tongue over his lips, savoring every drop of the warm honey she'd given up to him, he let himself go.

With a roar, he slammed himself up and into her, burying himself balls deep with his very first thrust. She clamped around him like a greedy fist, and his eyes nearly crossed at the pleasure and at the insanity that rocked him as he once again became a part of her.

She was slick and wet and burning hot, and for a moment he was truly convinced that he'd lose it before he could make her come one last time.

Gritting his teeth against the sensations gathering at the base of his spine, he worked to hold on to the ragged edges of his control. Then she whimpered—her hands pulling at his hair, her legs wrapping themselves around his waist, her cunt pulling at his cock—and he knew he'd reached the end of his patience.

He rode her hard, his hands braced on either side of her head as he kept his gaze on hers—forcing her to look at him. Making sure she knew that this was real, that he was more than a fantasy. Determined to ensure that she stayed in the here and now, that she knew exactly who it was that was making love to her.

Over and over he thrust into her satin heat until the fire threatened to consume him. Flames of pleasure flashed through him, burning him up with the intensity of the emotions and sensations that had taken over his body.

He needed the sanity that would come with a physical release, but he wanted to keep making love to Lacey. He wanted to stay like this forever, connected to her by his body and mind and the overwhelming, unbelievable pleasure that burned between them.

Sweat beaded on his chest, rolled down his back, but still he refused to stop. He thrust into her over and over again—trying to get as close to and as deep in her as he could. Trying to get inside more than her body. His arms trembled under the onslaught, his cock screamed for relief and still he continued to move inside her.

She was sobbing, screaming, her muscles contracting more and more tightly around him with every slam of his hips. Her nails dug into his back, her teeth into his shoulder, and still he kept at her. Her legs circled his hips, her hands clutched at his back and he knew that he couldn't hold on any longer. She felt too good, too alive, and he wanted to hold on to every single part of her.

He was buried deep, as close to her as he could get, when he felt the orgasm tear through her, a deep, dark wave of sensation so powerful that it swamped him, buried him, dragged him under before he could find the will to resist. His own climax welled up within him, the sweet clutch of her body sending him right over the edge and beyond, to a place where nothing existed but the infinite pain and pleasure of their joining. A place where he could do nothing but wallow in the need that arced between them.

It started at the base of his spine and spread out from there—through his dick, his stomach, up his back, around to his chest. Pleasure, pain, passion roaring through him, flowing from him to her and back again as he emptied himself inside her in a series of powerful, all-encompassing waves.

Stripped of all defenses, completely vulnerable, Byron poured everything that he was, everything that he felt, into Lacey. Then held her as he wished, hoped, prayed, that just once he would be enough. That just this once he had given her everything she needed to be happy.

Chapter Nine

S o, Lacey Adams had a lover. Gregory kept his face schooled into its normal implacable lines as he studied the brief report Jim had brought him a few minutes before. Though he was furious at the idea of some other man putting his hands on the little redhead he was already beginning to think of as his, he was smart enough to keep his reaction to himself.

Jim was concerned about his preoccupation with her; the look his bodyguard had sent him when he'd asked for information on her first thing this morning had been telling. But Jim hadn't said a word—and wouldn't. Not if he valued his tongue.

For the third time since he'd gotten the folder, he read over the sketchy details inside. His men had followed her to an apartment building on the out-skirts of the Quarter. Had found out her apartment number—2D—and had used that to track down her car and run the plates.

That's how they'd gotten her name. As they'd been hanging around, watch-ing the place, they'd seen a tall guy go in. When they'd finally left—five hours later—he had still been in there with her. The thought made Gregory's hands itch to curl into fists, but he controlled the impulse. He hadn't gotten where he was today by letting emotion rule him or his actions—no matter how tempting it might be. Still, how much could he be expected to take? How long could he be expected to tolerate her fucking some other man?

"Has Micah sent in his report yet?" He spoke through his teeth, keeping his voice steady through sheer strength of will. It wouldn't do for Jim to see just how anxious he was in reviewing the PI's report on his little Lacey.

"Not yet, sir."

"Did you tell him to put a rush on it?" He barely bothered to listen to the answer. He was too caught up in the pictures in the file—Lacey dressed in short-shorts and a skimpy tank top while she opened the door to her muscle-bound lover. Lacey silhouetted against her balcony doors, her nude body gleaming in the moonlight. Lacey backed against the wall while her lover plunged into her without even taking the time to disrobe. As if the actions themselves weren't infuriating, the look on her face was enough to send him right over the edge.

There was ecstasy on her face. Ecstasy and a depth of passion he couldn't help wanting to experience. Ecstasy he couldn't help wanting to kill the other man for giving her.

He wanted her focused on him and only him—an odd sentiment, admittedly, for a man who had never cared about anything enough to become attached to it. While it was true he didn't share his women and never had, that was more from a need to appear strong—to guard what was his—than out of any jealousy he might have felt. But no one took what was his, and watching Lacey share herself with this man, watching him take what Gregory had already claimed for himself, was unacceptable. And not to be tolerated—at least not for much longer.

But first—first he needed to know everything about Lacey Adams. Who she was, what she did for a living, if she'd be missed by anyone besides her Neanderthal lover. He hoped that wasn't the case, but . . . he shrugged. If she did have people waiting for her, then it could be taken care of.

Everything could be taken care of—for a price.

"I want to know who he is too."

"Sir?" Jim's voice was quiet, obsequious, but puzzled as well—as if he didn't know who Gregory was referring to.

"The boyfriend!" he snapped impatiently. "Have Micah put together a file on him as well." He'd gotten as far as he had in this business by knowing everything he could about his enemies, and this man who had dared to put his hands and mouth on the woman Gregory already considered his was definitely an enemy.

For long moments, he studied the picture of Lacey with her head thrown back in passion, her eyes sexily glazed as pleasure rushed through her. And imagined it was him putting that look on her face, imagined what it would feel like to be inside her tight little pussy while she came, her sweet body milking him again and again.

His fingers tightened on the picture as his dick hardened painfully. "Get Sophie." He barked the words to Jim, and his assistant was gone in the blink of an eye. He was back moments later with one of the girls from the club below. She had a smile on her face and anticipation in her eyes—something he saw regularly when one of the girls from the club was brought up here for his own private use. He was, after all, known for his generosity, in and out of bed.

And she was the closest thing to a redhead they had downstairs, but her stick-straight, strawberry-blond hair was a far cry from the gorgeous auburn waves that floated halfway down Lacey's back. Still . . .

"Get over here." It was an order, pure and simple. Hard, direct, without the normal softness he used with his lovers. *But then, she isn't really a lover, is she?* he wondered as he bent her over his desk. More like one small step up from using his hand. After pushing her skirt—he didn't know if he was disgusted or gratified that she wasn't wearing any underwear—he sheathed himself in a condom. With her history in the club, God only knew what diseases she might be carrying.

"Gregory, baby," she turned to look at him with a smile on her face. He ignored it, ignored her, except to shove her facedown into the desk. Hard. Then he thrust roughly inside of her, with no preamble or foreplay. He didn't want anything to distract him from his fantasy of Lacey. Certainly not this skinny, drugged-out little bitch who was out for everything she could get from him.

"Close your legs," he grunted as he pumped against her. "I like it tight."

"Whatever you wa—"

"Shut up!" He grabbed her hips and slammed her ass against his pelvis, excited when he heard her muffled gasp. Again and again he shoved himself into her—brutally hard and without compassion. With each thrust she cried out, and he imagined that it was Lacey beneath him. Lacey taking him so completely, holding him so tightly. Lacey whimpering, not in pain but desire, as he took her again and again and again.

Reaching beneath the girl, he grabbed her breasts and squeezed hard. She moaned, but didn't protest; simply pushed her ass more firmly against him, like she wanted even more. That's when he lost it. With one final thrust inside of her, he came—in long, powerful waves that nearly brought him to his knees.

When he was done, he sagged against her, relishing the feel of the soft, female body beneath his. But as the minutes ticked by, he became more and more aware of where he was and who he was with. It wasn't Lacey beneath him, wasn't Lacey who had taken him so fully and enthusiastically.

Pulling out, he yanked off the condom. "Get out!" His voice was harsh—much harsher than he usually used with the girls—but he couldn't bring himself to care. Jacking up his pants, he fastened them as Sophie stared at him, wide-eyed, her mouth gaping like a fish's.

"Did you hear me? Get your ass out of my office. Now!"

He settled behind his desk as she fled, yanking her skirt down while she ran. Then picked up the top photo of Lacey and ran a finger over her beautiful body.

"Soon," he murmured as he stroked her. It was a promise, but he didn't know whether it was to her or to himself.

"So, can I buy you breakfast, or is that against the rules?"

At Byron's voice, Lacey looked up from the morning paper she'd been studying for the last fifteen minutes. Too bad she'd read the first paragraph at least six times and still had no idea what it said.

"Breakfast?" She tried her damnedest to look him in the eye, but it was hard, especially when his heavily muscled chest was bare and still a little damp from the shower he'd just finished.

"Yeah, you know. Eggs, toast, pancakes. Ring a bell?"

"I just thought you'd . . ." Her voice trailed off lamely.

"Thought I'd what?" His eyes narrowed dangerously. "Slip out while you were in the shower?"

He walked over to her, took her lips in a long, hard kiss. "Sorry to disappoint you, but I've never been much of a wham, bam, thank you, ma'am kind of guy."

"That's not what I meant." She stared at his back in frustration as he sauntered past her into the kitchen. Then lifted a hand to her mouth and rubbed her fingers over her well-kissed mouth. Even as she did it, she knew it was going to take more than that to wipe away the toothpaste-and-lemon taste of him.

"There's fresh coffee," she called, striving to sound as relaxed as he obviously was.

"I already found it."

He appeared in the doorway, holding her favorite cup. The delicate fairy mug looked much too small for his hard, lean hands.

"Well, help yourself," she muttered, not sure whether she should be disgruntled at the fact that he'd made himself at home in her apartment.

"I usually do." He flopped down onto the dining chair next to hers, ran one long, tanned finger over the bridge of her nose. "So, what do you say?"

"To what?" She determinedly ignored the shivers sliding down her spine.

"To breakfast. There's a great little place on Chartres that serves the best—"

"I can't."

"Okay." Her refusal didn't break his stride. "How about lunch?"

"I have a meeting."

"Dinner?"

"Come on, Byron. Don't do this."

"Don't do what?" His grin was razor-sharp, but his eyes were amused. "Don't try to spend a little time with you outside of bed? Or don't buy you a meal?

"Come to think of it, every time I try to feed you, you turn me down. Are you on a hunger strike for world peace or something?"

Irritation skated through her. "I'm not a dog; I don't need you to feed me."

"You didn't answer the question."

"Do I look like Gandhi?"

He took a sip of coffee. "Not a hunger strike, then. Just a feminist's objection to letting a man do something for her? That's easy enough—you can buy me breakfast."

"No!"

"Well, if you're not a feminist or an activist or any other kind of *ist*, what, exactly, is your objection to sharing a meal with me?"

"We didn't agree to this!"

"Didn't agree to what? Consuming a few hundred calories together? God knows after the night we had, I think we both deserve several thousand."

"You're being deliberately dense."

"Well, enlighten me, then."

"I don't want . . ."

"What?" He raised a brow. "What don't you want?"

"I don't want this. I don't want to have to make conversation or worry about having morning breath or . . ." She trailed off, looked at him helplessly.

"Believe me, Lacey, after last night I've got a pretty clear picture of what you're looking for—and what you're not. But I didn't think a little breakfast was a declaration of intent. My mistake." He drained his coffee cup in one long gulp, then carried it to the kitchen. "Let me get my shirt and I'll be out of your way."

"I didn't say you had to go." She jumped to her feet, followed him back to the bedroom.

"Yeah, well, you've made it pretty obvious you don't want me to stay." Byron slipped his T-shirt over his head as he strode toward the front door. "Call me sometime if you want a repeat of last night. Otherwise, I guess I'll see you around."

He didn't even bother to slam the door on the way out, just closed it with a firm thud that was somehow all the more intimidating.

Lacey stood where she was for long moments, staring across her living room at the closed door, wondering how the morning had gone so wrong. She hadn't meant to piss him off, hadn't meant to make him feel like she wanted nothing more to do with him. But he'd made her nervous, walking around half dressed, poking in her cabinets like he belonged there. Kissing her like he meant it.

She could barely handle her own feelings; she sure as hell didn't want to be responsible for his as well. And yet she didn't feel nearly as good about this whole fuck-buddy thing as she'd thought she would.

Maybe it was because she'd broken her promise to herself to remain celibate until she could get her head on straight. Byron's eyes, haunted and angry, rose up in her mind's eye. Or maybe it was because she'd really wanted to go to breakfast with him—which was why she'd felt honor bound to say no. The idea of strolling hand in hand through the Quarter with him, of sitting across a breakfast table and talking to him about everything and nothing, had been way too appealing.

No, she told herself as she settled in front of her computer to write the day's blog entry. She'd done the right thing. Better to go on as she planned—fun and games in bed—but that was it. There was no way she was going to chance falling for someone right now, no way she was willing to give control over her heart and her emotions to a guy who could use and abuse them.

Satisfied that she'd done the only thing she could do, Lacey tried to put herself in the right frame of mind to write her blog. But for once, no fantasies were coming. She snorted. It was probably because Byron had done such a great job satisfying every craving she had the night before.

Still, she needed to write something. She didn't want to lose her following after she'd spent months building it up and responding to the comments she got there. Plus, she admitted, she really wanted to see if that new guy would comment again. Something about his response the other day had gotten to her, and she wanted to see what else he had to say.

But before she could do more than close her eyes, the phone rang. She thought about ignoring it—instead trying to stay in the zone—but she was expecting a call from her editor and really wanted to discuss with Melissa where she thought the book might be going.

Lunging for the phone, she answered with a breezy, "Hello."

"May I speak with Lacey Adams, please?"

Lacey's heart beat a little faster at the tentative female voice. "This is she."

"This is Carrie Winston. You called yesterday about my daughter. About Anne Marie."

There was such hope in the other woman's voice that Lacey winced. Any and all thoughts she had of something besides the investigation flew right out of her head.

Her hands were damp when she answered, "Yes, Mrs. Winston. I'm in New Orleans, and your daughter's name came up in reference to an investigation I'm doing—"

"You're a policewoman?"

"No, I'm a true-crime writer. I'm working on a book—"

"A writer? You're another reporter?" The hope died, replaced with disgust. And a bone-deep anger that had Lacey wincing in painful empathy. "I should have known."

The silence on the other line was absolute. Lacey cried, "Please don't hang up!" She blurted the words out as fast as she could, certain she would never get another chance to speak with the Winstons. "It's not what you think."

"That's what they all say. But it's always the same thing—someone, somewhere, looking for a new angle on my daughter's disappearance. Looking to exploit Anne Marie in one way or another."

Lacey winced as guilt once again assailed her, but she shoved it aside. She had a real chance to help Anne Marie here, and even if it caused her parents pain, she needed to take it. "That's not what I'm doing. I want to help Anne Marie."

"Really?" Carrie Winston's voice dripped sarcasm. "And how, exactly, do you think you'll be able to do that since she's dead?"

Lacey felt the blood drain from her face. "Anne Marie's dead?"

"Isn't that why you called?" Anger fairly vibrated through the phone lines.

"They found her body six weeks ago, though it took some time to—it took some time to identify it."

"I'm so sorry. I didn't know."

"You're not much of a reporter, are you? I'm not surprised. It's not like the NOPD is much of a police department."

"Technically, I've never worked as a reporter. I write books." She paused, then: "They haven't found anything?"

"Nothing. They don't even know how she died. Her skeleton—" The woman's voice broke and she started to cry softly.

Lacey started to apologize again, started to hang up, as she didn't want to cause the woman any more pain. But at the same time, she was starting to feel like she had a real chance of finding out what had happened to Anne Marie.

When the woman's sobs had quieted, Lacey said softly, "When I was in the Quarter yesterday, I saw Anne Marie's picture on a strip-club wall."

"You're wrong." The woman's voice broke again, and Lacey's heart broke along with it.

"I don't think so, Mrs. Winston. Believe me, I wish I was. She didn't look like she wanted to be there—a lot of the girls in the pictures didn't—and I can't help wondering what a girl who went missing from a university in western Canada ended up doing down here in New Orleans."

Carrie Winston didn't say a word, and the silence would have been eerie if not for the ragged sound of her breathing coming loud and clear through the telephone line. More than once Lacey started to say something, but in the end she kept her mouth shut.

Finally, Anne Marie's mother spoke. "You think whoever took my daughter forced her to do . . ."

"I think it's a strong possibility. Mrs. Winston, was there any indication that Anne Marie left school of her own free will?"

"No." The word was choked, barely understandable. "There were no withdrawals from her bank account, no charges on her credit card. None of her clothes were missing."

"There's a prostitution ring that got broken up here in New Orleans not very long ago, and a number of the girls from the ring didn't have identification on them when they were arrested. Plus, a few of them disappeared after being released on bail.

"When I found out about Anne Marie being taken and then working as a stripper, I couldn't help wondering if there was a connection. Couldn't help wondering if what had happened to your daughter had happened to other girls like her. If it has, I need to know why and how. I need to know if it's still happening to them. If there are more parents like you, who woke up one morning to find out that their entire world had caved in. If there are, if other parents are suffering as you and your husband have, then I have to try to stop it. I can't just let it keep happening, not if there's a chance I can do something about it."

Ragged, tortured sobs came from the other end of the phone, and Lacey held her breath as she waited for Anne Marie's mother to collect herself.

It took a few minutes, but finally the tears stopped. Carrie cleared her throat, and when she spoke, the anger was back. But this time it wasn't directed at Lacey. "What do you want to know? I'll tell you whatever I can."

Lacey's smile was grim as she reached for the notepad she'd recorded her questions on earlier that morning. Then she settled in for what she hoped would be a long and fruitful talk.

It was over an hour before Lacey hung up the phone, sickness and bile churning in her gut. That last day, when Anne Marie had called her mother, she had been hysterical. Had begged her parents to come find her. She'd told them that she'd run away, that one of the other girls had been killed and she was terrified they would kill her too. Then someone had hung up the phone before Anne Marie could say anything more.

Anger was a living, breathing animal inside Lacey as she shoved away from her desk and began to pace the narrow confines of her living room. The Winstons had flown to New Orleans within hours of receiving their daughter's phone

call, had talked to the police and the FBI, the district attorney and a private investigator they had hired. And nothing had been done. They hadn't heard from the
police again, except when they called for a status update, until the day they'd
received the call that their daughter's body had been identified.

No connections had been made between Anne Marie's death and the strip
clubs—or at least none that Mrs. Winston knew about. What Lacey needed, she
thought with a grim smile as she stared blindly at her living room walls, was to
get her hands on Anne Marie's file. Not that she had a chance in hell of getting
it; public disclosure laws obviously didn't allow cops to share open files.

Still, it wouldn't hurt to talk to the detectives who worked Anne Marie's case,
to see what they said. And in the meantime, she was going to rattle every contact
she'd managed to make in this case, was going to shake the trees and see what
fell out. Because there were only a few things she knew for sure, and one of them
was that if this had happened to Anne Marie, it had happened to other girls as
well. She just needed to find out which ones.

Settling behind her computer once again, she started running a search in the
Times-Picayune database on girls found dead in the French Quarter in the last
three years. Then nearly cried when she saw just how many there were.

Chapter Ten

S o, how's that piece for the governor's mansion going?" Mike asked as he reached into Byron's fridge and grabbed two beers. Mike was tall, skinny and could hold his liquor like a lumberjack.

"You don't want to know."

"Why not? You were really excited about it the last time you brought it up."

"That was before I fucked it up. I spent half the morning trying to figure out how to fix the mother of all scratches that runs down the center of it, but I think I'm just going to have to start over."

He flopped down on the couch and picked up the remote, doing his damnedest not to glance across the courtyard into Lacey's apartment as he flicked through stations. It wasn't like she was home anyway; the place was still dark as a tomb. Or at least it had been when he'd checked ten minutes before.

"Hey, what station's the game on, anyway?" he called to Mike, who was currently rifling through his pantry in search of some sports-worthy snacks.

"Seriously? It's on NBC." Mike pulled his head out of the cabinet long enough to toss him a disgusted look. "Grow a pair, why don't you?"

"I have a pair, thank you very much. Just because I prefer contact sports to watching a bunch of grown men wave a stick at a little white ball doesn't mean shit."

"Yeah, well, the Sox are playing, so keep a civil tongue in your head, all right?"

"You can take the boy out of Boston . . ."

"Damn straight." Mike finally settled on a bag of potato chips and headed for the other end of the couch, just in time to watch a beer commercial flash onto the screen. "Come on with the commercials already. Where are my guys?"

"You're calling a group of grown men your guys, and you think I need to grow a pair?" *Fuck it*—Byron gave up the fight and darted a look across the courtyard. Lacey's kitchen light was on.

"At least my pair is getting a workout, which is more than you can say. How long's it been for you anyway? You've been grumpy as shit lately."

Byron ignored him as he wondered what Lacey was doing over there. Was she writing on her damn blog again, or had she already posted something? He'd been dying to check all day, but had forced himself to avoid it.

Ignoring his instinct to head over there and demand that she talk to him was hard enough—especially after the way he'd left things that morning. If he read one of her fantasies, imagined Lacey in the positions she described in her blog, he'd be lost. Especially if some asshole posted a particularly graphic response in the comment section.

Just the thought of a bunch of guys sharing Lacey's fantasies had Byron across the room and logging on to the Internet before he thought twice about it. And sure enough, when he pulled up What a Girl Wants, there was a new fantasy there.

I want you naked, your body gleaming in the moonlight coming in from my window.

I strip you, pulling your shirt off slowly. I run my hands over the smooth muscles of your shoulders, the lean hardness of your abs. I kiss my way down your chest, over your stomach, to the raging erection of your cock.

I take my time undressing you, take my time slipping off your belt, feeding the button of your jeans through the buttonhole, pulling down your zipper until I take you in my hand.

I can feel your eagerness, feel how much you want me with every breath you take. But I'm not done, though I hold you in my hand. Though I stroke my thumb over and around your broad head and make you groan for me.

It's too soon, too quick, and I want to make you suffer a little. Want to turn you inside out. Want to tease you as you have so often teased me. Behind me, the radio is playing—something smooth and sexy and so very perfect that it is hard for me to resist.

I let you go, move away, watch the disappointment and the desire cloud your gaze. You think I'm taunting you, that I've brought you this far just to leave you. But this is just the beginning of the show.

I begin to sway to the music, my arms and hips and breasts and ass all moving in time with the sweet melody that fills the space between us. I reach for the hem of my T-shirt and pull it up slowly, revealing the soft skin of my stomach inch by inch. I hear you groan, hear your breathing speed up despite the music swelling between us.

Finally, I pull the shirt off and fling it away. I skim my fingers over my stomach, beneath the waistband of my skirt, and shiver at the feel of them on the raging heat of my skin. They feel good, but I wish it was you touching me. Want it to be you with a need that borders on the obscene.

I shimmy out of the skirt, let it fall in a puddle at my feet.

I stand before you in my scarlet bra and panties. A little obvious, I know, but I want to be your scarlet woman. Your exotic dancer. Your harem girl.

Your deepest, darkest fantasy.

As you are mine.

He stared at Lacey's blog with a bewildered frown, reading and rereading her newest post. Behind him, Mike yelled obscenities at the umpire, but Byron ignored him.

Skimming through the comments—many of them sexually explicit—he told himself not to get upset. Told himself that the fact that she was still posting fantasies—frank, exciting fantasies that would have at least half of her readers throwing wood—was no reflection on him. Just as he told himself it didn't matter that hundreds, maybe thousands, of men were reading this and imagining Lacey, imagining *his* woman, pleasuring them. Stripping for them. Dancing for them.

It didn't work, and he could feel the confusion inside him giving way to an anger he knew he wasn't going to be able to hide. It was stupid—ridiculous, really—to feel like this. Lacey had been running this blog for months. Why should she change her modus operandi just because they'd spent the night together?

Just because her sexy body and incredible responsiveness had fulfilled his deepest, darkest fantasies didn't mean he'd done the same for her. Judging from the way she'd kicked him out of her bed—and her apartment—with that no-strings-attached garbage, he hadn't come close to satisfying her. She obviously had more fantasies, obviously had—

He slammed his fist down on the desk so hard it made his laptop jump. *He* wanted to be the one to fulfill her fantasies. The idea of her being unsatisfied, of her needing more than he could give her—than he *had* given her—literally turned his stomach.

"Hey, what's got you so pissed off?" Mike swung off the couch as the TV cut once again to commercials.

Byron scrambled to close the window before Mike could see Lacey's distinctive home page, but he wasn't quick enough.

"Oh, man, are you still following this site?"

"Aren't you?" He tensed as he waited for his friend's answer.

"I would, but Janine's being kind of psycho about it lately. She says my interest in this blog makes her feel like she's not enough for me. Can you believe it?" He took a swig of his beer and reopened the window.

For once, Byron knew exactly where Mike's girlfriend was coming from—which was too fucked-up for words, as he'd always thought Janine was a little too emotional for comfort.

Mike read for a few seconds, then whistled low and long. "She's still cranking them out, huh, man? I swear, after reading this I'm ready to go home and make Janine a very happy woman. You should do the same."

"I don't think I'm Janine's type." Byron drained his beer, fighting the urge to smash his fist into his friend's face. But at least Mike was thinking about Janine while he was reading the blog; that meant he could let him live. Probably.

"Damn straight you're not—and you just remember that, okay? I don't need a pretty boy like you sniffing around, making me look bad. Janine's always had a thing for baby-faced white boys, and I don't need the competition."

"I haven't had a baby face since I was one. And when did you start caring who else Janine looked at? I thought one woman was as good as another."

A flush crept up Mike's cheeks, and Byron stared at him in surprise. "Are things getting serious between you two?"

The commentator came back on, announcing that one of Mike's favorite players was about to bat. When his friend didn't even turn around to look, Byron had a premonition about what was coming.

Sure enough, Mike reached into his pocket and pulled out a square black box.

"Dude, I didn't know you cared," Byron tried to joke.

"Shut the fuck up." He flicked the box open. "I just picked it up today. Do you think Janine's going to like it?"

Byron stared at the round diamond for a few seconds. It was big and shiny; what was there not to like? "Yeah, of course."

Mike studied it. "I don't know. I almost went for a kind of rectangular-shaped one, but this one sparkled more."

"Sparkle's important."

"That's what I thought." Mike glanced up, saw that Byron's tongue was tucked firmly into his cheek and groaned. "I sound like a total pussy, don't I?"

"Let me count the ways."

"That's what I figured." He shoved the box back into his pocket. "I'm gonna ask her tonight. I think she'll say yes—she's been hinting for a couple months now."

"Then let me be the first to congratulate you. Couldn't happen to a better guy." He crossed to the fridge, pulled out two more beers and tossed one to Mike. "To you and Janine. May there be a bunch of little Mikes running around soon."

"Let's not even go there. The whole marriage thing is creepy enough without bringing kids into it."

Mike stayed for the rest of the game, drinking beers and trading insults. When he finally left to meet Janine a couple hours later, Byron watched him go with mixed feelings. He was happy for the guy, but a little jealous too.

Not that he wanted to get married—not even close. But he sure as shit wanted to be something besides fuck buddies with the most intriguing woman he'd ever met, and he envied his friend a woman who was more open about her feelings than Lacey had been.

Of course, he was coming to believe an ice cube was more open about its feelings than Lacey, so maybe that wasn't saying much.

Flicking off the TV, he wandered his apartment for a few minutes, cursing himself. He never should have given in to temptation and read her blog. He'd been pissed at her all day over her attitude that morning, but that didn't seem to matter to his cock. He was hard and aching and more than willing to say, "To hell with sensibilities." Who cared if all she wanted was to screw around? All he wanted at the moment was to get her into bed again and relieve the never-ending ache—while taking care of every fantasy she had, once and for all.

And wasn't he jumping the gun a little with that one? Commitment? How the hell could he be thinking commitment when they'd never been on a real date? Never talked about their hopes or dreams, their pasts or their problems? It was ridiculous. And yet, as he eyed his computer, he felt like he knew her inside out. Like he knew the most important parts of her. Not just sexually, but also what she really wanted. What kind of woman she was. And it wasn't necessarily the persona she put forth on What a Girl Wants.

When they had been in bed the night before, he'd wanted her to tell him what she liked and how she liked it. Her persona from the blog would have had no problem with it, but the Lacey he'd been with hadn't been nearly so open.

She knew what she liked, knew what she wanted, but she'd had a terrible time saying it out loud. Almost as if she was completely unused to a man asking. Or caring.

It was something he'd thought about a lot while he'd lain in bed, watching her sleep. Something he'd tested out when he'd talked her into trying out his special brand of water sports in the shower.

And he'd discovered that he was right. His Lacey wasn't shy; she loved giving and receiving pleasure and wasn't the least bit reticent about touching him in every way imaginable. But she was leery of asking for her own pleasure, almost as if she expected it not to matter to him.

The thought still pissed him off, though he'd been brooding on it most of the day. Made him wonder what kind of bastards she'd previously hooked up with that her pleasure was an afterthought. Made him wonder if that's why she wrote the blog.

But that was a great big *if*, and if it wasn't true, then he'd feel like a total ass. Especially as her current fantasy was screaming at him like it was written in all caps. Making him wonder if he'd pushed her too far the night before, or not far enough. Maybe he was being stupid to spend so much time worrying over it, but he wanted her to be satisfied. Wanted her to get what she needed from him.

Fuck it! He stood up with a grimace, deciding he had to move on or the whole thing was going to drive him completely around the bend. One sexual encounter, no matter how fantastic, wasn't enough to change a person. Wasn't enough to base a commitment, any kind of commitment, on. And yet even with all the rationale, he felt surprisingly let down—like he'd been crazy to think that the night before had meant anything.

But it had meant something to him, and he'd be damned if he just disappeared into the woodwork after the best night of his life. Lacey might not be interested in more than fun and games, but that encompassed a whole range of activities. Activities he would be more than happy to share with her.

He strode to his balcony and looked out. Across the courtyard, Lacey's light beckoned like a siren's song. It was all the encouragement he needed. He headed for the bathroom and a quick shower to wash away the sweat and grime of the day.

Despite his pressing problems with the governor's table, he'd spent most of the day working on the rocking chair a young couple had commissioned from him. Originally, they hadn't needed it until mid-September, but she'd gone into labor three weeks early. The baby was fine, or so the dad said, but the mom was obsessed with having the rocking chair in the nursery when she brought her first son home in a couple of days.

So he'd rushed it, moved it up on the schedule and spent all day making sure the finishing touches were just perfect on it. When the dad had come to pick it up—he couldn't have been much more than a kid himself—he'd been so excited and so proud and so grateful that Byron hadn't been able to help responding. Any more than he'd been able to stop himself from giving the guy 20 percent off the agreed-upon price, as a baby gift.

And his father wondered why he was happy being a carpenter? How could he not be? The look on that young dad's face had been more than equal to the money he would have made on Wall Street for the same amount of hours.

Plus, the satisfaction that came with doing something that he loved, instead of just something he was good at, couldn't be denied. He loved building furniture, loved making something that might very well become a family heirloom one day. Loved making people happy in a way that didn't revolve around their wallets or bank balances.

If that made him a failure in his father's eyes, then so be it. It wasn't like he hadn't been fucking typecast for the role since the time he was a toddler anyway.

Annoyed all over again, he shrugged into a set of clothes that didn't have sawdust all over them before gathering up his wallet and heading for the door. He'd made an ass of himself this morning, and experience had taught him that flowers could go a long way toward healing the breach. Besides, she hadn't said flowers were against the rules.

With one last glance at the computer, he made a conscious decision to shrug off his crappy mood and enjoy the evening with his new lover.

Because one way or the other, Lacey was going to be his. Even if it was just for a little while.

Chapter Eleven

Lacey paced her apartment, a glass of wine in one hand and a Godiva chocolate bar in the other. This was just one more reason why she didn't like to get involved, didn't like to date. Once you let a man get inside your head, you were stuck wondering about him. Worrying about him and yourself and whatever petty little fight had started all the angst. The next thing you knew, you were drowning your sorrow in booze and chocolate, waking up the next morning with a hangover and a bad complexion.

She studied the chocolate in her hand; told herself she didn't need it. That she was going to throw it out. Then took a big bite anyway, washing it down with the port she'd splurged on a few weeks before.

This whole thing totally sucked. She was the one breaking her own rules to be with him—ending her self-imposed celibacy months earlier than she'd ever contemplated—and Byron had still managed to act like he was the offended party. All she'd done was set down a few rules—guidelines, really—and he'd gotten all pissy. Almost as if he'd wanted her to care about him. As if he'd wanted something more.

But that was ridiculous. They barely knew each other. Of course, that was her own fault. She was the one who'd cut him off when he'd tried to talk, tried to invite her out to eat. She was the one who insisted that sex was the only thing that mattered.

It is *all that matters,* she told herself, even as she took another bite of chocolate. It was all she would *let* matter, because there was no way she was getting involved with another gorgeous, brooding male with a chip on his shoulder. She'd already been there and done that, and she had the scars—emotional and physical—to prove it.

Determined to work, she sat down at her computer, but found herself pulling up her e-mail instead. Her agent had written to check up on how the book was progressing, and before she let herself think too long and hard about it, Lacey dashed off a breezy response about how her sources had turned to shit. If that didn't freak Kimberley out, nothing would.

Her next e-mail was from Becca, a wish-you-were-here note from her baby sister as she backpacked her way around the world. For one brief moment, Lacey wished she was in Greece too, especially when she saw the ominous title of her third e-mail, this one from her editor.

Melissa had written LET'S TALK TOMORROW in the subject line of the e-mail—a sure sign that she wasn't happy about the long e-mail Lacey had written her earlier in the day, explaining her dilemma. Not that she was surprised; it wasn't like she was pleased as punch herself.

Shoving away from the computer, she dragged her thoughts from Byron and onto the book she had already accepted a substantial advance for—an advance she'd already spent more than half of. She didn't have time to worry about a guy—not when her career was on the line.

Circling her dining room table, Lacey looked at the pictures she'd printed out throughout the day. Pictures she'd done her damnedest to avoid, since the implications had become obvious.

There were fifteen of them on the table. *Fifteen.*

Fifteen girls in the last four years—ranging from fourteen to nineteen—who had simply disappeared from their hometowns in Canada.

Fifteen girls who had gone missing from different parts of the country and then showed up dead in New Orleans weeks, months and sometimes years later.

Fifteen girls whose lives had been cut short because someone was doing his damnedest to keep the dots from being connected.

She was very interested in knowing who that someone was—not to mention the picture those dots made.

Most of the girls—at least the ones under eighteen—had been classified as runaways by the NOPD, a classification that stank to high heaven, as most of them had been good students from good families, with no history of aberrant behavior. How the hell the police—and the New Orleans FBI, for that matter— had gotten away with it was something she would never understand. Someone— probably more than just one—in both those offices had to know. It would take a few people in each organization to manipulate the evidence. Even then, the only way it could have worked was if they had made sure to keep each faction, from homicide to kidnapping, sex crimes and human trafficking, from knowing about what was being investigated by the other factions.

Still, this was insane. To do this—to keep the media from making a connection, to keep the families from discovering what had been going on—meant the cover-up had to be huge. And had to go at least as high as she'd originally feared. Maybe higher.

But who? And how many? New Orleans politics had been dirty since the dawn of time, and certainly since Huey Long had been governor in the late 1920s. But even if playing dirty was one of the state's recognized pastimes, that didn't make things any easier.

Not all the politicians were dirty, certainly, but a bunch were. The key was going to be finding out who was, and what connections they had, with Washington and with the underbelly of New Orleans crime. Because she would bet her whole damn career that whoever was involved in this cover-up was playing both sides against the middle, and benefiting like crazy from both. Otherwise—

A knock on her front door abruptly cut off her thoughts, and her eyes flew toward the balcony. Byron's apartment was dark, but it had been lit up like a firecracker for most of the night.

Her heart started to pound faster, even as she told herself it wasn't Byron on the other side of the door. Maybe Mr. Andalukis had stopped by with some of his wife's cookies, or maybe Sarah from next door wanted to run out to the store and needed her to babysit the twins for a few minutes.

Surely, after the way they'd left things this morning, it wasn't Byron. Still, she couldn't help smoothing a hand over her hair any more than she could stop herself from glancing down despairingly at her ragged leggings and tight tank top. Curtis always complained if she didn't look good, always hassled her if she wasn't dressed up whenever she was around him. She hoped Byron wasn't—

As soon as she realized what she was thinking, Lacey froze. When had she started thinking of Byron as the new guy in her life? When had she started thinking of what he wanted or liked over her own desires?

And comparing him to Curtis—she shuddered at the thought. For one, he was a much better lover, and that was saying something, as Curtis had been very smooth at the beginning of their relationship.

Besides, she wasn't in the market for a relationship—in any way, shape or form. Sure, last night had been great, but that didn't mean she wanted something serious. In fact, she was positive that she didn't.

How could she? Less than twenty-four hours after sleeping with Byron for the first time, she was worried about impressing him. Worried about him getting upset because her career was falling apart around her and she wasn't at her best. It was exactly what she'd sworn she wouldn't do, exactly the trap she'd promised herself she'd never fall into again.

And yet here she was, dithering away, both hoping and dreading that it was Byron on the other side of the door.

Well, she wasn't that woman anymore, she reminded herself as she marched toward the foyer. And she wasn't going to get herself worked up because some man might be unhappy with her. If Byron said one word, she'd tell him to go to hell and then slam the door in his face. She'd—

Lacey threw the door open with a flourish, prepared to tell Byron off if he so much as looked at her funny. But when she met his eyes over the hugest, most beautiful bouquet of fuchsia stargazers she had ever seen, she stopped dead. And prayed for the floor to open up and swallow her; she had a feeling that was the only way she was going to be able to keep from jumping him in her foyer. Again. How the hell was she supposed to resist a man who managed to guess her favorite flower his first time out of the gate?

"Oh, Byron, they're beautiful." She had a hard time speaking past the sudden lump in her throat, but somehow she managed. "Absolutely gorgeous."

"I'm glad you like them." He smiled as he handed her the bouquet.

She waited for him to say more—maybe something cheesy about them reminding him of her, or maybe that they weren't as beautiful as she was. Any of the old, tired lines would do, and then she wouldn't feel so bad about having worked herself into a snit about him.

But he didn't say a word, just stood in her doorway and smiled at her with warm eyes. Her heart melted just a little, despite her determination that it wouldn't.

"I'm sorry about this morning," she found herself apologizing.

"Why? I was the one who stormed out of here. I came here to apologize to you."

"Come on in." She stepped aside, her palms starting to sweat as he brushed past her. "I'm sorry I'm not dressed—I wasn't expecting company."

"Don't worry about it, and please don't change on my account." His gaze went from warm to hot in one second flat. "I think you look great."

It was all she could do to keep from gaping at him. As it was, surprise had her fumbling her grandmother's vase, and it would have crashed to the ground had he not caught it with nimble fingers.

"Thanks," she mumbled as she felt her cheeks flush almost as deep a fuchsia as the flowers. *Damn redheaded complexion.*

"Hey, that color looks pretty good on you," he said with a grin, setting the vase on the counter before pulling her into his arms.

"Ugh, don't make it worse." She buried her face in his chest, soaking in the licorice and sandalwood scent she was beginning to associate with him.

"Why not?" He bent down until his lips were mere centimeters from her ear. "I think it's sexy."

"Now I know you're just being nice. There is absolutely nothing sexy about blushing."

"Sure there is." He pulled away, then trailed a finger over the low-cut neckline of her tank top. As he did, she realized her blush had managed to cover her entire upper torso. "It's very sexy to stand here and wonder how low your blush goes—and whether or not I'll get to see the boundaries."

He dipped his fingers inside her shirt and stroked her nipple once, twice. "Whether I'll be able to touch them."

He skimmed his lips down her neck and over her bare shoulder. "Whether I'll be able to kiss them."

Lacey's knees turned weak at the first touch of his lips on her collarbone, and suddenly she was flushing for a whole different reason. "You know," she whispered, her body strung so tightly she didn't trust her regular voice to actually function. "You're making it really hard for me to keep my distance."

"Good." Byron grinned as he pulled her body flush against his own. "Right now, keeping my distance is the least of my priorities."

"Oh, really?" She met his eyes with a smirk of her own, wondering how this could be the same man who'd slammed out of her apartment this morning. Wondering what his change of heart meant. "What about the rules?"

He shrugged, a wicked glint in his eyes. "I figure there's something to be said for taking pleasure where we can get it."

"Really?" She searched his face, looking for the truth.

"Really. Now, do you want to keep talking about this or do something more interesting?"

"That depends on what you have in mind."

He leaned down until his face was only inches from her own. "Guess," he murmured, right before his lips closed over hers.

Chapter Twelve

L acey's lips moved under his, stroking, caressing, *teasing* him into a frenzy, and Byron was loving every minute of it—right up until she broke off the kiss and strolled deliberately out of the kitchen.

He stared after her for a few seconds, wondering what she was up to even as he struggled to get his body under control. How was it possible that one kiss from Lacey had him so hot that his hands trembled and his cock actually throbbed?

From the second she'd answered the door—though he'd promised himself he'd take tonight slow with her, get to know her despite her best efforts to the contrary—all he'd been able to think about was bending her over the nearest chair and having his wicked, wicked way with her. Climbing onto the nearest horizontal surface and letting her ride them both into the sunset. Lifting her onto the kitchen cabinets and getting something cooking.

As his thoughts registered, Byron could feel himself flushing. Had he somehow channeled his teenage self and been unaware of it? It was completely embarrassing how being around her wiped everything out of his head but the driving need to be inside her, any and every way she would let him.

Still struggling to get himself under control, he followed Lacey into the family room, where she was standing at the bar, pouring herself a glass of wine.

"Hey, what can I get you?" She glanced over her shoulder with a grin, and everything inside him seemed to freeze. God, she was beautiful. Not just in the conventional sense, but in so many small ways he couldn't fail to notice. Ways he'd never thought to look for before her.

It wasn't just her face, though, God, she looked good. It was the smattering of freckles across her nose and the patterns they formed. Her high cheekbones and the incredibly kissable hollows beneath them. The peekaboo dimple in her left cheek that flashed only when she smiled just right. And her smile, the one that lit up her whole face and made him feel—for a few seconds—like he was the only man in her world.

"Byron?" Lacey called his name for the second time, and he suddenly realized that he'd been standing there, gaping at her like a total idiot.

"I'm sorry. What did you ask?"

"Do you want a drink?"

"Oh, sure, sorry." He shook his head, made an effort to concentrate. "Do you have a beer?"

"Of course." She bent to open the small bar fridge, and her yoga pants stretched taut over her sweetly rounded ass. It took all his restraint not to drop to his knees behind her and take her right there. God knew, all the work he'd done in the kitchen to calm himself down had been totally undone in the two minutes since he'd been in the room with her.

"I've got Purple Haze, Strawberry Harvest and Red Ale."

He stared at her incredulously, wondering if he'd heard right. "Are those beers or song titles?"

She laughed. "Beers. Whenever I move to a new place, I like to try out the local breweries. These are all from Abita, and they're really good."

Figuring it wouldn't hurt to play along, he tried his damnedest not to look doubtful. One or two sips wasn't going to kill him, after all. "Okay. Which one is your favorite?"

"I like them all, but I guess it depends what you want. Are you in the mood for raspberries or strawberries?"

He didn't have to think twice, as a picture of her raspberry-colored nipples flashed before his eyes. "Raspberries."

"Somehow I knew you were going to say that." She tossed him a beer with a purple label, and he shook his head while twisting off the top.

"I don't know about this, Lacey. No self-respecting beer has a purple label."

"This one does. It used to be available only at Mardi Gras—hence the name and the color—but it got to be so popular that they brew it all year round now."

He stared at the bottle doubtfully for another minute before taking a swig, and was pleasantly surprised at how smoothly it went down. "It's actually pretty good."

"You don't have to sound so surprised." She led him over to the couch, then gestured for him to sit. "Are you sure you'd rather stay in tonight?"

He raised an eyebrow. "Is that a trick question?"

She laughed. "Good answer."

"So, you move around a lot?"

She cocked her head to the side, somehow managing to look like an inquisitive little cat—one he wanted to do nothing more with than to pull her into his lap and pet. But she obviously wanted to call the shots tonight, and he was intrigued enough to follow where she led. For a while anyway.

"Is that what you want to do with the evening?" she asked. "Play Twenty Questions?" Her voice was low and inviting and took the sting out of the question.

"Actually, I've got a better idea." God knew, he had a few of them. But tearing her clothes off before the first glass of wine—for the second time in as many days—seemed more than a little rude.

"And that is?" She took a sip of her wine and then shot him a smile that had his cock straining against the zipper of his jeans.

He studied her for a few seconds, running his eyes over her clothes and jewelry. "I call it *nine* questions."

"Nine?" She raised an eyebrow. "That's a fairly random number."

"Not really. It's the number of items you're wearing—if you don't go commando, I mean. It also"—he glanced down at himself—"happens to be the exact number of items I'm wearing as well."

"Well, isn't that convenient?" She pursed her lips into an inviting O.

Had he thought his dick was hard before? As he watched her lick her lips, the blood rushed from his head so fast that for a minute, he was afraid he might pass out.

And wouldn't that just be a kick in the ass, particularly on what promised to be one of the most erotic nights of his life?

"Am I correct in assuming that there's a fee for every question asked?"

"You are, indeed. One item per question."

"Are any subjects off-limits?"

He smiled then. "Let's cross that bridge when we come to it. *If* we come to it."

"Sounds like a plan."

Lust raked through him with vicious claws, had him clenching his fists and struggling for air as their gazes met—and held. She was so sexy, so interesting, so goddamn perfect for him that he couldn't help wondering if she'd slip away the second he dropped his guard, or woke up—whichever the case might be.

"So, do we have a deal?" She sat watching him, waiting, an air of expectation around her that he would do anything to uphold.

"We do," he murmured.

"Excellent." She held a smooth palm out for him to shake, and he laughed before pulling her into the circle of his arms.

"Sorry, baby. But there's only one way to cement deals like this."

"Oh yeah? And what is that?"

"I think you already know." With that cryptic pronouncement, he swept down and stole a kiss from the woman he had already decided he wanted to make his.

Lacey's lips were warm and firm, and so tempting that Byron almost decided to forget the whole thing. But he was determined to learn more about his wary lover before he once again tumbled her onto the nearest available surface. The game seemed like the perfect way to do just that and to keep things light, as she demanded.

Lacey lost herself in Byron's kiss, despite the skitter of unease working its way up her back. Why did he always have to ask questions? Why was he always trying to learn more about her?

A part of her told her to run in the other direction. It would be so much harder to keep Byron at arm's length—to keep herself from caring about him—if she learned more about him. If she shared herself with him.

But she didn't want to run, not when being with him was more exciting than anything she could remember. Not when he seemed to want to see the real her, not some figment of his own imagination.

Why she cared so much, she didn't know. But she did, and it was incredibly stupid all the way around. If all she wanted from Byron was a good time, why did it matter if she knew what his favorite color was? Or what had made him move to New Orleans. Or if he was an only child.

It didn't matter. Of course it didn't. And yet—

Byron broke off the kiss with just the right amount of reluctance, and she took a minute to give her spinning head a chance to focus. It was ridiculous, really, how crazy this man made her. Crazy and mixed-up and so aroused that half the time when she was around him, she didn't know which way was up.

Like now. She'd planned on sending him away, on telling him she couldn't see him anymore. Instead, she'd invited him in and started playing with him. Teasing him.

Of course, she was the one getting all hot and bothered. If they didn't get started on his question game pretty soon, she wouldn't be able to remember her own name, let alone any other pertinent information.

"So, who goes first?" Byron's voice was warm and his eyes hot as he watched her closely. He looked as out of control as she felt, and for the third time in as many minutes, she thought about just taking him to bed and saying to hell with the rest. But he'd started this thing, and she was determined to see it through— even if it killed her. No way was she chickening out.

"You do—it was your idea, after all." She settled back on the couch and took a long sip of wine, hoping that it would bring her down a notch. Or three. God knew she needed it.

"All right, then. I'd still like an answer to the question that started this whole thing." At her blank look, he continued, "You said that you like to check out the local flavor wherever you live. Do you move around a lot?"

"I do. I like to see different parts of the country—and the world. My feet get itchy if I stay in one place too long."

"Where else have you lived?"

"That's two questions—and I don't see the payment for the first yet."

"I thought this was just a friendly game between friends." His voice was warm and intimate and had her seeing stars by the second syllable; she was so dazzled that she almost acquiesced. But the small gleam of triumph lurking in the back of his eyes gave him away. He was as competitive as she was—and played just as dirty. The thought shouldn't be such a turn-on, but it was.

Determined to stay on top, she said sweetly, "Of course it's friendly. Or it will be as soon as you take off your shoes."

Lacey nearly laughed at the disgruntled look on his face, but when he sat back on the sofa and slipped off both of his tennis shoes, she knew she was in trouble. She'd never paid much attention to men's feet one way or the other, but one look at Byron's feet—still encased in socks—and her heartbeat was already speeding up. Maybe it was the implication that very soon the rest of his clothes would follow. Maybe it was the thought of having him naked for her viewing pleasure. And maybe it was just that she was completely, around-the-bend crazy. Tonight certainly wasn't the first time she'd had the thought in the past few days.

"Okay," he murmured, after drawing her attention to his discarded second shoe. "I did my part. What's the answer to the second question?"

"As an adult, I've lived in San Francisco, New York, Chicago, Paris, Phoenix, Boston, Milan and now New Orleans."

His eyes widened at her list, but all he said was, "Which one did you like best?"

"Wow, three questions in one turn. You're a lot easier than I thought you were going to be." She raised an eyebrow and gestured to his pants. "What's coming off next?"

He laughed. "Never mind. I'll save my questions for something I can't find out in casual conversation."

"That might be a good idea."

"All right, then. It's your turn." He leaned against the sofa, arms spread over the back as if he didn't have a care in the world. Only the sudden wariness that flickered briefly in his eyes told a different tale. It made her want to start out easy when she knew she should be going for the jugular—at least if she wanted to win their little game.

Deciding on a compromise, she asked, "What's a New York guy like yourself doing living in the Big Easy?"

"How'd you know I was from New York? I don't have an accent." He looked more than a little startled.

"It's the attitude, the way you hold your body. You've got New York written all over you. After you live there for a while, it's easy to recognize the signs."

"I guess so." But he still looked surprised, and less than pleased.

The investigator in her knew there was a story there and wanted to dig, but the woman didn't want to alienate him—or to take the fun out of the game. Not yet anyway. To distract them both, she reached down and pulled off a sock, twirling it above her head for a few second before letting it fly.

She watched as it landed on the potted palm she kept next to the balcony, then turned back to Byron with a grin. Her diversion must have worked, because the disgruntled look had been replaced with amused appreciation.

"Your turn," she said. "And just to show you what a generous person I am, I won't charge you for the question you just asked."

"I didn't—" He broke off, chagrined. "I didn't realize 'How'd you know' counted."

"They all count. Rules are rules, after all."

"So you're not a rule breaker?"

She paused, considering his question for a minute. "I never used to be."

"And now?"

"Now I think I'm learning to unbend a little bit. God knows I'm breaking all the rules sitting here with you."

His eyes changed from chocolate to obsidian and he leaned forward, a look of dark arousal on his face. "I'll be happy to help you break a few more rules, if you'd like." He reached for her hand, stroked his thumb back and forth across the sensitive skin of her palm.

Her body lit up from the inside, like a surge of electricity had whipped through her and turned on every part. "I don't know about that. I think the one I already broke is enough for me."

"And which one is that?" His voice was so low and gravelly, so dark and tempting, that she felt her palms and her panties go damp.

"Are you sure you want the answer to that? You're on question number five."

His gaze caught hers and held. He didn't look away for a second, even as he peeled off both his socks. Then he reached up and took off the little gold hoop he had in his right ear—the one she'd found incredibly sexy from the second she'd first laid eyes on it. "Oh, I definitely think it's worth it. Things are just getting interesting."

"I'm breaking the no-involvement rule," she said, as he reclaimed her hand. "I promised myself I'd stay away from men for two years—no relationships, no sex, nothing but friendships, if I even allowed myself that." She could see the question in his eyes and answered before he could ask it. "I managed to lose myself during my last relationship. I needed time to find me again, to figure out who I am now and what I want out of life."

"And did you figure it all out?" His hand tightened on hers, a silent offering of support that had her heart stuttering in her chest.

Because her reaction to him freaked her out, and because the question hit much closer to home than she was ready for, she did the only thing she could do: She dodged it. "Hey, no fair. It's my turn—you keep skipping me."

The rueful twist of his mouth said he knew exactly what she was doing—and that he wasn't going to call her on it. "All right, then. What's next?"

"Something easy." She wanted, needed, to lighten things up. "What's your favorite ice-cream flavor?"

He grinned. "Rocky Road."

She couldn't stop her knowing laugh. "Why does that not surprise me?"

"I don't know."

She reached down and took off her sock, did the same twirl-and-toss routine as she had with the first. Then waited for him to move on, but he merely stared at her with raised eyebrows.

"What?"

"That was two questions."

"No, it wasn't!"

"Sure it was. Think back."

She did, and was astounded to realize he was right. "Well, if the second one counts, I want something better than 'I don't know' as my answer." She lifted her pant leg and unhooked her ankle bracelet.

"But I don't know."

"Tough luck." She gave him a hard-ass look as she put the anklet on the end table next to her. "Make something up. And make it good."

"Well, then, let me think." When he finally spoke, it was with a wicked grin that put her instantly on edge. "Rocky Road is . . . complex. There are all these layers and textures to it that make it so much more interesting than plain old vanilla. The smooth, satiny chocolate that seduces your mouth from the very first bite. The crunchy, prickly nuts that add a lot of flavor and just the right hint of salt."

He brought her hand—the one she realized he'd never quite let go of—up to his mouth. Ran his lips across her palm in a tender kiss. "And then there's my favorite part."

"Which is?" Was that high-pitched breathless noise really her voice? It sounded like she'd swallowed a canary.

He grinned. "The marshmallows, of course. They're softer and sweeter than the rest of the ice cream. All warm and creamy and delicious." His tongue darted out, once, twice, and he licked her palm like he would an ice-cream cone—or a woman. Long, slow drags of his tongue that had her nipples pebbling and her already strained breathing shifting into hyperdrive.

"Yep, marshmallows are definitely my favorite." He delivered one well-placed nip over her mound of Venus that nearly had her eyes crossing, then pulled away to settle back on the couch, his breathing calm, his gaze completely unruffled.

He was good, so good that she would have totally bought the casual act—*if* she hadn't had a pretty damn good view of his *very* healthy erection. It made her mouth water even as it reassured her she wasn't the only one affected by the powerful sexual chemistry between them.

Once again she considered ending the game and taking him back to her bedroom. But if she did that, he would win, and she *so* wasn't ready to let that happen. She wanted him on his knees first.

So, while it took every ounce of concentration she had, she managed to get her body and her breathing under control.

When she was finally able to speak, there was nary a hint of the overwhelming arousal she felt in her speech. "That does sound good. Maybe I'll pick some up the next time I'm at the grocery store."

His eyes widened at her nonchalance, and she almost blew the whole thing by bursting out laughing. Somehow she managed to swallow back the giggles long enough to say, "I think it's your turn."

Her amusement must have shown through, though, because his lips twitched suspiciously. "All right, then." He nodded toward the long table behind them as he slipped off his watch. "What are all those pictures of girls for?"

"A book I'm writing."

"So, you're a writer? What kind?"

"True crime. And trust me when I tell you that you don't want to hear any more about it tonight. It's been a pretty crappy day."

He nodded. "Fair enough. Your turn."

She pulled off her bracelet. "Why do you always smell like sandalwood?"

He shrugged. "I smoke a lot of pot and burn incense to disguise the smell. Sandalwood is the most common ingredient in incense."

She could feel her eyes widening, though she tried her damnedest to look as blasé about the whole thing as he did. "Seriously?"

"That's another question. If you want an answer, you'd better pony up." He nodded to her camisole.

She slipped off her ponytail holder and handed it to him instead.

He grinned wickedly. "No, not seriously. I'm actually a carpenter, and I use sandalwood or its oils in some of the furniture I make. It repels moths and other insects."

"Ugh! That was totally uncool." She pretended to pout as she secretly admired his ingenuity.

"But so much more interesting than the truth. You did say I could make things up."

"True," she acknowledged. "But you asked two questions last time and I didn't make *you* take off two things."

"And how is that my fault?" His grin was self-satisfied and wicked as hell. It was also sexy enough to curl her toes. "You need to be more cutthroat."

She took a second to swallow, knowing the jig would be up if she actually drooled on the man. "So that's how you want to play it? I thought you said this was just a friendly little game between friends."

"You're the one who made it into something else. I'm just trying to keep up. Besides"—he shrugged, and she couldn't help admiring just how neatly he'd flipped the tables around on her— "I only play to win."

"Isn't that funny?" She dipped her index finger in her wine, then brought it to her lips, where she slowly sucked the delicious liquid off it before running her finger over her bottom lip. His eyes followed her every movement, and she couldn't help being gratified when they glazed over. "So do I."

He didn't say anything for long seconds, so she finally said, "Your question."

His voice was somehow even more hoarse than it had been when he asked, "Why me?"

"Why you?" She didn't understand the question.

Standing up, he slowly pulled off his shirt, and it was her turn to lose focus as all Byron's glorious muscles went on display. "You said you were breaking the rules by being with me. What made you choose me to break them with?"

Chapter Thirteen

Gregory stared down at the file in front of him in disbelief. For nearly a minute, he sat frozen, unable to think or move or breathe. Unable to act like the leader his men needed.

The last thought galvanized him, made him snap out of the unpleasant shock that had whipped through him as he'd gazed at the information Micah had unearthed on his little redhead.

He snorted. His little redhead—what a misnomer that was. Lacey Adams was a true-crime writer who had come to New Orleans to investigate the prostitution-ring debacle that had brought an end to one of his most lucrative business ventures.

Just the thought of Veronique and what had happened caused his fists to clench in annoyance. That whole thing should never have happened—would never have happened if the little whore he'd put in charge had been as good at keeping her mouth shut as she was at shoving shit up her nose.

The only reason she wasn't dead yet was because she had been smart enough, during the time the escort service was riding high, to secure herself the NOPD police commissioner as a lover. In exchange for free sex whenever the bastard wanted it and a closed mouth on Veronique's part, he had protected her.

Watched over her. So that even the very brief time she spent in prison had been at the best women's prison in the state—one where serving time was more of a pastime than the hard labor his men went through if they got caught.

For a while, her connections hadn't bothered him—hell, they had made the whole dismantling of the escort service easier, as the commissioner had been more than willing to help them protect the names of the clients. Names of some of the men who did more than just sleep with his whores. Names of men who were neck-deep in the other side of the business and would do anything to keep their extracurricular activities from being discovered.

But after the plea bargain was done and the evidence put away, when Veronique had been in prison, he had tried to have her taken out. After all, she knew far too much about him—about how his operation worked—and leaving her alive was a liability he just couldn't afford.

But Beauchamp, the bastard, had kept the bitch protected even in prison. And Gregory had lost two of his best female assassins before he'd figured that out and decided to leave her be—for a while.

But now, now Micah was telling him that the stupid whore was becoming a distinct liability. She had met with Lacey yesterday morning, had talked with her for nearly an hour. God only knew what the two of them had talked about, but if Veronique had let anything slip, she was a dead woman—important lover or not.

No, fuck that. She was a dead woman no matter what. He couldn't afford the liability of keeping her alive.

He glanced at Jim sharply, who was staring straight ahead while he went through the file. "Did you look at this before you gave it to me?"

"No, Mr. Alexandrov. I knew you wanted to see it as soon as it arrived. Should I have?"

"No, no, it's fine." He flipped through the pages of the report. "But I think we may have a problem."

Jim's eyes grew just a little more alert, and his body language changed until he went from looking like a mild-mannered assistant to the dangerous predator he was. His chameleonlike abilities and his skill with a knife were just two of the reasons Gregory kept him around.

"I think it's time to take care of the little problem we've been talking about. She's becoming a liability, one that I don't think we can afford any longer."

"I see. And is there any particular way you'd like it done?"

"Make it look like a mugging—or a rape. The last thing I need is her pain-in-the-ass lover up in my face. And make sure the body is found, quickly. I want it to serve as a warning to anyone else who is thinking of betraying me."

"Of course, sir. I'll take care of it today."

"You do that."

After Jim had excused himself, Gregory flipped through the file one last time. Reread all the information Micah had included on Lacey. Stared at the pictures his men had taken of her. And seethed that the one woman he'd truly wanted in more years than he could count might very well be the one who could cause him the most problems.

It wasn't an insurmountable problem; there were ways to secure her so that once she was in his world, she could never get out. Ways to keep her from writing the damn book even as he fucked her brainless.

With a muttered curse, he turned to his computer and typed in the Web address of the blog Micah said Lacey ran in her free time. Then stiffened as the hot-pink and black blog flashed on his screen, complete with Lacey's deepest, darkest fantasies.

He scrolled through the blog entries, noting, with rising fury, the number of comments on each one. Most entries had at least a hundred comments—a hundred men lusting after Lacey. A hundred men imagining what it would be like to fuck her.

It was enough to make him want to set the whole damn world on fire.

He stopped scrolling abruptly, read the fantasy he'd landed on with raven-ous eyes.

You follow me onto the elevator, your hands already on my ass. On my tits. And I know the second the doors close behind us, you'll be covering me, your body pressing against mine as you lift me up and sink your cock inside me.

I'm already wet and creamy at the thought, my pussy drenched with the need to feel your cock inside me. But I want you everywhere and don't know where to start—with my hand, my mouth. My cunt, my ass. I want to take you in every part of me, want you to brand me, to ride me. To fuck me.

Closing his eyes, Gregory imagined Lacey at his mercy. Imagined her on the floor in front of him, her glorious red hair streaming over her naked breasts as she fucked him with her mouth. He would be gentle with her the first few times, earn her trust. And then he would take her harder, make her scream his name in pain and pleasure. Make her want him until she didn't care where they were or what he did to her.

His dick hardened, punching a tent in the front of his tailor-made trousers. He reached a hand down, undid the zipper. Started to stroke himself as he imagined it was Lacey's hand around him.

Yes, he thought as his breathing grew ragged, it was definitely time to set things in motion. He was getting tired of waiting to make his fantasies a reality.

His question hung between them, and Byron watched as Lacey struggled to find the best way to answer it. Her teeth nibbled at her glorious lower lip, much as he liked to do, worrying it as she searched for the right words.

Finally, just when he was sure she wouldn't answer, she said, "I didn't choose you. I couldn't *resist* you. There's a difference."

His cock, which had been hard as hell for what seemed like hours now, somehow got even harder. His palms literally itched with the need to touch her, to hold her, to pull her to him and take her in all the very many ways he wanted to. But she was telling him things he'd never find out another way and he wasn't going to call a halt to that.

Still, there was so much he wanted to say to her, so much he wanted to do to her, that restraint was a physical ache within him. Somehow he managed to hold himself back, to simply say, "I'm glad," and leave it at that as he waited for her next question.

"Why do you want me?" she whispered.

For a second he was sure he had misheard the question, then nearly laughed when he realized she was serious. "How could I not?" he asked.

She never looked away, but he watched as her cheeks turned rosy with embarrassment. "Very easily."

He did laugh then. "I don't think so." He stepped closer, no longer giving a damn about the game or the rules or anything else that didn't involve touching Lacey. "I want you because you're the most exciting woman I've ever met. You're smart and charming and so beautiful that sometimes it hurts to look at you.

"You make me think, make me laugh. You shake me up and make me work for every smile I get from you. You're real in a way nothing has been for me in a very long time.

"Why do I want you?" he echoed her question. "Why on earth *wouldn't* I want you?"

For long seconds, she didn't do anything but stare a him with her shamrock eyes. Then, just as he'd decided she wouldn't respond, she whipped her camisole over her head and stood in front of him, bare from the waist up.

Heat exploded inside of him, both at the sight of her and at the vulnerability she was showing. The fantasy he'd read earlier on her blog—the one where she had imagined stripping for her lover—came back to him; tonight's game had been his effort at making that fantasy a reality. But the game had taken on a life of its own, and now they were both more vulnerable—more emotionally naked—than either had been expecting.

And still it wasn't enough for him. He wanted all of her exposed to him—every inch of her gorgeous, feminine body. Every emotion in her guarded, generous heart. Every thought in her agile, interesting mind. He wanted it all. And now, at this moment, knew he would do whatever it took to get it.

Without taking his eyes from hers, he unfastened his pants and let them—and his boxers—fall to the ground at his feet. He stood before her more vulnerable than he'd ever been in his life, and hoped she understood what he was offering.

She walked toward him slowly, her arm outstretched as if she couldn't wait to touch him. But then, when she was inches from him, she paused. Let her hand drop back to her side. Slowly shimmied out of her sweats and panties until she too was completely nude.

The sun had set at some point during their little game, and her skin gleamed like alabaster in the moonlight. Her long, silken hair tumbled over her shoulders in a fiery waterfall, and her beautiful body urged him forward like a siren's call.

Hunger rose in him—sharp, hot, all-encompassing—and he wanted nothing more than to take her with all the pent-up need he had inside him. But she wanted more than that tonight, and he wanted it for her. He would take it slow with her—savor her. Then maybe, just maybe, it would be enough to calm his raging instincts.

Pulling her into his arms, he kissed her until he was drowning in her. Kissed her until he didn't know where she left off and he began. Kissed her until she felt the same way.

He wanted her on fire, wanted her burning with the same need that threatened to eat him alive. He wanted to slip past her defenses, to see every secret part of her. He wanted—just once—for her to trust him enough to lose control.

He needed her to lose control. As he skimmed his lips over her razor-sharp cheekbones and down the delicate skin of her jaw, the world around him began caving in. He wanted her arms around him, her body beneath him, wanted to take over every part of her so that he knew that she was his. So that she knew it too.

Reaching for him, Lacey cupped his face in her hands and brought his mouth back to hers. The second their lips met, he gave himself over to the conflagration gathering between them, around them.

With a groan, he slid his tongue inside her mouth, thrusting between her lips like he wanted to thrust between her thighs. Demanding more and more from her, demanding all that she had to give.

Lacey whimpered at Byron's blatant invasion—his blatant claiming—and tried to pull away, to regroup. But he refused to let her go, his tongue stroking every inch of her mouth. His chest pressing against hers. His arms, holding her tightly to his long, lean body. His hips thrusting his hard, thick, long cock against her pussy until she was crazed with the need to have him fill her.

Tangling her tongue with his, she sucked him fully into her mouth and stroked the bottom of his tongue with her own. He growled deep in his throat while his hands tangled in her hair, holding her face to his.

Lacey relinquished his tongue with a moan, tilting her head back until she could see his face. Until their eyes had once again met. His were so black that the pupils had disappeared, so deep that she swore she could fall in and keep falling.

But wasn't that what she was doing already? Falling for him when she'd promised herself she wouldn't? Falling for him when she knew she would only get hurt again?

Usually, the threat of more pain was enough to get her to back off. Enough to let her convince herself that the blog was all she needed. Enough to let her believe that she didn't need to be held. Didn't need to be loved.

As she looked at Byron in that moment—at the tenderness and the desire that existed side by side on his face—she knew that she'd been lying to herself.

She didn't want to pretend anymore. Didn't want to get up in the morning and tell herself that it was better that she was alone. For a while it had been better, but not now. Not with Byron and his incredible lovemaking in her life.

No, she was much better off being with him than she was being alone. He made her happy. She knew, of course, that that also meant that he could make her sad. He *would* make her sad. She understood that, just like she understood that what they had wouldn't last.

But she was okay with that. Okay with having Byron for the six or seven months she was in New Orleans. Okay with letting him heal her battered body and soul. And when it was time to let go, she'd be okay with that too.

As she looked into his eyes and dared him to do whatever he wanted with her, she promised herself that she would be just fine when he left. Told herself—and him—that she could take anything he needed to give her and then some.

It was all the invitation he needed. Breathing harshly, he backed her up against the glass door that led to the balcony and held her there as his lips ran over her neck and shoulders and the hollow of her throat.

Fire raced through her wherever he touched, and she could tell he felt the same way. His breathing was harsh, his muscles tight, his cock huge as it nestled in the juncture of her thighs.

And he was staring at her, watching her, with eyes of liquid ebony. She glanced down, suddenly overwhelmed by the need to see herself through his eyes. To understand what made him lick his lips while he gazed at her, to know why his cock jerked and surged against her in such violent arousal.

Her breasts were full, swollen, her nipples bright pink and hard as rubies. Her skin was pale, the blue veins of her breasts evident beneath the oh, so delicate skin. Overwhelmed, aroused, operating on instinct and the need to drive him as completely insane as he was driving her, Lacey bent her head and trailed her tongue over the curve of her breast and down until she reached her nipple.

Byron didn't move, didn't betray his reaction by so much as a muscle twitch, and sudden embarrassment bloomed within her. Maybe she'd done the wrong—

"Do it again." His voice was rough, distorted, and she knew she had nothing to be embarrassed about.

His jaw was rigid and his teeth clenched, his skin pulled tautly over the sharp planes of his cheekbones. His hands had clamped around her upper arms, in a painless but unbreakable grip.

"I said, 'Do it again.'" The words were even darker, even lower than the first time.

"Do what?" She licked her finger, trailed it in lazy circles over her right breast and then the left. Then dipped lower to lightly graze first one distended nipple and then the other.

He growled low in his throat. It was a warning and a declaration, and she took delight in defying him. In seeing just how far she could push him.

"Do it!" It was an order, one she didn't mind following in the end. With a secret grin she complied. But this time, as she did it, she kept her eyes opened and fastened on his face.

His arms locked around her, caging her in a silken trap that for once she had no desire to escape.

"Touch yourself. I need to see—"

His voice trailed off as she reached down and cupped her breast in the palm of her hand while she squeezed the nipple between her thumb and forefinger. It felt good—really good—and her breath sighed out while she stroked her nipple.

"Fuuuuuck." It was one long, drawn-out syllable, and she relished this small example of her power over him. Then Byron was wrenching her hand away, replacing it with his mouth and showing her what power truly was.

His tongue licked over her—softly, gently, tenderly. Tears sprang to her eyes at the care he was taking with her, but she blinked them back. She wasn't going to cry—not this time. No matter how sweetly he made love to her.

His mouth turned rougher; darkness and flames licked their way from her nipples to her stomach, down her arms and legs, until they coalesced in the ache between her thighs.

"Byron, please." She thrashed against him, bucking and arching as she tried to coax him into giving her what she wanted. What she needed.

He only laughed and pulled his mouth away completely, his breath a soft breeze over her achingly aroused flesh. She grabbed his head in her hands, her fingers tangling in his silky, too-long hair as she tried to force his mouth back to her distended nipple.

"Don't tease me," she pleaded as she arched against him.

"Baby, I haven't begun to tease you." He curled his tongue around her areola, sucked it into his mouth with a power so strong he had her gasping. The pleasure was so intense she had to bite her lip to keep from screaming, the sharp nip of his teeth taking her arousal to a whole new level.

"Fuck me." She didn't care that she was begging, didn't care that she sounded hot and needy and completely overwhelmed. The only thing she could think about was getting him inside her, and she would do anything to get him there. Risk anything to have him where she so desperately needed him.

"That's what I'm doing." His breath was hot against her breast, his hair cool against her neck and chin. She was pushing against him, whimpering, pleading with every weapon she had for him to put her out of her misery.

He refused to be hurried, no matter how restlessly her legs moved against his or how desperately her hands clenched in his hair. He pushed her and pushed her, licking delicately, nibbling softly, until she was on the brink of sobbing. Only then, when she was strung tight and on the edge of madness, did he drop to his knees in front of her.

"Oh, God!" She couldn't stop the whimper that welled in her throat, any more than she could keep from twisting the blond hair in her suddenly tight fists.

Rough hands parted her trembling thighs, and he stared at her with burning, intense eyes. "God, Lacey, you're so fucking beautiful." He reached one calloused finger out and stroked right down the center of her.

She trembled again, his words and touch arrowing through her brain to her heart and onto her sex in one burning line. No man had ever looked at this most private part of her and called her beautiful before. No man had ever stared at her as if it was agony not to be inside her. The thought made heat explode within her, shooting her arousal from hot to feverish to downright frenzied. She could feel an orgasm welling powerfully within her and she stood there, shaking, while he brought her right to the brink with almost no effort at all.

"I like this," he murmured, leaning forward so his mouth brushed against her bare stomach and the small turquoise star tattoo. "I forgot to tell you that last night."

"I got it when I was in college—a reminder of where I wanted my writing to take me."

He nuzzled the small tattoo, licked it. "All the way to the stars?" he asked.

"Yes." She gasped the word—the best she could manage—as desire made her light-headed.

"And did you make it?" he asked right before he sank his teeth into her upper thigh.

She screamed his name as her arousal shot through the roof and her lithe body bowed against him.

He laughed—a low, wicked sound that sent razor blades of need through her. "Well, did you?"

"Did I what?" Her voice was hoarse, but she figured she should be grateful that she still had the power of speech. As his lips skimmed over her hip bone and abdomen, stopping to nibble at each birthmark and freckle, she feared that soon even that ability would fail her.

"Reach the stars?" His mouth closed softly over her navel, his tongue incredibly gentle as it probed her belly button and the soft skin of her abdomen.

"Not—" *Not yet* was what she had wanted to say, but her voice truly was gone, her ability to concentrate evaporating beneath the gentle suction of his mouth.

And then he was moving on, moving down, his lips skimming over the top of her mons, down the side of her hip. His tongue made little forays underneath her hip bone, delicate little touches that lit her up like a Roman candle. Sharp little nips that had her gasping for air with lungs that had forgotten how to breathe.

"Byron." It was a cry of agony, a plea born of desperation, and his hands clenched on her thighs as he realized just how far he had pushed her.

Shudders racked his body as Byron buried his face between Lacey's thighs. She smelled delicious, like honey and cinnamon and sweet, sweet strawberries. He paused for a minute; simply absorbed her smell into himself. He took a deep breath, then another and another, while his thumbs stroked closer and closer to the slick folds of her pussy.

With each slide of his thumb, she trembled more. With each clasp of his hands, she took a shuddering breath. And when he moved forward, blowing one long, warm stream of air against her clit, she started to cry, to sob, her body spasming with even the lightest touch of his against it.

His cock was on fire, his balls pulled so tightly against his body that he feared he might explode if he didn't take her soon. But he wasn't ready for it to end, wasn't ready to send her careening over the edge so he could follow behind.

He wanted to savor her, to push her, push himself, higher than they'd ever gone before.

But she was coming apart, her body so sensitive and responsive that it humbled him even as it made him sweat.

"You're unbelievable," he muttered as he delivered one long lick along her gorgeous, ruby-red slit. "So fucking responsive I could just—" He stopped talking as Lacey screamed, her hands clutching his hair as flames ripped through her. He licked her a second time. And then a third, lingering on her clit.

Sliding his hands up her thighs, he gripped her ass in his hands and squeezed. When she moaned, he moved his thumb over her anus and pressed in slowly, gently. At the same time, he pulled her clit into his mouth and suckled.

She sobbed as she hurtled over the edge, orgasm after orgasm roaring through her body like a series of shooting stars. He held her while she came, stoking the flames higher and higher until she was screaming silently, her hands clutching at his shoulders in an effort to pull him up and into her.

Her need sent him over his own edge, and he stood in a rush, one hand reaching for his pants and fumbling the condom out of the pocket, as he used his other to spin her around. "I've got to fuck you," he growled, as he threw open the balcony door and walked her out to the railings.

It was still raining; the thunderstorm that had moved in while they'd been playing the question game had decided to stay. He pressed her against the rain-soaked railing, and Lacey gasped as wind whipped against her, lashing her with warm raindrops that felt cool against her heated skin.

Words from one of her older fantasies played in his head as he rolled the condom over his dick, tormenting him with the power and the pleasure of her words, driving his own need to stratospheric heights.

You come to me in a flash of lightning, as rain pounds the burning streets beneath my balcony. A stranger who grabs me from behind and presses me against the wet and slippery iron of the railing. You raise my skirt, rip my underwear from my burning pussy and take me right there, before I ever have a chance to see your face.

Again and again you take me as the hot rain falls on my face.

Again and again you take me—with your hands and mouth and cock—until my knees quiver and my soul is satisfied.

He wasn't a stranger and she wasn't dressed, but the other parts of the fantasy were right on and he wanted to give it to her, needed to give it to her—and himself—with a desperation that bordered on the obsessive.

Skimming his mouth over her neck, he reached between her legs to make sure that she was ready for him. She was slick, swollen and so hot he shuddered with a desperate need to be inside her.

With a groan, he placed a hand on the nape of her neck and another on the small of her back, bending her forward over the railing until she was at the perfect angle. And then, with his knees shaking and cock throbbing, he sank into her, the broad tip of his cock working its way into her one slow inch at a time.

She felt amazing, smooth and silky and so hot he feared she would burn him alive—but, God, what a way for him to go. With her wrapped around him like a fist, her strong body quivering against his, and the wind lashing them with rain-soaked sweetness, he wanted nothing more than to stay like this forever. Working his way inside her as she had found her way inside him. Taking her as she took all of him.

Lacey moaned as Byron entered her, his thickness an invasion that stretched her beyond comfort and into a pleasure-pain that was unbelievably exciting. She arched backward, desperate to get away, to get closer, to make the agony of unfulfilled desire go away.

He held her steady, thrusting slowly, pulling out, thrusting a little harder, pulling out, until he'd worked another inch of himself inside her. He was gentle, more gentle than she'd expected him to be, certainly more gentle than he had been the night before, and she struggled to find her voice.

"It's okay," she gasped, pressing her ass into his stomach. "You won't hurt me. I can take all of you."

His only answer was a low, deep groan as he thrust and retreated, thrust and retreated. Fucking her with more care and reverence than he could have imagined possible.

"Byron," she gasped. "Please."

And then he was all the way in her, his cock a strong, undeniable presence within her. She'd never known anything could feel so good.

Leaning forward, he rested his cheek against her temple. "Is this okay?" he asked through gritted teeth, his breath coming in harsh pants against her ears. "Am I hurting you? You're swollen, tight, from last night."

"No, God, no!" She answered in a series of tortured gasps, so turned on by the care he was taking with her that she would have fallen if Byron hadn't been there to support her. She was trapped between a rock and a hard place—the stationary, unyielding balcony at her front, and his strong, immovable body behind her. She was trembling, shaking, barely able to hold herself up.

And then she didn't have to, because he was there, supporting her—his cock an exquisite pressure within her. He began to move, gentle thrusts at first that glided in and out of her. The pleasure built and built until she was once again on the edge.

He was deliberately keeping her there, suspended on a precipice she couldn't cross without his permission. And no matter how hard she pressed, how much she struggled, he kept up the same, easy, in-and-out rhythm that was setting her hair on fire.

When she could take no more, when need was a screaming obsession inside her, she clenched her vaginal walls around him. Once, twice, again and again she squeezed his cock within her, until she elicited one long, deep groan from him.

"Fuck, Lacey. You can't do that." He leaned forward, pressing her hips into the railing with all of his considerable weight, while his hips pistoned back and forth against hers. "I'll lose it—"

"Good." She reached back and around, clasping his ass in her rain-soaked palms. With the last of her waning strength, she pulled him against her as hard as she could, clenching down with her vagina as she did so.

He wasn't expecting it, and the move broke his composure, his unbelievable control. He began thrusting against her, the power of his hips actually moving her up and down on the railing as he came at her with everything he had.

And she loved every second of it, her cunt running with the slick proof of her desire for him. He brought his hands up and cupped her breasts, squeezing her nipples between his thumbs and index fingers until she nearly screamed with the pleasure and the pain of his possession.

Reaching up, she grabbed on to his thick wrists, trying to keep herself in place beneath the powerful hammering of his hips. It was no use; she was being swept away. Carried off by the rising tide of an orgasm that was almost within her reach.

"I can't hold on—" He ground out the words as he thrust harder and harder. "Come with me, baby. Come with me!"

It was the order that did it, the rough command in his voice that sent her spiraling off the highest edge yet. The climax ripped through her, taking over her entire body until all she could feel or see or hear was him.

In those moments, Byron was all around her, inside her. Not just in her body, but in her mind and heart and soul. And though she tried to keep him out, to slam walls down around her out-of-control emotions, it was too late.

The sensations kept coming, never-ending waves of ecstasy that shot up her spine, her arms and legs, through every part of her. In a small part of her mind, she was conscious of him stiffening against her, of his body jerking inside hers while he came in a series of long, beautiful pulses.

When it was over, he didn't collapse on her as she'd expected. As she'd craved. Instead, he leaned down and swept her feet out from under her, cradling her against his powerful chest. Then he ducked back into her apartment and carried her through the living room to her bedroom.

He laid her gently on the hot-pink comforter, then joined her, tracing the raindrops on her arms with his tongue.

"You're so goddamned beautiful," he said between kisses. His voice was gravelly, rusty, as if it had been too long since he'd last spoken.

"You don't have to say that," she answered, rolling to her side and pulling her knees up so she wouldn't feel so exposed.

"I don't *have* to say anything. But that doesn't make it any less true."

With a smile, she pulled him into her arms and reveled in the feel of his big, warm body against her heart—even as he wondered how long this fantasy could last.

Chapter Fourteen

Gregory hung up the phone with a growl.

"Boss?"

Gregory looked up from the picture of Lacey Adams that he was very quickly growing obsessed with. "Yes, Jim?"

"The new shipment has arrived at the airport. Dimitri wants to know if the merchandise should be delivered to the regular warehouse, or if any of his current load should be sent on to the auction house."

Shit. Gregory froze as he realized he'd been so obsessed with Lacey that he'd failed to look over the newest files. He didn't even know what kind of merchandise was being delivered, and that sure as hell didn't say much about him as a businessman.

Furious with himself—and the red-haired witch who was slowly turning him inside out—he barked, "Do you have the files?"

Jim held out a small group of manila folders to him. "They're right here, sir."

"Are they secure?"

"I've kept them with me all day, so that I would have them when you were ready for them. They haven't been out of my sight." There was no censure in

Jim's voice, but since his assistant valued his life, Gregory didn't take that as a particularly encouraging sign.

He had dropped the ball today and could only hope Jim was the only one who had noticed. He could always tell the others that he'd been too busy to get to it before then. It sounded so much better than saying he'd been too busy looking at a woman to do the job he'd made a fortune doing.

He glanced through the merchandise files quickly, wanting to make up for his blunder. "How fresh is the merchandise?"

"Not very, from what I understand."

He looked up sharply, growled his displeasure. "There are no pure ones in the whole shipment?"

His annoyance must have been obvious, because Jim took a cautious step back. Gregory almost smiled when he saw that small retreat—how nice it was to have men who appreciated how dangerous he really was, despite the fact that he rarely chose to handle the dirtier aspects of his job anymore. Nice to know that Jim realized he could still handle it when he needed to.

"No, sir. They thought they had secured one, but it was tainted."

"Damn it, I have a whole host of clients coming who are expecting something special this time around. We need to deliver it." He cursed; the problem with being successful was you became a victim of your own success. Do something good once and you ended up with clients who wanted something even better. Do something spectacular, and the fucking sky was the limit.

Still, success was a hell of a lot better than where he'd started out—in life and in this business. He sure as shit wouldn't do things any differently. "All right, then. We still have a few days to figure out what to do for the auction. In the meantime, have all of these delivered to the warehouse and get them processed immediately."

"Yes, sir."

"And that other matter we spoke of earlier—is it taken care of?"

"Yes. The story should run on the news tonight."

"Excellent. You may go."

But as his bodyguard walked toward the door, he called after him, "And, Jim, start thinking about ways to get the redhead. I've decided I want her for my collection."

"Of course, sir." Not by so much as a flicker did he reveal what he was thinking. But Gregory recognized the gleam in his bodyguard's eyes, the lust that said he would be more than happy to do what his boss asked, if for no other reason than to get his shot with Lacey when Gregory tired of her.

Gregory glanced down at the photos he never kept far from his desk. Like that was going to happen anytime soon.

Byron and Lacey ended up going out despite all her previous objections, though it was for a midnight snack instead of breakfast. A stroll through the French Quarter instead of the morning window shopping he'd originally planned.

After they'd eaten, he'd bought her an ice-cream cone—Rocky Road, of course—then shared it with her as they strolled hand in hand down Chartres Street.

"So, you said you write true-crime books," he said as they traded licks of the frosty treat. "Is that why you move around so much? For research?"

She nodded. "I usually like to live in the city I'm writing about. It helps with the background information and insight. It usually makes it easier for me to get into the mind-set of the people I write about."

"So what are you writing about here? God knows this city has enough crime to stock a library full of books."

She took another lick of the ice cream, and he enjoyed watching her pale pink tongue scoop up a little of the tasty treat. Leaning in, he swept his tongue over hers and savored the cool, chocolate taste of her.

"If you keep that up, I'm not going to remember my own name, let alone what question you want me to answer," she murmured breathlessly.

"That's not necessarily a bad thing." He skimmed his lips over hers.

"No, it's not." He heard the smile in her voice and reluctantly pulled away. "So, tell me, what are you writing about?"

She seemed to hesitate for a minute before she said, "The Mardi Gras Madam case. I'm sure you've probably heard of it."

He laughed as they turned a corner. "It's pretty hard to live in America—and New Orleans, specifically—without hearing about it. Half the state congress is still reeling under the allegations."

"Right. Anyway, I'm looking into a bunch of stuff in the case that just doesn't seem right. Parts of the investigation don't make much sense and I'm trying to dig a little deeper, see what's there."

"Gotta love the NOPD," he said with a grin, steering her from St. Louis onto Royal. "There's always something going on over there."

"I know." She shook her head. "You'd think they'd clean house or something."

"I think they have—more than once. But there's always a group that just doesn't understand that the rules apply to them too. I think it's that way in any busy police force."

"Maybe. But it seems to be more prevalent here. There's a larger percentage of dirty cops. Dirty DAs. Dirty politicians. It goes all the way up."

"Is that what you're looking at?" He was curious at the vehemence in her tone—like she'd had personal experience with the problem.

"I'm investigating a lot of things, actually, and I really don't have any idea how it's all going to pan out."

"Is that normal?"

She snorted. "Not usually. But then, everything in this city is just a little south of normal."

She paused in front of a ladies' boutique and admired the group of fancy hats in the window. "Look at that one there," Lacey said with a laugh as she pointed to a red one that was decorated with miles of lace and fancy beads. "Isn't it pretty?"

"Do you want it?" He started to reach for the door handle before he remembered that the only places open after midnight were bars and restaurants. Glancing up, he made a note of the name, Miss Hattie's.

"Yeah, right. What would I do with a hat like that?"

"Play dress-up?" He wiggled his brows suggestively.

"I bet you'd like that."

"Hell, yes, I would. I bet you'd look fabulous in nothing but a little red nightie and that hat. Oh, and maybe a feather boa or two," he said as he remembered the template she used for her blog. "You would look fantastic."

"Yeah, well, keep dreaming. If you're nice, I might strip for you, but I draw the line at feather boas." She continued down the street.

"Now, that's a damn shame," he said as he caught up to her.

"Isn't it, though?"

They walked a few more blocks in silence, smiling at the occasional tourist—or local—who wandered by. After a year and a half in New Orleans, he still found it fascinating that while Bourbon and its cross streets were alive with color and music and throngs of people, the other streets died down after dark, once the stores closed down. The quiet so close to the chaos was a dichotomy that never failed to interest him.

"You want to head toward Bourbon Street?" he asked, after they'd wandered past five or six cross streets. As they stood on the corner of Royal and St. Ann, he could hear the jazz and rock floating down from the club-lined street.

She paused, seeming to consider the question for an inordinately long time before finally answering, "All right."

But the closer they got to Bourbon, the more tense she got. Finally, he had to ask, "What's wrong, Lacey? If you don't want to head this way, we can go back."

"No, I'm sorry. It's fine. I just started thinking about my book. I wouldn't mind grabbing a jungle juice or something."

"You sure?" He studied her closely, surprised at the pallor of her normally healthy-looking complexion. Maybe it was just a trick of the moonlight, but the longer he stared at her, the more obvious it became that something was wrong.

"Lacey, I'm serious. We don't—"

"Come on, silly. Let's go." She grabbed his hand and started dragging him toward the bright street.

She smelled Bourbon Street about half a block before they actually got there—the mixture of sweat and alcohol, piss and puke that helped lend the street its ambience. By the time they actually turned left off St. Ann, Lacey was vaguely nauseous from the combination of the smell and her churning stomach.

It was stupid, she knew, to be this freaked-out about walking on Bourbon Street with Byron. But the last time she'd been here, she'd made the connection between the missing girls and New Orleans.

And while she was still anxious to dig deeper, she didn't want to do it with Byron around. Starting a relationship—even one based purely on sex—was difficult at the best of times. Doing it while investigating the shady world of sexual slavery and human trafficking seemed a lot to ask of anyone.

But once she was there, on the street, a small jungle juice in her hand, she couldn't help but look around and wonder. Was the teenage girl leaning against the outside of Cat's Meow just an underage kid waiting for her friends, or was she a runaway? How about the little boy tap-dancing for tips, with bottle caps glued to the bottom of his shoes? What was his story?

As they walked slowly down the street—people-watching and drinking and occasionally boogying when they came across a song they liked—Lacey did her best to ignore the sex shops and clubs the city was known for. Even so, she found her gaze drawn to them time and again as she wondered which ones were involved with her story. Wondered which ones pimped out drugged, kidnapped girls and called it business.

Perspiration rolled down her back as they walked, pooled between her breasts and in the hollow of her throat, but she didn't know whether it was the heat making her sweat or the complete train wreck of her thoughts. Forcing herself to uncurl the fists she hadn't been aware of making, one slow finger at a time, she lifted a hand to her eyes and rubbed them tiredly.

How long was this going to go on? How long before she found the evidence she needed to write her book? How long before she found a way to help those poor girls—to save the living and find justice for the dead?

"Hey, Lacey, you okay?" Byron asked, stopping dead. "You've been walking in a stupor for two blocks now."

It took a minute for her to focus on his concerned face, to bring her thoughts back from the nightmare they'd wandered into. "Yeah, I'm sorry. I was just looking at some of these places and thinking about my book."

He glanced toward the curb uneasily, and for the first time, she realized they'd stopped in front of the strip club where she's seen Anne Marie's picture earlier in the week.

"You think some of these places are involved in that prostitution ring?" he asked incredulously. "I thought they shut that whole thing down last year."

"They did, ostensibly." She found herself walking toward the strip club, her feet moving of their own volition even as her mind warned her that she was wrecking their date. But now that she had fifteen dead girls staring at her from her breakfast table, she couldn't just move past the club without at least looking at the pictures.

Stepping up to the window, she moved her fingers over the photos one by one, tempted to skim for expediency's sake, but knowing she would probably miss something if she did.

"Hey, what are you doing?" Byron asked, bewildered, as he stopped beside her and began to study the pictures too. "What exactly are we looking for?"

She shook her head. "Pictures of the girls on my table."

His eyes widened, but it only took him a second to catch on. "Those girls didn't work for the Mardi Gras Madam. Those girls—"

"Were all reported missing from Vancouver, Toronto, Quebec and Calgary." She finished his statement. "And they were all found dead in New Orleans over the past four years."

"Jesus Christ." It was Byron's turn to look sick. "What the hell has been going on down here?"

But before she could answer his question, he handed her his cell phone and hissed, "Quick, take a picture."

"What?" She stared at the black phone uncomprehendingly.

"Hurry up. I think someone's taking exception to the interest we're paying his girls."

Lacey glanced around Byron's shoulder and saw a gigantic guy baring down on them. Huge and heavily muscled, he was dressed in jeans and a leather vest and had tattoos covering every visible inch of skin on his body, including his bald head. And he was barreling toward her like a monster truck at a demolition derby.

"Oh, shit." Panic raced through her at the thought of anyone finding out what they were looking at. The pictures would be gone in a heartbeat—and so would her proof. "What do we do?"

"Take the damn pictures—make sure to get the club's name in if you can—or at least a bunch of distinguishing stuff from the building, so they can't argue that you're making things up."

"Right." She lifted the cell phone, clicked off a picture that took in the top of the window display and the neon sign that proclaimed its name, Seductions, and then continued taking panel shots of the window. There were hundreds and hundreds of shots up there and she tried to get them all. Who knew which other missing girls were up there, waiting to be found?

She was on the last section when Grave Digger asked, "Hey, what the hell are you two doing?"

Byron opened his mouth, but Lacey stepped around him with a smile. Pulling her innocent-little-me smile out of storage—the one she'd discovered four or five books ago worked wonders on the opposite sex—she said, "I was just taking a few photos for my scrapbook."

Unfortunately, Grave Digger seemed immune to her charms. Maybe he wasn't human after all. "Yeah, well, don't."

"Why not?" She added a slightly breathless, completely dim-witted voice to the look, and swore she could actually hear the guy gnashing his teeth. Of course, the sound might have been coming from Byron.

"Because they're not meant for you." He stopped less than a foot from them and looked her over with suspicious eyes. "Unless you and your date want to pay the cover charge and come sit through a set or two."

At that moment, there was nothing she wanted more—even if it meant being watched by a bouncer with all the charm of a natural disaster. There could be evidence in that building—pictures of other missing girls or even the girls themselves. But her internal radar was going off, warning her to get as far from the club as she could, in the least amount of time possible. Warning her that walking into that strip joint, alone and without anyone knowing where she was, was akin to suicide.

Behind her, Byron radiated enough fury to light up a small state, and she knew there'd be hell to pay when they finally got out of the situation. But she'd been around the block enough to know that if she'd let him handle it, he and Grave Digger would have ended up in a pissing contest, or worse, a fight. And for a woman who wanted to be as unmemorable as possible, both of those possibilities were the kiss of death. Literally as well as figuratively.

"Another time?" She tried a more normal smile on the guy this time, but once again it fell short. Way short.

"I don't think so." He looked down his misshapen nose at both of them. "Now, what's it going to be?"

"Okay." Byron wrapped an arm around her and told Grave Digger, "I'd like to see the inside of a real, live strip club, wouldn't you, sugar pie?"

"Uhh—"

"I know you would. Just think of what you'll be able to tell the folks back home." He reached for his wallet with a slightly vacuous smile of his own. "How much do I owe you?"

Grave Digger stared at him suspiciously for a minute, but finally said, "Ten bucks apiece. Plus there's a two-drink minimum."

"No problem. The little woman gets kind of frisky when she drinks, if you know what I mean." Byron winked at him. "Maybe I'll get lucky tonight."

That proved to be the last straw for the guy, and he walked away shaking his head and muttering God only knew what.

"Come on, sugar pie, let's go on in." Byron's hand was a too-tight manacle around her arm as he led her to the door.

She shot him a look promising that she'd be getting even, and soon, but he only grinned. Lacey shook her head as she followed him into the club. The poor man didn't even know when to be afraid.

Chapter Fifteen

n hour later, Lacey stumbled onto the curb in front of the club and sucked in huge gulps of air. It said a lot for the atmosphere of the place that the stink of Bourbon Street felt positively pristine in comparison.

Byron coughed. "Jesus, my lungs may never be the same."

"It was your brilliant idea to go in there, buddy. So don't you start complaining. I'm the one who should be pissed off."

"And are you?" He put his arm around her shoulders and started guiding her toward home.

"Yes. That was a waste of time I couldn't afford."

"I don't know about that. You got pictures of most of the girls performing—which was why I wanted to get in there in the first place. You can compare the latest group that are dancing there to the photos you've got at home. Maybe something will pop."

"You mean, maybe we can save some of the girls if we know where they came from."

"Exactly. But you need to make sure they aren't there voluntarily before you kick up a stink." His mouth was grim, his eyes shadowed with disgust, and Lacey couldn't help falling just a little deeper under his spell.

Not all men would understand what was going on here. Not all men would want to understand. Byron not only grasped the concept and was sickened by it, but he also wanted to do something to help. Needed to do something, if the anger and frustration radiating from him were any indication.

As they walked through the still-lively throng of tourists and locals alike, she cuddled closer to him and marveled at how different he was from Curtis. Curtis had thrown fits about her job, had tried to get her to quit or to pick a different occupation numerous times. And while she'd remained firm on her career choice, it was the only area of their life together where she hadn't given in to him. The only area where she'd managed to keep a small part of her separate and untouched. Of course, that had only made him hate the whole thing more.

But she was ruining this moment thinking about him, and it wasn't worth it. She didn't have forever with Byron, probably didn't have very long at all, and she didn't want to spend the time she did have thinking about her bastard of an ex-boyfriend. Not now that she'd finally gotten away from him.

"Hey, Lacey, wait up!" Lacey turned, surprised to see Sandra barreling through the crowds toward them, her boyfriend, Tony, behind her.

"Hey, Sandra," she said as her friend approached.

"I thought that was you. We've been trailing you two for three blocks." Sandra turned her baby blues on Byron and batted them for all she was worth. "And who is *this*?"

"This is Byron Hawthorne—he's my neighbor from across the courtyard."

"How nice to meet you. I've been trying to set Lacey up with a guy for months, but she keeps refusing. Now I know why."

"Come on, Sandra." Tony weaved a hand through hers, pulling her closer to his side. "Leave the poor guy alone—he's not used to you yet."

Lacey shot him a grateful look before asking, "So, what have you been to?"

"We're about to check out that new club Voodoo Heaven. It's supposed to be fabulous." Sandra paused. "Why don't you two come along?"

"Oh, I don't think so. We were just heading home."

"Come on—we've still got a couple of hours before things slow down. Let's go dance."

She glanced questioningly at Byron, who nodded amiably. "Sure. If you want to dance, let's go."

It's not that she wanted to dance so much as she wanted to wipe the feel of the strip club from her brain and body. Part of her wanted to head home, climb in the shower and have crazy, mad sex with Byron under the pounding spray. But another part of her didn't want to bring the bone-deep stink of that club back to her apartment. She wanted to put a little time and distance between her home and the images she'd just seen.

As they slipped into the noisy club, Sandra grabbed her arm. "Why don't you guys go get some drinks? Lacey and I are going to go dance."

"Already?" she asked as Sandra pulled her toward the tightly packed dance floor.

"Is there a better time?"

The new Beyoncé mix started just as they hit the floor, and Sandra laughed. "Come on! I love this song!"

As they danced to the song and then another, Lacey found herself laughing right alongside her friend. But Sandra was like that—fun, happy, with an enthusiasm that was completely infectious.

By the time Byron caught up to her three songs later, Lacey was drenched with sweat and feeling much better about life in general. "Dance with me?" he murmured against her ear as his arms circled her waist from behind.

"Sure." She started to turn toward him, but he held her in place—his chest against her back, his erect cock nestling against the curve of her ass.

As if on command, the music turned slow and dreamy, and Lacey let her body relax against the hardness of his. He splayed his right hand across her abdomen, to keep her hips flush against his, and cupped her right breast with his left hand. His thumb glanced over her nipple—once, twice, then again and again.

Her nipple pebbled tightly under his attentions, her pussy growing damp as he pulled her ass more firmly against his cock and began to move. She'd never danced this way before—her body pressed against his from shoulder to thigh, but facing outward.

She liked it. Liked the freedom it gave her to look out over everyone; liked even more the feeling of being trapped against him as people danced all around them. They were in a hugely public place, but completely shielded by the crush of bodies on the dance floor.

Relaxing her neck, she let her head loll on Byron's shoulders as she arched her back so that her breast fit more completely in his hand. The music was loud, so she didn't hear his groan, but she felt it in the vibration of his chest against her back and the whisper of his breath past her ear.

She felt her own breath catch, felt desire humming through her bloodstream as she rubbed her ass against him. He was hot and hard and felt so good it was all she could do not to beg him to take her right there. To fuck her in the middle of the throbbing crowd, and to hell with public-decency laws.

His hand tightened on her breast, his fingers squeezing her nipple until she gasped—proof that he was as affected by what they were doing as she was. She whimpered at the pressure, and liquid pooled between her thighs.

"Byron."

It was a whisper, but somehow he heard her. Pressing his mouth to her ear, he said, "Do you want to get out of here?"

She nodded, even as she prayed that her shaky legs would carry her that far. He must have read her mind—or maybe he was just as anxious as she was—because he said, "I'll go flag down a cab."

"I'll go tell Sandra we're cutting out, and meet you out front."

He turned her around until she faced him, took her mouth in a brief but bruising kiss that had her fingers tangling in his shirt as her knees buckled. "We've got a table against the back wall. Don't be long."

"Believe me, I won't."

She watched him walk away, his broad shoulders cutting a swath through the gyrating bodies as he headed for the door. He was eventually swallowed by the crowd, so she started making her way in the direction he'd pointed. She'd made it off the dance floor and halfway across the room when she felt a hand grab her elbow.

Expecting it to be Sandra, she turned around with a smile—and found herself looking at a guy who made Grave Digger look like a friendly, neighborhood Smurf.

"Hey, let go!" She spoke loudly, but when he made no move to show he understood her, she tried to yank her arm away. His grip tightened to the point of pain.

A ripple of unease went through her, though she told herself she was being ridiculous. What could he do to her in such a crowded place? The thought might have comforted her more if she and Byron hadn't just engaged in some heavy petting without drawing anyone's notice.

"I mean it. Stop it." She yanked harder, but his grip still didn't budge.

"Leave me alone!" She raised her voice to a yell, but the current song was heavy on the bass, extremely popular and extra-loud. Nobody paid any attention to her.

The man started propelling her toward the back door of the club, his long legs eating up the ground as he dragged her in his wake.

"Help!" She screamed it now, but he'd made his move at the right time. The area around them was dark and nearly deserted as people flocked toward the dance floor to groove to the song.

She tried to dig her heels into the carpet, but the guy was huge and any resistance she put up was barely noticed. As they passed close to a table, she grabbed on to a chair. Surely someone would notice a huge guy towing a woman towing a chair and screaming.

But he simply shook his head and grabbed her other arm so hard that her fingers went numb and the chair clattered harmlessly to the ground.

"Look, lady." He let go of one arm and leaned down until he was close enough for her to hear him. "If you're going to cause trouble, I'll just knock you out and carry you out of here. Everyone'll think you passed out."

His words exacerbated her fear, and pure instinct made her go for his eyes. Curling the fingers of her free hand into rigid claws, she slashed at whatever portion of his face she could get at.

She didn't know who this guy was or what he planned on doing with her, but there was no way she was leaving this club with him without kicking up the mother of all protests.

"Fuck!" For one brief second his grip loosened as he tried to protect his eyes, and she yanked herself free. Without looking back, she ran for the dance floor and relative safety. This time, when a hand grabbed her from behind, she screamed her head off even as she started swinging.

"Get away from me!" she screamed, kicking out at the bastard. Smiling when she caught him in the shins. Glancing up, she nearly sagged in relief as she saw Byron barreling toward them.

"You bitch." His fist came up and headed for her jaw, and she braced herself.

"What the fuck is going on here?" Byron roared, putting himself in front of her and taking on the jaw the punch meant for her.

He didn't even flinch, just shoved the guy, who stumbled but caught himself before he fell to the floor. At the same time, the song ended and people started heading back to their tables.

"You're going to regret that," he muttered, then took off, blending into the crowd.

Byron watched him leave, then turned furious eyes on her. "What the hell was that?"

She shook her head. "I don't know."

"Come on! I'm getting you out of here." For the second time in five minutes, she was dragged toward a door, but this time she was more than willing. Fear was setting in, and she was deathly afraid she was going to be sick.

Was that what had happened to all those girls? she wondered as she scrambled to keep up with Byron. *Were they abducted in plain sight, while life went on around them?* The thought caused her to panic all over again, so that by the time they made it outside, she was all but hyperventilating.

"Shit." Byron cursed, shoving her toward the taxi he had waiting on the cross street. Opening the door, he flung her inside.

"Are you all right?" he demanded, after spitting their address at the cabdriver. "Who the hell was that guy?"

"I don't know!" She tried to tell him more, but she couldn't get enough air. The world was going black around the edges.

Byron cursed again, then shoved her head between her legs. "Try to take a few deep breaths," he said.

"Hey, man, if she hurls, you're cleaning it up."

"Just drive the fucking car. She's not going to get sick."

She was glad he sounded so sure, but she was nowhere near as optimistic. In fact, she was pretty sure the only thing that kept her from tossing her cookies all over the cab's backseat was the fact that she didn't want Byron to see her puke, let alone have to clean it up.

By the time the cab screeched to a halt in front of their apartment building, she had almost recovered from her panic attack. But Byron still helped her out after paying the driver, then insisted on carrying her to her apartment.

"I'm fine," she insisted as he headed for the stairs. "I can walk."

"That's why you nearly passed out on me back there—because you're fine."

"I'm not the one who got punched."

"And I'm not the one who nearly puked in the back of a cab."

That shut her up, as she was sure he had intended. Neither of them spoke again until he got her into her apartment and settled on the couch.

"Now, do you want to tell me what the hell happened back there?" he demanded as he flicked on a lamp.

"Oh, my God, look at your jaw!" She reached for him, but he shrugged her off.

"It's fine."

"It doesn't look fine."

He shrugged. "I bruise easily."

"He hits hard."

His eyes narrowed dangerously. "Did he hit you?"

"No. But he sure scared the hell out of me when he grabbed me."

"We need to call the police." He headed for the phone.

"And tell them what? Some big guy with an attitude got a little too frisky with me at a club?"

"He did more than get frisky," he said angrily.

"Yeah, but the cops won't believe that."

"They will if you tell them about your book—"

"That's the last thing I want to do. The NOPD totally mishandled that whole case. Don't you think there's a reason for that? If I tell them what I've found so far, what's to stop them from scrambling into total CYA mode?"

She shook her head. "No. We're not calling the police. I can't risk it."

"You'd rather risk your life? Over a book?"

"You know it's not just a book, Byron. Hundreds of girls' lives are at stake."

He didn't like what she was suggesting; his fury was evident in his rapid breathing and clenched jaw. But he didn't argue anymore.

When he did finally speak again, he ordered, "So, tell me what happened."

"I already told you—"

"Exactly what happened." His voice was as cold as a glacier—and as immovable. "And don't leave anything out. Or I'm going to the police and to hell with what might happen. I want *you* safe."

By the time she was done telling Byron what had happened—and answering all of his questions—he was furious and she was exhausted. The adrenaline that had carried her this far had obviously worn off.

"Come on, Sleeping Beauty," he said with a grin that did nothing to detract from the anger in his eyes.

"Where are we going?"

"To get you into a shower and then into bed. You look like you're about to fall flat on your face."

"Nice to know there's still truth in advertising."

He laughed as he guided her through her bedroom and into her bathroom. Closing the toilet lid, he parked her there while he turned on the water. "Now, just sit there until the water warms up."

"I want to load the pictures, start looking at them. Maybe there's something on there we can use."

"And maybe there isn't. Either way, they'll wait until tomorrow." He stripped her sundress over her head, then disposed of her bra and panties with equal efficiency. "Now, into the shower with you."

She was so tired that she didn't argue, though the small part of her brain still working did wonder if she was going to fall asleep under the spray. But then Byron was stepping naked into the shower and she forgot all about sleeping.

Turning, she pressed herself against him, exhausted but still enjoying the feel of his hard muscles against her softness. She shifted her hands to cup his ass. Maybe she could work up the energy—

Byron laughed as he pulled away. "I don't think you're up for water sports tonight, sweetheart."

Then he guided her head beneath the shower spray as his fingers tenderly combed through her hair. "That feels good," she murmured as he started to massage her scalp.

"It'll feel better, I promise."

He reached for her shampoo, squirted some on his hand and then worked it through her hair. Did the same for her conditioner, rubbing and rinsing until she was so drowsy it was all she could do to stay on her feet.

By the time he'd squirted some of her strawberry-scented lotion on a puff and washed every part of her, she was completely blissed out. He turned off the water with a laugh, wrapping her hair in one towel and her body in another before propelling her back into the bedroom.

"Where do you keep your pj's?" he asked as he towel-dried her hair.

"In the top drawer over there."

He found the old, oversized shirt she liked to sleep in and slipped it over her head. Then pulled down the covers on the bed and eased her inside.

"Aren't you coming?" she asked as he covered her up. She was already half asleep.

"In a few minutes. I'm going to lock up first."

"Don't take too long. I—"

Lacey was asleep before she could finish the sentence. Byron stood over her for long minutes, studying her beautiful face while he went over what she'd told him about the club.

He should have chased after the guy—should have found out what the hell he wanted. But at the time, he'd cared more about getting Lacey out of there, getting her someplace safe, than he had about catching the bastard who'd been messing with her. But that was before he'd realized that the asshole had actually tried to abduct her.

Turning out the light, he headed toward the kitchen and—hopefully—an ice pack. That asshole had packed a punch like an eighteen-wheeler, and his jaw ached like hell.

After filling a plastic bag with ice, he pulled his cell phone out of his pocket and started flipping through the pictures Lacey had taken. Each was more disgusting than the last, but as he flipped through them, his admiration for Lacey grew.

Yeah, he wanted her. Absolutely, he imagined taking her in each and every way she fantasized. But it was more than that—more than the sex and her big green eyes. More than her killer body and no-holds-barred attitude.

He loved her dedication to her job, loved the fact that once she'd found out what had really been going on down here, she hadn't shied away from it. She'd met it head-on, determined to do whatever it took to find out what had happened to girls she didn't know but cared about all the same.

As they'd sat at the club and the story had poured out of her in bursts and fits, he'd been awed and horrified and more furious than he could ever remember being. These men were animals—worse than animals—and the idea that they had gotten away with something like this for so long was anathema to him.

Tossing the phone on the desk next to her computer, he prowled the apartment, too wound up and pissed off to sleep. Walking the length of her dining room table, he stared at the faces of the fifteen dead girls looking back at him and wondered what the hell he could do to help make this right.

Because one thing was for certain: after what had happened tonight, there was no way in hell Lacey was going to do this on her own.

Chapter Sixteen

*I*n every touch of your lips I feel the strength and the sweetness that is your power over me. Your lips find mine, again and again, as we stand in your kitchen, the sun setting in the windows behind us.

With each caress of your lips on mine, each slick of your tongue over and around my own, I feel the fire inside me burn hotter. Fiercer. Stronger than before.

You slide your fingers inside my shirt, ripping the buttons off in your quest to touch me, to be as close as two bodies can be. I arch my back, offer myself to you. Revel in the feel of your mouth on the soft skin of my throat, the delicate flesh of my breasts.

On the counter next to us is the drink you made for me earlier—a margarita. My favorite. You lift it to your mouth, take a sip, then press your lips to mine so that I too can enjoy the tart sweetness that comes with the mingling of the tequila and the strawberries.

The mingling of you and me.

Your cold mouth trails kisses over my shoulder, down my chest, to my nipple. You take it in your mouth, bite softly, then suck with a strength that has me crying out. A strength that almost brings me to my knees.

My hands pull at your shirt and I nearly shred it in my effort to get closer to you, my desire to feel your skin—slick with lust—against my own nearly overwhelming.

Your laugh is low and husky as you scoop the frozen mixture out of the glass with your fingers. You rub the sugary treat over my lips, groaning, as I suck your finger inside my mouth and refuse to relinquish it. I know that I should let go, know that you have so much more in store for me, but you taste too good.

But you are wilier than I am. Better prepared. Better controlled. You dip your other hand into my drink, leave it there for long seconds. Then you rub my nipple with your icy fingers, coating it with strawberries. With sweetness.

"Look," you whisper to me. "Look at how beautiful you are."

I don't want to look away from you, from the darkness of your eyes, the intensity that is the only constant in the maelstrom of emotions overtaking me. You're pushing my boundaries, taking me further than I've ever gone before, and I'm afraid to look away.

You understand my fear, my hesitation, but still you push. Your hand anchors mine, holds me tightly. "I've got you," you say. "I won't let you go."

It's the reassurance I need, the promise I was looking for. I want to make you happy, to arouse you as you have so thoroughly done to me, so I look. I glance down and see my rosy nipples hard as diamonds as they beg for your attention.

They are covered in my drink, covered in strawberries, and redder than I've ever seen them. I feel you lick your lips and know that I am beautiful to you. I am desired by you. And that is all that matters.

You begin by licking the juice off my breasts, the little rivulets that have crept over the rounded globes, dribbling down onto my stomach and my sides as the heat between us causes the ice to melt. You work your way slowly—oh, so slowly—to my nipples, laving first one, then the other, with your wicked, wonderful tongue. I moan, clench my fists in your hair and surrender.

Lacey took a bracing sip of coffee and logged on to her blog, feelings of anticipation and nervousness mingling in her stomach. The anticipation was usual, but the nerves were new and she couldn't help wondering if they had to do with Byron and his strangely sudden role in her life.

She'd posted a new entry yesterday and she wanted to see what her readers thought of it.

Just looking at the responses had her glancing guiltily toward the bedroom. Toward Byron. Though she told herself it didn't matter, that this was all fun and games, she wasn't so sure anymore. He'd been so tender with her last night, so careful. So concerned. Less like a fuck buddy and more like a lover.

Suddenly, putting her fantasies out there for the whole world to see felt a little like cheating on him. He didn't know she was describing her sexual desires to a bunch of men who answered in kind. And when she'd been determined to keep things purely casual between them, she hadn't cared.

But now . . . she kept remembering what it felt like to be held by him. How it felt to let him take care of her. Though she still wasn't looking for anything serious, she was smart enough to know they'd crossed a line last night, one it wouldn't be that easy to step back over.

Besides, Byron wasn't like Curtis or the other guys she'd slept with. He loved her sensuality, wanted to know what she liked and how she liked it. With him, she didn't have to pretend, to hide her desires. She could be herself.

She skimmed the comments—there were almost two hundred today—and it took a few minutes to read them and respond to the interesting ones. Even that felt a little uncomfortable, and she cursed herself for being an idiot. It wasn't like she was interested in any of the guys the way she was in Byron, so who cared what they said to her and what she answered?

But the more comments she addressed, the more uncomfortable she became, until she didn't even want to read any more.

Should she tell Byron about the blog and hope he understood what she was doing and why? Or should she keep writing in secret and hope that when he found out—if he found out—that he would understand?

Or, an insidious little voice inside of her whispered, *you could stop writing*

*the blog. Just end it cold turkey, and really give a relationship with Byron
a chance.*

She was shying away from the idea even before it had fully formed. Had she
really learned nothing after those two and a half years with Curtis? She'd given
up everything for him, and in the end had been left with nothing—not even her
self-esteem. There was no way in hell she was going to do that again.

But the blog wasn't everything, she admitted. It was just a little piece of who
she was. Would giving it up be such a terrible thing?

She reached for her coffee cup and took a long sip as she stared at the computer with blind eyes. Where would it end? If she gave up the blog, what would
she feel the need to change next? How she dressed? How she talked? Who she
hung out with?

No. She shook her head. Better to keep all the pieces of herself intact and see
if Byron could deal. If he couldn't, well, then, he knew where the door was, and
he was more than welcome to use it.

Satisfied, she went back to answering questions. And did her best to ignore
the hollow feeling in the pit of her stomach.

Byron woke up slowly, aware that for the first time in the long, sex-filled night,
Lacey was not beside him in bed. He'd planned on letting her sleep, but she'd
had other ideas and he'd lost track of how many times she'd woken him up to
make love.

She'd obviously had her fill, however. They'd both fallen into a stuporlike
sleep sometime around dawn, and now late-morning sunlight streamed through
the window. It had been at least six hours since she'd reached for him.

Stretching lazily, he enjoyed the pleasant heat of the rays touching his skin,
even as he wondered where Lacey had wandered off to.

As he became more awake, his brain kicked into gear and images of the night
before ran through his head. Lacey slipping her T-shirt over her head. Lacey

kneeling before him, taking him into her mouth. Lacey crying out as he brought her to orgasm with his mouth and hands before sliding inside her and taking her all the way up again.

His early morning erection grew harder, the throb in his balls more urgent, and he couldn't help contemplating what it would take to get Lacey back to bed. He'd had her again and again through the night, so many times that he'd been certain it would take a miracle for him to get aroused again. Yet one sniff of her cinnamon sweetness, one thought of her beautiful, honest reactions to him, and he was right back where he started from; hot and hard and hungrier than he could ever remember being.

Rolling out of bed, he slipped into the jeans he'd left lying on the floor by the nightstand, then went in search of his wayward lover. If things went according to plan, maybe he'd be able to convince her to try out an encore before he had to head in to work.

He cruised into the living room, then stopped dead when he saw her sitting at the table, her glorious legs drawn up beneath her as she typed rapidly on the keyboard of the laptop computer she had set up in front of her.

His gut clenched at the sight, an overwhelming jealousy sweeping through him at the idea of her typing her newest fantasy into her blog. At the idea of other men reading Lacey's desires and getting off on them.

Was she writing a new fantasy, or simply responding to comments on the one she had posted yesterday? The jealousy ratcheted up a notch, or ten, and he wanted nothing more than to storm across the room and rip the laptop from her hands.

The feeling blindsided him, had him feeling stupid as all hell.

But that didn't make the jealousy go away, didn't change how he felt at all. Maybe it was stupid, considering the provisos she'd put on their relationship, but after the night they'd shared, he didn't like the idea of her opening herself up sexually to all the men who read her blog. Hated the idea of her engaging them in dialogue—reading their answering fantasies and responding to them. It felt too personal to him, too intimate, as if she was giving away a piece of herself that should belong to him.

He thought of some of the comments he'd read when he'd been on the blog yesterday, and had to grit his teeth against the urge to ask her why she was still writing it. Still answering her fans.

Wasn't he satisfying her? After all the hours they'd spent together, making love and whispering in the dark, hadn't she figured out that there was no fantasy she could ask for that he wouldn't be willing to help make come true? What did she get from those men—and their desires—that she couldn't get from him?

Jaw tight, his good mood draining from him like it had never been, he forced himself to walk toward her as if he didn't have a care in the world. "Good morning."

"Oh, good morning," she answered in surprise, as if she'd had no idea he'd been standing there, studying her for long moments. God, sometimes she was hard on the ego.

"Whatcha doing?" he asked, careful to keep his voice casual as he leaned down to brush his lips over her hair, all the time hoping to get a glimpse of what she was writing. But Lacey had blanked the screen as he bent down, a move that made him distinctly itchy even as it convinced him she really had been posting a new blog.

"Just working." She lifted her face for a kiss, and he was more than happy to oblige.

Leaning down, he brushed her lips with his, once, twice, three times before taking the kiss deeper. He knew she'd been looking for a brief good-morning kiss, but with his suspicions—and petty jealousies—circling his head like a pack of slavering wolves, he couldn't ignore the need to mark her. To brand her as his.

To show her how much he wanted her.

With a groan, he took the kiss deeper, sucked her lower lip between his teeth and nipped lightly. Her answering moan was all the encouragement he needed, especially as she wound her arms around his neck and pulled him closer. Sweeping his tongue over her lips, then dipping inside, he savored the incredibly sweet taste of her. Like caramel and strawberries and dark, warm cinnamon. He wanted to eat her up, to take her inside himself and hold her there until the fire raging between them finally subsided.

She ended the kiss with a laugh, but the eyes she turned on him were as dark and turbulent as an Atlantic storm. And as dangerous.

He stepped back at the thought, releasing her slowly, and was gratified when she stood up, following him, as anxious to maintain body contact as he was.

"Where you going?" she asked, slipping her hand into the back pocket of his jeans.

"To get dressed. I figured I'd run out and get us something for breakfast." He slung an arm over her shoulder and pulled her against his body. Even after the past two nights they'd shared, he was shocked at how small and delicate she felt against him. Because he was tall and strong, he usually went for women who were closer to six feet. Women who had some muscle on them so he didn't have to worry about breaking them.

With Lacey, he'd always have to worry about tempering his strength, about not holding her too tightly or taking her too roughly. And yet she felt nice against him—soft and delicate and so sexy, he wanted nothing more than to lift her and bury himself in her one more time.

But she looked tired, and after everything that had happened last night, that wasn't a surprise. Better that he hold back a little bit, feed her and pamper her. There would always be time later to make love to her again.

"I was going to make Belgian waffles," she said, tugging him away from the bedroom and toward the kitchen. "I've already got everything prepped—I was just waiting for you to wake up before actually getting started on them."

"You didn't have to do that. I could've run out to get something."

"I know." The smile she gave him was equal parts temptress and angel. "But I wanted to. Pour yourself a cup of coffee," she added as she slipped out from under his arm. "This will only take a couple of minutes."

With a grin, he did as he was told, picking up the large mug she'd obviously set on the counter for his use and pouring coffee into it. Life was pretty damn good with a woman who woke up early to prepare breakfast for him—even if she did have a secret life she wanted him to know nothing about.

"Can I help?" he asked, watching her move around the kitchen with admiring eyes. She was wearing a short, black silk robe that left her glorious legs bare for his perusal, even as it cupped her pert little ass in a way that made his blood pressure skyrocket. Maybe he'd been hasty before when he'd decided to give her a little space. . . .

"There are fresh strawberries and whipped cream in the fridge. Put them on the table—and syrup, if you want it." She nodded toward her pantry.

He followed her directions, then topped off her coffee cup and set it on the table, just as she slid the first golden brown waffle onto the plate. "Here, start with this," she said. "Mine'll be done in a couple of minutes."

"I can wait." He set the plate on the table, then cuddled up behind her, wrapping his arms around her waist and nibbling his way up her slender neck.

She giggled and tilted her head to the side to give him better access. "You're supposed to be eating."

"I am." He darted out his tongue, swirled it in the hollow of her throat.

"The food, I mean. You're supposed to be eating *the food*."

"This is more fun . . . and infinitely more delicious." He gave her one last lingering lick before reluctantly lifting his head. "But if you insist."

"I do. I'm starving." She slipped her waffle onto a second plate, unplugged the waffle iron and then slid into her chair at the table. He followed her lead, smiling as she heaped strawberries and whipped cream on her plate.

"I love waffles," she said as she cut off a big bite. "The bigger the better. But I only let myself have them on special occasions."

He lifted an eyebrow. "And this is a special occasion?"

"With all the calories we burned off last night, I should say so."

"You didn't seem to mind at the time."

She laughed. "I don't mind now. I'm just saying that last night was a marathon, and this morning I feel the need for as many calories as I can sink my teeth into. To keep my strength up, you know? I have a lot of data to analyze today."

"I do know, actually," he answered, loading up his own plate.

"How are you feeling, by the way?" He watched her carefully from his spot across the breakfast table.

"Are you kidding me? I'm great. You have that effect on a girl."

"I meant about the—"

"I know what you meant. And it's fine. I'm fine." She smiled teasingly. "You're great medicine."

"Well, I try."

"You succeed—very well."

They ate in companionable silence for a couple minutes before Lacey looked at his near-empty plate. "Do you want me to make you another waffle?" she asked. "I didn't think about the fact that you're twice my size and probably eat double what I do."

"I'm fine."

"Are you sure?" She stood up and started toward the counter and the now-cold waffle iron, but he grabbed her hand and pulled her onto his lap.

"I'm positive. Another waffle isn't what I want."

"Oh, really?" She shifted until she was straddling him, and he nearly groaned out loud as it became apparent she was completely naked under her robe. "And what do you want, if you don't mind my asking?"

"Oh, I think you've got a pretty good idea." He untied the belt holding her robe closed, then slid the black silk off her shoulders, watching as it pooled at her feet.

God, she was so fucking beautiful it nearly ripped him in two just to look at her. With her pale, creamy skin, raspberry-pink nipples and scattering of freckles, she turned him on like no one ever had before.

Lowering his head, he traced his tongue lightly over her shoulder, playing connect the dots with the freckles grouped there. From the time he was little more than a kid, he'd had a thing for freckles—or sun kisses, as his first girlfriend had called them. He didn't know why, but to him, there was something incredibly sexy about the little groupings that appeared at some of the most intimate and beautiful places on his lover's body. Like she was a pretty birthday package just waiting to be unwrapped.

Lacey shivered as he made patterns on her skin with his tongue, her legs tightening on his while a low, keening cry came from between her lips. He nearly lost it at the sound, nearly reached between them, unzipped his jeans and thrust into her harder and faster than he had last night.

But she tasted too good to rush, felt too amazing against him to end it just that quickly. Not when her mouth was cold and tantalizingly sweet from a combination of the strawberries and the whipped cream.

Keeping his mouth on hers—like he had the fucking willpower to break away—he reached behind Lacey to the table and grabbed a handful of strawberries. Then stood up and balanced her perfect little ass on the edge of the table.

"Byron?"

Her beautiful green eyes blinked open in confusion and he didn't do anything to reassure her, didn't say anything to put her at ease. He wanted her off balance, wanted her watching him with those wary cat eyes that made him hotter and harder than anything ever had.

"Lie back," he said instead, exerting pressure on her shoulders with his empty hand.

"What, here?" she demanded breathlessly, even as she complied with the order.

"Of course here." He watched as she braced herself on her elbows, a move that had her pretty breasts jutting forward invitingly. "Haven't you ever done it on a table before?"

Her eyes widened. "No."

Her admission soothed the jealousy that had been riding him hard ever since he'd seen her sitting at her computer, and he smiled in relief and satisfaction. "Then just relax and let me do all the work."

He took her long, lingering sigh as acquiescence, and reached behind her to the bowl of strawberries still on the table. Picked one out and ran it across her lips. Her mouth opened up automatically and she bit the pretty red berry in half, then giggled as some of its sweet juice ran down her chin.

He licked it up with one long, slow swipe of his tongue, and she stopped laughing, her eyes darkening and her body growing tense. Good. He liked it when she was a little on edge—it made the seduction all the sweeter.

He picked up another couple of berries, and her mouth opened invitingly, but he merely shook his head. Holding them above her body, he squeezed hard, then watched as all their lovely juice leaked out of his fist and ran in rivulets down her pale, beautiful body.

Lacey gasped at the first touch of the cold juice on her breasts and her stomach. Gasped again as Byron smeared the strawberry pulp around first one areola and then the second. Her nipples went pebble hard at the contact, though she wasn't sure if it was from the cold berries or Byron's fingers or simply the anticipation of what was coming next.

There was a wicked gleam in Byron's eyes, one that hadn't been there last night as he'd taken her again and again, giving her more pleasure than any woman had a right to expect. It made him look even handsomer, more dangerous. And when he bent his head to her breast, she nearly sighed in delight.

But he didn't stop there. Instead he picked up more strawberries and once again crushed them in his palm, allowing the juice to drip over her abdomen, down to her mons and between her thighs. The contrast of the ice-cold strawberry juice and Byron's warm mouth had her writhing in seconds, begging for him to finish the game.

He wasn't willing to be rushed this morning, however, and he took his time teasing her with little flicks of his tongue over her breasts, down her belly, over her sex. He followed these with more demanding nips, that had her blood boiling and her hands fisting in his hair.

"Come on," she whimpered as she tried to pull him over her. "Do it already."

His laugh was low and taunting. "Baby, I'm just getting started. There won't be anything *to do* for quite a while."

And then he set about teasing her, giving her no more time to talk or plead or even think. She could only feel, only revel in the sensations of unbelievable pleasure that the feel of the strawberries and his tongue brought to her.

He leaned over her on the table, so that he was touching her in one long line from her shoulders to her toes. The roughness of his jeans scraped against the tender skin of her stomach and outer thigh, but she relished the contact. Embraced the burn that he was so carefully stoking inside her.

Rising on one elbow, he picked up the loaded spoon from the whipped-cream bowl and held it suspended over her. He didn't move, didn't flick it over her, didn't do anything until he was sure he had her complete and total attention.

Pushing up on her elbows, she looked at him warily. "What are you going to do with that?" she asked warily.

He grinned, and it was a scandalous, shameless thing. Her heart beat faster and then she was arching, her head falling back as he dropped the cool cream onto her lower abdomen.

"Byron!" It was a squeal. A protest. An invitation for him to do whatever he wanted. For him to do everything he wanted.

"Do you know," he whispered, as he dipped one finger into the mound of whipped cream, "I always loved finger-painting as a child?"

"F-finger-painting?" She could barely form the words, all of her energy focused on the calloused finger currently drawing figure eights on her stomach.

"Yes. I loved to make designs with the paint, to create something beautiful out of nothing." His finger dipped lower, across her mons and down, until he was painting her pussy with the whipped cream. Circling her clit with it and then moving down to rub the sweet stuff over her labia.

"Of course, you're already so beautiful it makes my head spin," he murmured as he applied more and more cream to her aching sex. "But there's something to be said for making a little treat for myself, isn't there?"

She whimpered—the only sound she could make as rational speech was suddenly beyond her.

"Isn't there, Lacey?" His finger dipped inside of her and she nearly came from the contrast of hot and cold against the walls of her vagina. His burning-hot finger covered in cold whipped cream was taking her higher than she'd ever been before. He was scrambling her brains, making her crazy, and she was loving every second of it.

"Lacey?" he murmured again, delving a little deeper with his cream-covered finger. "Yes or no?"

"Yes," she whispered through dry lips, not knowing—and not caring—what she was agreeing to. All that she had, all that she was, was focused on this man and the wicked, wonderful things he was doing to her body. Things she'd only fantasized about. Things she would never have let another man do to her.

And then he was leaning down, his tongue licking the cream from her stomach like she was a piece of fine china. He traced patterns on her quivering stomach, and whatever limited thoughts she'd managed to string together dried up and she could think no more. Only feel.

She moaned, a soft, breathless sigh that seemed to snap his control. And he was on her, his body covering hers, his shoulders flexing as he trailed hot, moist kisses down her body. He followed the trail he'd painted with the whipped cream, his talented tongue doing things to her that she had only read about before. He was everywhere—everywhere—and as his tongue thrust inside her, she lost the last remnants of control she'd been clinging to so desperately.

Her elbows went out from under her and she sank back onto the table—collapsed, really—and let him have his wicked, wicked way with her.

And what a way it was. He played her like a finely tuned instrument, loved her in those moments like she was the only woman he'd ever had. He was endlessly curious, unbelievably giving, his mouth bringing her to one whipped-cream orgasm after another as he explored her body, taking the time to learn what she liked, what she loved and what drove her absolutely insane.

He licked her in long strokes, again and again, like she was the sweetest ice cream he'd ever tasted and he could never get enough. His tongue explored every crease, lingered for long minutes at her clit until she was clawing the table in search of relief.

But there was none, only more of the torturous pleasure that went on and on. His thumb pressed against her from the back, entering her at the same time his tongue thrust inside her pussy like a spear.

She screamed, bucked frantically against him, rode the orgasm out as wave after wave of pleasure crashed through her. And still he wasn't done. His face was buried between her thighs, his lips and tongue and breath coming at her again and again until sanity was only an abstract concept. Until the world around her ceased to exist and Byron was the only steady thing in it.

She was going beyond individual orgasms to a place where the overwhelming pleasure went on and on and on. She twisted desperately, tugged at his shoulders, begged for him to end the torture with the satisfaction of his thick cock within her. But he only laughed and continued to push her and push her until she was sobbing, mindless, an animal driven by the sweet, hot edge of pleasure-pain and the promise of completion.

Her body was no longer her own. It was under his complete control, enthralled, desperate, dying. In those moments, she would have followed him anywhere, done anything, been anyone he wanted her to be. That he only wanted to bring her joy—incredible, mind-boggling joy—was the biggest turn-on of them all, after everything she'd suffered at another man's hands.

Byron spiked his tongue, swirled it inside her before pulling out and going for her clit again. As he did, another wave snuck up on her, slammed through her, and she knew she couldn't take any more. She pushed him away and into the discarded breakfast chair. Then dropped to her knees in front of him, unzipped his jeans and took his glorious, incredibly hot cock in her mouth.

"Fuck, Lacey," he groaned, his hands fisting in her hair as she got her first taste of him. He was delicious and it was her turn to tease, her turn to swirl her tongue down and around him until he was breathing in great shudders, his lower body arching off the chair, desperate for something more. Desperate for everything she had to give him and more. "Have mercy."

But there was no mercy in her, nothing but the driving need to take him as high as he had taken her. She slipped her mouth down the hard length of him, lingered at the base for a moment as he slid down her throat. Then pulled back with a long, lingering swipe of her tongue.

"Don't tease, baby." It was a gasp, sweat pouring off him as his body shuddered beneath her. "Please, just do it."

But she couldn't. She wasn't ready for it to end yet, wasn't ready to see his passion-glazed features go lax with satisfaction. She wanted him as needy as she had been—and still was. She had to have him as desperate for her as she was for him.

And so she continued her ministrations, slipping and sliding over him. Relinquishing his cock for a moment, she slipped farther down his body to take his balls in her mouth, to lick them with gentle strokes of her tongue that had him arching and pleading much as she had done only minutes before.

The power was a beautiful thing, the understanding that she could drive this beautiful specimen of manhood to insanity and beyond a joy that she never wanted to give up.

"Do it!" His voice was harsh, his hands tight and unyielding in her hair as he pulled her up. He was beyond gentleness, beyond thinking, and she loved him this way. As she licked her way back up to where he wanted her, she noticed the clear drops of fluid on the head of his cock and nearly whimpered in desire. Finally, she had driven him beyond control, to the brink of an orgasm he refused to take without her.

But the choice wasn't his anymore. *She* was in control now, and his body *would* give her what she demanded.

Licking the pre-ejaculate off, she dawdled for a few long moments over the sexy length of him as he writhed beneath me, his hands in her hair a snare she had no wish to escape. "You have to . . . Lacey, please . . . I can't . . . Baby—"

There it was, the note of surrender and desperation she had been waiting for—the same desperation that he had evoked in her time and again. Even as he'd done it, she'd wanted to give him the same thing and was thrilled that she'd been able to. Thrilled that he'd let her.

With a secret grin, she swallowed him whole, sucking him all the way inside her. She used her mouth and tongue and throat on him, lightly scraped her teeth across his great length. It was that moment of combined pleasure and pain that did it, that sent him careening over the edge he'd been clinging to with battered fingers.

With a hoarse shout, he arched up, thrusting again and again against her seeking mouth. And then he was pouring into her with long, brutal jerks of his hips, and she was loving every second of it.

His orgasm went on and on and on, until nothing existed besides him and her and the fire that burned between them.

When it was over and Byron finally pulled out, he was still semihard, his strong body trembling as wave after wave of sensation swept through him. She held him as he recovered, her head resting on his stomach, her arm around a powerful thigh.

They stayed that way for long moments, and a sense of peace she'd never felt before stole through her. Her body was content, her mind at rest.

Her eyes started to close. Then he was shifting, pulling her up and into his arms and then walking down the long hall to her bedroom, where he tucked her under the covers before climbing in behind her.

She cuddled up to him until she was sheltered in the curve of his arm, then slid into sleep, perfectly happy for the first time in a very, very long time.

Chapter Seventeen

The next time Byron woke up, it was to find Lacey climbing out of bed beside him.

"Hey, what's the hurry?" he protested as he wrapped a hand around her wrist and held her in place.

"We've been in bed half the day." She shot him a sweet smile. "And, thanks to you, I have work to do, which I'm sure you do as well."

The warmth in her eyes startled him—and turned him on. But even as his cock hardened, he knew it was more than physical. That she made something come alive in him that had been dormant for far too long—maybe his whole life; he wasn't sure. All he knew was that being with her felt right in a way nothing had in as long as he could remember.

"Oh no," she said with a laugh, as she tried to pull her wrist away from him. "I know what that sexy, heavy-lidded look in your eyes means. And seriously, I *have* to work."

"Really? What does the look mean?" He started to exert a little pressure on her wrist, to pull her back into bed with him, where he could touch her, kiss her, hold her. Where he could just be with her.

"It means that I am not getting in that bed with you. It's noon. We've slept half the day away." She reached for the controller on the nightstand, flicked on the TV and watched for a second as the newscaster droned on about the city's rising crime rate.

"See, the midday news is already on."

Byron glanced at the clock, shocked to realize that she was right. He hadn't been in bed at noon in he didn't remember how long. But now that he knew how nice it was, he was going to make a habit of lingering in bed every once in a while—as long as Lacey was in there with him, that was.

"Well, then, ten more minutes won't matter," he said, as he gave a sharp tug that made her tumble back onto the bed. Another tug and she was cuddled into his chest, exactly where he wanted her.

"Now, see," he said after a minute. "Isn't this nice?"

It was. Nicer than Lacey wanted to admit, and more worrisome than she knew how to handle. She was getting attached to Byron in a way she'd sworn she wouldn't, and she was deathly afraid that it would shatter her when he left.

But all she said was, "It feels guilty."

"Guilty? About what?" He leaned to the side, tried to get her to look at him, but she refused to lift her face from his chest. He waited for a while, long seconds that ticked by in slow motion. Eventually, he must have figured out that she wasn't going to answer him, but he didn't let her go; just cuddled her more closely against him.

She knew her refusal to answer bothered him, but she didn't know what to say. How did she explain that she felt guilty about being with him? About breaking every promise she'd made to herself? Telling him would only hurt him. Besides, worrying about it now wouldn't do her any good. She'd just have to keep her chin up and hope for the best, because she couldn't stand the idea of shattering all over again, not after she'd spent so long picking up the pieces after she'd left Curtis.

Closing her eyes, she drifted along, listening as the newscasters reported new construction in the ninth ward and tests being done on the Pontchartrain levies. She was paying more attention to the feel of Byron against her—long, lean and so comfortable that she never wanted to move—when she felt Byron stiffen. Jerking her head up, she stared at the TV with blurry eyes.

"What's the matter?" she asked sleepily.

"Sssh. Listen."

"In other violent news," the newscaster said with just the right touch of chagrin and nonchalance, "the Mardi Gras Madam's body was discovered in the middle of Jackson Square this morning. The police say nothing has been confirmed, but they believe Veronique Rosen was the victim of a mugging turned nasty. Her body was taken—"

An ugly buzzing started in her ears, and Lacey grabbed on to Byron as the world around her started to spin. "I just had lunch with her a couple of days ago."

He looked at her sharply. "Did she tell you anything about the escort service? About the girls?"

"No. She told me to leave things alone, not to push. That someone was going to get hurt if I didn't back off.

"I didn't listen to her. I kept pushing, kept investigating. That's what I do—poke and prod until something comes loose." She stared at Byron with stricken eyes. "Is this my fault? Did I do this to her? She didn't talk to me, didn't say anything, but maybe someone thought—"

"Don't go there, Lacey."

"How can I not go there? She warned me, told me someone was going to end up dead. I didn't believe her." She was having trouble breathing.

Byron sat up, gave her a little shake. "It's not your fault."

"It is. It—"

"No." He pulled her up, made her look him in the face. "It's not. She chose to live her life a certain way. Yes, you talked to her, but that doesn't mean she wouldn't have ended up like this anyway. You told me yourself she was scared to death of someone, and that she was a serious junkie. It's a miracle something didn't happen to her sooner."

"But I pushed it, pushed her. And now she's dead and I—"

"And you are going to try to get justice for her the only way you know how—by finding out who did this to her and the other girls. Now, let's take a quick shower and get dressed. Then I'll help you get started weeding through those numbers you mentioned that you found."

"Don't you have your own work to do?" Her voice was shaky, but at least the walls had stopped spinning. Byron's pep talk had calmed her down, gotten her to focus.

"I'll get to it. But"—he cast a grim look at the TV set and the newscaster who was blithely continuing on with the day's stories—"at the moment, you're a hell of a lot more important. I think we need to get to the bottom of this and quickly. Before *you* become the story on tomorrow's newscast."

Hours later, they were still searching, but this time at Byron's apartment and on his very fast, wholly tricked-out computer. When she'd been poring over the evidence files she'd managed to finagle from the NOPD, she'd found strings of numbers the police had done nothing with during their investigation. She'd been determined to find out what they meant, but hadn't had a clue where to start.

When she'd showed them to Byron, he'd poked around a little and proclaimed them bank account numbers. Which is why they were now sitting here with his friend, Mike—a tall, beautiful, African-American man who ran a computer-security firm—as the two men tried to unravel the miles of security codes built into the banking sites they'd traced the numbers to. Curses were flying left and right as they tried to hack the network.

"Come on, you son of a bitch," Mike muttered through clenched teeth as his fingers flew over the keyboard. "Let me in."

"No, don't go there. Check out that piece of code down—"

"I've got it." More typing. "Now, let's see what this baby can really do."

Lacey watched them in bemused silence, shocked at just how much enjoyment the two of them were getting out of pitting themselves against a security program. When Byron had first mentioned bringing Mike in, she'd been more than a little leery—after all, the last person she'd talked to about the case had ended up dead, and she couldn't handle it if someone else died while trying to help her.

But Byron had been insistent. Mike was the best of the best, a retired super-hacker who now made his living keeping others out of places he'd spent years breaking in to. If anyone could find a back way through the security and find out who the accounts belonged to, it would be Mike.

He'd been right. They were making progress—already they'd identified two of the feeder bank accounts as belonging to a U.S. senator who had professed to be "the moral choice" in the election he had just won, as well as a high-placed Washington lobbyist. And from the amount of money flowing into their accounts, it looked like they were actually involved in the ring somehow. Besides regular monthly deposits in the tens of thousands, each also had a few large deposits of over a hundred thousand dollars—a well as a couple of big withdrawals.

She couldn't help wondering if those big additions and subtractions had more to do with the buying and selling of sex slaves to rich perverts than it did with the thousand-dollar-a-night fees Crescent City Escort Service charged.

As she took notes on how to follow up, Lacey's stomach was in knots. God only knew what else they were going to find before this was done. But she knew whatever it was, was all bad. And she'd brought Byron—and now Mike—more trouble than she'd originally imagined possible.

Besides, what was she going to do with this information when she eventually got it? Write a book, obviously, but the stuff they were talking about was really heavy, criminal stuff. She needed to find out who to call, who to report this to. Right now, all she knew was that it needed to be someone not from New Orleans or Louisiana or D.C. Someone who wasn't involved.

Because, as things were unraveling, it was becoming more and more apparent that she'd been right about the human-trafficking ring, right about the sex slavery. She'd been going through the pictures from the strip club one at a time, trying to match them to the photos she had of the girls who had been reported missing from Canada and Mexico.

She'd found three so far besides Anne Marie, all from Canada—Beth Coulter from Toronto, Michelle Donovan from Windsor and Stacy LaRue from Quebec—but she knew she'd find more. These bastards had been doing this for a while—definitely since Katrina, but maybe before it. And with a lot more girls than the fifteen she'd managed to track; there were probably hundreds, maybe thousands, of girls they'd managed to kidnap in the past four years. The fifteen who had turned up dead were their failed experiments—girls who, for whatever reason, had been more trouble than they were worth.

Girls who were easier to eliminate than sell.

Her stomach turned as she tried to puzzle things out. At one point she'd run out to the nearest drugstore and bought a map of the U.S., and had begun to map out places and times and dates the girls were taken, followed by the times and dates their bodies had been found in and around New Orleans.

For a brief moment, she'd played with the idea of taking this to the FBI and praying that she got an agent who wasn't on the take. But when Byron traced one of the bank account numbers to the NOPD police commissioner, she gave up. There was just no way to know who was involved with what—not right now anyway, and maybe not ever.

From what she could see, the only other option they had was the press, and she was prepared to take that option if she had to. But before she went to them, all her ducks had to be in a row, and she had to be able to lay them all out—with evidence. Otherwise, she and Byron and even Mike would be the ones to pay the price.

The idea that these girls were being triply victimized—first by the bastards who took them and sold them, second by the men who paid for them and third by the system that allowed it to go on—was infuriating, maddening, so awful she could barely wrap her mind around it.

Her thoughts were interrupted when Mike called a dinner break around eleven, and the three of them stood around Byron's kitchen island, eating roast-beef sandwiches and talking about anything but what they'd spent the entire day doing. The reality was too disturbing, too disgusting, but as they looked at one another, there didn't seem to be much else to say. What did a baseball score mean when weighed against the agonies these girls had suffered?

Soon after midnight, Mike left, promising to come back the next day after work. Lacey had planned to work after he left, but as the door shut behind him, she dissolved into hopeless tears.

"Lacey, baby." Byron pulled her into his arms, onto his lap, and rocked her much like he would a child. She felt so small in his hands, so fragile, and he wanted nothing more than to take her pain away. Yet that was impossible; she was crying like her whole world was crashing in on her and there was nothing she could do to stop it.

He wanted to say something, anything, to take her pain away. But how could he? He was sick—sick at heart, sick to his stomach, sick in every way possible at what they were finding. He could only imagine how much worse it would be for Lacey, whose job it was to crawl into the gutter with these monsters and make some sense out of what they were doing.

In the end, he didn't say anything at all. Just held her while she sobbed like her heart was breaking, then took her into the shower and held her while she cried some more. Finally, he put her to bed. She'd clutched at him, begging him to climb in beside her. Which he did—then held her as she slept. But he stayed awake, watching over her, counting down the hours until daylight. Trying to figure out how the hell he was going to make this okay for her.

As night bled slowly into dawn, he was as miserable as she had been. Because he had no new ideas—no ideas at all—that might somehow help Lacey fix what was going on down here. At least, not without getting her killed.

He was a failure, just like his father so often told him. Because it didn't really matter what he was good at if he couldn't do the one thing he needed to do above all else: keep his woman safe.

Chapter Eighteen

Lacey awoke the next morning to a steaming cup of coffee under her nose, and Byron's face inches from her own. He looked tired, his eyes dark and shadowed, his handsome face drawn taut, and so worried that she felt her heart break just a little bit as her brain slowly kicked into gear.

"I have to go into work this morning, but I didn't want to just leave without talking to you first. I'd stay, but I have this piece I have to finish and—"

She placed a soft hand over his mouth. "Go. It's fine; I know you need to work. I've got enough stuff here to keep me busy for a long time to come."

He handed her the mug and she took a long sip of the steaming brew. "I'll try to knock off early and come back to help. Maybe we can—"

"Byron, over the course of my career, I've researched six books without you. And while any and all help you can give me on this one is completely appreciated, I understand you have other commitments. I'll be fine until you get back."

She took another sip of coffee. "Of course, I wouldn't object if you wanted to start the shower for me."

"Sure." He got up and headed into the bathroom. When he came back into the bedroom a minute later, he was shirtless and Lacey's mouth began to water.

"You know, I do some of my best work in the shower," he said as he unbuttoned his jeans.

"I thought you had something to build." She shot him an amused look as she strolled, naked, into the bathroom.

He shrugged. "I make my own hours—kind of a perk that comes with being self-employed. It won't matter if I'm an hour late." Plus, when he'd left the stock exchange, he'd sworn to himself that he'd never be a slave to a schedule again. He'd work when he wanted, for how long he wanted, and when he wanted to go home, he'd damn well go home. In the year and a half he'd been in New Orleans, he'd kept that promise to himself.

He didn't say any of that to Lacey, though, didn't know how to say it without coming across as a shiftless loser to a woman who worked twenty-four/seven. Besides, he did have to get to work—that table he'd screwed up the other day wasn't going to fix itself.

The look she shot him over her shoulder was somehow completely deadpan and smolderingly hot at the same time. "Yes, well I'm taking this shower alone, so you'll have to save your talent demonstration for another time."

"Alone?" He made a grab for her, but she eluded him. "Don't you know we're in the middle of a drought? We should do our best to conserve."

She snorted. "It's rained every day for the last six weeks—I think the drought is all in your head. Besides, if I let you in this shower with me, I have no doubt that water conservation will be the last thing on your mind."

"You might be right," he allowed with a grin.

"I am right." She started to close the door behind her, but his arm shot out and stopped it before she got more than halfway.

"Still," he said as he pushed his way into the small bathroom. "Won't you be lonely in that great big shower all by yourself?"

"I think I can manage."

"Yeah, but why settle for just managing?" He pulled her into his arms, ran his hands up and down her satin skin before cupping her glorious ass and pressing her body to his.

"You've got ten minutes," she said, as stepped into the shower, pulling him with her.

"Ten minutes is all I'll need."

It turned out, he needed only three. The last seven, she told him with a laugh, were all about showing off.

Byron ran the sander over the top of the table yet again, praying that this time would be the charm. That this time he would look down and the gouge would magically be gone. He'd been over the table numerous times with the machine already, and he didn't have much more room to try to correct his mistake. If the gouge didn't come out soon, he'd have to start over—a prospect that left him both annoyed and frustrated, especially with the time he needed to put in with Lacey and her research.

But when he moved the sander off the spot where his hand had slipped and accidentally driven his screwdriver into the carefully carved wood, he sighed with disgust. The mark was slighter than it had been before this last run with the sander, but it was far from gone.

Didn't it just figure? He was always so careful, always so meticulous when it came to his work, that it was totally ironic that when he finally made a mistake, it was on the most important piece he'd ever done.

Reaching out, he ran a finger over the long slice. He still couldn't believe it had happened, that he'd managed to screw up weeks of hard work in the blink of an eye.

The whole thing was stupid, completely ridiculous. For the first time since he'd become a carpenter—for the first time since he'd walked away from his Ivy League education and seven-figure job—he'd been working while focused on something other than the job. Which was more than stupid; it was reckless. He was damn lucky he'd screwed up only the table instead of losing a finger or three.

But he hadn't been able to help himself. Hadn't been able to rip his mind away from Lacey and the heat they generated whenever they were in the same room with each other. At the time, he'd been wondering what he could possibly do to get into her hot little pants. Just the image had had him slipping—it was a good thing he hadn't known the reality the other day, or he might have punched a hole right through the damn tabletop.

With a groan that was part disgust and part satisfaction that at least the most important thing in his life was going right, he started the sander up again and ran it over the table in a final run-through that was more of a Hail Mary than the final pass in last year's Super Bowl. It hadn't worked for the NFC team then, and he doubted it was going to work for him this time. But he loved this table and couldn't see junking it—not if there was even the slightest chance that he could fix what he'd ruined.

As he worked, he tried like hell to concentrate, but couldn't keep his mind from wandering to Lacey time and again. With everything else that was going on, it was stupid of him to be concerned about what she did or didn't do on that damn blog of hers. But he did care; he gritted his teeth as annoyance ripped through him. He'd checked a couple of hours ago, and sure enough, she'd uploaded another fantasy. One that involved a moonlight beach, a blanket and an audience. Now, how the hell was he supposed to live up to that? While he didn't necessarily mind the first two, the third set him on edge. Not that it should surprise him; she obviously had an exhibitionist streak in her, or she wouldn't be posting to the blog to begin with.

But she'd never had such a public fantasy before, not in all of the blogs she'd ever written. And he should know—he'd read them all. So what was this new fantasy, and why was she posting it less than an hour after making love to him? And what did it say about his lovemaking that she couldn't talk to him about what she wanted in bed, but she could post it for her slobbering audience of adoring fans?

He shook his head, tried to snap himself out of this ridiculous fit of jealousy. A few days ago, he'd been jumping for joy at having found his fantasy woman, and now he was envious because she wasn't sharing herself exclusively with him. How ridiculous was that? One week, no matter how spectacular, did not a relationship make. Especially not under the conditions they were facing.

But it *did* make a relationship for him—that was the problem. He was crazy about Lacey, absolutely, positively in love with the brave, funny, heart-wrenching woman she was. And the idea that he wasn't enough for her—that once again he loved someone who wanted more than he could give—had thrown him into a complete and total tailspin.

Brooding, out of sorts, he continued to work on the table until he caught a movement out of the corner of his eye. At the first glimpse, Byron froze, as it sunk in that he was no longer alone. Stopping the saw, he pulled off his gloves and slapped them on the table before heading to the front of the shop, where a man was waiting.

Byron felt himself tense as he looked at the guy, though he couldn't put his finger on why. The guy looked perfectly normal—dressed in a pair of dark pants and a silk T-shirt—but there was something about him that rubbed Byron the wrong way.

It wasn't that he was in his shop, as he wasn't the first customer to stop by the address listed on his business card, and hopefully wouldn't be the last. Maybe it was the way he was looking around Byron's work space, like he was analyzing every detail—and found it lacking.

But this was a working woodshop, not an upscale New York office building, and he'd treated it as such. When he'd moved here, he'd wanted to get as far away from his former life as he could—from the stress and the phoniness and the all-around ugliness. This place had been the result.

But when the man looked at him, there was no censure in his face, no disgust. In fact, the only thing Byron could see was a lively curiosity that drained some of his own tension.

Putting his paranoia down to residual angst because of Lacey's blog, he extended a hand as he asked, "Can I help you?"

"I sure hope so." The man's handshake was firm and brief. "My wife saw your work spotlighted in this month's edition of *Southern Living* and fell in love with it. It's all she's talked about for days."

His voice was low, the Southern accent smooth as molasses. Everything about him screamed good ol' boy, and Byron felt himself relaxing despite his earlier suspicions. "Thank you. I appreciate that."

"No, *thank you*. I've racked my brain for days trying to figure out what to get her for our tenth anniversary, and that article helped me make up my mind. I want my gift to be really special—really unique. You know, something that she remembers forever."

"Of course." Byron gestured around his workshop. "But what you're describing sounds more like a piece of art. I'm a carpenter, Mr. . . . ?"

"Call me Mark. I know you're a carpenter, Byron. But you make the most beautiful furniture around. I would love it if you could make my wife something really special."

He raised an eyebrow. "Like what?"

Mark shrugged. "Now, that's where I'm not exactly sure. I was thinking maybe a beautifully carved trunk—you know, the kind they used to have in the old days."

"A hope chest?"

"Yeah, something like that's exactly what I mean. A hope chest. But I don't want it to be just a plain box. It needs to be beautiful—really well made. Hand carved and stained—like that table you were just working on. You know what I'm saying?"

"Yeah, of course. But a piece like that's going to cost you around a thousand dollars, maybe a little more, depending on the kind of detail you want."

"Doesn't matter. The sky's the limit. Just make it beautiful. My wife deserves something beautiful after putting up with me for all these years."

"All right, then." Byron walked over to the desk he kept in the corner, pulled out an invoice slip. "I'll need you to fill this out—name, address, all that. Plus if you have any special instructions—minimum and maximum size for the piece, type of wood, what kind of stain you want on it." He gestured to the corner. "I've got samples over here for you to take a look at."

"Excellent."

Byron spent about half an hour with Mark Cavanaugh. And when he left, Byron couldn't help staring after him. Envying him the fact that he had a woman he loved, who loved him in return. One who not only wanted an acknowledgment of his feelings, but expected it.

Soon, he told himself as he began putting his tools away for the night. *Soon, Lacey will be ready to give me what I want*. A hint of unease niggled at the base of his spine, but he ignored it. Lacey did care about him—he was sure of it. He just had to give her a good enough reason to admit it.

Chapter Nineteen

C ome on, Derek. Talk to me." Lacey smiled up at the lean black man who towered over her. She'd met him months before, when she'd made her first trip to New Orleans to investigate Crescent City Escort Service, back when she'd been trying to decide if she wanted to write the book.

He'd spent three years working as chauffeur for the escort service, though when she'd met him, he'd been unemployed. At the beginning, Lacey had been skeptical of the depth of the story, and when she'd dug a little, hoping to prove the allegations false, she'd run into Derek.

"Last time I talked to you, it got me in trouble. I don't want to talk to you no more."

"What kind of trouble?"

"Now, you know better than that. Do I look like the kind of guy to kiss and tell?"

No, he looked like the kind of guy who had fallen far since she'd last seen him. When she'd first met him, Derek had dressed in suits and spoken with a kindness and courtesy that had immediately set her at ease, despite the circumstances. Now he looked like the big, bad wolf out for whatever he could get, and the implication that she had done this to him made her sorrier than she could say.

"You look like the kind of guy who knows a lot more than he's saying. About a lot of things."

He flashed a smile, and for the first time he looked like the same man she'd met a lifetime before. "Too true, girl. Too true."

"So how about swinging a little bit of that knowledge my way? I won't quote you—unless you want me to. I just need you to point me in the right direction."

"Hell, no, I don't want you to quote me. The only reason I even decided to come meet you is 'cuz you said you'd be here, just in case I showed up. I couldn't stand the idea of you waiting around out here all by yourself. This isn't the kind of neighborhood a girl like you should be hanging in."

Like she hadn't been able to figure that out by the number of drug deals and john hookups that had happened in the few minutes the two of them had been talking. Keeping a lid on her sarcastic side, she said, "So why don't we go somewhere else? You can come to my place, or we can get a cup of coffee somewhere." When he didn't bother to disguise his snort, she added hastily, "Or a drink. We can go to whatever bar you want—my treat."

"No offense, Lacey. I mean, you know I like you, right? But I would rather have a drink with a stone-cold killer than sit down at a bar with you. There's a much bigger chance I'd get to leave the bar alive."

Skitters of alarm ran down her spine and had her shivering, despite the oppressive heat. "What is that supposed to mean?"

Derek sighed, then leaned in close to her. "It means that if anyone found out I was talking about what you want to talk about, if anyone found out I'd talked about that shit, I'd be a dead man. Hell, if I'm seen with you and it gets around that you're asking about this stuff, I'll be dead anyway. Even if I don't tell you a thing. I know what happened to Veronique—I'm not stupid."

Lacey's stomach clenched and her heart beat double time. "I thought this was just a story about a prostitution ring, one that's already been broken up." She tossed out the bait and waited for him to bite.

It didn't take long. Derek's look was filled with reproof. "Don't kid a kidder, girl. If this was just the story of a little old N'Awlins escort service, we wouldn't be here, where nobody knows us, waiting to get stormed on."

"You picked the meeting place, not me."

"Yeah, because I wanted to scare you off. You don't want to get mixed up in this."

"I'm already mixed up in it—you know that. Besides, I signed a contract to write this book."

"Well, unsign it, then. Or you're going to be as dead as those girls you're researching."

His words hit her like a blow. Lacey tried to steel herself so he wouldn't see how much he'd affected her, but Derek was a pretty smart guy and he knew exactly what he'd said—and how she'd respond to it. "I'm sorry, Lacey. I know you don't want to hear that. But it's the truth. These guys you're messing with are bad business."

She let the rest of his warning go—after all, it wasn't like she was going to back off now—and latched on to the last thing he'd said. "Bad news how?"

"Bad news like, if you cross them, you end up dead."

"You already said that. Can you be a little more specific?"

He laughed, but this time the sound was far from pleasant. "You want more specific? How about raped and dumped on the side of the road with your throat slit? How about broken into so many pieces even your mama won't recognize you? How about sold to some guy with perversions that make the freaks in this town look like altar boys? Is that specific enough for you?"

He was angry, agitated; his hands clenched into fists so tight it was amazing he hadn't broken something. She wanted to let it go, wanted to let him go, but what he'd said echoed everything she already knew.

"What do you mean *sold*, Derek?" *God, please let him know something that could help her.*

"There's only one kind of sold, girl. Sold like you're a piece of meat to the highest bidder. And once he's bought you, he owns you—body and soul."

"So these bad guys, the ones I'm pissing off by asking about the escort service, they have their fingers in the slave trade?" She thought of all those young, missing girls. Stolen girls. Thought about them being drugged and raped and beaten until they had no more will to fight. Until prostitution and drug running and everything else seemed the lesser of the evils inflicted on them.

"Hey, whoa." Derek started backing up. "I didn't say that."

"Sure you did. You said bad news, like I'd be sold to some weird pervert guy. That sounds like human trafficking—sex trafficking—to me."

"Give me a break." He nodded a little down the street, to where a john was hooking up with a girl for twenty bucks. "That's sex trafficking right there. Same thing that happens at the escort service, just cheaper. Don't put words in my mouth."

"That's not what you were talking about, Derek, and we both know it. Don't insult my intelligence."

"Look, Lacey." He cast a nervous look behind him. "You can't be saying things like that."

"Like what?"

"Like fucking sex slavery. You're not listening to me. They'll get you."

"Who'll get me?"

"The fucking Russians. They moved in here after Katrina, took over half the city. You know what they do to people who fuck with them?"

A sliver of unease worked its way through the calm reserve Lacey was trying so hard to project. She did know what the Russians were like; at one point she'd considered doing a book on the Russian Mafia's takeover of Brighton Beach in New York, but she'd scrapped it when she realized just how dangerous the project was.

Nice to know she'd run from the organized crime up there, and had ended up down here in something much more dangerous, much more disgusting.

Didn't it just figure?

Despite her nervousness, she kept poking at Derek, hoping to make him slip.

"That's a lot of power you're giving these guys credit for. You really think they can do everything you said?"

"Damn right they can. And more. These guys will fuck you up, Lacey. And laugh while they're doing it."

"You seem pretty sure of that. What kind of run-ins have you had with them?"

"Me? I haven't had any run-ins at all. I'm obviously a lot smarter than you are—I keep my head down and mind my own damn business. You go looking for the shit like it's a goddamn prize."

"Are you telling me, seriously, that you've never had a problem with these men? And you're still scared to death of them? That doesn't make any sense to me."

"I've never seen a nuclear warhead either, but that shit scares me too. Some things you don't have to experience firsthand to know they'll fuck you up—and fuck you up good."

Lacey schooled her voice to remain calm as she said, "Yes, but we've all heard about what a nuclear bomb can do. What have you heard about these guys?"

He shook his head. "I've heard enough."

"Like what? Do you know who they are? What they do?"

"I know they kill anyone who gets in their way, and that's been more than enough reason for me to fly under the radar. They hurt girls, Lacey. They sell them, and if the girls don't do what they want, they drug them. Beat them. Sometimes kill them, if they don't fall in line."

"Do they kidnap them?"

The look he shot her was completely incredulous. "Well, you know a bunch of girls who up and volunteer to be the love slave of some sick old fuck?"

"I don't know. There's a lot of women who marry men much older than they are."

He snorted, shaking his head as if he was totally disgusted with her. "This isn't marriage. This is ownership, pure and simple. Those girls don't have any rights. It's like they're pets and the second they step out of line, they get beat with the newspaper. Or the belt. Or a fucking gun."

"And the escort service?" she whispered. "What about those girls?"

Derek started, as if he suddenly remembered who he was talking to. And what he was talking about. He started backpedaling as fast as he could. "I'm not talking about them, Lacey. I was just speaking in general. I mean—"

"Don't bullshit me, Derek. Don't start lying to me now—not after you put all those horrific pictures in my head."

"I was trying to warn you. I don't want you to end up like those other girls."

"What other girls? Girls like Anne Marie Winston?" She leaned forward, put a hand on his arm. "What happened to Anne Marie, Derek? How did she really die?"

"I don't know." He pulled away from her hand, shook his head as if dazed. "I haven't worked for the service since Veronique and the other girls got busted."

Derek sighed, then thrust a frustrated hand through his close-cropped hair. "Lacey, you don't know what you're asking. You don't know—"

"Sure I do. I need to know what happened to those dead girls."

"No, you don't. All these questions ain't gonna bring those girls back. All they're going to do is get you in hot water." He paused, cleared his throat. "I don't want to see that happen to you. I like you, Lacey."

"Come on, Derek." She was close; she could feel it. He wanted to tell her, wanted to help her out, but was too afraid. She needed to know what he was afraid of—who he was afraid of. "Point me in the right direction. Give me a name."

"I'm not going there."

"Derek." She reached out a hand, closed it over his own. "Please. I won't tell anyone where I got the information. I won't—"

His laugh, when it came, was so low and harsh, she wasn't sure that it wasn't a sob. "I keep telling you, you don't know what you're asking for. If these guys set their sights on you, you'll spill everything you know in thirty seconds flat. And if that ain't good enough, you'll make shit up just so that the pain will stop. And then—more than likely— they'll kill you anyway."

"You sound like you know that from personal experience." She kept the statement brief, casual, though her heart beat like a metronome as she waited for his answer.

But she must have gone too far, because he pulled his hand back so fast he nearly stumbled. "Don't do that. Don't play me like that. Not when I'm being as honest as I can be with you."

"I'm not playing you."

"Sure you are." He backed away, his eyes as angry as they were frightened. "Acting all nice and concerned and desperate when all you really want is a story. A story that'll get both of us killed."

"I won't tell anyone—"

"Bullshit." He spat the word at her right before his hands closed over her upper arms, hard. "You won't need to tell. You'll just go snooping around and they'll come looking for whoever pointed you in their direction."

Convinced he'd done his best on the table and eager to get home and see Lacey again, Byron locked up his workshop in a hurry. It had been a long day, but a good one. He'd managed to salvage his piece for the governor's mansion, without having to replace the ornately carved tabletop, and had also done some preliminary sketches for the trunk Cavanaugh had commissioned that morning. Tomorrow, he'd fax them over to the guy and see if he liked the concept Byron had come up with.

As he stepped away from the building and into the street, the heat blasted him like a furnace working overtime. Wet, sticky and hotter than the proverbial frying pan or fire, it sucked the air from his lungs and had him cursing under his breath.

He started toward the truck he'd parked in a little alley a block away, doing his best to ignore the drug deals and prostitutes that lined every corner. Normally he made a point of getting out of here earlier, before the sun went down and all this crap started, but he'd worked late today in an effort to make up for the many and varied screwups that had happened as the week progressed.

He snorted. Like that was possible. Lacey was taking him on one hell of a chase, and the fact that he'd spent the last few nights in her bed didn't mean that the game was over. Not by a long shot—she wasn't ready for a commitment yet, and he didn't want a relationship with her without one. So where did that leave them but shit out of luck?

He tried to shake off the melancholy mood, but it had been with him ever since he'd seen her blog today. And since it was driving him crazy, he knew he was going to have to confront her about it and tell her he knew. He sure as shit wasn't looking forward to that discussion.

Sidestepping an addict on the make, he continued down the dirty, pitted street, avoiding potholes and prostitutes alike. As he did, an overwhelming sadness filled him. He'd thought he'd left all this behind when he'd left New York and his high-paying job on Wall Street, had thought seeing the hookers and the drugs on a daily basis was over. But if he'd learned anything from his move to this city, it was that misery and degradation were everywhere. On these streets, women sold themselves for twenty or fifty bucks, whereas the women he'd known in his other life had held out for diamonds and expensive clothes.

And the addictions—they were just different faces of the same old poison. The drugs might differ—crack instead of pure cocaine, beer instead of hundred-year-old Scotch, but the results were all the same.

It was one of the reasons he'd left, one of the reasons he'd "thrown it all away" according to his father. One morning he'd woken up and realized that alcohol had become a crutch he used to deal with the high-stress stakes of his job, a crutch that was becoming more and more necessary for him to function.

Since he'd watched his father spend his life in the first stages of a drunken haze—had seen him drive and prescribe meds and treat patients with a steady stream of alcohol in his blood—his own growing reliance on the stuff had scared the shit out of him.

So he'd said "Fuck it," and had walked away—to something different, something better. Or so he'd thought at the time.

Byron shook his head as he skirted a drug deal neither party even bothered to try to hide. New Orleans was different, all right. But better? Only sometimes. Especially now that he knew about all those dead girls. He couldn't help looking at the prostitutes and wondering what their stories were. Wondering if the same thing had happened to them that had happened to Anne Marie Winston and the others.

Still, the closer he got to his truck, the more relieved he became. Another minute and he'd be able to hop in, drive a couple blocks north and spend a few minutes thinking about something besides how much trouble these young girls were in.

Sweat slid from his forehead onto his left cheek and he reached up, wiped it away. And in doing so, broke his first rule. He actually looked at the people around him, and as he did, he couldn't help noticing a huge ape of a man hassling a woman half his size.

Anger exploded in his gut, a by-product of heat and frustration and his bone-deep disgust with any man who needed to pick on someone smaller and weaker than he was just to feel powerful. Just because he could. These girls suffered enough—more than enough—and the idea that they had to put up with some john beating on them hit him where he lived.

His older sister's husband had beat the crap out of her when Byron had been just a kid, and he still remembered what she'd looked like all busted up. She'd barely been able to walk without flinching for weeks.

He was crossing the street before his conscious mind could catch up with his feet. "Hey," he shouted, "Leave her alone." Even as he said the words, he prayed he wasn't doing the girl a disservice. Hoped that she wouldn't get beat on later because he'd tried to be her fucking savior now.

But as he got closer, the guy dragged the woman back a few feet, until they were under the dingy streetlight, and for the first time he caught a glimpse of red hair. Bright red, like a living flame.

Bright red, like Lacey's.

That was when he started to run toward her.

Chapter Twenty

H ey! Let her go!"

At the familiar voice, Lacey glanced up in shock, just in time to see Byron heading for them at a dead run. Derek glanced behind him, but didn't relinquish his hold. "You need to stop asking these questions, do you understand me?" His fingers dug into the soft flesh of her arms, hard, and she had to bite her lip to keep from crying out.

"Do you understand me?" he repeated, the vise around her arm growing even tighter. "For your own good. The next time you come around here, I'm not going to be this nice. Do you feel me?"

When she didn't answer, he dug his fingers in even tighter. "Do you feel me?"

She nodded, afraid that if she spoke she'd end up crying out. She was pretty sure Derek wouldn't hurt her—that he was just trying to make an impression—but she couldn't be positive, especially not with Byron barreling down on them like a sinner in need of salvation.

"I said, 'Let her go.'" Byron's voice was as hard as steel, as cold as ice, and Lacey actually saw Derek recoil. But he must have been more upset than she thought, because his hand on her arm never faltered—it only got tighter at this new threat, and suddenly she wasn't nearly as convinced of her safety.

"Hey, man. This isn't your business." Derek's voice was full of bravado.

"The hell it isn't." He glanced at Lacey, and the fury on his face had her breath catching in her throat. "The lady doesn't look like she's enjoying herself."

"I don't give a shit what the bitch enjoys. She comes down here, dressed for the stroll and messing with my girls, she deserves whatever the fuck she gets."

Lacey winced. Though she knew Derek was just doing his thing—protecting himself and trying to keep his role in her research quiet by looking like any other drug dealer or pimp working the street—his words took Byron from enraged to murderous in less than one second. If she didn't do something, and quickly—

"Byron, it's no big deal. I'm fine." With a mighty tug, she wrenched her arm from Derek's grip, ignoring the pain that such a movement induced. As his nails raked against the tender skin of her inner elbow, she fought hard not to wince. And thanked God she was up-to-date on all her shots—Derek might be the cleanest, most decent of the bunch, but in this area of town, that really wasn't saying a whole hell of a lot.

"Whoa, you know this guy?" Derek blanched and he took a couple of steps back, the look he shot her full of betrayal and disgust. "I thought you weren't telling anyone about this. Isn't that what you just told me—no one has to know?"

"I didn't tell anyone." Frustration ripped through her as she saw her best chance at getting information slip right down the drain. She was going to kill Byron for this.

"Then what's he doing—"

"Think, Derek. If my friend"—and she was using the term loosely here—"knew that we were just having a harmless little chat, do you think he would have barged in like that?"

"I don't know." Derek shook his head and backed up even more. "It doesn't matter anyway. I'm done with this."

"No. Please—don't do this."

He shot her a hard look, one filled with resolve and something even more dangerous. "Stay away from me, Lacey. I don't want to see you again."

"But—"

"I mean it. Don't come around here again. Nobody will talk to you."

"Derek." She started after him, but Byron grabbed her wrist. Held her in place. She struggled against his hold, but it was as implacable as the look on his face. "Come on," she pleaded.

Her source just shook his head as he turned and headed down the dirty street at a fast clip. "Someone's going to get hurt, and I'd just as soon it not be you or me."

"Derek!" She yelled after him as he put more distance between them, more desperate than she would have thought possible. But he just flipped her the bird and kept walking.

She stared after him for long seconds, trying to control the disappointment and fear racing through her, as well as rein in her temper. It wouldn't do any good to explode—not out here, where the night had ears and streets could talk. But she couldn't remember ever being this furious, this sick. It's not like contacts in this industry were a dime a dozen, what with every source she had clamming up on her. Derek had been her best shot, and now he was gone—thanks to Byron and his high-handed hero tactics.

Taking a few deep breaths, she really tried not to explode. Not to tell Byron off.

But it wasn't easy. By the time Derek had disappeared into the darkness, blending into the night like the chameleon he was, she was shaking with rage. He knew something—about Anne Marie, about the whole damn operation. She could have gotten a handle on what was going on—could have gotten the goods that would help her blow this thing sky-high—if Byron hadn't interrupted. If she'd had just a few more minutes with him.

Oh, Derek had been putting up a struggle with her, but he hadn't walked away. He had a good heart, which is why he'd been trying to warn her. It was that good heart that would have had him spilling the goods—or at least some small part of the story—whether he'd wanted to or not. It was obvious he was no happier than she was about what had been happening with those girls.

Which meant, as long as he felt that way, that she'd still had a chance at him, still had a shot at getting him to give her something. Anything. But he'd freaked when he'd seen Byron, and she knew she didn't have a chance in hell of getting him to talk to her again. Derek as a source was now totally blown, and she was right back to where she'd started this morning.

At the thought, fury flared inside her all over again and she turned on Byron before she could stop herself. "What the hell do you think you're doing?"

"Me?" He grabbed her arms and pulled her against him as he gave his own anger free rein. "I think that's my question, don't you?"

"No, I don't!" For the second time she tried to wrench her arm from a man's grip, but Byron wasn't nearly as easily displaced as Derek. His grip wasn't painful as Derek's had been, but it *was* completely solid. No matter how she twisted, his hand didn't budge so much as a millimeter.

When he brought his face down until it was only an inch from hers, she would have shrunk from the rage in his eyes if she hadn't been just as angry as he was. She was getting damn sick of men manhandling her and telling her what was good for her. Sick enough of it that if Byron didn't let her go, he was going to wish that he had.

"What the fuck are you doing down here, dressed like that?" He looked over her short skirt and tube top with derision.

"It's none of your goddamn business what I'm doing down here." Again she tried to wrench her arm away; again he held fast, his grip unbreakable. "Maybe I was just asking for directions. Shouldn't you have waited to see what was going on before you came barging in like some jealous moron?"

"Don't pull that shit with me, Lacey. You look like a damn hooker, and that guy was no Good Samaritan. So you'd better start talking, and quick." His hand tightened infinitesimally on her arm—not enough to hurt, but more than enough to serve as a warning. As did the look in his eyes: dangerous, demanding, determined to learn the truth, no matter what he had to do to get it.

As the realization washed over her, she flashed back to any number of conversations she'd had with Curtis through the years—conversations where he'd used his strength and attitude to try to intimidate her into doing whatever he wanted. Conversations where she'd been forced to give in to him, just to keep the peace.

Her old feelings of anger and helplessness came back, making her even angrier. Making her even more frightened, and she went crazy—struggling to break free of him even if it meant hurting herself. "Get off of me! Right now." She pulled against Byron, more determined than ever to get back control of her own body.

"Lacey, stop it! I was only trying to help."

"You stop it!" She continued to wrestle with him, desperate to get free of his grip. Desperate to free herself from the memories and feelings of inadequacy that were circling her like wolves.

"I didn't ask for you to come down here and get involved in this! I didn't ask you for a damn thing!"

Byron glanced around, and for the first time seemed to notice that they were attracting more than their fair share of attention. He started walking back the way he'd come, his grip on her wrist ensuring that she would follow.

"I don't want to go anywhere with you." She tried to dig her heels into the scarred pavement, but he just kept walking—as if her resistance was of absolutely no consequence to him.

"Tough shit."

Overhead, thunder boomed, right before the sky opened up and started to pour on them.

"Byron, this is kidnapping."

He paused, once again got in her face. "No, Lacey. This is me taking you—my lover—to a quiet place so we can talk like rational human beings, without half of New Orleans looking on."

"I don't want to talk to you."

"At this exact moment, I don't really give a shit what you want." He paused beside a big maroon truck with blacked-out windows while he pressed the unlock button on his keychain.

The second the locks disengaged, he whipped open the door and all but threw her into the front seat. Then he slammed the door and headed around the truck to the driver's side.

By the time he'd opened his door, she had hers open again and was scrambling to get out of the truck, not caring how wet she got.

"Don't do it!" His voice was low, tough, and she was struck—again—by the difference between this man and the one she'd slept with for the last two nights. Gone was the playful Byron with the sweet kisses and gentle lovemaking. Gone was the man who teased her, touched her, made her laugh. In his place was this commanding, dictatorial hard-ass who seemed more than willing to fight dirty if it meant getting his way.

"Don't tell me what to do."

"Goddamn it, Lacey!" he roared, obviously a man pushed past his limits. "I just want to talk to you for a few minutes."

"You want to order me around." She stared at him with smoldering yes. "You don't have that right."

He reached across her and slammed her door before starting the truck and pulling onto the road with barely a look in his rearview mirror. "I'm your lover; that gives me the right to be concerned about you."

"You're a one-night stand that got a little out of hand." She didn't know who she was hurting more with her words—him or herself. Still, as her wrist throbbed from where he'd held her, his implacable resolve blended in her head with Curtis' cruelty, until she couldn't stop the words from pouring out. "That doesn't make you my lover."

As soon as she'd spoken, she knew she'd made a mistake. Knew she'd thrown down the gauntlet to this fire-breathing alpha male.

The look on his face only confirmed what she'd just begun to figure out. He glanced at her with eyes that shot sparks, his sensual mouth curling into a snarl that could only be described as predatory.

She knew she should be frightened—of the look and the man. After all, it was more than obvious that she'd pushed Byron right up to the edge of civilized behavior. But she wasn't frightened, wasn't concerned, as they barreled through New Orleans' rain-slicked streets.

Instead, much to her dismay, she was relieved. Exhilarated. Aroused. He was furious—certainly more furious than she had ever seen him—and he hadn't laid a hand on her in anger, hadn't said one word to tear down the fragile self-esteem she was still in the process of building up.

"I am your lover."

The cockiness of the statement set her teeth on edge, had her answering with a snarl. "You're the guy across the courtyard. We've had fun these last few days, but—"

She never got a chance to finish the sentence, as he slammed to a stop outside their apartment building. His mouth crushed down on hers with all the finesse of an out-of-control freight train, hard and hot and unforgiving.

Lacey told herself to pull away. Told herself she didn't want this. But the truth was she was already wet, and at this exact moment, there was nothing in the world she wanted more than him.

In a last-ditch effort at self-preservation, she threw herself at the truck door and slid out onto the slick pavement.

He was around the truck in five seconds flat—angrier than she'd ever seen him. More enraged than she thought a man could be without lashing out with his words or his fists. "Go home, Byron. I don't need—"

He cut her words off with a kiss—his lips, his tongue, his teeth working in concert to devour her lips. He tasted like licorice; smelled like sandalwood and wet, wild rain. He kissed her like he meant it, like he wanted to absorb her into his body, into his soul. The anger and sense of betrayal that had been riding her drained away, leaving only desire in their wake. Cupping his face in her hands, she gave him everything she'd been afraid to give to anyone for far too long.

Ripping his mouth from Lacey's, Byron trailed his lips across her cheek and down her throat. She moaned softly—though it could have been the wind—and he lifted her until she was wrapped around him. Her arms encircled his shoulders while her ravenous mouth covered every inch of his face, every centimeter of his neck. It was his turn to groan when her tongue found his collarbone and began licking the water off it; he'd never have guessed it was an erogenous zone, but then again, with Lacey, everything turned him on.

Her legs were twined around his waist so that she was completely open to him, and his cock hardened to the point of pain. Her energy was explosive—passion, desire, need poured from her and enveloped him as the storm continued to rage.

Pulling back from her grasping hands and seeking lips for a second—just a second—Byron stared at her. Mesmerized by her. He wanted to be able to remember her just like this: soaking wet, desperate for him, the elements around them as frenzied as she was.

Tears were streaming down her face, sobs wracking her body, but he didn't stop. Somehow he knew she needed this elemental connection between them even more than he did.

"Baby, you have to stop." It was his turn to run his lips over her face, sipping the cool rain and hot tears from her cheeks as he did so.

"I can't."

"You have to. You'll make yourself sick."

She simply wrapped herself more tightly around him, until her hot, wet center was pressed directly over his aching cock. Whimpering, crying, she rode him, her hips lifting again and again as she tried desperately to find surcease—and oblivion—in his arms.

He wanted to give them to her, even if just for the moment. He didn't know what was tearing her apart, but he knew that he would do whatever it took to get her through it.

The realization hit him hard, and the sudden, urgent need to be inside her hit him even harder. Carrying her, he stumbled around the side of the building and into the heavily shaded courtyard.

"Byron!"

"I know, sweetheart." They weren't going to make it upstairs, so he pulled her into the darkest area and shoved her back against the wall.

He tore at her flimsy underwear like a man possessed, and it gave way with one powerful jerk of his hand. Her skirt was bunched around her waist, and the only thing that separated them was the wet, clinging material of his jeans. He ripped at them until his zipper was open, and then he slammed into her with one powerful thrust.

Joy. Ecstasy. Need. And a hunger he was afraid would never be satisfied. He thrust into her again and again, a powerful slamming of his body that he would have worried about any other time. But she was taking it, taking him, as if she craved his unrestrained desire. As if she needed it. Needed him.

"Harder. Harder. Harder." She repeated the words again and again, her hips rising and falling with every thrust of his. He tried to hold back as he usually did, worried about hurting her with his unrestrained strength.

But she was having none of it, her body moving over and above his in a way designed to make him completely insane. He groaned, tried to hold her still until he could regain some control.

"No," she gasped, struggling against his restraining hands. "I want it all. Give it to me."

Still he hesitated. "Lacey—"

Her inner muscles suddenly clenched around him so tightly that he saw stars, the movement like a velvet fist over and around his highly sensitized cock.

"Fuck, Lacey," he groaned before he could stop himself. He didn't say anything more, couldn't say anything, as he waited for her to do it again.

She did and the stars grew brighter in front of his eyes, spinning and turning in an unconstrained pattern unlike anything he'd seen before. He grew longer, bigger, heavier as emotions he'd never felt before ripped through him.

She belonged to him, and he would kill anyone or anything that tried to take her from him. She was his, and he would protect her with the last breath in his body.

His thrusts grew harder, less restrained, more animalistic, and she took them. Took him—in a way no one else ever had before or ever would again.

The need to come rose inside of him—urgent and intense, a painful ecstasy raking him with sugared claws. But even more intense was his need to make sure Lacey came first. Slipping a hand between their bodies, he stroked his thumb over her clit once, twice. Then again and again as he leaned down and took her nipple in his mouth, right through her sodden tube top.

She screamed and bucked against him. Because of his rough penetration, she was swollen and more sensitive than she had ever been before, and he felt fully every shiver of her body. It made him even crazier, until he was biting her, slamming into her, bruising her with the power of his need. Her sobs grew louder, more violent and finally—finally—he felt her inner contractions pulling at him. Milking him. Taking him somewhere he'd never been before. Finally he gave himself to her, flooding her with all that he had, all that he was, while he took all that she was inside him and sheltered her close to his soul.

When it was done, when the raging conflagration between the two of them had cooled to a reasonable level, Lacey fumbled her panties up her legs with unsteady hands. She didn't know whether it was the leftover desire that was making her shake, or if she was trembling because of what she'd done. All she knew was that the ramifications of what had happened tonight couldn't be denied.

"Hey, are you okay?" He grabbed her hand, but she jerked away.

How could she have done that? How could she have made love to him when she was so furious with him? How could she have enjoyed it so much, when he'd made love to her in an effort to dominate her rather than because he wanted her? When Curtis had done that, she'd always hated it. Always felt violated and angry and hurt.

But with Byron it had been wonderful—sexy, sizzling and erotic as hell. But what did that make her? When she had set out on her quest for self-discovery eighteen months ago, she'd sworn to herself that she would never be with another man who tried to bend her to his will. Who didn't want her to be herself. Who manhandled her.

And yet here she was, in love with a man who had just done all of those things. So the new question was, What was she going to do about it?

How could she have fallen for him and not seen the similarities to Curtis? Oh, Byron didn't fight dirty, didn't try to control her with words and pinches and little slaps the way Curtis had, but that only made his dominance all the more frightening. Byron didn't have to resort to petty threats to get his point across, to see that his will was enforced. All he had to do was smile in that unamused, implacable way of his and go forward, full speed ahead with no consideration or worry about what she wanted. What she needed.

As she stood with him in the rain, his warmth seeping through her, she realized that she had made a huge mistake. She wasn't ready for this—wasn't ready for him. Not by a long shot. She wasn't strong enough yet, mentally or emotionally.

Because when he looked at her with those smoldering eyes, all she really wanted to do was to give in to him. To let him have his way.

She shuddered as she realized she hadn't come nearly as far as she thought she had in the last year. Just because she'd kicked Curtis out, just because she'd been determined to rebuild her life one small step at a time, didn't mean she was ready to face off with another dominant male. Didn't mean she'd gained enough of herself back to risk losing it to a guy—no matter how sexy and charming he was.

No, she thought as she started backing away, *I'm better off on my own*. Better off fighting the loneliness and the desire than trying to resist the advances of a man hell-bent on controlling her.

She flew across the courtyard as fast as she could go, determined to reach the safety of her own apartment before Byron could catch up with her. It was stupid, childish, but she knew she couldn't fight him tonight. Knew, after that brutal and mind-numbing lovemaking they'd shared, that she was more likely to tell him everything than she was to tell him to go to hell. And that, considering the circumstances, was far from acceptable.

"Lacey, wait." She heard Byron's voice behind her, heard his footsteps as he pounded the pavement after her. But she was almost to her door, almost to freedom, and she wasn't giving that up for anyone. Not even Byron.

Especially not Byron.

Putting on one last burst of speed, she slammed into her apartment on the fly, shutting and locking the door behind her like the hounds of hell were on her heels.

Which they were, in a very real way. With her past rearing its ugly head—and her fantasies scattered around her feet in ruins—she needed time to regroup. Time to strengthen her defenses. Time to convince herself that her heart wasn't breaking wide open for the last time.

Chapter Twenty-one

Mr. Alexandrov?" Jim's obsequious voice drew Gregory from his contemplations of Lacey Adams' blog and her young, dumb and full-of-cum lover. A carpenter, for God's sake. She let a carpenter take her, let him put his hands all over her, like he had that right. Like they weren't dirty and calloused and far, far beneath her.

He slammed a fist down on the desk, ignoring Jim's startled look. She would pay for letting that laborer touch her, for letting him come inside her. What was wrong with her, with her self-esteem, that she would sell herself so cheaply? This carpenter wasn't the only man she could get—not by a long shot—so why would she choose *him*? He could give her nothing except sex, and surely that alone wasn't good enough for a woman like her.

Then again, judging from the way she looked as he fucked her, she really enjoyed the sex. Which was yet another bonus in his mind; he liked a lover who was as into physical pleasure as he was himself. It made things so much more interesting, especially when he introduced her to a few of his acquired tastes.

But what kind of man let his woman post sexually explicit fantasies for the whole world to see? Gregory reread the day's blog for what had to be the fifth time since he'd pulled up What a Girl Wants. Despite the ridiculous title, the blog was the sexiest thing he'd ever read, and reading it was getting to be the best part of his day.

Imagining Lacey spread out before him while he did all the things she described had become his favorite pastime; thinking up new ways to keep her satisfied became his greatest pleasure. When she was his, there was no way she'd keep writing that stupid blog. No way he'd allow it. No way she'd need to do it anyway.

Spinning away from the computer, he glanced down at the photos that littered his desk. Photos of Lacey looking content. Well pleasured. Satisfied by the day laborer and his pedestrian lovemaking.

Rage, shocking in its intensity, trembled through Gregory at the thought. He never let himself get angry, never let himself get upset. What was the point? All anger did was dull the thinking and increase the odds that one would make a mistake.

Gregory didn't make mistakes—in his business, there was no room for them. In the grand scheme of things, the occasional blunder might be excused. But if you made too many of them, you became weak. A liability. Incapable of handling your business. Therefore, it was better all around to just avoid making mistakes at all. Life expectancies were so much better that way.

"Mr. Alexandrov." Jim's voice intruded for the second time, and Gregory looked up, furious at the interruption. Now that he finally had Lacey's folder in front of him—filled with pictures and intimate details and conversations she'd had with her peers—he wanted nothing more than to be left alone with it. Needed nothing more than to read the file cover to cover and do his damnedest to figure out the best way to approach her. The best way to take her from her muscle-bound lover.

The best way to make her his.

Because if he had learned nothing else in this business, he'd learned to take—and, in turn, protect—what was his, at all costs. Men who didn't know that code or who didn't live by it were more than stupid. More than ignorant. They were careless, and in his mind, there was no bigger insult.

"Marina is here to see you. Again."

"Tell her to come back later." He never took his eyes off the file in front of him. "I don't have time to talk to her now."

"She insists, sir. Says—"

He slammed the file on the desk and stared at Jim with incredulous eyes. "She insists? Who is she to insist? I'll see her when I want to see her, and coming here, badgering me for money twice in three days, is not the way to get my attention!"

Cheeky little bitch. He'd cared about her for a while, had treated her well, and as such she thought it gave her rights to him that no one else had. And while that might have been true—once again, he took care of what was his—she was going to find out that any favor she curried from him had long since come to an end. Especially since she was working hard to make a nuisance of herself.

"She says it's not about the money. She says she heard something disturbing today—something about a redheaded writer who is new to the city."

His hand froze in midair, halfway to the folder. "Lacey? She knows something of Lacey?"

"I don't know," Jim said calmly. "But I thought it best to ask you before I sent her away."

"Yes, thank you. I would very much like to hear what Marina has to say about my little writer."

"I'll escort her right in."

"Yes, do that." Gregory waited until Jim had left the room before he shoved the folder containing information on Lacey into the top drawer of his desk. Marina might now be a junkie and a sometimes whore, but she'd been trained as a computer programmer. Her attention to detail was truly impressive, even when she was half drugged out of her mind.

The door opened again and in walked Jim, closely followed by Marina. He had schooled himself not to show shock at her appearance, but even so, it was

hard not to respond negatively. When she'd been with him, she'd been a beautiful woman. Tall, blond, curvaceous, she'd held his attention longer than any
woman had before her. He'd broken it off when he got bored, as he always did,
but had kept in touch because of a strange affection he had for her. He'd often
thought it was because she was so much like him—resilient, resourceful and
downright wicked when the situation called for it.

But looking at her now, he was hard-pressed to find the beautiful woman
he'd once shared so many intimate moments with. She was thinner than she had
been even a week before—which was saying something, as it had been months
since he'd seen a curve on that long body—and was also a lot more strung-out.
Dressed as she was—in a tank top and short-shorts—he could see the track lines
on the inside of her arm. She had a sore—red and oozing—on the left arm that
looked like an infected injection site.

"Marina, love." He kept his voice warm, even though he was completely disgusted by her appearance. But he knew just how twisted Marina was—it was what
had attracted him to her in the first place years ago—and the more eager he was
for the information she had, the longer it would take to get it out of her.

"Gregory." Even her voice was different—lower, raspier, as if she was severely
dehydrated. Or had been downing vodka like a Russian sailor.

Normally he would have extended a hand to her, but frankly, he was afraid
of catching something. So he simply nodded to the chair across the desk from
him and said, "Sit, please. Can I have Jim get you something to drink?"

"Vodka on the rocks." She pulled out a cigarette and lit it, her hands shaking
like she was in the middle of a particularly bad bout of the DTs. But the glazed
look in her eyes told a different story; she was on the downside of a pretty good
high. Years of selling the stuff—and watching his girls use it—had made him somewhat of an expert.

He nodded toward Jim, who filled a glass from the bar in the side of the
room and handed it to her before discreetly leaving them alone together.

"So, Marina, what can I do for you? I'm not used to having the pleasure of
your company twice in one week."

She knew him well enough to recognize the threat in the cultured tone, but was either too high to care or thought she had something so good that he would overlook his annoyance. All she said was, "I knew you'd want to hear this right away."

"Really?" He steepled his hands in front of him and did his best to look uninterested—which he would have been, if she hadn't mentioned to Jim that she had info on a small redheaded writer. The promise in that statement had him chomping at the bit, but he refused to give her the satisfaction of knowing it.

"There's a reporter in town," she said, after taking another shaky drag on her cigarette. "And she's investigating Crescent City Escort Service. Says she wants to know what happened to some of the girls who worked for them, and who either disappeared or turned up dead."

Shock stiffened his spine, had him dying to shove his fist into Marina's face. Surely she knew something of what had made Lacey suspicious. Surely she wasn't here just to deliver the nerve-racking news. Surely she knew more.

"Really? And where did you hear this?"

"She was meeting with Derek earlier today—down off of Magazine. He told her to leave stuff alone, and she told him she couldn't stand not knowing what had happened to all the girls who'd ended up escorts against their will."

Beneath the desk, his hand clenched as he fought desperately to remain calm. Lacey, investigating the disappearance of girls from his escort service for a book? It couldn't be.

And yet how many true-crime writers were there in New Orleans with red hair and a killer smile? He could think of only one, and he'd lived in this shithole his whole life.

"Derek? Who's Derek?"

"You know, the black guy who used to drive the girls around. He hasn't worked since everyone got busted, but he's a good guy. Probably too good, if he's telling tales to some reporter chick who plans on putting everything in her book or on the Internet."

He had some vague recollection of the man, but nothing really concrete.

Then again, how could he actually be expected to know all of his employees? There were just too many of them.

Crossing to the corner bar, he poured himself a double shot of Stoli, then drank it in three slow, measured sips. It wouldn't do to show his consternation or concern.

"And he knows this true-crime writer? This redhead you were talking about?"

Too high to sense the danger in his tone, she shrugged. "I guess. At first I thought she was on the stroll, you know, but then I heard them arguing about some dead girl."

His fingers tightened reflexively on the glass as he debated pouring another shot. Normally, he would forgo it—once again, it never paid to show weakness—but in this case, he figured it was okay. Marina was so high she probably wouldn't notice if he guzzled the entire bottle—without benefit of a glass.

"What dead girl were they talking about, Marina? Can you be a little more specific?"

"I don't know. Do you know how many fucking dead girls show up in this city? Some girl who got whacked by a junkie a couple years back, I think. Derek knew her and so did the redhead. I think she was related or something.

"Anyway, Derek got a little rough with the slut—"

"What slut?"

She rolled her eyes, then said, in a voice that implied she was talking to a child, "You know, the redhead. Derek shook her hard enough to leave a few bruises, I bet. And then some hot blond guy came rushing up. He broke up the whole thing."

Yes, the redhead in question was definitely Lacey, and the blond, her erstwhile lover. It was an interesting turn of events, but not one that was particularly worrisome. At least not yet.

"Did they say anything else?"

The look she shot him was sly. "Maybe."

He let a few, silent seconds pass, then pulled out his money clip. Laid two hundred-dollar bills in front of Marina and watched her mouth all but water.

"The redhead said she had to find out what happened to some dead girl, and how the escort service was connected. That she was writing a book about it, but that it was about more than that now." She snapped her fingers suddenly. "I guess she'd already talked to Veronique, but V didn't give anything up."

A skitter of alarm worked its way down his spine, as he remembered Lacey standing outside his club, staring at the flyer on the light pole like she'd seen a ghost. Was that the girl she was talking about? If she'd managed to track down Veronique and the chauffeur, she obviously knew what she was doing.

Which still wouldn't have worried him; he was covered all the way up the line, with enough dummy corporations between him and the various escort services he owned that it would take a miracle for her to find him.

But the way she had been looking at the photos on his wall—the way she had ripped that flyer off the post outside—had convinced him she was connecting dots he hadn't thought could be connected. He'd tried to arrange a meeting with Lacey the other night, but Jim had sent an imbecile to collect her. He'd let it go; hadn't wanted to spook her. But if even half of what Marina said was true, he couldn't wait any longer to meet his little redhead—and bring her into the fold, so to speak.

"Did anything else happen?" He turned to Marina with a smooth smile. "Anything you might have forgotten to tell me."

She shrugged. "Not really. Unless you count the fight she got into with the guy who butted in with Derek. They went at it pretty hot and heavy—"

Well, that sounded promising. Maybe Lacey's tastes were growing more refined. If she had no emotional entanglements, it would make things easier—

"And then he threw her in his truck and took off." She laughed, the sound like nails scraping down a chalkboard. "It doesn't take a genius to know what happened when he got her alone."

At her words, his fingers clenched so tightly on the glass in his hand that he feared he was going to break the crystal. Deciding it was better to be safe than sorry, Gregory placed the delicate glass on the bar and walked back to his desk.

Pulling open the bottom drawer of his desk, he yanked out a syringe, a spoon and a bag of the really pure stuff he usually kept for special visitors.

Her eyes lit up at the sight, like he knew they would. "Thank you so much for coming to me with this information," he said, as he sprinkled some of the heroin onto the spoon. "Can I offer you a reward?"

She watched his hands, mesmerized by the sight of the white powder. Thrilled—he could tell—by the thought of shooting such good stuff into her collapsing veins.

He flicked his solid-gold lighter on, ran the flame under the spoon until the powder was liquid and bubbling. Then he filled the syringe.

"Here, Marina. Let me help you with this."

She held out her arm, and after a minute or two, he managed to find a vein he could use. He watched her eyes as he injected her, watched the pleasure take her. Then stood and poured himself one more drink.

He had just finished it when her eyes rolled back in her head. Without glancing in her direction—junkies were so unattractive, after all—he walked out of his office, shutting the door behind him. Jim was waiting in the next room, and Gregory nodded to the closed office door.

"Give her a few minutes, and then take out the trash. I don't care what you do with her, but I want her gone by the time I get back. And I don't want to see her again." He turned away, then stopped when he was halfway out the door. "Oh, and I think it's time for us to move on that other project we had going on. Trouble seems to be brewing."

"Of course, sir."

Byron stared after Lacey for long seconds, shock ricocheting through his body, before he recovered enough to stuff himself back into his jeans.

He started after her as soon as he pulled up his zipper, but those few precious seconds cost him, and cost him big. He trailed Lacey into the building, but her small head start afforded her the extra time she needed to get her key in the lock.

By the time he caught up with her, she was disappearing into her apartment, her long, red hair flying behind her.

"Lacey!" he pounded on the door with a closed fist. "Open up."

There was no answer, and the shock he'd felt at watching her run started to give way to anger. What the hell had he done that was so bad, she felt the need to run away from him? And why couldn't she be bothered to talk to him, instead of hiding in her apartment like a thirteen-year-old in the middle of a tantrum?

He wasn't used to this. When his girlfriends in Manhattan had a problem with him, they were more than willing to tell him exactly what he'd done to piss them off. And running sure as hell had never occurred to any of those women. They'd rather be boiled in oil.

So what the hell was wrong with Lacey? She was no wallflower who couldn't speak her mind. Yes, they'd had an argument, but he'd pretty much figured the amazing sex that had come after it had negated many of the harsh things they'd said to each other.

His anger ratcheted up a few notches at the thought, though he didn't know what pissed him off more: the fact that she'd had sex with him and made him think everything was okay, or the fact that she'd jumped out of a moving vehicle to get away from him without so much as a fuck-you to his face.

The thought had him redoubling his efforts—had him pounding harder on the door even as he felt like an idiot for doing it.

"Goddamn it, Lacey. Let me in. I'm not going away until you talk to me."

Still nothing, but if he was quiet, he could hear her moving around. "I'm going to knock this door down, Lacey. I'm not kidding. You're acting like a child. If you're upset—"

The door flew open before he could finish the sentence. Lacey stood there looking very much like a cross between an avenging angel and a gypsy. She'd changed out of the skimpy outfit she'd been wearing on the street earlier and into a long white skirt and tank top that showed off her light golden tan.

Before he could say anything or demand to know what the hell had gotten into her, she let him have it with both barrels. "I am *not* a child, and I really don't appreciate you treating me as if I am one. Especially since you have the intelligence level and sensitivity of a rabid goat."

Determination alone kept his jaw from dropping open at her blatant attack. Grinding his teeth together, he stared at her incredulously before finally getting it together enough to speak. "Then stop acting like a child. What adult actually runs away instead of having a fucking conversation?"

"How exactly am I supposed to talk to you?" she demanded, stepping back from the door to let him in. "Every time I try to say something to you, you distract me with sex."

"You didn't exactly seem to mind while it was happening."

She rolled her eyes. "Well, that's a typical male answer." She looked down her pert little nose at him, and it turned him on all over again, despite the fury coursing through him.

"Well, here's a news flash, baby. I'm a fairly typical kind of guy."

"Not that typical—if you were, I wouldn't be having this problem."

Frustrated, he shoved a rough hand through his hair. "And what problem is that?"

"You make me—" Her voice broke, and she swallowed nervously before starting again. "You make me forget that this is only supposed to be casual."

His cock hardened at her words, even as his heart melted. "I didn't realize that casual was still the arrangement. I thought we were moving beyond that."

"Oh, come on, Byron. We're glorified fuck buddies. We decided that at the beginning."

"You decided. You never gave me a choice in the matter. I went along with it because I figured having fantastic sex with you was better than having nothing at all. But that doesn't mean I don't want more."

"Yeah, right." The look she shot him was full of disbelief. "It's not like we've done much else. I mean, how much more do you know about me, besides that I'm flexible as hell and like to fuck? Oh yeah, and that I'm easy to control?"

Once again he was speechless. There was so much to take issue with in her statement that he didn't know where to start. With her ridiculous accusations that he didn't know anything about her, or the fact that she thought he wanted to control her?

Or maybe he should just focus on the fact that she wasn't happy with the knowledge that their relationship was getting more serious?

Not wanting to make things any worse than they already were, he took a few seconds to sort out his feelings. He was angry; he knew that. But underneath the anger was a very real disappointment. Not to mention a healthy dose of hurt and embarrassment. He'd been falling in love with her, and she'd been hell-bent on stopping herself from falling for him.

Maybe he should have figured it out—after all, she'd continued to post those damn fantasies, a surefire sign that he wasn't satisfying her. Only he'd been too stupid to believe it. He'd been sure that if he gave her a little time, she would realize she didn't need the blog anymore.

He was more of an idiot than he'd thought.

How could he have been so stupid? He knew how to treat a woman. Knew how to wine and dine her with the best of them. And yet the only time he'd taken Lacey out, they'd ended up in a strip joint. He hadn't cooked her dinner or breakfast. Hadn't done anything besides—and she was dead-on when she'd hurled the accusation at him—fuck her.

But he hadn't meant to overlook that stuff. He'd been trying to give her more, trying to give her everything she wanted and needed. He'd thought by helping her live out her fantasies—one sexy scenario at a time—that she'd understand. That she'd realize he was willing to do whatever it took to make her happy. By helping her with her work, he'd thought he was being supportive.

But he'd screwed up. She thought the sex was all that mattered to him. He almost laughed at the thought. He wanted her for so many things that it was hard to imagine she'd gotten it so very wrong. Yes, he loved having sex with her—he'd have to be insane not to—but at the same time he just loved being with her.

He loved how her eyes lit up when she was talking about something that mattered to her, loved how they turned dark as a trans-Atlantic storm when she was upset. Truth be told, he loved everything about her, and it bothered him a great deal that she thought he took her for granted. Worse, that she thought he didn't care about her.

"Lacey, I'm sorry I didn't do a better job of taking care of you. I—"

"That's just it: I don't want you to take care of me. I can take care of myself."

Warning bells went off in his head, but he ignored them as he tried to feel his way around his lover's volatile mood. "All right. Then I'm sorry I didn't tell you that my expectations for this relationship had changed—I should have. But things have been so intense between us—surely you know I care about you."

"*I* don't want you to care about me, and I sure as hell don't want to care about you. I'm not looking for all this sexual intensity and angst. I just want to have a little fun."

Her words hit him like an earthquake, shaking him up and bringing up insecurities he'd spent years trying to bury.

What the hell was so fucking wrong with him that no one he loved ever loved him back?

Pushing the question—and the hurt that came with it—to the back of his mind, he said, "So, let me get this straight: You ran away like I had the plague because you *don't* want to get serious?"

"No!"

"Then what? Help me out here, Lacey, because I'm pretty damn confused."

"I want—" She stopped.

"What do you want?"

"I don't want to get emotionally involved. I don't want to have to think about anything but having a good time when we're together. I don't want to lose control." There were tears in her eyes, but he was too angry—and too hurt—to pay attention.

"Is that why you write those fantasies and post them on the Internet? So you can stay in control? Or so you can control hundreds—thousands—of men you've never even met?"

She froze, her eyes going wide at his words. But he was too far gone to care. "That's what this is all about, isn't it, sweetheart? You want power, and the only way you think you can get it is by staying in control."

"How do you know about my blog?" she whispered. "Nobody knows about it."

"Everybody knows about it. How many hits do you get a day—a hundred? A thousand? Ten thousand, maybe?"

"That's not what I meant. Nobody's supposed to know it's me!"

"Why not?" He advanced on her. "Why isn't anyone supposed to know what you want? You hide that part of yourself from everyone—even your lovers. Why?"

"I don't want to talk about this." She was backing up, eyes wide, hand held out in front of her.

"Of course you don't. You're much better on the offensive, aren't you, sweetheart? Telling what you don't want. Telling what you don't like. God forbid anyone should look close enough to figure out what it is you really do want. Because you don't have a clue, do you?"

Lacey bit her lip hard in an effort to keep her tears from falling. It worked, barely, but she didn't know how long she could keep her emotions in check. Not with Byron stripping her raw, battering away her defenses with each well-placed accusation.

"It's not like that!"

"Then what is it like? Tell me—because from the second I found out that you were the one writing those fantasies, I wanted to know *why*. Why would a beautiful woman like you—who could have any man she wants—resort to living vicariously through her fantasies? Why would you choose fake emotions, fake encounters, over real ones?"

He laughed bitterly. "Of course, that's not exactly what happens, is it? You're one of those have-your-cake-and-eat-it-too kind of girls, aren't you? The kind who wants a lover dancing to her tune while she keeps hundreds of other men on a string."

"That's not true!"

"Isn't it?" His lips twisted. "Then tell me, please, what's it all about?"

Lacey started to answer, but his words were tearing her to ribbons. She wasn't the way he was accusing her of being. Dangling a bunch of men on a string, watching them dance over her thoughts and desires, even as she gave her body to another man. One she didn't want to share any part of herself with. One she trusted with her body but not with her emotions.

"You don't understand."

"So make me understand." He raised one brow sardonically. "If you can."

"How long have you known about the fantasies?"

He shrugged. "Long enough."

Her stomach twisted and turned. "Have you known all along?"

"Does it matter?"

"No. I don't know." She glanced away, refused to look at him. "My whole life, I've been a good little girl. Always doing what I'm supposed to, never asking the hard questions except at work, never causing any trouble for anyone. Not my parents, not my friends, not my lover."

"I don't know about that—I think you've given your lover plenty of trouble."

"Not you." His face turned pale, and she realized in an instant how he must have interpreted her words. "I mean, not now. You're my only lover now, but a couple years ago, there was this guy . . ." Her voice trailed off.

"Ah yes. The ubiquitous other guy. The one the good guys always have to pay for." He took a step closer to her, but this time it was about comfort instead of control. Still, she shrugged him off. She'd never get through this if he was touching her—she might not even get through it with him across the room.

"Anyway, he was smart, successful, everyone loved him. My friends, my parents, everyone."

Something flickered in Byron's eyes and his jaw tightened, but he didn't say anything. She stared at him for a minute, waiting, but when he continued to regard her in silence, she continued. "Curtis was a real charmer—and very sexually magnetic. Like you."

His eyebrows rose at her description of him, but he didn't interrupt.

"But he was different in private. Meaner. More controlling. He kept up a great face outside, but the second we were alone, it was his way, no exceptions. I didn't even get the highway option, and believe me, after a few months, I would have begged for it.

"At first I told myself it was no big deal. He never really hurt me—just little pinches, some hair pulling when I put up a fuss. Everyone else loved him, so I figured it was my fault. Especially when he kept telling me that it was. But then—" She paused, worked up the nerve to look at Byron. He was so rigid he might be confused for a statue, if he wasn't wearing clothes. "I'm sorry. You don't want to hear about this."

"Yes, I do."

She stared at him for long seconds, at his rigidly working jaw and clenched fists. "Anyway, same old story. He started to bitch about my job, my friends, everything. He didn't want me to go out without him. And at the same time he worked on my self-esteem, convinced me that I was nothing without him. For a long time, I believed him. Then my dad died and my mom needed me. Curtis didn't want me to go, didn't want me to attend my own father's funeral. Can you imagine? For the first time in a long time, I didn't care. I just walked out. And with every step I took away from him, I remembered who I was. Remembered what I wanted from my life."

She shrugged. "I've spent the last eighteen months trying to figure out who I am."

"And have you succeeded?"

"I thought I had. And then I met you, and my head got all messed up again. I don't want to lose myself again. If I give in to you, I don't think I'll ever make it back."

"What about being involved with me makes you think that you'll lose yourself?"

"You're so strong, so in control all the time. You want to rule me, and I don't want to be ruled. Not now. Not ever again."

"Lacey, that's absurd. I have never tried to rule you."

"You do it in bed all the time, but that never really bothered me. Today, though, you did it."

He stared at her blankly. "What does that mean? When?"

"On the street. With Derek. You dragged me away like I was a dog; threw me in your truck like I was something you owned."

"That's ridiculous."

"Don't tell me my feelings are ridiculous!" He looked like he wanted to argue some more, but she walked to her front door and opened it. "I want you to leave now."

"You don't mean that." He reached for her, but she evaded him.

"I do mean it."

"Lacey."

"Go, Byron."

He stared at her for long seconds, but then finally turned and left—like she'd known he would all along.

Chapter Twenty-two

Byron slammed into his apartment, fury and anger twisting inside him as he headed straight for the refrigerator and a cold beer.

What the hell just happened? he wondered as he popped the top of the bottle and drank half the beer in one swallow. How the fuck had they gone from making love in the shower this morning to that debacle of a scene in Lacey's apartment? More important, what the hell was he going to do about it?

She'd asked him to leave her apartment like he was some kind of animal—some kind of monster. Like he couldn't be trusted around her, or something. *What had he done that was so bad?* he wondered for what had to be the fiftieth time.

He'd tried to replay in his head the scene that had happened down the street from his workshop, but most of it was a red haze. He remembered seeing that bastard shaking Lacey, remembered getting in the middle of the two of them, remembered pulling her away, but much of the rest—right up until he'd ripped Lacey's panties down her legs and thrust inside her—was blurry.

Had he hurt her somehow, in the midst of all that fury? Done something to scare her? Except she hadn't seemed scared; she'd seemed as irritated and unsettled as he had been. And up until a half hour ago, he would have sworn that she had given as good as she'd gotten.

Control? He downed the rest of the beer and then reached for a second one. She thought he wanted to control her, thought he would control her. What a fucking crock that was. She'd obviously underestimated him—and herself. There was nothing he would change about her, nothing he wanted to control. And then to find out she was comparing him—unfavorably—to that jackass she'd been with before? He couldn't ever remember being more pissed off.

When she'd been telling him about the guy, he'd wanted nothing better than to find him and rip his fucking head off. To teach him some manners. To explain in words of one syllable that there was a right way and a wrong way to treat a lady, and that his way had been way fucking wrong. The idea of Lacey at the mercy of some prick infuriated him. The idea that he'd ripped apart her self-esteem like a fucking Weedwhacker, until she didn't know where to turn, was even worse. Guys like that didn't deserve the fucking title.

And she thought he was like this guy. Like fucking Curtis, with his little dick and his fucked-up power plays? How was that possible?

A little of the hurt he'd been doing his damnedest to suppress leaked through at the thought. Maybe he shouldn't take it personally, maybe he should try harder to see it from her point of view, but it was difficult when she'd compared him to a guy who was the antithesis of everything he respected.

When the fuck was this nightmare going to end? When the hell was somebody going to see him for who he was instead of what they expected to see? His whole fucking life his father had told him he was a failure, that he wasn't good enough, that he'd never measure up. He'd worked his ass off to prove to the old man that he was wrong, had nearly worked himself into an early grave.

And when he'd explained to his dad—the doctor—about his stress levels and insomnia and everything else that went hand in hand with the life, the guy had called him a pussy. Told him he needed to toughen the fuck up.

Like thirty-two years with that man wouldn't toughen up a fucking marshmallow.

Eventually, he'd told his father to screw off and had moved down here. Had started a new life for himself. Had thought he was doing pretty damn good—right up until Lacey had coldcocked him with her accusations. Suddenly, he was right back where he'd started, trying to prove himself to someone who had no desire to see him succeed.

And for what? Her approval? Her body? Her love? Setting his beer down with a resounding thud, he crossed to the balcony. Stripped off his wet clothes and pulled on a pair of ratty old jeans. Threw open the door and stepped outside.

The rain had stopped and the picturesque courtyard with its fountain and bouquets of flowers and wrought-iron benches was back to its normal tranquillity.

He let his eyes wander to Lacey's apartment. There was a light on in her bedroom, and if he looked hard enough, he was almost certain he could see her silhouette against her curtains. But that made him feel too much like the perverted bastard she'd accused him of being—not to mention took him right back to where they'd been a week ago—so he forced himself to look away.

He was so goddamned tired of living down to someone else's expectations of him, so tired of trying to prove himself to people who expected him to fail. Expected him to be an asshole. Expected him to be unlovable.

And isn't this just a fucking righteous pity party? he asked himself with a snarl as he went back in to get his beer. Absolutely pathetic to be sitting here, waiting for a woman who thought he was a complete and total loser.

His anger didn't stop him from grabbing his beer and heading back to the balcony, any more than it kept him from willing Lacey to come out. To look for him as he was looking for her. But her balcony remained quiet, the only movement in the courtyard that of the owl who made his home in the big tree near the gate.

He didn't know how long he sat out on the balcony, watching, waiting for Lacey to come out. When he was about to give up, to go back into his apartment and say to hell with women, her bedroom light flickered out. Great; so she was going to get a good night's sleep while he was torturing himself with everything he'd done wrong. Wasn't that just—

A scream pierced the air—one high-pitched, terrified shriek that had his blood pumping and his adrenaline soaring. He recognized it instinctively as Lacey's, though he'd never heard her yell like that before, as if she had just found a very big, very hairy, fanged monster in her closet.

Or a sex trader.

The thought had his blood running cold, and he wasted precious seconds trying to see what was happening inside her apartment. But it was pitch-black and he couldn't see a damn thing. By the time it registered that Lacey always—always—had a small light burning, he was already moving toward the door.

He took the stairs three at a time, his heart pounding with a fear he had never felt before in his thirty-four years. If he didn't get to her in time, if those bastards took her, he might never find her. She could end up like—

He cut himself off in midthought, pushing himself to run harder, faster. But by the time he got to Lacey's apartment, it was empty, the door gaping wide open in accusation.

Acting on instinct alone, he raced down the stairs, hitting the ground running as he jumped from the landing halfway down the flight of steps. But again he was too late; by the time he got to the small parking lot behind the building, he saw a flash of red hair as Lacey was loaded into a black SUV.

"Hey!" He ran screaming across the pavement, barely noticing the heat of the asphalt on his bare feet as he tried desperately to reach her in time, knowing even as he ran flat-out that he didn't have a chance.

The SUV careened out of the lot and sped down Burgundy. His keys were in his apartment, so he ran after it for five blocks, memorizing the license plate when he was close and then just trying to keep the vehicle in sight as it got farther and farther from him. It made a screeching right onto Canal Street, and though by that time he knew it was hopeless, he kept running, praying for a miracle. For something, anything to stop them.

But when he made it to the corner of Canal, which was bustling on the busy Friday night, the SUV had blended into the hundreds of other SUVs on the street, and Lacey was gone.

Fuck, fuck, fuck. He stopped dead, bracing his hands on his knees as he dragged air into his starving lungs. Panic was a living, breathing animal inside him, raking him with razor-sharp claws as he tried desperately to think. To figure out what to do.

He reached for his cell phone, only to realize he didn't have it with him. He didn't have anything—no shirt, no shoes, no wallet, no phone. Nothing. Jesus Christ, Lacey was totally screwed.

There were people on the street, and he asked to borrow a cell phone, but they all looked at him like he was crazy and gave him a wide berth. Not that he blamed them—he probably looked as homicidal as he felt.

Crossing Burgundy at a jog, he swept into the Ritz-Carlton on the corner and made a beeline for the courtesy phone. A security guard tried to intercept him, but he shrugged him off as he dialed 911.

As soon as the operator answered, he said, "A woman's just been abducted. She's in a black Ford Expedition heading north on Canal Street, license plate 6V7 8A9. Her name is Lacey Adams. Red hair, green eyes, five foot two inches, one hundred and five pounds." He hung up the phone without giving the operator any more information—at this point, he didn't know who the hell he could trust in the NOPD, so he figured the less info they had, the better. At the same time, he wanted them looking for Lacey. Looking for those bastards who had taken her.

Before the security guards could say anything to him—or hopefully remember anything about him but his shirtless state—he took off. The cops would be here in minutes, and he was pretty damn conspicuous as he was.

Booking it back to his apartment, Byron ignored the cuts and bruises on the bottoms of his feet as his mind circled around itself. Again and again, he tried to figure out how to get Lacey back. Again and again, he came up blank.

All he knew was that he had to act quickly. If he'd learned anything these last couple of days, it was that these guys were experts at making girls disappear, and disappear fast. He refused to let that happen to Lacey.

It didn't matter what he had to do, or who he had to take on; he *would* find her. And when he did, the men who had her were going to pay for hurting her.

Lacey came to slowly, unsure of where she was. Her head was throbbing, her stomach rolling and her mouth tasted so bad she was afraid something had crawled in there and died while she was asleep.

Did she have too much to drink? She remembered pouring herself a glass of wine after her fight with Byron, but one glass of wine wasn't enough to make her feel like her entire head was going to explode. Or at least, it never had been before.

Maybe it was the crying jag or the fight or the fact that she'd never been so miserable in her life. She didn't know, and at the moment, as the room spun around her, she didn't particularly care. She just wanted it to stop.

With a low groan, she reached for her nightstand in the hopes of turning off her bedside lamp before she opened her eyes; the way she was feeling, the first glimpse of the light would send gigantic spikes of pain through her head.

"Hello, Lacey." She froze at the unfamiliar voice. Could she possibly have gotten so drunk the night before that she'd gone out and picked up a guy she had no memory of? Muttering a prayer that that wasn't the case, she cautiously opened her eyes.

The first thing that registered was that she'd been dead-on about the spikes. The second thing that hit her was that she wasn't in her room. And the third realization she had—and it was a big one—was that she was in serious trouble.

Adrenaline surged through her, and she jerked up in the bed. But as soon as she did, her stomach turned and she was desperately afraid that she was going to puke.

"Take it slow," the low, lightly accented voice told her. She struggled for a minute to place the accent, but she was too disoriented to figure it out.

Taking a deep breath, and with a sinking feeling in the pit of her stomach, she gingerly turned her head toward the voice. Her first glimpse of the man's face made panic race through her. She recognized him, remembered his face, though she wasn't sure from where.

Wherever she knew him from, she knew it wasn't good. The instinctive adrenaline rush that had hit her as soon as she saw him told her that much. "Where am I?" she demanded.

"At one of my houses. I thought it would be more comfortable for you than the warehouse."

"Warehouse? What warehouse? What do you mean?"

"Come on, now, Lacey, don't play coy. I know you've been investigating me for quite some time. I thought I would speed up the process a little. Give you the answers you've been looking for."

His words had her heart pumping even faster, had the bile in her stomach boiling into her throat as she recognized him. He was the man she'd seen last week—after she'd had her meeting with Veronique. The one who had been watching her from the top floor of Seductions.

Oh, fuck. Dismay slammed through her, followed quickly by a shot of terror that had a scream rising in her throat. She was totally screwed, and more than smart enough to know it. Too bad she hadn't been smart enough to figure out that the guy she was looking for had been in front of her all along.

"What do you want with me?" She tried to keep the quiver from her voice, but from the pleased look on his face she knew she'd failed.

"Come on, *limaya moya*," he murmured in Russian as he lit a cigarette with a fancy lighter. "Let's not play these games. I think you know exactly what I want you for. You'll be a nice change of pace from the teenagers I usually get around here."

He ran a finger up her arm, and it was all she could do not to shudder in revulsion. "So, what do you say? I promise I'll take much better care of you than that laborer you normally let touch you."

"Do I have a choice?" Her head was spinning, every part of her screaming in horror at the predicament she'd landed in. But the drugs were still in her system, confusing her. Making her weak.

"Of course. There's always a choice, Lacey. In this case, your choice is me, or ending up like all those other girls—a whore in some brothel until you piss someone off and end up dead. Or you OD and end up dead. Or—"

His alternatives were just making her sicker, which, of course, was exactly what he intended. "I think I understand."

"I thought you might—you seem like a smart girl."

He smiled smugly as he spoke, his voice charming, intelligent and absolutely, positively remorseless. The combination was more chilling than anything she had run across in eight years of writing true crime.

Think, Lacey, she told herself. There had to be something she could do, some way she could get out of this. Some way she could escape. But she was too sick, too disoriented, too petrified to do anything but panic.

She wasn't ready to die—and certainly not like this. Tied to a bed, forced to endure being raped and drugged and brutalized. She wanted to scream, to rage, but some instinct she hadn't known existed warned her that to do either would only make things worse.

"So what's it going to be?" His hand ran over her shoulder, down her arm, before cupping her breast. His thumb flicked against her nipple, and she had to bite the inside of her lip to keep from crying out.

She itched to hit him, to claw the smug look from his face with her fingernails. But with the drugs in her system, she didn't have the strength. Better to wait until she had her strength and a snowball's chance in hell to escape.

"You're not fighting me," he said as he massaged her breast a little harder. "Is it because you like that?"

She hated it, hated him, and didn't know how much longer she could hold it in.

Pictures of Anne Marie danced in her head, and pictures of the other girls who had been killed by this monster. She knew if she had any chance of surviving, she had to put up a good front.

But when he ripped open the buttons on the front of her tank, she cried out. She couldn't help herself. Then wanted to die when she realized her fear excited him.

"*Ti tak Aya kras Ivaya*, Lacey. You have lovely breasts for such a small woman. Very full. And your nipples are gorgeous." He reached down and roughly squeezed one between his thumb and index finger, and in that moment, she knew she was going to be sick.

She looked around desperately for something, anything, to throw up in. Her captor must have figured out her distress, because he shoved a small bowl on the floor beside the bed before crossing the room to stand as far away from her as he could.

"That's the drugs," he said with distaste. "It happens to everyone. They should be out of your system by tomorrow, and then you'll be feeling better." He nodded to the nightstand. "There's water there, if you want to wash your mouth."

"Thank you." For a moment she thought she was going to choke on the words, when what she really wanted to do was tell him to go to hell. To beg and plead for him to let her go. To tell him what a vile bastard she thought he was. But none of those things would endear her to him, and she had told herself that she would have a better chance of escape if he thought he had her cowed.

"You're welcome." His voice was low, pleased. "You have impeccable manners."

Too bad she couldn't say the same for him. "Thank you," she repeated through teeth clenched so hard, she was afraid she might crack one in half.

"Still, with that red hair, I expected a little more fire. Hmm." He shrugged. "Maybe tomorrow, when you are feeling better."

She nodded, but wasn't sure how much fire she had left. She was terrified. The images of the girls who had gone missing, only to turn up dead, ran through her head in a brutally graphic montage. She wanted to fight him, wanted to do whatever it took to escape. But this was real life, not fiction, and she had never had call to fight someone in her life.

As her captor left the room, she gave in to the despair whipping through her. Violent sobs shook her body as she wondered how she was going to get out of this.

The sick feeling in the pit of her stomach warned her that she didn't have a chance in hell.

Chapter Twenty-three

Byron paid the ten-dollar cover charge to get into the strip club, ignoring his jangling nerves as he did so. Coming here was a long shot—he knew that—but it was the best chance he had of finding Lacey.

He'd spent the morning poring over the evidence she had left at his apartment, speaking to the police who had been assigned to Lacey's case after his frantic phone call the night before, and generally trying to figure out how to find her. He'd even gone down to the area around his workshop and asked for Derek, the guy she'd been talking to when they had had their fight. But no one he'd spoken to had been willing to help him. Not that he was surprised; they could barely help themselves.

It hadn't stopped him from trying, though. He'd talked to everyone he could find working the streets on the seedy side of town, had called every escort service in the yellow pages and hassled them. So far he hadn't had any luck, and it tormented him that she'd been in these bastards' hands for twenty-four hours now. God only knew what they'd done to her.

His hands shook at the thought, and he shoved them in his pockets as he looked for a place to sit. Finally settling on a spot at the bar that surrounded the stage—better for him to watch and be watched—he ordered a stiff drink that he had absolutely no intention of drinking. If things worked out here the way he planned, he'd need all his wits about him.

As soon as his drink was delivered, he took a quick sip, in case the bartender was watching, and then dumped the rest of it in the abandoned beer mug beside him. He ordered another one and did the same thing. Then another one, until it was entirely plausible that he was drunk.

"Hey, bartender," he yelled loudly, so that he could be heard over the music. "You're watering down my drinks."

The man's eyebrows hit his forehead like an exclamation point. "Excuse me, sir? Is there a problem?"

"Yes, there is. And I want to see your manager. I'm paying ten bucks a drink here, and I'm getting nothing but flavored fucking water."

"I'm sorry. Let you get me another one."

Byron knocked the glass out of his hand. "I don't want another one. I want to see your fucking manager."

"He isn't around right now. But if you'll let me—"

"No! I don't want another one of these fucked-up drinks." He reached out and swept a hand over the bar, knocking over a couple more drinks as he did so.

"Hey, man! That's not cool!" The guy next to him, who had been watching the show, jumped up as his drink hit his crotch. "I ought to kick your ass!"

"All right, let's go."

"No one's going to be fighting, not in my establishment." Byron froze at the smooth, cultured voice that sounded behind him. Turning, still pretending to be inebriated, he stared at a large man in a suit, who was flanked by two hugely muscled guys. One of them he recognized from the other night. The other was brand-new to him.

"Now, if you would like to come with me, I'll be happy to refund your money, with the understanding that you take your patronage elsewhere. You are no longer welcome here."

The man escorted him to the door, where he handed him thirty dollars. "Ivan, see this man out, if you please. And impress upon him the fact that we don't want to see him in here again."

"Sure thing, Jim."

Byron didn't like the sound of Jim's instructions, and as Ivan and his no-neck buddy took him to the back alley, he knew his instincts had been right on. Expecting the beat-down of his life, he was pleasantly surprised when all he got was a meaty fist to the gut and another, less couth, warning.

"Stay the fuck out of this bar. The next time I see you I'll rip your balls off and feed them to you. We clear?"

Byron was too busy trying to catch his breath to answer. But he'd gotten what he'd come for; he now knew who the guy in charge was, and if he had to, he would hang around the bar all fucking night, waiting for him to leave. Praying that when he did, the guy would take him straight to Lacey.

Settling into the back of the alley, his truck parked right around the corner, he waited in the dark for the bastard to come out. About forty-five minutes later—earlier than he'd expected—his patience was rewarded. The guy in the suit—Jim, the bouncer had called him—strolled into the alley from the club's back door and climbed into one of the black BMWs that were parked in the alley.

Byron watched him leave, then ran for his truck and started to follow him. He could only hope this worked, hope that the guy wasn't knocking off early for the night but instead was going to meet someone. Even if it wasn't the right place, Byron was willing to follow this bastard all over the fucking city if it meant he had a shot at finding Lacey.

The guy's first stop was another strip club a couple blocks up the Quarter. He stayed there for about half an hour or so, then climbed back into his car and made a quick U-turn, heading toward uptown.

When he stopped his car a few minutes later, it was in front of a big house on one of the side streets off St. Charles. There was a lot of activity on the street—frat boys coming and going, as they were close to Loyola and Tulane—and for a minute, Byron was afraid the guy had driven home.

But when he looked more closely at the men walking by his truck, he realized they were all coming from the same house. The one his guy, Jim, had just gone into. A closer look at the men made him realize they weren't all college kids, after all.

Excitement and horror hit him as he realized he was probably looking at one of the houses set up specifically to sell sex. That there were girls in that house who were, very likely, being forced into prostitution.

He was out of the car in a flash, grabbing a baseball cap from the back and pulling it over his head, to cover as much of his face as possible. Then he was joining the line of men—young and old—waiting to go into the house with twenty-dollar bills clenched in their fists.

Bile rose in his throat, even as he pulled out a twenty. Adrenaline was racing through him, combining with the fear that was a tight fist around his gut. What if Lacey wasn't in there? What if she was? The questions tormented him as he waited his turn; the idea that one—or more—of the men in front of him might end up raping her before he could get in was a sickness inside him.

Finally, finally, it was his turn. He paid his twenty bucks and followed the directions they'd given him. Inside, he found a bunch of cubicles set up, a different girl in each one. He walked up and down looking in each one, praying he would find Lacey, praying he wouldn't. Not here.

All of the girls were young, a lot younger than Lacey, and they all looked drugged-out, spaced-out and just completely used up. His stomach turned, and for the first time in his life, he was ashamed of his gender.

He kept looking, fighting back his horror at what he was seeing, but Lacey wasn't there. Then he realized that there were more rooms at the top of the stairs, and that a few men were headed up that way. Adrenaline coursed through him and he started to follow, but another no-neck guy stopped him at the bottom of the stairs. "Where's your ticket?"

"What ticket?" he demanded, as he tried to look like every inch of him wasn't straining to get up those stairs. To see if Lacey was up there.

"These are VIP rooms. You want in, you gotta pay more."

"How much?" Byron pulled out his wallet.

"Two hundred bucks."

"Sure, okay." He shoved the money into the guy's hands and started up the stairs, forcing himself not to run. "What do I do?" he asked the guy as he passed him.

"Pick a room—each one has a girl in it. Decide which one you like."

"All right." Figuring he'd start at the last room and work his way down, he got to the top of the stairs and headed to the end of the hallway.

He opened the first door and nearly freaked out; a girl was handcuffed to the bed, dressed in nothing but her underwear. Next to the bed was a whip and a riding crop. Judging from the bruises and welts on her body, he wasn't the first one to open her door tonight.

He was shaking, shuddering, when he slammed the door, so disturbed that he thought he might lose it right in the middle of the fucking hallway. Only the thought that Lacey was here, in one of these rooms, kept him from getting the hell out as fast as he could.

Taking a deep breath, steeling himself, he opened the next door gingerly, his hand shaking with the fear of what he would find.

"She's taken!" A gruff voice sounded from inside, and the door slammed shut in his face. But not before he'd seen the drugged-out blonde in the middle of the bed.

He continued down the hallway, looking in each room. Finding something more depraved, more horrifying, in each room he entered. Normally, he didn't consider himself squeamish; he was all for two adults doing whatever made them happy. But this—this drugging and raping and abusing of girls—there was nothing consensual about it, and it turned his fucking stomach.

He was at the end of the hallway, had checked every room, and hadn't found Lacey. Appalled, discouraged, and sicker than he'd been in his entire life, he stood there for a minute, unsure of what to do. Of how to find her.

As he stood there, he realized there was another staircase leading up to a third floor. Sure, that it was another wild-goose chase, but he wasn't willing to leave until he'd checked every alternative, so he headed up the stairs.

He tried the door, but it was locked—unlike any of the others. Hope, painful in its intensity, started to pump in his chest as he tried the door a second time.

Suddenly, it swung open and a well-dressed man in a suit was standing there. "This room is not part of the sales." His voice was low and smooth and finely accented. "Go back downstairs and pick one of the girls from there." Then he shut the door, but by then Byron had gotten a glimpse of flame-red hair on the bed across from the door.

Fury exploded in him like a wild thing, and he wanted nothing more than to ram his shoulder into the door until it gave. He almost did, would have, if not for the certain knowledge that doing so was a death sentence. Which might not have bothered him, except for the fact that no one would be able to help Lacey if something happened to him.

Trying to control the rage eating him from the inside, he took the stairs down two at a time. Once he was outside, he ran to his truck, pulling out his cell phone as he did. He dialed 911 for the second time in two days, and this time, when the operator answered, he gave her the house's address. "There's a major fire. I don't know how it started, but I think the whole house is going to go. Please, hurry."

Then he reached into the back of his truck, pulled out the gasoline and box of newspapers he had put there earlier in the day. He walked casually to the house next to the little shop of horrors where Lacey was being held, and went through the side gate. Once there, he raced through the backyard to the fence that separated the two houses. Flinging the box of newspapers over the fence, he climbed it—gasoline can in hand—in two quick pulls, then jumped down to the other side.

Dousing the box of newspapers in gasoline, he set it far enough away from the fence that it wouldn't cause the thing to light up accidentally, but close enough for it to be seen from the house. Then he reached into his pocket for the matchbook he'd stuck there earlier and lit the whole thing up.

It caught, and he jumped the fence, then went to stand back in line to get into the house. After a minute, as the flames were starting to show above the line of the fence, he yelled, "Fire! Jesus Christ, there's a fire!" And was nearly trampled in the stampede of men trying to get away from what they thought was a burning house.

In the confusion, he was able to slip inside. He heard girls screaming, men yelling in Russian and, in the distance, the sound of police cars and fire engines racing toward the blaze.

He took the stairs two at a time, completely focused on Lacey. As he made it to the third floor, he barreled toward the lone door at the end of the hallway and kicked it as hard as he could. The door splintered, and, suddenly, there she was, lying naked and trembling on the bed.

She was alone.

"Oh, my God. Oh, Lacey."

He bent down and picked her up, wrapping the sheet around her as he did. She was drugged and fairly out of it, but lucid enough to know that it was him. Tears leaked from her eyes, and she started to sob, "Byron. You came for me. You came for me."

"Of course I did." He hurried down the stairs, hiding Lacey's red hair under the sheet and hoping to God the fire and imminent threat of police would keep everyone too busy to question him.

It almost worked. He was on the bottom floor, halfway to the front door, when someone grabbed him from behind. It was the same man who had been in Lacey's room. Byron lashed out, kicking him hard in the stomach, and the guy hit the ground hard. But before Byron could move, he'd pulled out a gun and leveled it straight at him. Straight at Lacey.

"Put the girl down," he said in clipped, heavily accented English. "She stays. She's mine."

Byron did as he was told, but put his body in front of Lacey's as a shield. "Run, Lacey."

"But—"

"Do it," he ordered.

"Don't move!" The asshole with the gun shouted. "Don't you fucking move."

"Lacey, go!" He gave her a shove in the direction of the door and headed toward the guy with the pistol. He wasn't thinking straight, wasn't thinking at all. He knew only that there was no way he was leaving Lacey here in this hellhole to suffer a fate worse than death.

Byron heard the gun go off, felt a searing pain in his chest. His legs went out from under him and he collapsed right in the middle of the dirty floor. The last thing he heard as he lost consciousness was Lacey screaming his name.

Chapter Twenty-four

Lacey was scared to death as she sat by Byron's hospital bed. It had been three days since he'd burst into Gregory's lair and rescued her, and still she couldn't help looking over her shoulder. Despite the fact that the house had been raided and Gregory arrested, part of her expected him to show up and drag her back to that hellhole.

Even worse was the guilt that filled her as she stared down at Byron, willing him to wake up. She couldn't believe he'd rescued her. That he'd cared enough about her to risk his life—even after all the ugly things she'd said to him the night of her abduction.

When she'd seen him lying there in his own blood, her life had flashed before her eyes. And when Gregory had taken aim at him again . . . thank God the fireman had burst into the house before he'd been able to pull the trigger a second time.

She'd never been more ashamed of her behavior in her life—even before the kidnapping, when she'd been sitting in her apartment, absolutely miserable and missing Byron more than she'd thought it possible to miss a person, she'd known that she'd wronged him. That she'd projected her fears onto him.

But she had been afraid, deathly afraid of making another mistake. Deathly afraid of losing her heart to another man who wielded affection—and the lack thereof—like a weapon.

Deathly afraid of opening herself up and being vulnerable again.

When she'd fought with Byron, it had been because he made her realize just how susceptible she was, and she hadn't liked it at all. Had, in fact, been damn sick of feeling out of control—or worse, like someone else in her life had control over her.

She smiled, a rueful little upturning of her lips that had a lot more to do with acknowledgment than it did happiness. But one day in Gregory's sadistic, psychotic clutches had changed how she thought about the world—especially when she saw everything Byron had sacrificed for her.

Leaning forward, she smoothed his hair away from his face and prayed for him to get better quickly. He was in a drug-induced coma—the doctors had put him in it to give his brain time to heal—and they had told her his prognosis was good. That he was young and healthy and more than likely going to recover from his injuries. But he hadn't provided any guarantees, and when it came to Byron, that's what she wanted. She wanted everything wrapped up in a neat little bow, with the promise of his recovery the pièce de résistance sitting on top.

They'd know more after he was awake, the doctor had promised when they'd spoken again last night, and had told her that today might be that day. They were easing back on the drugs and giving him the chance to wake up on his own.

She was dying for him to wake up, but at the same time, was absolutely petrified at the thought of facing him with all of the harsh words between them. She didn't know where to start apologizing—or, for that matter, how to thank him for coming for her.

What was she supposed to say? What *could* she say that would explain all of the complex feelings inside her?

The day passed slowly as she waited for Byron to open his eyes, each hour that ticked by leaving her more and more anxious. His friend Mike had stopped by to check on him in the morning, as he had every morning since the shooting, and the doctor had come by twice. The first time he had been relatively uncon-cerned about Byron's prolonged unconsciousness, but the second time he hadn't been happy. That much had been obvious from the way he'd looked Byron over. It was different than the other times he'd been in during the past four days. As if he'd been expecting something more from Byron.

It made her nervous. Very, very nervous.

Getting to her feet, Lacey crossed the room to look out the window. The ambulance had rushed him to Tulane Medical Center, and outside she could see the skyscrapers of downtown. Cars were driving down the street, people walking on the narrow sidewalks.

The world going on as normal. Amazing, wasn't it, that her entire world was crashing in on her, yet for other people it was just another day as usual.

"God, Byron. Come on. Wake up." She muttered the words to herself, not even bothering to say them aloud as she wrapped her arms around herself and started to rock. She'd been talking to Byron for days now, and it had done abso-lutely no good.

Leaning against the window, she touched the cool glass with shaky fingertips. *How is this going to work out?* she wondered for at least the hundredth time in the last few days. Had she finally found the man for her, just to lose him because she'd been too stupid to trust him?

Losing him seemed a worthy punishment, but not like this. Please, God, not like this—Byron in a hospital bed, slowly slipping away.

She heard a noise behind her and turned, heart in her throat. Maybe he was waking up, maybe it would be like all those cheesy shows, and— Miranda, Byron's nurse for this shift, stood in the doorway, bearing a tray of food.

"You need to eat, Ms. Adams. You've been here almost nonstop for three days, and I know you're not taking proper care of yourself."

Lacey knew she was right. Except for the time she'd left to go home and shower Byron's blood off her, and talk to the police and the press about the shooting and her kidnapping, she hadn't left the room. "Thanks." Lacey smiled briefly at her, then watched as she put the tray on the table next to Byron.

"No problem. I'll be back in an hour to collect this—make sure you've eaten at least some of it."

Lacey nodded, though she didn't know if she could choke anything past the huge lump in her throat. It had first appeared as she'd watched Byron gunned down in front of her, and it hadn't gone away yet. If Byron died, she didn't think it ever would.

There was a muffin and a cup of coffee on the tray—a large, paper one that she knew hadn't come from the cafeteria. Figuring Miranda had gone out of her way to get her coffee, then the least she could do was drink it. Lacey crossed the room and picked up the cup. Took a long sip of the fragrant brew and felt her insides begin to thaw out.

She didn't know if that was a good thing or a bad one. The numbness had been her constant companion for the last few days. It had kept her safe. The idea of losing it so abruptly was disquieting, to put it mildly.

That numbness had helped her talk calmly to police—somehow, in Lieutenant Genevieve Delacroix, she'd gotten one of the few honest cops in the NOPD, and that had made a huge difference in how the case was handled.

It had also helped her to talk to the press. She hadn't wanted to, but she'd wanted Byron as safe as she could make him from retaliation from Alexandrov's organization. Putting him in the spotlight had seemed the best way to accomplish that.

On the plus side, between Byron and the police raid the other night, Alexandrov's men seemed to be in chaos. She could only hope things stayed that way for a while.

Taking another sip of the hot coffee, savoring the warmth as it spread through her, she sank back into the chair by Byron's bed. She didn't know what made her look at him at that exact moment—maybe fate, maybe desperation, maybe hope—but as she glanced at Byron's face, she realized that his eyes had just opened.

"Oh, my God, Byron." She threw herself at him without conscious thought, draping her body gently over his legs in an effort not to hurt his wounds. She reached for his hand and squeezed, and was reassured on a purely visceral level when he squeezed back. It was faint—more a twitch than an actual squeeze, but she would take it. God, would she ever.

"Lace—" His voice was a croak as he tried to talk, his eyes panicked as the pain began to register.

"Hold on," she murmured, pressing the button for the nurse. "You're fine. You're in the hospital, but you're doing fine. You're going to be fine." She reached over and smoothed a thick lock of blond hair from his forehead. "You're going to be just fine."

When the intercom by his bed crackled a minute later, she told the nurse, "He's awake. Oh, God, he's awake."

Within minutes, the room had filled up—two nurses, Byron's doctor and three medical students had all come to evaluate him. They were more than satisfied with what they saw—for a man waking up for the first time in three days, he was doing great. Or so the doctor said.

Of course, *great* was a relative concept—Byron was still pasty gray, and he was sweating a little despite the frigid temperature of the room. The doctor had assured her it was a side effect of the pain, and had ordered more medicine to be given to him through his IV.

When the exam was all finished, when the room had been vacated and Byron was drifting peacefully from the new pain medication, Lacey laid her head on the bed railing and wept for long minutes, so relieved that it was a physical ache within her.

"Lacey."

She looked up to see Miranda standing at the door again, a smile on her face. "He's going to be out of it for a while. Why don't you take this chance to go home and change, take a shower. He should be pretty much gone for the next couple of hours."

"Okay. Maybe I will." She said the words, but even as she did, she knew she wouldn't take Miranda's advice. If Byron did wake up again, she wanted to be right there, next to him, when it happened.

"Don't—" She jumped when she felt Byron's calloused palm glance over the back of the hand she had resting on this thigh.

His eyes were closed; his color still wasn't good, but at least it was a little better than the pasty gray it had been when he'd first woken up. "What's the matter, Byron?" She leaned forward until her ear was almost directly above his mouth. "What do you need?"

He smiled then, a brief, heartbreaking twist of his lips. "You," he whispered. "Don't go. I need . . . you."

"Oh, love." She gently cradled his beat-up face in her hand. "I'm not going anywhere."

The next few days passed in a blur as Byron became more alert. He was still on pain medication—a bullet in the chest could do that to a guy—but at least he was able to stay awake for a little more each day. His color was back to normal, and for the past two days they'd actually let him get out of bed and walk the halls for a while.

On the fourth day after he'd woken up, Lacey had deemed it safe to leave for a while, and had run home to take a quick shower and change her clothes. Her apartment was a mess, and a fine film of dust they'd used to check for fingerprints after her disappearance covered every surface. But she wasn't complaining, not now that she and Byron were safe.

She'd also taken a few minutes to call her editor, and fill her in on the change in the scope of the book. Melissa had been excited about the changes and was waiting anxiously for the final manuscript. Of course, she'd have to wait a while longer, as Lacey was a lot more concerned about getting Byron well than she was her fast-approaching deadline.

When she returned to the hospital, freshly washed and with a huge cup of coffee and a box of doughnuts for the nurses, Byron was once again up. And clearly out of sorts.

"I don't want a damn sponge bath," he was telling the young nurse's aide, who was standing over him with a basin of soapy water. "I want to get up and take a shower like a real man."

"You can't, Mr. Hawthorne," the girl argued with him. "You're not able to get your incision wet yet." She gestured to the giant bandage on his chest, under which there was a large cut that ran the length of his sternum, where the surgical team had worked to save his life.

Recognizing the obstinate look on Byron's face, Lacey figured she'd better intervene before things went down the drain fast. "Stop hassling the pretty woman," she told him, "and I'll let you have a sip of my coffee."

His eyes lit up when he saw her. "Is it the real thing, or more of that decaf shit they keep giving me?"

"Wow." Her eyes met the poor nurse's aide's. "You are in a mood today."

The girl's vigorous nod wasn't lost on Byron, who seemed to be gearing up for another tantrum. "Tell you what," she said in an attempt to head him off before he got started. "How about you cooperate with her while she gets your vitals, and then I'll give you the sponge bath myself." She held her cup of coffee to his lips so he could have the sip she'd promised him.

She glanced at the aide. "Is that okay?"

"Absolutely." She seemed relieved—and a little disappointed that she wouldn't be getting her hands on Byron's glorious body, but Lacey chose to ignore that. After the girl had gotten Byron's temperature, blood pressure and the other stuff, Lacey settled in the chair by his bed.

"Hey," he complained, "I thought I was getting a bath."

"Do you want one?"

His eyes darkened. "From you, absolutely. From the eighteen-year-old teeny-bopper from hell, no, thank you!"

"I'm glad to hear that." Shrugging out of her sweater, Lacey murmured, "I guess the first thing we need to do is get this gown off you." She helped him slip the hospital gown down his arms, grateful that the nurse had unhooked the IV the night before, though she'd left the capped-off port in his vein in case of an emergency.

"I actually brought you some stuff—a couple pairs of pajamas, a few books," she said as she dipped her hand into the large basin of warm water the girl had left next to Byron's bed. How ridiculous was it that she was breathless at the thought of bathing Byron? It wasn't like there was going to be anything sexual to it.

Trying to concentrate on the task at had, she wrung out the washcloth, then smoothed it gently over Byron's face before moving lower to his powerful shoulders and arms.

"Is the water warm enough for you?" she asked.

"Yes." His voice was low, deep. Glancing up at his eyes, she saw him staring at her with an intensity that belied the wound in his chest.

He reached for her, but she danced out of his grasp. "Oh no, none of that," she said lightly, even as her nipples peaked against the soft cotton of her tank top. "You were at death's door a few days ago. This is a bath, and that's all."

"Yeah, but I'm better now." He reached for her hand—the one that wasn't wet—and pulled it to his mouth. She shivered as he kissed her dead center in her palm.

She dipped the washcloth in the basin again, and took back the hand he was holding so that she could wring it out again. Then she swept the rag down the right side of his chest, and the left, being extra careful not to get the gauze covering his wound wet.

Moving lower, she brushed the cloth over his taut, rock-hard abdomen, watching as the muscles jumped and flexed at her touch. The sight was arousing, and she tried to hurry through the area without looking at him.

What did it say about her that she was ready to jump a man who, a few days before, had been at death's door?

But he isn't there now, a little voice in the back of her head reminded her. Now he was feeling well enough to argue with nurses and steal kisses from her. They hadn't talked about their fight, hadn't talked about the future, but she knew he'd forgiven her for the ugly things she'd said to him—and everything that had come after.

If only she could forgive herself.

"Hey, Lacey, are you okay?" Byron's hand moved to cover hers, and when she looked up at him, he was watching her with concern.

She cleared her throat. "Yeah, I'm fine."

"Are you sure? Because you've been stalled out at my stomach for a couple of minutes now."

"Oh, sorry. I was just . . . thinking."

His hand covered hers. "If you don't want to—"

"It's not that."

"Did that bastard—" His voice broke.

"No, Byron!" She shuddered, in relief and remembered terror. "You got me out before Gregory could do anything but scare the hell out of me. He was waiting for the drugs to wear off before he—" It was her turn to stop midsentence.

"I'm sorry it took me so long."

"I'm sorry you got shot."

"It was worth it." He grinned, then gazed meaningfully at where her hand still rested on his belly. "It did get me here, after all."

Lacey blushed, but didn't look away as Byron eased the covers down past his lower abdomen, all the way to midthigh. She shuddered as she realized he was full, hard, as achingly aroused as she was. Maybe more. His cock was lying against his stomach, stretching all the way to his navel, and she could feel her hands begin to shake.

When she made no move to touch him, to bring the washcloth lower, Byron cleared his throat. "Does it bother you? It's just that when you touch me, I—"

"That's all right." She cut him off. "Are you sure you're feeling okay?" She didn't want to kill the guy, not after spending seven days beside him, trying to help him recover.

"I feel fine, Lacey."

She worried her lower lip between her teeth. "Are you sure?"

"Yes." He hissed the word between his teeth as she drew the washcloth down his abdomen—first on the right side of his erection, then the left, being careful not to touch it. "God, yes. Lacey, please."

Wetting her lips, still not believing she was all but molesting a hospital patient, she ran the washcloth lower, over his balls and behind them, sweeping over the sensitive spot she knew was there.

Byron sucked air in through his mouth at the touch of the washcloth as it ran over his most private places. He would prefer it to be Lacey's hands, would die to have her touch him, but for now he would take what he could get.

She washed him thoroughly, the washcloth moving closer and closer to his cock with each sweep of her hand, until he was ready to beg her to touch him, beg her to finish him off.

When her knuckle grazed across his hard-as-nails cock, he groaned. His hips flexed, arching involuntarily, and his cock twitched with the need for her to touch it. To touch him.

"Lacey," he groaned, trapping her hand against his thigh and then sliding it up and over his straining flesh. "Please, baby. I need—"

His breath rushed out as her hand closed around him and began to stroke. "Are you sure you're okay? I don't want to hurt you—"

"I'm fine, baby, better than fine." She was working him slowly, sweetly—her touch soft and tentative and so arousing he thought he would lose his mind.

For long seconds, he let her go at it, tangling his hands in the bed coverings in an effort to keep from taking over. From taking control. The last words she'd said to him before the kidnapping still echoed in his head, and he didn't want to drive her away. Didn't want to chance losing her again, not now when he knew how much she meant to him.

But it was torture to lay there as she stroked him, torture to have her small palm run up and down his length without ever giving him the friction that he needed. Within minutes, he was a seething mess of arousal and need, his body arching and quivering, flexing and thrusting against her palm.

"Ssh," she said, putting her other hand on his shoulder and pushing him back against the bed. "You need to relax."

His laughter was a harsh shout in the room. "I can't relax. You're killing me."

"I don't want to hurt—"

"Lacey, if you don't do it right now, I swear to God I'm going to have a fucking heart attack."

When she still seemed undecided, he put his hand over hers, squeezed tightly and pumped. Once, twice, a third time. And then he was coming, the orgasm ripping through him with the force of fully loaded tank. The fact that Lacey was watching him, her pink tongue brushing against her lips again and again, as if she was staring at a particularly delicious treat, only made him come harder.

When it was over, she cleaned him up, helped him slip into the pajamas she'd brought with her.

"Come here," he murmured, patting the spot next to him on the bed.

"No way. I don't want to hurt you."

"You won't. But I want to feel you next to me."

She didn't move, just continued to watch him dubiously, until he got impatient. Reaching for her hand, he yanked her out of the chair and onto the bed. The movement made his chest burn, but the pain was well worth it as Lacey curled up beside him.

"Tell me if I'm hurting you."

"You feel fabulous," he murmured, running a soft finger over her lips. "I'm so glad you're all right."

Tears welled in her eyes. "Thanks to you. Byron—"

"Ssh." He tugged her closer, until her lips met his. He kept the kiss light, sweet, determined not to pressure her, though every instinct he had clamored for him to make her his.

She whimpered and pressed closer, careful not to jostle his chest, but he didn't give a shit about the discomfort. All he wanted was to feel her.

Bringing his hand up, he cupped her breast, flicking his thumb over her nipple again and again.

"Byron, stop!" She shot an anxious look at the closed door, but didn't pull away.

"I don't have another vitals check for a couple hours—we have plenty of time."

"I am not having sex with you in the middle of the hospital!"

"Who asked you to?" he teased, even as he increased the pressure on her nipple.

"Byron!"

"Lacey." He shoved her shirt out of the way and lowered his mouth to her pouting nipple, taking care to lick around the edges of her areola as she liked.

"Oh, my God! You need to stop!" But her back was arching and she was pressing her nipple more firmly against his tongue.

He continued to pleasure her, to nip and suck and kiss until she was trembling and nearly incoherent. Then he slid his hand under her long peasant skirt. Shoving her underwear out of the way, he rubbed her clit with firm strokes, reveling in the way her breath caught. The way her hands clutched at his biceps.

His chest was starting to ache, but he wanted to give this to her. Needed desperately to see her come after the sexual depravity he had witnessed at that hellhole where she'd been held.

"Come for me, Lacey." He whispered the words against her breast. Her lower body arched into his hand and he slid first one finger and then a second inside her.

"Kiss me. Please, Byron, kiss me."

She lowered her head, and he took her mouth ravenously, sucking her tongue into his mouth and stroking it with his own. She started to come on the third pass of his tongue, her body tightening and releasing around his fingers in a rhythm that had his dick twitching back to life.

When it was over, she collapsed against him and he held her for a long time, tenderly stroking her hair away from her face. She curled against him, but as time passed, it occurred to him that she was refusing to look at him.

"Lacey, come on." He placed two fingers under her chin, tilted her face up so that he could see her eyes. "Look at me."

"I'm sorry, Byron. For all the horrible things I said to you. For pushing you away. For getting myself kidnapped and needing you to rescue me. For—" Her voice broke on a sob, and he felt his own heart crack wide open in a response that had absolutely nothing to do with the bullet they'd pulled out of his chest a few days before.

"Hey, now, you're going to make yourself sick. It's okay. I'm okay. We're okay."

And in his mind, they were. Everyone fought, everyone had problems. That didn't mean things were over. The fact that Lacey had stayed with him these last seven days had told him all he needed to know about her feelings. And if she wasn't ready to admit it—wasn't ready to give everything to him yet—he could wait. He was a fairly patient guy, after all.

He stroked her hair as she cried, knowing that this was about more than the fight, more than their relationship. It was about the kidnapping and everything she'd endured at the hands of that animal. If he could have killed him a second time, he would have done it in a heartbeat. The idea of that bastard anywhere near Lacey caused a murderous rage in him like nothing he'd ever felt—even now, after the guy had been dead for nearly two weeks.

When she'd finished crying, she went to the bathroom and rinsed off her face. Then settled next to him on the bed, once again being careful not to jostle him. "I love you." She said the words that arrowed straight through his heart. "I fell for you that first night on the balcony and then just kept falling. And it scared the hell out of me. I didn't want to feel that way about a man—about anyone. Not if it meant opening myself up to pain and fear and all those emotions that come with love."

He started to interrupt, but she stopped him with her fingers on his lips. "I know you were upset about the fantasies I posted on the Internet—you thought I wasn't getting what I needed from you. But that's not true. Like you said that last day at my apartment, all those fantasies I posted on the Internet were just one more way I was striving for control. One more way I wanted to be the one calling the shots in my world."

His heart filled with love for her until it was an actual ache inside of him.

Pulling her closer to him, he murmured, "It doesn't bother me anymore. You can be in control like that anytime, baby. As long as I'm the guy you're fantasizing about."

"They're all you, Byron, and have been for quite a while now. From the second I first saw you six weeks ago, you were the one I thought of when I fantasized. The one I imagined being with."

Shy now that she was looking into his warm eyes, she didn't know how to do what she needed to do. Finally, she decided to just suck it up, and pulled out her laptop. "I posted a new fantasy yesterday. Do you want to see it?"

"Does it involve Rocky Road ice cream?" he asked wickedly, his hand covering hers as she carried the computer.

"No, but I'm hoping it's something you'll like even better."

"Better than Rocky Road? That's a pretty big promise to live up to."

She shrugged, then surreptitiously tried to wipe her sweaty palms on her jeans. "Yeah, well, you be the judge."

He grinned as she slid the computer in front of him. As he read, his grin slowly disappeared. Once he glanced at her with razor-sharp eyes, but then he went back to reading what she'd written. She waited nervously, going over the words of the fantasy in her head as he read it. Wondering if he would understand what she was saying. What she was asking for.

You come to me, bearing gifts, as a shooting star streaks across the inky blackness outside my window. You ply me with wine and chocolate and crazy, sexy poems from people who lived—and loved—long before we were conceived.

You tease me, with glancing touches of your forearm against my erect and aching nipples. Torment me, with brazen sweeps of your fingertips against my wet and swollen folds. Kiss me—a long, lingering, luscious melding of lips and tongues and teeth that wipes out all that came before—or will come after.

Together we sit on the porch of the house we built. You've built me a swing, and we sit on it now, my feet in your lap, your hands in my hair. You tell me of your day, of the wonderful pieces you made. I tell you about my research and how the book is going.

You gather me in your arms, hold me against you so that I can feel your heartbeat. Your hand strokes over mine, and I know that I am safe. That I am exactly where I've always wanted to be.

When he finished reading, the eyes that met hers were full of questions, full of hope, and Lacey couldn't help laughing with pure, undiluted joy. Leaning over Byron, she placed her lips on his and murmured, "I'm not afraid anymore. I want everything you want to give me."

He laughed as well, for the same reasons. Then pulled her into his arms and said, "I want everything. Are you sure you're up for that?"

"You have no idea just how ready I am."

Then she laid her head on his chest, being careful, very careful, of his still-healing wound, and whispered another fantasy to him, one that involved him and her and the life she was more than ready to begin.

It was good, for once, to be unafraid.

About the Author

Tracy Wolff lives in Texas and is a writing professor at her local community college. She is married and the mother of three young sons. Visit her at tracywolff.com.

If you enjoyed this seductive story, look for Tracy Wolff's

TIE ME **DOWN**

Available now from NAL Heat.
Read on for a sneak peek. . . .

I t was hot as only New Orleans could be.

Hotter than a cat on a tin roof.

Hotter than the Cajun cooking her mother used to make.

Hotter than hell.

And she was burning up, fury and sorrow eating her from the inside out.

More than ready for the day from hell to be over, Genevieve Delacroix slammed out of the precinct on the fly, then cursed as she plowed straight into the sticky heat the city was known for. It rose up to meet her like a wall—thick and heavy and all-consuming.

Pausing to catch her breath, she stared blindly at the planters full of cheerful posies that lined the front of the precinct. Her partner, Shawn, had picked a hell of a time to take a vacation—in the middle of the busiest week homicide had seen in years. After working four homicide scenes in as many days, it was a miracle she could still put one foot in front of the other.

Today, she'd awakened to a ringing phone, news of a brutal, sexual homicide the first thing she'd heard as she surfaced from a sleep so deep it was almost like death itself. Yesterday it had been a murder-suicide. Two days before that, a domestic dispute turned deadly.

Not to mention the bizarre call she'd gotten earlier that afternoon promising her—with sexually graphic delight—that the caller would be seeing her very soon. As the only female on the homicide squad, she got her share of calls from weirdos, and this one was nothing unusual—but it still put her back up.

Sighing, she rubbed a weary hand over her eyes. This week, the Big Easy was anything but.

Taking the precinct steps two at a time, Genevieve glanced around the French Quarter where she'd worked and lived for most of her life.

Tonight she could see none of the beauty the Quarter was known for—the architecture, the colors, the history. It all faded beside the sickness she'd witnessed that morning. The most recent in a long line of sick and twisted crimes that ate away at the city's population like a cancer.

Her argument with the lieutenant rang clearly in her head as her long legs ate up Royal Street's narrow sidewalks.

Not enough similarities in the causes of death in the murders.

Not enough similarities in the three victims.

Not enough evidence, in her boss's not-so-humble opinion.

But in the eleven years she'd been on the force, Genevieve's gut had never been wrong, and right now her instincts were screaming that the case she'd caught this morning—the brutal rape and murder of a nineteen-year-old Tulane student—wasn't a freak event. A serial killer was at large.

True, the cause of deaths in all three murders had been different, as had the body dumps—Jackson Square, Jean Lafitte's Blacksmith Shop, Senator Mouline's house—but the feel of the scenes had felt too similar for it to be a fluke. The evident, full-out rage the killer had been in when he'd inflicted the wounds had been the same, as had the desperate need to cause as much pain and humiliation to his victims as possible.

Without knowing where she was going, Genevieve made a quick left on St. Peter. She knew only that that she couldn't face going home and reliving the whole damn day over and over in her head until she wanted to scream—or sob.

The image of Jessica Robbins' body was in front of her eyes, the atrocities done to her burned into Genevieve's brain by the hours and hours she'd spent working the case. By the helpless anger she felt at not being able to stop the crime.

By the failure she was already anticipating.

If this was the work of a serial killer—and her experience and instincts shouted that it was—then he was damn good at his job. Maybe the best she'd ever run across. And she'd need more than a condescending smile and a load of denial from her egotistical boss if she was going to catch the bastard.

Sickness churned in her stomach and turned her legs weak. Chastian couldn't be allowed to sweep this under the rug, like he did so many of the other ideas she went to him with. He couldn't be allowed to discount her ideas, just because she was a woman and, in his screwed-up opinion, didn't belong in homicide. She knew how to do her job and would be damned if she was going to let his sexist bullshit stand in the way of her doing what she knew was right.

A couple of frat boys cruised by, jostling her, and Genevieve nearly jumped out of her skin. One more sign that she was wound tight enough to break.

"Hey, baby, let me buy you a drink." One of them leered at her, his vacant eyes testimony to just how many drinks he'd already bought.

"I think you've had enough." She started to move away from him.

"Aww, come on, darlin', don't be like that." The second one blocked her way, and Genevieve sighed as she saw her day going from miserable to excruciating in the blink of an eye.

"Guys, you're already drunk off your asses and it's only"—she glanced at her watch—"seven thirty. Why don't you head back uptown and sleep it off?"

"Is that an invitation?" the first one asked, leaning in so close that she could almost identify the brand of beer he'd been slamming back.

"Not the kind you're looking for." Straightening up, she shoved past them. "Now scram."

With much grumbling, they did, and Genevieve started to walk away, but now the idea of a drink had begun to sound entirely too good to pass up. Maybe a hurricane—or three—would help get Jessica out of her head.

Shouldering around the crush of tourists standing in front of Pat O's, she slunk into the much less raucous bar a few doors down. If she couldn't force the memories out of her head, maybe she could drink them away. At least for tonight.

Cole Adams slid onto the barstool next to the blond bombshell with more curves than a baseball, and wondered how to start up the conversation he was dying to have.

Should he open with the truth? He wasn't sure how well this beautiful woman would take to the fact that he'd been researching her for months. That he'd followed her from the police station. That he'd been lurking around outside the precinct, waiting for her to come out for nearly an hour.

That he wanted a whole lot more from her than she'd be willing to give.

He'd meant to stop her there, to tell her what he wanted right from the start. But she'd looked so enraged—and miserable—that he couldn't help wondering what had caused the devastation written so clearly on her face.

But before he could decide how to approach her, Genevieve had started off at a walk so fast it was nearly a run, and he'd been forced to follow her or lose his chance.

He couldn't afford to mess this up. Not now, when he'd finally gotten everything set up the way he wanted it.

Glancing at Genevieve out of the corner of his eye, he nearly snorted. Yeah, right. Things were going exactly as he'd planned.

Except that she looked more likely to shoot him than listen to him.

Plus, the speech he'd prepared sounded incredibly stupid now. Like a bad pickup line instead of the appeal to her conscience he'd intended.

Maybe he was just paranoid—and who could blame him? He'd done his homework on the NOPD so thoroughly that the face of every homicide detective on the force was familiar to him by now. But Genevieve's picture hadn't done her justice. On the computer screen, her hair had looked more of a dirty gray than the honey blond it really was, and her ample curves had been hidden under an ill-fitting suit. Now Cole was struggling to deal with the arousal that had wrapped around his gut like a fist at his first sight of her and had only gotten worse as he'd watched her sinuous glide through the Quarter.

Looking at her from beneath his lashes, he watched her long, unpainted fingers tap an impatient rhythm on the bar as she leaned back in her barstool in a parody of relaxation. What did it say about him that the guarded accessibility of her frame—combined with the sight of those loose, feminine fingers—had him longing for the feel of her against him? For the feel of her hand on his suddenly—and unexpectedly— hard cock?

Fuck, damn, shit. What was he—a horny teenager who couldn't keep his dick under control? Or a man who knew what he wanted, one with a secret to unravel and only one woman who could help him do it?

This couldn't be happening. Not now, when he was so close to getting the ball rolling. Not now, when he had Detective Genevieve Delacroix almost exactly where he wanted her.

But it *was* happening, his body spinning rapidly out of control while his mind struggled to find a way to approach her that she wouldn't find threatening—or annoying.

"So, can I buy you a drink?" Her question came out of nowhere, in a no-nonsense tone and a voice that was pure, sugary Georgia peach. Smooth and silky and sweetly delicious, despite the hint of hard-ass he heard just below the surface.

Surprise swept through him, and he wondered if she would taste as good as she sounded. The contrast between her voice and her tone intrigued him, one more example of the numerous contradictions that seemed to make her up.

The lush body covered by that ridiculous suit.

The indolent pose belied by the watchful eyes.

The gorgeous voice with the don't-fuck-with-me tone.

It made him wonder who the real Genevieve Delacroix was. Made him want to fuck with her—to fuck her—and to hell with the consequences.

As he struggled to regain control—to keep his eye on the prize—the wicked curve of her lips kept interfering with his concentration.

"What are you offering?" He kept his voice low as he angled his body toward hers, savoring the rush of arousal pouring through him. Inconvenient or not, it had been far too long since he'd felt this instantaneous reaction to a woman.

Her barely there smile turned into a smirk. "That depends what you ask for."

He nodded to the bartender, who had sidled up to the other side of the bar. "A shot of Patrón Silver."

"Interesting choice." Genevieve quirked a brow before turning to the bartender. "I'll take an Absolut and cranberry."

After the bartender had moved away, she leveled a pair of deep blue eyes at him, and he fought the urge to squirm. Genevieve had cop eyes—world-weary, cynical and more than willing to believe the worst.

For a split second, it was like looking in a mirror—his own tormented emotions of the past few years staring back at him. But then a shutter came down, blocking him from seeing anything but a sardonic amusement that sent shivers up his spine.

"So," she demanded as she leaned forward until her mouth was only inches from his own. "Do you often drink alone?"

It was his turn to raise a brow. "I'm new in town. I don't have anyone else to drink with."

"I'd feel sorry for you, but I get the impression that's more by choice than necessity." Her cerulean eyes glowed as they swept over him, and he couldn't stop his body from clenching in response.

"So, what about you?"

She inclined her head. "What about me?" Her peaches-and-cream voice was ripe with approval, and he felt his cock throb. Shifting a little, he tried to adjust himself so his hard-on wasn't so obvious—or painful. But a quick glance at Genevieve told him she was more than aware of his dilemma—and she was enjoying it.

"Do *you* often drink alone?" He parroted her words back at her, determined to gain control of the conversation.

"Who says I'm alone? I could be waiting for someone."

She was bluffing—pushing him hard with her fuck-off voice and come-hither body language—and normally he'd be more than happy to go along for the ride. But now wasn't the time for this, he reminded himself forcibly.

"Should I leave?" He started to stand.

"No!" For just a moment her facade slipped, giving him one more glimpse of the frustrated, tired, too-pissed-off-to-be-alone woman behind the mask.

He sank back into his chair. "I'm Cole, by the way." He held out a hand.

"Genevieve." She hesitated before placing her hand against his.

"Afraid?" he asked, with a smirk, unable to stop himself.

"Of you?" Her hand met his in a firm, no-nonsense clasp, her eyes narrowing in derision.

"Is there someone else here?" She tried to tug her hand back, but he didn't let go. Couldn't let go, any more than he could stop the cocky, shit-eating grin from crossing his face. It was going to be fun as hell testing her, seeing what she was made of.

Seeing just how far he could push before she began to shove back.

It might not be the wisest course of action, but then again, he'd given up being smart when he came to this hellhole of a city, intent on finding a truth that had eluded him for seven long years.

"I don't know." She glanced around the bar, let her eyes linger teasingly on some guy near the door. "Is there?"

As the guy straightened up and made a move toward them, Cole scowled fiercely. Then gave a sharp tug on Genevieve's hand that had her out of her chair and between his legs before she knew what was happening. He wrapped his free hand around her hip and pulled her even closer, so that her thighs rested against his aroused cock.

Those blue eyes sparked with a fury that was cold as ice, and he expected her to struggle—for one brief moment, even wanted her to. His brain was sending all kinds of messages, calling him every name in the book, even as it warned him that he was blowing everything before his plan had a chance to get off the ground.

But for the first time in his life, his body had sole possession of the driver's seat, his suddenly unruly libido shrugging off the warning signs like they didn't exist—even as he struggled for control.

For one brief, terrifying moment, he thought about forgetting the whole thing, about saying "Fuck it" and just reveling in the moment. About taking this woman any and every way he could have her, and letting the chips fall where they may.

How had she gotten him so hot so quickly? In the long years following Samantha's death, he'd never let anyone get under his skin. Ever.

And this wasn't how their first meeting was supposed to turn out—with him fantasizing about what she looked like in the throes of one orgasm after another.

He was supposed to be laying the groundwork. Feeling her out. Checking to see if she really was as good as her record said she was. An hour ago her competence—or lack thereof—had been the most important thing on his mind. But now all he could think about was what it would feel like to come in her mouth. In her pussy. In her lush, gorgeous ass.

He tried to tamp down on the arousal, but that was like trying to put out a wildfire with a spray bottle—especially since he could feel the heat and arousal coming off her. Could see her nipples peaking beneath the thin material of her blouse. Could hear the hitch in her breathing as she too struggled for control.

He'd come to New Orleans looking for peace; had sought Genevieve out for just that purpose. But the aroused, out-of-control, gotta-have-her-now feeling that had grabbed him by the balls the second he laid eyes on her was anything but peaceful.

Gritting his teeth, he pulled himself back from the edge. It wasn't easy when he wanted to be inside her more than he wanted his next breath. More than he wanted the answers he'd come here to get.

But the look on Genevieve's face said she'd been pushed—or pulled—as far as she was going to allow. Aroused or not, her next move would be to take a swing at him.

For a minute, he could almost taste the coppery tang of blood in his mouth. It might be worth it.

"You're going to want to let go of me." Her voice was low and hot, a warning if he'd ever heard one.

"I'm not so sure about that." His hands tightened—on her hip and her palm—holding her to him for one endless moment. The image of what she would look like spread-eagled on his bed roared through him, her pale skin gleaming against the midnight silk of the sheets. For a second, he was afraid he wouldn't be able to let her go.

But his brain was screaming at him, the warning signals having turned into bright red flags of alarm, and somehow he found the strength to release her.

The bartender chose that second to drop their drinks on the bar, and he grabbed the ice-cold shot of tequila like it was a lifeline. Slammed it back and gestured for another one. He was teetering on the brink of madness, his body out of his control. His desire for Genevieve nearly palpable in the small distance she'd created between them.

What is wrong with me? he wondered, tossing back the second shot as quickly as he had the first. He'd never reacted like this to a woman before, had never felt like he would give anything—and everything—just to be inside her.

But Genevieve—in just a few brief moments, Genevieve had turned him inside out. It was ridiculous, absurd. And he—

"You're not as uncomplicated as you look." Her voice broke into his self-flagellation, had him turning to her with hot eyes he couldn't hope to cool down.

"I could say the same thing about you." He forced a calm into his voice that he was far from feeling.

"Yeah, well, I had a crappy day." She stuck out her chin at him. "What's your excuse?"

"I wasn't aware I needed one."

Very deliberately, she glanced down at where his hands were clenched into fists, before taking a long sip of her drink. "It's pretty obvious that you need something."

Her words—ice-cold and taunting—slammed through him. God, she was amazing—her icy control housed a hot fire, tempting as hell.

"And what is it you think I need?"

For the first time, he saw a flash of uncertainty in her eyes and couldn't help wondering at its cause. A heavy silence stretched between them, long and taut and more than a little uncomfortable. Just when he'd decided that he'd blown it—that she wasn't going to answer—Genevieve took a deep breath.

"Me," she said in a voice that was as steady as it was unexpected.